TRUMPETS FROM OBLIVION

H. BEDFORD-JONES

TRUMPETS FROM OBLIVION

H. BEDFORD-JONES

COVER BY
HERBERT MORTON STOOPS

ILLUSTRATIONS BY
JOHN CLYMER
AUSTIN BRIGGS
HERBERT MORTON STOOPS
JOHN RICHARD FLANAGAN
ROBERT. L. LAMBDIN
J. CLINTON SHEPHERD

STEEGER BOOKS • 2025

TABLE OF CONTENTS

TRUMPETS FROM OBLIVION

THE STAGNANT DEATH

IN THIS FASCINATING NEW SERIES THE FAMOUS AUTHOR
OF "ARMS AND MEN" GIVES A REALISTIC EXPLANATION
FOR THE STRANGE LEGENDS THAT HAVE COME DOWN
THE AGES.... THIS FIRST STORY, "THE STAGNANT DEATH,"
DEALS WITH THE TRADITION OF THE SARGASSO SEA.

A DOZEN OF us, members of the Inventors' Club, received invitations to that first amazing seance with Norman Fletcher. None of us knew the man, but all had heard astonishing reports of him, of his wealth, and of his strange—almost weird—accomplishments.

A tight-lipped old Yankee,—there was a Fletcher on the *Mayflower*,—he had a walled and guarded estate some miles outside the city, and seldom stirred from it. Some termed him a madman, an eccentric dabbler in dark and devious things. Others stated he had inherited the electrical genius of the late great Steinmetz, and would some day startle the world with his discoveries.

Well, we accepted his invitation. We passed the massive gates, arrived at the enormous granite mansion, and were ushered into Norman Fletcher's presence.

He greeted us genially. He was a spare, alert, ruddy-cheeked old man with white hair and twinkling eyes, erect as an arrow. We had a cocktail, and passed into a gorgeous dining room where we enjoyed a dinner that would have shamed the reputed banquet board of Kublai Khan himself....

Norman Fletcher proved a charming host. He discussed everything from local politics to the bombardment of the atom with insight and keen intelligence, but gave no hint as to the reason of this invitation until coffee and liqueurs had been served. Then he stood up and spoke abruptly, without any preliminaries.

"Gentlemen, let me state bluntly that I did not call you here to explain any of my discoveries; merely to lay them before you and to demonstrate certain theories of mine. You're aware, of course, that sound and light never perish, but go on and on. With the proper apparatus it is theoretically possible to overtake these ether waves, so to speak, and to bring back whatever we wish from the past—for example, shall we say, the voice of dying Caesar."

He paused, to beam at us, and Cromer, who was the radio genius of our little club, spoke up in his skeptical manner.

"Yes, but light and sound don't travel at the same speed. And by the same theory, you'd be two thousand years bringing back the voice of Caesar! What goes out and is on its way, must be overtaken."

Norman Fletcher smiled indulgently. "Quite right, Mr. Cromer. You're acquainted with ultrasonic waves, I believe? I've been working with them for years; and by my use of these waves, I have developed the apparatus mentioned. What's more, it evokes sight as well as sound, from the depths of the past. And that has led to an interesting discovery."

He paused, in his casual, calm manner, to sip his brandy, as though his stupefying announcement were quite ordinary.

*"Three dimensions, whatever it
is!" I heard Cromer gasp.*

Cromer muttered to me that the old boy had gone nuts, and most of us agreed.

PHYSICISTS HAVE long been working on ultrasonic waves, the so-called "death ray," and have not more than skirted the subject, which has appalling possibilities. Yet these very waves have been known to mankind for ages, under the name of the Evil Eye.

"My apparatus, gentlemen," went on our host, "evokes, by a process somewhat akin to television, the startling truths behind ancient myths and fables. I made this discovery by accident, and found it so interesting that I invited you to witness a demonstration."

"Oh!" exclaimed Cromer. "I suppose you can make us see St. George's dragon, and hear the songs of the sirens?"

"Certainly," affirmed Norman Fletcher urbanely. "Men are not fools. All such old fables are based on fact: if mankind believed such tales, it was with reason. I find in some cases that the facts were deliberately distorted to make the yarns. This basic reality lingers in human consciousness. If you could delve into the subconscious of anyone you care to name, you'd find startling half-beliefs in what we pleasantly call Old Wives' Tales. The world has laughed at Shakespeare for his alleged 'seacoast of Bohemia,' but my apparatus will demonstrate that Bohemia did at one time have a seacoast. Were there ever sirens, 'little people,' mermaids? Certainly."

"I know something I'd like you to demonstrate," began Cromer ominously.

"Very gladly, but at another time," smoothly broke in Norman Fletcher. "As you yourself mentioned, the difficulty in overtaking both light and sound, and synchronizing their return, is sometimes quite vexatious. To obtain any given subject requires delicate tuning and adjustments, as you can appreciate. Tonight I've prepared a demonstration of the supposed myth sometimes called the Stagnant Death—probably the most ancient of all fabulous tales, since it goes back beyond Aristotle, beyond Sidon and Egypt, to the very earliest peoples. And it has persisted to very recent days. Will you gentlemen come to my laboratory?"

We did, and pretty skeptical we were. In fact, we were like an audience watching a sleight-of-hand artist and hoping eagerly to catch him tripping....

Fletcher led us into a huge stonewalled room. On three sides were apparatus; one wall was left bare, and chairs faced it. We seated ourselves, and Norman Fletcher sat at an instrument no larger than an organ manual. We were anticipating anything, from a hoax to a clever trick, but he turned negligently to us and switched off the lights to a glow.

"The tubes require some moments to heat," he observed apologetically. "Keep your cigars, by all means."

"Just what," I asked, "is the Stagnant Death you mentioned?"

"The ancient myth that from the lost continent of Atlantis grew a sea of weeds so thick that it stopped navigation and caught ships. In other words, the Sargasso Sea, so called from the Portuguese word for seaweed, *sargaco.*"

"But that's no myth, Mr. Fletcher!" I exclaimed. "Why, Columbus was caught in it!"

He laughed heartily. "And told marvelous tales of it, too. For hundreds of years mankind has credited the story of dead waters, of stagnant silence where ships and hulks drifted, their crews eaten by monsters who lived under the weed! Only within recent years has the Sargasso Sea been proven to be thin and harmless patches of kelp floating on the Atlantic; although, even today, scientists are not agreed whether this weed grows up from the bottom or is swept there from the Gulf Stream. The ancient myth, you see, is true. The fabulous stories built around it—are they, also, true? If not, how did they begin? Whence came this legend of stagnant deathly silence, where old Spanish galleons may still be found floating? That, gentlemen, is what I'm about to demonstrate."

His voice died, as light began to grow upon the blank stone wall facing us. A glittering, shimmering, palpitating light that seemed alive; it broke and separated in rolling, tumbling wave-crests; it became the ocean, most treacherous and mysterious of all man's servants. The wall seemed to dissolve. It disappeared. The ocean was before us. There was no projected light, no beam, no screen—we were looking through that wall upon the ocean. And, by heavens, the very rush and surge of the sea was audible! Television? There was nothing to indicate it. We were looking, as through a window, upon the ancient ocean itself. Was it my imagination, or did the salt-tanged fishy breath of the sea come to us?

"Three dimensions, whatever it is!" I heard Cromer gasp.

JUST THROUGH the wall, it seemed, a ship's deck grew. Here was a man, a young man, ankles and wrists chained together, walking up and down the deck, two guards beside him; he had yellow hair and very quick, eager eyes. A group of officers stood together, men were in the waist. All, men and officers, stared over the rail. I could have sworn they were real live people moving before us. Old Spanish costumes and armor, the ship a galleon of Spain.

Day after day, day after day,
We stuck, nor breath nor motion;
As idle as a painted ship
Upon a painted ocean.

"It's death, it's death!" broke out one of the men. "The ship is scarce moving at all! Go back while we can!"

"Master pilot!" called one of the officers, looking as frightened as the men. "Is it true that you know yonder hulk?"

A grizzled pilot crossed himself, with terror in his eyes.

"True, *señor capitan*," he replied. "The *San Tomas;* she left Havana five years ago, in 1587, with three hundred souls aboard, and was never heard from again. I navigated her to Cuba. I'd be aboard her now, but for the quinsy that by God's grace kept me from sailing with her. If we go closer to her, we'll be lost as she is. Look—look at the second hulk!"

"It's the Stagnant Death!" grew the mutter of voices. "Look, look!"

The sea, at which they stared, had no waves despite the breeze, but seemed all curiously still. The surface undulated gently; this surface consisted of seaweed extending over the horizon. Brownish-green kelp, enormous trailing lengths hiding the water from sight, except where channels cut through it. A sinister, unearthly and ominous vision.

A mile or two distant, in the thickest of the weed as though held in its massy vortex, lay a great ship. Beyond was a smaller

The very deep did rot: O Christ!
That ever this should be!
Yea, slimy things did
crawl with legs
Upon the slimy sea.

one; but the first was plainer to the sight—a huge galleon, dismasted, its high stern jutting into the air. Something indefinable about the outlines of that hulk, something queer, suggested horror.

"By the nails of God, go no closer!" cried one of the officers. "The water has no current; we'll be bound here helpless in another five minutes!"

The captain gave an order. Men leaped to the lines; the big ship sluggishly began to come around. From the man in chains burst a ringing, scornful laugh:

"Ha, *caballeros!* Cowardly dogs, to fear seaweed and a motionless ship!"

ATTENTION WAS focused upon him instantly. At an order from the captain, he was led aft, and the officers gathered around. The stately Spanish captain eyed him furiously.

"So, Don Balthasar de Soto! Sent home to Spain in chains, disgraced, doomed to trial for treason—and still a braggart! Perhaps you would like to explore yonder ship and make report of what you find aboard her?"

"I'd like nothing better," retorted Don Balthasar, "if it were only to prove that all Spanish blood is not craven and debased!"

The words stung. Disgraced and doomed Don Balthasar might be, for defying the viceroy sent out from Spain to the New World; but he had the yellow hair and blue eyes of ancient Gothic blood, and with them a certain wisdom that laughed at terrors seen or unseen.

The captain angrily snapped out orders. The ship's one boat, a stout pinnace, was cleared and lowered into the grassy water; six hapless seamen, white with fear, were ordered to the oars. The chains were removed from Don Balthasar's wrists and ankles; he swept the officers on the quarterdeck an ironical bow.

"Farewell, brave *caballeros!* The King will reward you well for news from the lost galleon! I'll bring back a few skeletons with me!" And he was gone into the waiting boat, with a mocking laugh.

The ship behind him was all filled with terror of the supernatural; as the stout little pinnace crept toward that towering hulk, surging and sliding through the weedy masses, the six rowers sweated with panic fear. The sight of those two empty, desolate hulks, so motionless under the bright sun and wind, and the inability of the ship herself to make headway through the kelp, was all bad enough. Worse yet was the stagnant unstirred water and stink of the weed; and still worse, the ghastly hulk ahead. At closer view, even the firm lips of Don Balthasar tightened, his eyes grew wary and alert, for realization of the grisly thing was chilling.

Her two rusted anchor cables hung straight down as though she lay anchored, but here was no bottom in a hundred fathom. Her lower ports were tight shut. Some of the upper ports were open, and from them curled branches and tendrils of growing things. Leaves decked her broken mast-stubs as though they had sprouted; and along her high poop trailed green growths. The whole ship seemed to have taken horrible root, by some hideous wizardry.

Rotted cordage hung from the shattered rails; at her waist was lowered a gangway ladder, and for this Don Balthasar steered. He hailed, but had no reply. She was silent as death, yet filled with hushed uneasy sounds. They lay hooked to the ladder, listening to the eerie noises—the faint low groans, bubbling squeaks, wheezy sighs. The six men blenched, but Balthasar stood up.

"Devils, avaunt!" he cried cheerfully. "Come along, men! The ladder's sound."

Aye, sound enough; and as he mounted, he observed that here and there it had been crudely but freshly repaired. No ghostly hands had done such work, and a laugh broke upon his lips. He topped the rail and leaped over to the deck; and there his laugh died, and chill dread lashed across his soul.

For, at either side, appeared a swaying, ghastly figure in boots and armor and steel cap, with skeleton face below the cap. Two of the men came tumbling over the rail, a third followed and hung there poised in paralysis of horror. Across the deck, toward them, a skull came rolling, and another followed it.

From the men burst one yell of shrill and awful terror. A gush of white smoke erupted from the poop, an arquebus roared, and a hail of bullets whipped the air. The man on the rail screamed out and fell, still screaming, from sight. Don Balthasar pitched forward. One of those swaying, ghastly-faced figures lurched down on top of him. The other two men went all asprawl for the pinnace below.

Now, upon the rail, leaped into sight the figure of a slim girl, draped in seaweed. She was directly above the boat. Seeing her outlined against the sky, the men broke into wild cries and shrieks; she held something, and let it drop. A cannon-ball, hurtling down at them, striking the very bows of the boat and shattering its rail.

The five remaining men pushed out in frantic horror, dug in oars for dear life, and pulled like mad. The girl, still on the wide rail, straightened up and watched them go. The dead man floated in the weed until something pulled him down. On the deck, Don Balthasar lay senseless, abandoned.

The girl watched until the boat drew near the ship. The five

men piled aboard her in mad haste, with their tale of throbbing fright; canvas was hoisted again, and without pause even to take the pinnace aboard, the ship surged away from this place of death and stagnation.

BUT BALTHASAR, aboard the hulk, was neither dead nor alone.

One of those bullets had raked his scalp. Another had cut the rope sustaining one of the swaying deathly figures, letting it fall upon him. Now came the girl. She pulled the dummy away, and knife in hand looked down at him.

A girl? Rather, a woman; a slender, lissom little woman, a very miniature of loveliness, a woman with the haunting wistful charm of a Chopin nocturne. Youth and tenderness ineffable breathed from her. Seaweed, fresh-plucked and glistening in the morning sunlight, encircled her proud slim throat, dripped down her slight pointed breasts, clung against her slim thighs. Eyes and hair were glossy dark; her features were chiseled in soft, delicate perfection.

She stood staring down at Don Balthasar with widening eyes. He looked very young, and his yellow hair was like spun

silk. She reached to his shirt, tore it open, and looked curiously at his chest, touching the white skin.

Darting up, she disappeared at a run. A moment and she returned, a ragged gown fluttering about her eager young body, the seaweed gone. She held a pannikin of water.

Balthasar, wakening, looked up into her face. She smiled, and spoke.

"I'M SO sorry that you're English!" she murmured in liquid Andalusian. "Even if you're not all hairy under your clothes, like the others, you're still English. Yet you're not like them at all, you don't look like them, and I'm not afraid of you. Why must you be English, with yellow hair?"

"Ha, little angel! I don't know or care whether this is Paradise or dream," responded Balthasar with enthusiasm. "In case it's Paradise, and St. Peter sent you to inquire, tell him that I'm certainly not English. I'm Balthasar de Soto by name, a Viejo Cristiano of the ancient Spanish blood; and I'd rather be dead here with you, than dead at Madrid!"

As the girl comprehended his words, mingled emotions passed across her face; a wild amazement, a forlorn bitter chagrin. Her eyes dilated; she gasped:

"Spaniard? You? But I thought—I thought all Spaniards were dark, like the pictures in the great cabin! Donna Luisa never said Spaniards had yellow hair!"

Balthasar suddenly sensed a quivering peril in her. This untamed virginal creature must be kept from any emotional despair; he could feel her frantic dismay, could see the impetuous beating of her heart. Swiftly, gently, he caught her hand and spoke.

"Look, little angel! Have pity upon me: tell me how you came to be here, why you took me for English! Who struck me down? Where are my men?"

"Gone, and your ship as well," she exclaimed, and her lips trembled. "Oh, miserable fool that I am! God forgive me, I tried to kill you. I thought you were like those other men, that you'd pursue me and mistreat me as they did Donna Luisa!"

"The ship gone? Hold on! Help me up."

Still gripping her hand, Balthasar came to his feet. One look at his ship's sails, barely showing on the horizon, and he turned with wild joyous laughter. When he met her eyes, the marvel of her again drove all else from his brain.

"Good! Gone, and good riddance!" he cried gayly. "Come, little angel! Who are you?"

Her wide eyes fastened wonderingly upon him, she spoke like a child, parrot-like, repeating words dinned into her ears.

"My name is Donna Ysabella Maria de Avelando, Countess of St. Jago, Lady of Las Cruces in Nuevo Granada—at least, that's what Donna Luisa taught me to say. My mother called me Conchita, and I like it much better. You may call me Conchita if you wish."

"Thank you, Señorita Conchita." With an effort, Balthasar clutched at slipping reason. "How old are you?"

"I don't know. Donna Luisa said I was twelve when the ship came here."

"Five years ago; you're seventeen, then. *Diantre!* I'm twenty-two. Stripped of my estates, imprisoned by that accursed viceroy, robbed of everything my father won in New Spain—well, we're a good couple. Ha! This head hurts. I'd give my right arm for a cup of wine!"

"Oh!" Contrite again, she caught his arm. "And you're hurt! Come into the cabin. I'm sorry I hurt you, Don Balthasar, truly sorry! Come along; I'll bandage your head, too. I have plenty of wine."

BALTHASAR, SOMEWHAT doubting his own sanity at first, doubted no longer when he sat in the cool stately cabin, a massive golden cup of wine before him, and listened to the girl. She had been aboard with her family when the galleon sailed out of Havana, and was torn from the fleet by sudden storm.

The masts gone, mad panic in the crew, revolt and mutiny—
she remembered little of those wild happenings. Later, she
had awakened to calm, finding herself in the arms of Donna
Luisa, a young matron passenger. Every other soul was dead—
or departed with the ship's boat; and the galleon drifted here in
the weedy sea, her anchors grappling the thick growths.

Thus began the years for woman and child, lost here out of
the world, prisoned by the stagnant death; other ships avoided
this patch of weedy sea.

The galleon was new and sound, provisioned, wined and
watered for hundreds; it made a secure home. Storms burst, but
no waves battered the sea of weeds. All was loneliness, a living
death, denied only by the child's growth.

Donna Luisa had fostered the young girl tenderly, nobly,
bravely; a great woman, that unknown Donna Luisa!

THEN THE Englishmen had come; that smaller ship,
yonder, had been theirs. They boarded the galleon hulk. What
happened? Conchita was not sure, but Balthasar could guess at
the nightmare deeds. The hacked portraits on the cabin walls
bore witness to carouse and rapine.

Judgment had overtaken those men swiftly. They were
crowded in their boat, alongside, when Donna Luisa dropped
a cannon-ball into it. Men could not swim in that sea of weed,
which clutched at them and bore them down; also, beneath the
weed were deathly things. Yet three of the Englishmen scrambled back aboard and wounded Donna Luisa to death.

They did not live long, for doom came out of the sea and
took them. How? Conchita did not know, but shivered and
paled as she told of it. Some grisly thing from the weed-bound
deeps, that came at night and took them. She had heard them
screaming.

"Sometimes it comes now. I can hear it, and the ship leans
over to it," she said, breathing hard. "I shut everything tight, and
in the morning it's gone. I was afraid more Englishmen would
come, so I fixed up those dummy men with skulls, and loaded

some fire-
arms. When
you came, I
thought you
were English,
with the yellow
hair—"

She regarded
Balthasar with
a pitiful twisted
smile, and began
weeping madly.

He was not
slow to under-
stand. No
longer alone
now, she had
found a friend,
all the desperate
lonely tension
was broken, and
life had flooded
back upon
her full force.
The violence
of her reac-
tion, however,
alarmed him.
He caught her
in his arms and
dinned harsh

She stood staring at Don Balthasar.

words at her, striving to halt her sobs.

"Stop it, I say! Stop it! Do you know you've saved my life?"

Finally she comprehended what he was saying and stared at
him from tear-wet eyes, startled. As he held her close, her eager

palpitant heart against his own, the swift madness of desire swirled upon him.

"Balthasar! How—how could that be?" she stammered. "Saved your life?"

His name on her lips, her kinship and warm friendliness and radiant youth, her nearness, her slim exquisite body between his hands, all fed the flame within him. He quenched it, upon a muttered oath; and touched his lips to her forehead, as to that of a child. But all too well he perceived she was no child.

"I was in chains aboard that ship, a prisoner, doomed," he said. "I had dared to oppose the tyranny of the viceroy, the great man who ruled the New World. The men aboard the ship dared not investigate this hulk; they were afraid. They sent me. And now—ah!" A great joyous laugh shook him. His eyes kindled upon her. "Now I'm accounted dead, and all the horizon opens again!"

"Then you're happy, after all? I'm glad, glad!" She leaned forward, kissed him on the lips, and went dancing away like a fairy sprite. "Come! I'll show you our ship. It's yours now, as well as mine; your home and mine, Balthasar!"

He had forgotten his hurt head, now and altogether.

I F H E were tempted to any fantastic visions concerning this galleon hulk, they speedily faded before cold reason; Balthasar was no fool when it came to practical affairs. One brief inspection of this majestic Spanish sea-castle, and he was filled with acute alarm.

Beneath the apparent security was an appalling rottenness. Fruits, seeds and plants, being carried to Spain, had vegetated and rotted and sprouted. The main hold was one hideous tangle of pallid white growths, deprived of sunlight, and it also stank with water. The pumps were long since rotted and useless.

Penetrated by roots from within, by worms and stress from without, the seams of the galleon were gradually opening. Only her stout newness had preserved her this long against the stagnant death.

When he pointed this out to Conchita, she assented, her

Sargasso Sea

face troubled. The English ship was quite obviously doomed; she had observed in recent days that the other craft was lying lower in the water.

Once on deck again, Balthasar looked for the sails of his ship, and laughed to see that they had clear disappeared. But something else remained. This was the little pinnace, abandoned, left adrift.

His brain leaped as he saw it. A scant mile away, with the wind gradually setting it through the weed in their direction. A stout little shallop, too—why not? There was salvation, to his hand!

"Look! There's escape for us both; not to Spain, but to some other land, some isle of the Indies, anywhere at all! When she comes a bit closer, I'll swim to her and fetch her alongside."

"No, no!" She caught at him in sharp protest. "You must not! A swimmer cannot live amid the seaweed!"

"But I can." Balthasar pointed to one of the channels. "That channel is fairly clear. A panicked man would drown in the weed, yes; a cool head survives."

"But it's death, Balthasar! The things under the weed—not fish, not sharks, but other things—I don't know what they are, but I know they're down there." She was lost in a wild and frantic alarm. "No, you must not!"

"We must not lose that pinnace, either." He eyed the grassy sea, the sky, and nodded. "Very well. Wait until evening, until morning. She's drifting closer. If the wind doesn't change, we can afford to wait. By heavens, that boat has been sent to us in vital need!"

So, for the moment, the matter was put aside. As for mysterious things under the weed—Balthasar only laughed.

He laughed at more than this. As the day drew on, Conchita developed an almost delirious exuberance, in a joy and delight of companionship that knew no bounds. Balthasar flung himself into her mood; they clambered about the high carven stern and galleries, fired off arquebuses, even poured powder into one of the rusted ship's guns and sent a ball skipping across the surface of the weed.

From the cabins, the girl lugged out silks, jewels, and women's gauds, decking herself with them, finding fine linen and lace and court dress for Balthasar. One of the chests yielded a lute; taking this, Balthasar strummed it and sang to her while she made ready a meal. The music, a new thing to her, moved her to tears and laughter of sheer emotion.

But to Balthasar the music brought realization. They two had come together out of the wide world's chaos; they had found one another, and for ever.

TIME PASSED, and the extravagant abandon wore itself out. Late in the afternoon, clad ridiculously in a garish flaunting gown of Moorish fabric, Conchita flung herself down on the deck beside him. She was all grave and serious, now.

"Does your head hurt? Do you want some wine? What do you want?"

"Only that." Balthasar pointed to the floating pinnace. "You see? It's closer now. Morning will find it near enough for me to get. And none too soon. This rotting home of yours has a lot of water in the hold."

"Supposing we get somewhere,"—and her gaze searched him thoughtfully,—"what will we do then?"

"Live." He smiled, strummed the lute, and smiled again. "Live, and face life together. It has problems, always. Do you know, you look like a monkey in that absurd dress! Pick out another."

"I like this one. It's pretty." She frowned. "What's a monkey?"

He explained the nature of a monkey. With a sudden gasp, she leaped up. White with anger, she darted away at a run and disappeared in an after cabin, with slam of door and grate of bolt.

Balthasar, laughing heartily, idled about. He watched the sun draw down in the west, while the pinnace moved ever closer before the urging breeze. Conchita did not reappear. Her absence, her silence, gave him an eerie sense of desolation and uneasiness.

"Balthasar!" In the gathering twilight he heard her voice, still firm with anger. "You can't stay out there after the sun goes down; it's dangerous. You may come into the first cabin and sleep there. I've opened the door. Be sure to lock and bar it after you. It's the cabin where the gold is piled. The Englishmen brought it up from the lazaretto."

He called to her swiftly, but again a door slammed for her only response.

Gold? Balthasar hurried to the lower deck cabins that opened off the waist. The first one was open; the doors beyond were closed and barred.

Royal gold from the mint, each heavy bar stamped with the royal seal and carefully wrapped—a whole pile of the bars were here. Gold for ballast, the stout pinnace with food and wine, water that was not yet spoiled from rain caught by the girl— why, here was everything! Fortune, adventure, security, the whole future glorious!

Balthasar was late in falling asleep, that night....

With morning, he wakened to her touch. She was here beside him, her fingers caressing his cheek, her voice at his ear, penitent and tender.

"Dear Balthasar, you won't ever call me a horrid hairy animal again? Then I'll be nice; it's a promise. Now come along outside.

The tendril flicked across
her shoulder and settled
there.... A sinuous arm fell
upon Balthasar, encircling
him with crushing force.

I've caught a fish, it's cooked and ready, and we'll have a grand meal. The little boat is close, too."

WHEN HE emerged on deck, she was radiant, eager, bubbling with high spirits, laughing as she pointed to the pinnace that was now within a quarter-mile. Then a change fell upon her, a queer look came into her face; she gazed at him blankly, questioningly, and glanced again across the weedy sea. Balthasar followed her eyes, and understood.

Where the other hulk had been, was nothing. The English vessel had disappeared during the night; the kelp had closed above her.

"This home of yours will go the same way, without warning, and before very long," he said gravely, as they ate. "Those noises from below, the sucking of water, mean danger. The pinnace is safer for us, and I wouldn't lose an hour getting away. We'll put

in all the king's gold we can take; you'll not be afraid to trust to me?"

"Afraid of what?" She laughed gayly, a ringing peal of merriment, but it died out in gray misery when his gaze went appraisingly to the pinnace. "Balthasar, you must not, you must not! I can't have you go into the water. Let it drift closer."

"It won't. The breeze is changing." He pointed to the streamers of seaweed that spread out along the surface according to the wind's direction. "Little angel, it's now or never, so don't be silly. I'll reach that craft in ten minutes."

She relapsed in dumb, stricken despair and uttered not another word.

He was, indeed, in frantic haste to get the little boat alongside. The galleon was assuredly lower in the water than she had been, the wheezings and bubblings from her hold came stronger, and he was afraid the hulk might go down under them at any time.

Stripping to loin-cloth and knife, he waved a hand to her and went his way down the ladder. Her fear-set eyes followed him, and something of her own terror was imparted to his heart; at the touch of the slimy weeds, he shrank in loathing. Then all fear was gone, he swam on and reached an open channel, and gained the pinnace with no difficulty whatever. Clambering aboard, he got out an oar. Mast and sail were stowed under the thwarts, and his heart sang again to golden destiny.

In ten minutes he made fast alongside the hulk. Mounting to the deck, he found Conchita overjoyed, but with tear-streaked cheeks. He laughed and took her in his arms, all wet as he was.

"All's well, little angel! Upon my word, there's no danger in the depths. Now kiss me, banish all fears, and we'll get to work."

So he dried her tears, she laughed anew and clung to him, and presently they fell to the task.

Throughout that long day they labored, ballasting the pinnace with gold, stowing away wine and food and what unspoiled water they had. There were chests to be searched for jewels and garments, packages to be stowed, weapons and powder to be placed aboard; the pick of the galleon's loot was theirs for the choosing. With morning, they would get off, spending the last night aboard in luxury and comfort.

THE SUN was westering when they finished. Balthasar made a final selection from some weapons found in a cabin. He loaded an arquebus, putting a handful of bullets down the bell-mouthed muzzle, and laid it by, then fell to fingering a dama-scened Moorish scimitar that was keen as a razor.

They sat resting by the rail, and he told her of the outside world and the things thereof. All fine things and glorious, as in a roseate glow of beauty and high fortune and splendor illimitable. With her youth and loveliness beside him, treasure in the boat below, his own ambition and assurance all aflame, how could he see the world except as magnificent? All the future was golden as the sunset, to his laughing blue eyes.

They had food and wine here on deck, strumming of the lute and gentle Spanish song; the red sun was touching the rim of the weedy sea, whose odor of briny kelp hung heavily on the air. Between them, friendliness had ripened into something stron-ger. Balthasar could not deny his heart-hunger for the girl at his side; in her eyes, in all she did and said, he read her answering awareness. When she stood up and he reached out, spanning her little waist with his two hands, and she looked into his face, a perfect comprehension passed between them. He put it into gentle stumbling words.

"Conchita, little angel! The past is closed out and dead. Horri-ble tales already are told of this weedy sea; those men who sent me aboard here will confirm all the stories. Mariners will avoid this part of the ocean. None will suspect that I've escaped. All's clear ahead. On some far shore we'll find new destiny together. It must be forever, little angel. I love you, I want you always."

"Why not?" she said simply, putting out her hands to him. "As I want you, dear Balthasar. Why not?"

They stood enfolded, heart to trembling heart, lost in the rush of youth and passionate destiny, all the mysteries of earth dwindling to naught before the tumultuous surges of emotion that mounted within them. Balthasar felt very humble before this woman, before her dearness, her proud sweet self that so trusted to him. Half below the horizon, the red sun hung poised and swollen.

Suddenly, the deck lurched a little.

He felt her change within his embrace. A chill quivered through her body.

"Did you feel it?" came her breathless gasp. "That's the way the ship moves at night. When the things from the deep come aboard!"

Her swift terror drew a laugh from him; but, even as he laughed, a queer realization jerked at him. The hulk had lurched toward the bows, as though some huge unseen weight had come upon her there. He recollected those two enormous cables of rusted chain, hanging with their anchors straight down and down, like ladders reaching far into the heart of the sinuous growths below.

IN THE instant, across his mind swept old stories, bits of classical lore told by pedants and by wise men, fearsome yarns whispered by mariners and pilots. From the ancient days of the earth and from the haunts of seamen alike came those tales: How this tideless sea marked the lost continent of Atlantis, whence upgrew the undulant masses of weed in a stagnant death, and how, from that far submarine forest down below, emerged strange loathsome monsters to grip ships and men down to doom.

The instant passed. His mind wakened, his brain cleared. Before him in the stark realism of dying day, were etched clear-cut details that put to flight those childish fancies. The lightly floating masses of weed, blood-red in the sunset, the galleon lurching to the gentle oily swell of weed and water, the small boat scraping below. Once more a quick laugh broke from him.

"Come along, little angel! Come along and repel boarders!" he exclaimed gayly.

"Into the cabins and close the doors, Balthasar!"

"No, *por Dios!* Up into the bows, and chase your fancies! Should a *caballero* of Spain fear the unseen? Not a bit of it. Set your fears at rest, then we'll seek the cabins and get the lamps alight for our last night aboard. Here!" He picked up the heavy arquebus and thrust it at her; with it was the slow-match he had lighted, half burned away by this time. He caught up a long pike, and whirled his razor-keen scimitar, some loot from the old Moorish wars.

"Ha! Down with all dragons and fish that climb in air!" he cried merrily. "I'll take the van, with pike and scimitar. Follow, army! Shoot at whatever you see!"

He led the way. They mounted from the waist to the low forward deck, Conchita half-heartedly joining in his gay whim. There, pausing, she laid down the arquebus and its slow-match.

"My shoulder would be black and blue for a week, if I fired this thing with the load you put into it!" she exclaimed. "Give me the pike. I'll face the enemy to starboard; you take the larboard bow."

Plucking the long-handled pike from him, she darted into the bows. Balthasar, with his scimitar, went to the larboard rail. As he did so, the hulk lurched again. He distinctly felt the dip of her, as though some gigantic weight—nonsense! He glanced down at the water, at the weedy trailing masses below him, where the anchor cable disappeared.

Something, neither water nor weed, was moving there.

ASTONISHMENT SEIZED him. He craned forward, looking at the swirling water, the moving kelp; something was there, yet he could find no definite shape. A queer sound startled him—a catch of the breath, a wordless groaning gasp. He turned, to glance at the girl.

What he saw, remained bitten forever into his brain.

She stood in absolute paralysis of terror. Across her outstretched arm, binding it to the rail, was what seemed to be a trailing length of giant seaweed. Her single garment was fluttering wildly. Another tendril of seaweed had licked over her shoulder, fastening upon the cloth. It ripped the slight robe clear away, lifting it in air. The thing was fantastic, impossible, like some necromantic conjuration; but her eyes, fastened upon Balthasar, were dilated in frozen speechless horror.

HER SLENDER little body was bare, rigid as golden bronze. The tendril of giant seaweed, waving in the air above her, dropped the fluttering garment; it flicked across her naked shoulder and settled there. A quiver, a terrible involuntary shudder, shook her; it rippled across her breasts, down her sides, down her slim thighs; from her lips burst a frightful incoherent cry of blind panic.

All this in one glance, one flash of time. Balthasar hurled himself forward as the awful truth burst upon him. Not seaweed at all, but arms, tentacles of some hideous monster from the depths!

She screamed again. His blade slashed at the tentacle gripped to her arm; the steel shored through it and bit into the rail. There was a convulsion. The hulk lurched again. A sinuous arm darted high in air and fell upon Balthasar, encircling him with crushing force. Freeing his blade, he struck again, but not for himself. The tentacle clinging to her shoulder was severed. She was free. He shouted hoarsely at her, and she went stumbling away. The pike fell from her hand and clattered on the deck.

Balthasar lifted his weapon for another stroke, and it hung poised. Something caught at his arm, twining about it and about the scimitar. He was like a child in that winding embrace. Then, like the sheer ravening ghoul of a dream, the thing itself came, following its arms.

It came silent, monstrous, incredible, a great mass sliding up and up above the rail, a formless, shapeless bulk of outflung weaving tentacles—a giant octopus, with hideous staring eyes and horny curved parrot-beak, almost within touch of him.

At this appalling vision, utter madness seized upon Balthasar. He tried to struggle, in spasmodic, superhuman effort; it availed him nothing. Instead, he felt the sucking cups of those tentacles drawing him inexorably toward that devil's beak. He saw it open, felt the paralyzing effect of those diabolical eyes upon him.

Conchita had darted up beside him, touching him; he glimpsed her wild set features, heard a moan of terror from her parted lips, yet she forced herself forward. A tentacle swerved out and caught hold upon her legs. The bell-mouthed arquebus was in her hand, she was lifting the slow-match.

Balthasar screamed his frothing protest. Ignoring it, she thrust the weapon almost against that fearsome beak, and set the match to the pan. The priming spurted smoke. The weapon roared, with a vomit of red flame and blinding smoke smack into that parrot-beak, while the load of bullets shredded the huge shapeless thing.

The tentacles leaped in wild convulsions; then they loosened and fell away. Balthasar felt his numbed arm free, and struck out frenziedly with the scimitar. In the thinning smoke, he glimpsed the body of Conchita passing him, being drawn to the rail and overboard. He struck and struck again, desperately. His blade severed the ghastly clutching tentacle and he dragged her away, senseless.

Balthasar stood panting, weak-kneed, faint with sheer horror. He looked at the rail; the grisly thing had gone. Upon his brain rushed wild desire to get away from here at all costs, quickly, quickly!

He stooped, lifted the naked senseless figure in his arms, and staggered to the ladder. With his burden, he descended to the pinnace. Something heaved and rolled the masses of kelp alongside. In mad panic, in fury of haste, he loosed the boat, shoved her out and away. The mast was already stepped. With the sail let free, the boat caught the breeze and slid away and away, into the starlit peace and quiet of these meadows of the sea.

LIGHTS FLASHED on in the room. My gripped hands loosened; I relaxed and sat back in my chair. The others, around me, were exchanging quick glances, faces tensed and questioning. When I looked where the scene had been, there was only blank wall of stone—solid stone, as I later made certain.

"The demonstration, I perceive, was successful." Norman Fletcher swept us with his twinkling eyes. His voice was quite placid. "Well, Mr. Cromer? You seem to be a trifle upset."

"A trick!" burst out Cromer, who had quite lost his poise. "Some kind of motion-picture—a trick, I call it!"

"No," said our host gravely. "A scene from the past; a trumpet from oblivion, Mr. Cromer! A glimpse at what actually took place in the Sargasso Sea, centuries ago. Now we may comprehend how ghastly tales were told of that sea, and sworn as fact. And, mind you, with a certain basic truth."

"What we just saw was an illusion, a picture, a trick!" repeated Cromer angrily. "Why, the language alone—"

"Yes?" Norman Fletcher eyed him for a moment. "I must convince you that this invention is no trick. A week from tonight, you and these other gentlemen shall return here. At that time I undertake to present another scene from the fabulous past; but you, here and now, shall choose the subject!"

CROMER, ASHAMED of his outburst, pulled himself together. Some one else intervened.

"Here, hold on! Why should Cromer get to choose the subject? There are things we'd all like to have cleared up. What about the Gilded Man, for example, or the unicorn?"

"What about the singing sands of the Gobi desert?" exclaimed another voice. "What about satyrs and mermaids?"

Norman Fletcher, with a hearty laugh, threw up his hands.

"Gentlemen, gentlemen! Very well. Each of you shall have his turn, I promise it. First let Mr. Cromer choose his subject. I guarantee to have the reception tuned in by next week."

Cromer leaned forward, speaking quietly, impressively:

"I'll just call your bluff, Mr. Fletcher. During all the Middle Ages, and long before, there were wild stories about Scythian lambs. Lambs that came out of the sea; lambs that grew from the ground, to which their umbilical cord was fastened. From their wool were made marvelous silken stuffs. Jewish legend turned the lamb into a man-monster called the Yedua.... You've heard the tales?"

"I vaguely recall some such fable," Norman Fletcher admitted frowningly.

"All right; suppose you demonstrate it," said Cromer with a slight sneer. "The whole world believed in that fable. The Chinese of a thousand years ago went into details about it. The Arab writers were definite about it. Sir John Mandeville, the world's champion liar, claimed to have eaten those very lambs, roasted. If such a wild yarn as that had any foundation in fact, I'll eat my hat!"

Norman Fletcher, his bright old eyes dancing, bowed slightly.

"I trust, Mr. Cromer," he said, "that one week from tonight you'll wear a hat."

THE SCYTHIAN LAMB

"THE SCYTHIAN LAMB" IS THE SECOND STORY IN THIS UNIQUE
SERIES WHEREIN THE STRANGE ANCIENT MYTHS THAT HAVE
COME DOWN THE AGES ARE MADE REAL AND REASONABLE.

"GENTLEMEN, I'M prepared to display before you the actual scenes, the happenings, the very voices, of a thousand years ago."

A dozen of us, all members of the Inventors' Club, were gathered in Norman Fletcher's laboratory when our host uttered those amazing words. Tall, dignified, white-haired, he eyed us quizzically for a moment, and smiled.

"I undertook to let each of you gentlemen challenge me in turn, to demonstrate my apparatus," he went on. "I shall keep that agreement. This evening I pick up the gauntlet flung down last week by Mr. Cromer. Ah, the cigars! Let us be comfortable, gentlemen."

I must confess that most of us agreed with Cromer, the electrical genius of our circle, that Norman Fletcher's inventions and discoveries dealt rather with illusion or trickery than with science. Yet—the damnable uncertainty!

Fletcher was no fool. An old Yankee of great wealth, he was said to have at his fingertips all the resources of science; it was no secret that he had carried the later discoveries of Marconi to amazing lengths. In his relations with us, he was applying his findings to some of his own decidedly odd theories.

One such theory was that all the fabulous legends and great myths of mankind were based on fact. The human race, he liked to say, was credulous but by no means were men to be reckoned as dunces. And he undertook to prove it, in a manner absolutely

bewildering. All of us were inventors; most of us were familiar with electricity; and we were certainly skeptics; but we could not explain the results Norman Fletcher obtained.

"Mr. Cromer, your challenge proved very interesting," said our host, lighting his cigar and surveying us placidly. If he were conscious of our skepticism,—I might almost say our underlying hostility,—he gave no sign of it, but went on in his calm manner:

"During the credulous Middle Ages there was a universal belief from China to Europe in a certain fabulous wonder, which had various forms. Some said lambs came out of the sea, rubbed themselves on rocks, and left behind a fine wool. The more accepted version was that lambs grew out of the earth, to which each was attached by an umbilical cord; these lambs produced a golden gossamer wool like silk. Travelers swore they had seen

such lambs, had even eaten them roasted. Am I correct, Mr. Cromer?"

"You are," Cromer rejoined. "And you certainly can't find any factual basis for that lunatic story, in your television!"

"BUT IT'S not television," Norman Fletcher insisted gently. "We know that no sound, no light, is ever lost; it travels on and on into the infinity of space and time. My ultrasonic wave studies have enabled me to overtake and bring back scenes that the world has forgotten, voices and happenings lost in the far distant past. These trumpets from oblivion, as I term them, are far from perfect; but I think my presentation of them is rather good."

He leaned forward, to the switchboard before him, and pulled a switch. The room lights sank low.

"Rather good" was no name for it; we who had witnessed his unbelievable demonstration, were eager to see it afresh and strive to pierce its mystery. He had refused any explanation of his process, though entirely willing to show it in use. No wonder that some of us assigned it all to trickery or illusion!

We were seated facing a perfectly blank stone wall; the entire house was built of granite. There was no visible apparatus, there was no chance for any light projection.

"The tubes require some little time to heat," Norman Fletcher observed casually. "I suppose you're aware, gentlemen, that a thousand years ago Sicily was in the hands of the Arabs, and one of the great world centers of education and commerce. Even long before that time, a mysterious textile had come upon the markets of the world in small quantities; a material that was neither linen, silk nor wool, but somewhat like all three. From it were woven garments of golden hue and of almost incredible fineness, which were eagerly bought by kings and emperors at tremendous prices. Charlemagne had one; and the Arab caliphs of Cordova paid a thousand gold-pieces each, for such robes."

"What's this got to do with my mythical-lamb yarn?" demanded Cromer.

"Everything. The origin of this byssus fabric, as it was named, remained unknown until recently. You may see ancient fragments of it in the South Kensington and other museums today; it is usually marked as a mysterious textile of uncertain origin. Ah! Now you'll see for yourself where the connection lies."

Upon the blank, rough stone wall before us was spreading a spot of colored light.

Now, there was no projected light; of this we were certain—yet so staggering were Fletcher's claims that most of us were convinced of trickery of some kind. As we watched the soft, iridescent play of colors on the stone wall, Wallach nudged me and spoke under his breath. Wallach had been a technical man in Hollywood, and had invented the new color camera taken over by the Army Air Corps.

"Listen! If this is some sort of picture, I'm going to put the bee on the old boy. You back me up. I want to suggest the subject for the next seance. I'll guarantee that he could make no movie of it in a week's time—or in six months either!"

I nodded assent, then leaned forward eagerly. Wallach caught his breath. That solid stone wall before us was dissolving!

It did just that—it dissolved, under our very eyes. The stones vanished. As through a window, a glassless window, we were looking out upon olive groves, white buildings, a blue sickle-sweep of bay, cloud-flecked skies. It was no flat picture, but rounded life and distance in full three dimensions. More, I recognized the spot: it was Palermo; the Palermo of a thousand years ago under the tolerant rule of the early Arabs, in the days when the Saracens held all Sicily.

BENEATH THOSE olive trees walked a rugged man, a seaman, by his rolling gait; with him was a woman. She was robed in white and wore a Moslem veil that hid all her face except the eyes. None the less she conveyed a peculiar sense of grace and sweetness. Her hands, clasped at her breast, were very white and firm with youth.

"Lady Daphne, you ordered me to come at the last moment for your private instructions," said the man. "I'm here. The ship's ready to sail the minute I go aboard."

She halted, facing him, and put out a hand to his arm as though in appeal.

"Captain Petros, I've a hard thing to say, but you're the one man in the world whom I can trust absolutely," she said, and paused.

HER VOICE whetted the curiosity to look upon her face, so musical was it. In that voice were the whispering rush of ocean waves, the low fluted cadences of wood doves.

"Funny thing if you couldn't," he rejoined. "I've served the Lochias interests these forty years. The men of my family have captained the ships of your family for generations back!"

"But now the Lochias interests face evil days," she said

Motionless, she watched the craft of Captain
Petros head out to sea. The children were safe!

bitterly. "My husband is dead. I alone remain, and my two children. Look! There are the twins, the last of the house of Lochias."

She pointed to a fountain below them, where two small children and a nurse played in the sunlight. Two boys, yellow-haired, alike as peas.

"The last of that family which for hundreds of years has held a monopoly upon the commerce of kings," she said softly. "Today, peril threatens them and me, destruction threatens our industry and wealth. The Emir Al Mansur is determined to wrest the secret from us, Petros; I've had sure warning from one of his Greek slaves."

Astonishment filled the rugged bearded features. "But you have protection from the Caliph himself!"

"The Caliph's far away; Al Mansur, the Victorious, is Emir and ruler here. I want you to take the nurse and the two boys straight aboard the ship; land them in Tarentum, across in Christian Italy. Now!"

"You go with us, then?" The seaman's eyes searched her keenly.

"No; perhaps by the next ship. The *Pollux* is due from Ostia in two days. Now, I've converted most of our cash, jewels and property into bills of exchange; they're carried by the nurse, a faithful woman who was my own nurse. If I can evade the Emir Al Mansur, I'll transfer the entire business to Italy, to Tarentum."

Captain Petros clucked his tongue. Transfer this business, which for many generations had centered here in Palermo! Knowing as he did the many agents involved, the almost incredible care with which its vital secrets were guarded, he was highly dubious.

"Can that be done, Lady Daphne? You hold a monopoly on the precious garments of byssus fabric, true, but the very secrecy surrounding it has caused the business to become so intricate and involved—"

"It can be done," she interrupted with decision. "I'm the one person here who knows where the material comes from; we ship it in, prepared and ready for weaving, from Byzantium and

Aleppo. The shops here can be abandoned and set up again at Tarentum."

"Then why not go with me now, today, with your two children?"

She made an impatient gesture. "I cannot! I hold this great business in trust for those two babes. I can't do everything on short notice. There are accounts to settle, letters and books to destroy, agents to be notified—in another two days I can finish and get off by the *Pollux*, with the help of Odoric."

His face changed. "Oh!" he grunted. "Yes, your manager's an able fellow—"

"Well, get off, get off!" she broke in. "Take them and go, and hold the ship at Tarentum. The nurse is ready. Get off! And God keep you."

Knowing her proud, imperious spirit, realizing that she could not endure the agony of farewells, the seaman saluted her and went. The nurse picked up one child, he the other. They went down to the gates of the estate and out of sight.

M O T I O N L E S S , S H E stood, while time dragged, while the morning sun waxed toward the zenith, while the brown-sailed fishing-boats toiled across the bay. Then she sighted a lordly dromon heading seaward, with the golden yellow canvas that denoted a Lochias ship. She caught her breath, clasped her hands again at her breast, and watched the craft of Captain Petros head out to sea and away. The children were safe!

She turned back through the olive trees to a range of low buildings below the villa that was her home. In these buildings were the shops and offices of the company. She entered them, looked at the weavers busy with their looms and shuttles, and passed on to the main office. Here three secretaries were at work under a tall, lean-faced young man with crisp yellow hair, who rose as she appeared. With a gesture, he dismissed the scribes. The two remained alone.

"The children are gone, Odoric," she said dully, and sank down on a seat before the table. It was littered with parchments.

"Gone. The ship's gone. They're safe. Now we must prepare letters to all our agents, telling them to make no more shipments until they hear from us."

"I did that last night," said Odoric quietly. "I could not find you this morning, so I applied your seal and got the letters off by the dromon."

"Oh!" Her head lifted. Her dark eyes, above the edge of the veil, struck at him. "How did you know the addresses of the various agents? No one knows who they are!"

"I've known that for a long time." A slight smile touched the firmly chiseled lips of the Goth. "Since your husband died, over a year ago, you've run this business with splendid efficiency. Today, Lady Daphne, you face disaster; here is needed a man's arm, a man's advice, a man's help. Now—off with the mask! Shall I speak plainly?"

She made a gesture of assent.

"Why have I, a man bred to arms and command, been working in this place like some Egyptian clerk, these two years and more?" he broke out. His voice was firm; only the tense features betrayed his inner emotion. "Because, Lady Daphne, from the first moment I saw you, there was no other woman on this earth for me. Aye, though you were another man's wife, though I could never let you guess my feeling—I loved you. I went to work here, that I might be near you, the fairest of Greek women."

He paused, as though expecting some angry reply; but she stirred or spoke not.

"Then," he went on, "in that sudden squall when your boat was upset and your husband drowned, you were washed up on the rocks and lay between death and life for days. I managed the business till you recovered, and ever since have helped to manage it. Since that day, you've worn that accursed veil like a Moorish woman, in mourning for your husband; hiding your lovely face from the world. Oh, I know you loved him! I know you'd never look twice at me, a Goth, a barbarian from the north," he added with bitter passion. "I've asked nothing from you. I ask nothing now, except to serve you."

STILL SHE remained silent. He resumed, less vehemently:

"I've seen disaster coming. Here in Sicily, Moslem and Christian live amicably, as Muhammad ordered; but the Emir Al Mansur cares little for the teachings of his own prophet. He's a tyrant. More than your wealth and property, he wants you. He has long desired you—"

"No, no!" An abrupt cry escaped her. "You're mad, Odoric!"

"You're blind to it, as you're blind to my devotion. But I've seen it. Even when your husband was alive, Al Mansur desired you; since then, his desire has grown. I've seen it in his eyes when he looked at you. Now he is ready to take you and all the Lochias wealth at one swoop."

"You wrong him!"

"Wrong that accursed Saracen? I'd like to wrong him, sword in hand!" flamed the Goth. "Well, I tell you that today you need me! I know your secrets, all of them; I've learned them, in order to help protect them for you. I know whence comes this mysterious tissue woven into the robes of kings. I know every angle of the business; how the secret has been guarded, too. The false stories about sheep that come out of the sea and yield their wool—bah! Childish tales, but people credit them. Yesterday I begged you to get away, aboard the ship of Captain Petros; you refused. Now it's too late. I tell you the Emir wants you, you yourself!"

"Wait." Her word, her upraised hand, checked him. "First speak of ourselves. It hasn't occurred to you, apparently, that you'd not have been here all this time unless you were wanted, appreciated, trusted. You give me singularly little credit for intelligence, Odoric. What's the advice you urge upon me?"

"To get rid of that veil. Forget your mourning. Be yourself once more. I know a sure, trusty man with a stout fishing-boat, who can take us to Italy. Flee tonight, before all is lost; abandon everything here and go! If you'd only listen and trust me!"

"And, perhaps, love you?" she added softly. All the rich music of her voice was stirred and shaken by swift emotion. "Ah, Odoric, what woman could know you day by day, and not trust you, not love you?"

He started, violently. "What?" he burst out hoarsely. "Do you know what you're saying?"

"Only too well, dear faithful friend. But on that day when my husband was drowned, when I was swept by the waves on the rocky coast and rescued, I finished with love forever, and all life was put behind me. You shall never see my face, Odoric, neither you nor any other man. Even though I love you, even though I've learned to value you above all others—"

She halted abruptly, as startled cries resounded. The door was flung open. A slave burst in to fall at her feet.

"Lady! They're here—soldiers of the Emir!"

NO CHANCE to escape. Next instant half a dozen men were crowding in, dark armed men. Their officer, in glittering mail, made curt demand.

"Where is the man Odoric, the Goth?"

"I am he," said Odoric calmly. The officer gestured; his men fell upon Odoric, bound him, dragged him away. The officer turned to Lady Daphne.

"I've a litter outside; I'm ordered to bring you to the presence of the Emir."

"How dare you invade my property?" she flashed angrily. "I have protection under the seal of the Caliph himself!"

"Lady, Al Mansur rules here. We do no hurt, either to you or this place. Do you go with me, or do I take you?"

"When I've dressed, I'll go."

Her quick eye had already perceived that this was no raid for plunder. Guards were posted, the weavers were kept at work, two Arab scribes were taking possession of all documents in the office. Not loot, but orderly seizure.

A CALM, veiled figure, inscrutable, she went her way. When she came forth, she was still veiled, but she wore one of those priceless robes that the house of Lochias, alone in all the world, manufactured. It was of a light, pure golden hue, incredibly strong yet so filmy as to seem of cobweb.

From beneath the hood curled a tendril of her dark hair; above the veil gleamed her dark eyes. And through that gossamer fabric, whose glorious golden sheen had the faint iridescence of a dove's plumage, could vaguely be glimpsed the rosy

*"Lord, give order to loosen the cords, and
I'll tell everything!" groaned Odoric.*

glow of her long-limbed slender body. She, who was famed as
the loveliest of all fair women, disdained regally to conceal what
God had made to delight mankind. Only Moslem women did
this; the Greeks knew better.

When they brought her, the Victorious was seated in the
Court of the Gazelles, conversing with his secretaries and cadis
and officials. To Daphne, who knew the palace intimately and
had frequently been a guest here in happier days, this was the

sweetest of all sweet places in Palermo—palace rooms on two sides, the other two open to a glorious view of the bay and town.

The tiles of the floor and walls and of the plashing fountain in the center were of Persian make—gorgeous in coloring, representing gazelles at play. The roof-columns were of sculptured old marble from some Greek temple. Soft glowing Eastern rugs were strewn about, and pillow-seats of carved Moroccan leather.

Al Mansur, seeing the approach of his enforced guest, rose very courteously to receive her. He was a lean, hawk-faced man, sparsely bearded, darkly handsome, with thinly cruel lips and imperious, passionate eyes; a warrior, every inch of him, and a prince. He wore a turban with jeweled aigrette, a simple robe of pure white, and was girded with the weapon which it was said never left him by day or night, the most glorious, the most famous, weapon in all the world, sung by poets and coveted by kings—the Bride of Islam, it was named. To all appearance a plain, unadorned sword in a plain silver scabbard.

With a word, Al Mansur dismissed most of those around him, only a secretary and the guards remaining, and went to meet his guest. A flush darkened his face, his alert gaze swept her figure, then he bowed and touched his fingers to brow, lips and breast.

"Greeting and welcome, most beautiful of all women!" he exclaimed, taking her hand and leading her toward the leather seat. "As Allah lives, your presence brings a new light into this place, a new glory to the sunlight itself—"

"A truce to compliments, Al Mansur," she broke in, halting abruptly. "You've seized my property and brought me here by force, despite the protection from your master the Caliph which I hold. How dare you do such a thing? Answer that question, first of all!"

"Very well, since you demand it." He bent a swift, ardent gaze upon her; they were standing by the fountain, all others were beyond earshot. His voice leaped at her. "Dare? By Allah, I dare anything in such a cause! Lady, I knew you well in other days, and your husband also; since his death, I've scarcely seen you. You've mourned him, wearing this veil which conceals your face; the greatest glory of Palermo is behind that veil. I'm a man; Allah gave me ambition, desire! Is it a crime to love you?"

"Love?" she said, and the word held lingering acid mockery. "You misuse the word, Al Mansur. Your harem holds a hundred women! How dare you—"

"Only you are the one I desire," he said bluntly. "How dare I do this? Because I love you. Because I've waited and waited—"

"Al Mansur, the Victorious—what a mockery!" she jeered. "Did you bring me here to whine, like a puling boy?"

Deeper burned his color beneath her whiplash of contempt.

"No, I did not! You ordered, and I lost my head." He bit his lip; with an effort, he got control of himself and motioned to the leather cushions. "Come, be seated; let me set forth the whole matter to you."

She assented, silently seating herself. Al Mansur remained standing. From the palace room behind them, a sound pierced the closed doors; a thin, febrile sound like the sobbing voice of a man in agony. Al Mansur darted one glance at those doors, then turned to her.

"Lady, I am confiscating all the Lochias properties; the business passes into my hands. Your two children shall become my adopted sons. You yourself shall be the absolute mistress of my harem. At your feet shall be heaped the treasures of Europe, of Africa, of Byzantium! Sicily is yours; say the word, and I'll lead my men into Rome and make you its mistress!"

"You'd have led them there already, if you could," she said, faintly ironic. "No, Al Mansur; you have struck too late. The Lochias properties have nearly all been sold. My children have been sent away. Money and babes are beyond your reach."

For one instant, a flame of astonished fury lit up his face, then was gone.

"Indeed? But you remain; you're the chief thing. And the business itself."

"Whose secrets you'll never learn," came her voice, proud and disdainful. "I alone know them; nothing can make me reveal them, nor can any power compel me to your arms."

A smile stole into his eyes, a smile so crafty and assured that she, seeing it, felt her heart sink.

"Dear lady, do you think I'd have you by force?" said he. "Allah forbid! This night you sup with me, and when we have eaten and drunk together, the mullah of the chief mosque will make us man and wife, and your face shall no longer be veiled from me. And this shall be of your own free will. If you desire, you shall bring back your children; they'll not be harmed. You're in this palace, and you go not forth but remain here—and of your own will."

"Surely Allah has touched your brain!" came her voice, uneasy. He laughed lightly.

"I've watched you, lady; I know all that's gone on in your house, in your business, these many months. Compel you, when your heart is given to another? No! Well do I know your devotion to the house of Lochias and its interests. The new east wing of the palace has been prepared for you; presently you shall go there, where slaves await your commands, and at moonrise you shall receive me there—very gladly."

HE HAD a strong, cruel will, this man of steel; it shone forth from him as he spoke, and behind her veil Daphne whitened with boding terror. She forced a laugh.

"You seem sure of yourself, Al Mansur!"

"Come with me, and you shall know why," said he, and motioned to the guards. "Open the doors!"

She refused his hand, but accompanied him to the doors; these were opened, and they stepped into the room beyond. At first, with the change from bright sunlight, she saw nothing. Then she saw everything, and a low, stifled gasp escaped her. A slave placed a seat, and she sank upon it weakly.

Two scribes sat at a table, ready to write, but they had written nothing. There was an odor of scorched flesh in the air. Upon the bright tiles lay a whip, dripping blood. And stretched upon what seemed to be a table, was a white thing; but the table was a rack, with torturers at head and feet, and the white thing was Odoric the Goth.

"BELOVED OF Allah," said one of the tormentors, "he has fainted. Shall I revive him?"

The Emir nodded, and they set about doing it.

He lay there naked, fastened by wrists and ankles, his head lolling, his face all drawn and asweat with agony, his body scarred and welted.

"A stubborn fellow," coolly observed Al Mansur. "Evidently they've not begun to tear him apart yet. Of course, Lady Daphne, at a word from you—"

He paused; a shiver took her, but she replied with indifferent voice.

"He is nothing to me. Why should I speak?"

"But I think he knows your secrets, lady," came the smooth reply.

Odoric was revived. His head came up, a low groan burst from him; he saw her sitting there, and his tortured eyes dilated.

"Do not speak, do not speak!" she cried out, with a sudden heart-break of agony. "Silence, Odoric, silence! Let them do their worst—"

"Easy for you to say," he gasped. A wailing scream escaped him, as the cords were tightened. "Stop! Stop! I'll tell!"

"Ease the cords." Al Mansur stood looking down at him. "So you do know the secret of the fabric, eh? No lies, you dog, or I'll have your eyes burned out! All these stories about sheep from the sea, about wool from the sea—these have concealed the truth long enough. Now speak! Whence comes this material?"

"Silence, Odoric! For the love of God, keep silence!" burst out the woman. But the man, looking up into the cruel features of Al Mansur, made response.

"From Scythia, Lord; from the shores beyond the Bosphorus, beyond Byzantium."

"Whence it is shipped here, eh? Very good." The Arab's eyes glittered, and he made a gesture to the scribes, who were already at work. "What animal produces this material?"

"It comes from a certain breed of lambs in that country," groaned Odoric. "Lord, give order to loosen the cords, and I'll tell everything. I can stand the torture no longer!"

Al Mansur nodded to the torturers. But Lady Daphne had lifted her head; her eyes, above the veil, were fastened upon the Goth in a certain stupefied amazement; when Al Mansur darted one triumphant glance at her, she dropped her head and slumped helplessly.

Odoric, loosened, a mantle flung over his body, was given a drink. Then, sitting on the edge of the rack, he spoke freely.

"Lord, in that far country are many wondrous things, but most wonderful of all are these lambs, which are produced from the ground of certain valleys—"

"From the ground?" broke in Al Mansur angrily. "You Christian dog, do you dare to mock me?"

Odoric cringed. "Heaven forbid, Lord! I tell the truth. These are not lambs of flesh and blood; they are a certain fern or vegetable, in the shape of young lambs curled up, covered with a long hairy growth. The people of those parts gather this growth, which is pale gold in color, and after certain washings, ship it to our agents—"

Al Mansur flew into a rage. "By Allah, you shall be flayed alive and then impaled, if this be a lie! And I can get the truth of it." He whirled. "Send for the Hadji Khalid ibn Batuta, of Khorassan—quickly, quickly!" Servants darted away, and he looked down at Odoric with flaming eyes. "That man has traveled through all countries. He'll know if there's any truth in this fantastic story. Meantime, go on; give a list of the Lochias agents, and where to reach them."

ODORIC WAS straining haggard eyes at the woman's figure.

"Pardon, lady, pardon! I had to tell," he broke out imploringly.

"Better if you had let your tongue be cut out—or if I had done it for you!" she replied bitterly. "Now all is lost, all!" And dropping her head in her hands, she was shaken by sobbing grief. Al Mansur glanced from one to the other, snapped an order at the Goth, and Odoric began to dictate the names and addresses of the Lochias agents who gathered and shipped this fabulous material.

In the midst, arrived the breathless Hadji, a wrinkled, filthy old Persian, but a holy man who had made the great pilgrimage, as his green turban signified. He was, indeed, a traveler of high renown in his day.

Al Mansur put the matter before him; and stroking his white beard, he nodded.

"Beloved of Allah, I have not been in that far land of Tartary beyond the Bosporus, but I have been close to it, even past Byzantium," he said gravely. "I know not about the golden wool, but I have heard tales of such lambs. Some say they are real lambs, whose navels are attached to the ground; men who had seen them, informed me that they were a certain fern or vegetable which bore a fancied resemblance to the foetus of a sheep.* It is evident this man speaks the truth."

IN THE silence, the sobs of the Lady Daphne became audible. Al Mansur stooped, took her hands, and gently lifted her to her feet.

"Grieve not, dear lady," said he, joyously exultant. "This infidel, on whom you had set your heart, has told everything. Because he has betrayed you, I'll have him drawn apart by four horses—"

"No, no!" she exclaimed. "Let the infamous wretch go free, this minute!"

---

* *The old Persian had it right; the botanical name is Cibotium Barometz.*

"Allah!" The gasping cry was torn from him. "Allah!"

"The last and greatest name, as you so truly said!"

"Yes?" He endeavored to pierce the veil that hid her face. "Very well—if you promise to receive me at moonrise."

"I promise," she replied in broken humility. "Everything is lost, now that you've learned the secret; all is lost, lost! Let me have one last word with this coward, whom I was so blind as to love."

Al Mansur laughed. "A dozen, if you like!"

Slipping a hand beneath her robe, she went to the tortured white figure. From her lips came swift words in Latin, which none of the Arabs understood.

"My dear, my dear, you've done nobly; I'm proud of you! Get the boat ready. Be under the windows of the east wing, a little after moonrise—"

Then her voice shrilled up in vehement, furious reproaches. Her hand flashed from under her robe; in it was a slender jeweled stiletto, a deadly little weapon. She was in the very act of stabbing Odoric, when Al Mansur caught her wrist and wrested the dagger away.

"What, your love for him has so soon turned to hatred?" he cried, laughing. "Then your hatred for me may as quickly turn to love, if Allah wills! Now tell us how this wool of the Scythian lamb is prepared. Sea-wool, it has been called until now—"

She described how the wool was plucked from those lambs, growing out of the earth, how it was washed and made ready for weaving. The scribes took down all she said, while oil was applied to the hurts of the groaning Odoric. Then Al Mansur took her hand and led her to an inner door, where two of the palace women were waiting.

"Go with them, fair lady," he said. "An oath is an oath; the Goth goes free here and now, with rewards. And you?"

"Lord, I have promised," she averred. "Come at moonrise; I will await you."

She was gone. Odoric the Goth, stumbling painfully away, was given gold and let go forth where he willed. The Emir Al Mansur, exultant, dictated to his scribes letters to be sent at once to merchants of Syria and Damascus, regarding shipments of wool from the Scythian lambs. And the sun drew down into the western sea....

Two hours later, the Emir came to the apartments where his bride awaited him. This eastern wing of the palace, newly built, was beyond the gardens and its latticed windows looked out to the bay and the sea; but those windows were above the old *suk*, the animal-market of the city. The richer the odors that lifted from the *suk*, the sweeter were the perfumes burned in the palace rooms.

Learning from the guards that Lady Daphne had sent away the women and awaited him alone, Al Mansur's heart was glad. He stepped into the room where the feast was set, and then stopped short, at sight of her figure.

"What? Still veiled? And where are the robes I ordered for you?"

A low, rich peal of laughter came from her, as she stood up.

"Could you give me a richer robe than the one I wear? But see—beneath it I wear the silken garments you sent me! As for the veil, is it not the Moslem custom that the husband looks not on the face of his bride until after the ceremony?"

His face cleared. "Ha! But I have seen your face in other days! Well, well, have it as you like." He took her hand and kissed it.

The soft, rich light of a hanging lamp touched his lithe figure; he now wore a long *kaftan* and robe of embroidered silk, girt with his sword-belt, and jewels glittered on his hands. At his gesture, she seated herself on the divan, and he beside her.

THIS DIVAN, spread below the carved wooden lattice of the windows, was composed of cushions and rugs and a profusion of soft rich fabrics. Before it were set taborets of cedar inlaid with pearl and ivory, bearing all manner of dishes and fruits.

They sat side by side, and ate a little, talking the while; and ever the fragrance of the woman and the tender music of her voice quickened the passion of Al Mansur. When he unbuckled the belt and laid by the silver-sheathed sword, she put her hand to it.

"Lord, is that the famous sword of which I've heard so much?"

"The Bride of Islam," said he, and laughed. "Aye, famous enough!"

"Show it to me. And in return, you may remove my veil."

"By Allah, a bargain!" cried he quickly, and caught up the sword. "The scabbard is nothing; the blade is everything. It was made for the Caliph Abu Bekr—"

So, eagerly, he bared the blade and let her take it. Wondrous indeed it was: the steel was marked like watered silk; and inlaid, up and down the blade, were solid golden symbols in Persian writing. The ninety-nine most excellent names of Allah, said he.

"But the name of Allah itself—where is that?" she asked.

His laugh broke forth.

"That, sweet lady, is the jest, and a rare one! The name of God is not there; it is only on the lips of him whom this blade smites. And now, turn this way! The veil!"

"Wait!" she exclaimed. "First, there is something I must tell you. When my husband was drowned, and I was washed ashore senseless, the sharp rocks somewhat marked my face. That's why, ever since, I've worn this veil; not in mourning, as you and others have thought, but because of scars that marred my beauty."

"Nonsense!" He leaned forward, forgetting that she still held the curved sword, forgetting all save the flaming passion that engulfed him. His hands went to the hood and ripped at it, ripping at the veil. "Nothing could spoil your lovely face—"

His words died, as her head and face were bared to sight; he sat transfixed, while she regarded him gravely, silently. Her face, that should have been so soft and young and tender, was marred by appalling scars.

As he sat with horror creeping into his eyes, she leaned forward and spoke, mockingly; and he was too fascinated by that hideous sight to note how she was holding the point of the sword toward him, in both her hands.

"What, Al Mansur!" she breathed. "Is the face of your bride so lovely that it leaves you speechless? See, how young and perfect is my body—look how exquisite and firm—"

He shrank back; and—suddenly she drove the curved blade through and through him.

"Allah!" The gasping, bursting cry was torn from him. *"Allah!"*

"The last and greatest name of God, as you so truly said!" She leaped up, and he twisted in a convulsion across the divan. "A fitting bride for the great Emir Al Mansur—the Bride of Islam, no less!"

Her wild laugh rang out, but he heard it not; he heard nothing more.

AS THE moon rose higher and higher above the minarets and gardens and terraces of Palermo, it struck down a silvery flood upon the new east wing of the palace, and upon the broken latticework of the windows; it fell upon a swinging knotted rope made from strips of garments and rugs, that dropped toward the deserted animal-market and was lost in shadow.

It shone upon a sturdy, battered fishing-boat setting forth upon the tide, with men singing as they worked the sweeps, and high-piled nets in the stern. It illumined two people there, who flung back the concealing nets as the boat cleared out from the shore and the brown sails went creaking up. It struck down upon the two of them, as they looked one at another, and the woman drew aside her veil.

"There's the reason, dear Odoric! Look at me now, and never again in this life," she said softly. But he, laughing a little, took her in his hurt arms and kissed her on the lips.

"You are what I always thought you, dear lady, what I always knew you to be—the most beautiful woman in this world!" he said, and they sailed on out of the bay toward Italy, and the future.

VISION OF sea and moonlight waned and died. Where it had been, was now but the blank stone wall again. The lights flashed up.

We sat in Norman Fletcher's great room once more, and romance was dead and gone. We stared at our host, at one another, in bewildered surmise, until Cromer voiced the question that was in every mind.

"Marvelous, Mr. Fletcher—marvelous! But look here, what's the answer? Maybe I'm just too dumb to get it; still, I didn't find any explanation of the yarn about the lambs!"

"Nor I," chimed the rest of us. "Nor I!"

Norman Fletcher bit into a fresh cigar and surveyed us slowly, with his placid smile.

"Sorry, gentlemen," he said. "You put the case amiss. The explanation of the lamb fable was there; the fable that went around the world and was believed for centuries, while at Tarentum the marvelous byssus fabric was manufactured anew—as I believe it is still manufactured. Only, today, it doesn't seem so wonderful as it did a thousand years ago. What you want, is the explanation of that fabric, eh?"

"Right," spoke up my neighbor, Wallach. "Just what's the catch in the story?"

Norman Fletcher chuckled. "Why, the man Odoric lied like a good one, that's all! He started a new story that's been accepted more or less until recent years. Along the southern coasts of Italy is found a shellfish, the *pinna,* which is anchored to rocks by a foot or filament. This fibrous filament was gathered, dried, prepared, and woven into a golden silk; that's the whole secret."

"Sea-wool!" I exclaimed. "Sheep from the sea—why, of course!"

"And no one guessed it for centuries," went on our host. "The secret was jealously guarded. The fabulous stories were carefully propagated. The material was carried afar and then shipped back, presumably from Scythia or Russia. And there you are."

Again we all exchanged glances, this time of comprehension; then Wallach laughed softly.

"Well, Mr. Fletcher, you're good; I'll say you're good! But am I correct in thinking that you'll bring up out of the forgotten past the actual facts about any fable or legend or wild yarn that we may care to name?"

"That," said Norman Fletcher amiably, "was my invitation to each and all of you gentlemen."

"Swell!" exclaimed Wallach. "Then there's something I'd like to have cleared up by your machine, whether it's trickery, illusion, backfiring television, or what you will."

"Gladly, sir, gladly!" our host rejoined. He did not catch Wallach's wicked smile, but I did, and remembered what Wallach had said about proposing something that could not be fixed up with any camera trick. "Name your subject, Mr. Wallach; if a trumpet-blast from oblivion can clear it up for you, consider it done!"

"All right," said Wallach. "It's perhaps the oldest and most universal human myth, that of the dragon. When Marquette explored the Mississippi, he found huge dragons painted on the cliffs; in China, the dragon has symbolized sovereignty for centuries; in Switzerland, dragon-caves are still pointed out, among the Alps; hero myths of all races touch upon it. The latest explanations, more or less scientific, claim that it was just an allegory. That looks merely silly to me."

"I agree with you," said Norman Fletcher. "The ancient myths and vestigial memories of mankind are based on facts, not upon allegories. Very well, sir! If you gentlemen will do me the honor of meeting here a week from this evening, we'll see about it. I promise nothing, but I shall do my best."

WHEN WE departed, Wallach gripped my arm exultantly.

"Promise nothing—huh! The old boy is weakening. This time, I've got the heat on full blast, and you bet he knows it! He can't pull any dragon out of his hip pocket and flash it on me. He can't work any camera hokum and get by with it. Mark my words, next week he's going to climb off his perch or else get shown up proper!"

And I was inclined to think Wallach was probably right about it.

WRATH OF THE THUNDERBIRD

THE WORLD-WIDESPREAD MYTH OF THE DRAGON IS THE SUBJECT
OF THIS BRILLIANT THIRD STORY IN "TRUMPETS FROM OBLIVION."

WALLACH, WHO had arranged to drive me to Fletcher's, was a former technical man in Hollywood; his inventions in the way of camera-craft were legion; he was past president of our Inventors' Club, and a dry, active, shrewd sort of man. But he was nervous.

"Confound it! That old Yankee Norman Fletcher has me puzzled!" he broke out. "I don't know what to make of his hocus-pocus. We know he's an electrical genius, a scientist, a wizard with high-frequency and ultrasonic waves; but I can't believe what he shows us!"

I shrugged. "Same here; yet why not accept his words? When he invited the Inventors' Club to witness his discoveries in recovering sound and scenes from the past,—when he lets us challenge him as he does,—he must have something on the ball. He offers to prove that all the great myths and legends of mankind are founded on fact, and reproduces the fact. Last week, you challenged him to show us what was behind the dragon-myth of early ages. Well—"

"I know. I figured he was tricking us with movies, perhaps. I knew he couldn't get or make a movie inside a week, on the subject of dragons—not, at least, one that would fool me. But now the time has come, I wonder what he'll show us!"

Passing the gates of Norman Fletcher's guarded estate, we joined our friends of the Inventors' Club in the enormous granite mansion where Fletcher resided alone with his work. He

had invited us for dinner; a magnificent dinner, sparkling with
the finest wines, fragranced with the most inimitable Havanas.
Our host, handsome, white-haired, affable, refused to discuss
the evening's program; instead, he kept the table in animated
talk on technical subjects. His erudition and his flaming genius,
his vigorous outlook, his unconventional views, kept us all on
the alert.

Not until we adjourned with our cigars to the big laboratory

*Into the very flame of the torch that Red Stone
flung aloft, came that incredible beak.*

with its walls of cut stone, did Norman Fletcher come to the
point. Our seats were ranged facing one of those blank granite
walls. There was no projector or other apparatus here. Fletcher
sat at his control keyboard, similar to an organ manual, and
surveyed us with twinkling eyes.

"Well, gentlemen, I have a confession to make. I began these meetings in order to demonstrate certain experiments of no practical value but of much interest; now I'm the one who finds them so fascinating that I've abandoned all other work to follow them! You must pardon me for not explaining any process involved.

"You persist in calling this a process of television. It is no such thing, let me insist. It is the overtaking, the bringing back, of sounds, light, scenes, which have passed on into infinity. On one occasion, I recalled the drums and trumpets of the Crusaders at Jerusalem, and this suggested the title of my discovery—Trumpets from Oblivion.... The tubes used in these ultrasonic waves require some time to warm up; one moment, before we discuss tonight's demonstration."

HE FELL to work at his switchboard, then turned the room lights low. He leaned back, took a fresh cigar, and bit at it. Wallach spoke up, in his pleasant but keen manner.

"I don't know which to find the more interesting, Mr. Fletcher—your discoveries or your theories. Frankly, I'm a bit skeptical of both."

"I know you are." Fletcher smiled unconcernedly, and lit his cigar. "My theory that all the famous old myths of the world are founded on fact; and my endeavors to prove it, might lead anyone to suspect me of some illusion or trickery. You suggested that tonight I attempt to recreate the foundation of the great dragon myth, common to all mankind. I've succeeded in doing so; and to me, the results have been startling and unexpected. Professor Smythe, I know you've published a monograph on the subject of dragons. Will you give us a brief word?"

Smythe, also a past president of the club, was a college professor whose inventions in certain mechanical lines were noteworthy. He nodded, and complied.

"The belief in dragons was universal, from the earliest ages. We know, of course, that it is probably a survival from the dawn of mankind—a memory of giant lizards which, in different parts of the world, has taken on different forms. Reduced to a common denominator, as it were, the dragon becomes a sort of dying serpent, a carnivorous and frightful racial memory. By the way, I brought with me sketches of the only known prehistoric pictures of dragons. Would you care to see them?"

We would, and we said so. Norman Fletcher, in fact, grew almost excited about them.

THE CRUDE sketches, as the professor explained, had been made before the Civil War. When exploring the Mississippi, Joliet and Marquette had discovered these huge dragons carved and painted on a bluff near what is now Alton, Illinois; the figures were destroyed when a stone quarry was opened on the spot, in the eighteen-fifties.

"But these are remarkable!" cried Norman Fletcher, gazing at the sketches. "They're exactly similar to Chinese dragons, Professor—bearded, horned heads, scaly bodies and tails! I've heard of these glyphs. They're supposed to represent the thunderbird, the American Indian counterpart of the dragon."

"So they undoubtedly do," said Professor Smythe. "Now, I have another picture here, this time a photograph recently sent me. You may recall that last July the Government increased the area of the Dinosaur National Monument in Utah to the extent of three hundred and twenty square miles? In all this region, the fossils of dinosaurs and other primitive creatures abound. But here is a photograph taken by amateur hunters who found something else. Unfortunately, they ruined the site before it could be explored by scientists; yet this photograph—"

At a faint, crackling noise, Norman Fletcher lifted his hand and broke in.

"Hold it, if you please!" he exclaimed, and turned more switches. "Wait until after my demonstration, Professor."

"Very gladly," murmured Smythe, and put away the envelope he had produced.

"Here, gentlemen!" spoke up our host. "As it chanced, I've brought back the happenings of bygone ages in America itself—

even, as I believe, in what is now the great desert of the Southwest, and what was then a vast inland sea. Look for yourselves; according to my indicators, we go back four thousand years or more—"

His voice died. I noted Wallach leaning forward, intent and absorbed; upon all of us fell a hush, as a spot of light flickered

"She who was, is returned to the Great Spirit."

and grew upon the solid stone wall fronting us.

Before our very eyes, the naked granite wall was dissolving in a glow of light, of white, intense, electric sunlight such as beats down in the great deserts of the Southwest. Here, however, no desert came to view. In the light, things took form and shape, as though we were looking through a window in that wall.

The scene was rounded, in three dimensions; it was no flat picture. These naked, sun-swept rocks fairly radiated heat. Below them was water that rippled off across the horizon. A cliff above the sea—a cliff of peculiar shape, with square angular top, and halfway up, a rounded, jutting boss of black obsidian. Beside this huge black boss was the mouth of a cave. Flocks of birds flitted about the water. Off to the right, at the end of the rocky cliffs, towered a gigantic forest of redwoods.

Something moved at the cave entrance, came out into the

sunlight, and stood erect. A woman, a girl, glorious to see. Except for moccasins and strips of hide protecting her, all her body was a golden copper that glinted aureate in the sunlight. Her hair was a reddish bronze and her face was eager with life.

"Red Stone!" she called. "Answer me. I heard you. Where are you?"

Momentary silence as she gazed about; then from a clump of rocks leaped a man, waving exultant hand, and dragged into view a deer, new-killed.

"Gray Snake is losing his influence with the Great Spirit!" he called, as the girl came hastening down the almost invisible path along the cliff. "He swore that we'd starve, but we're still doing well; and here's a fine deer to prove it. Ha, Bright Sky! Luck's with us, and now we can let hunting go for a bit, and get some work done on the boat that will take us across the great water!"

He caught her in his arms; she yielded to his embrace, then pushed him away and looked into his eyes.

"Little Flower hasn't come; something's happened, Red Stone! She promised to be here last evening. Do you suppose she came by way of the swamp? It's the shortest, you know."

Red Stone started, glancing over toward the towering redwoods and the lower land behind them. He too was golden copper in hue. He wore only moccasins, breech-clout, a necklace of huge claws, and a quiver of arrows at his hip. Despite an air of hawk-like alertness, his features were thoughtful.

"Your sister would hardly have been so foolish, Bright Sky. Still, who knows? It thundered last night; and only when it thunders, only by night, does the Thunderbird come. Well, there's food for a few days. Come along and look at the boat."

A smile, another embrace, and they passed among the rocks to where a section of a tree-trunk waited.

LONG MILES in the distance lay the village of their people. Bright Sky had been ejected from that village because of her ugliness; she did not conform to the standard of the squat, wide-hipped flat-faced women. Red Stone had been ejected because of his contumacy toward the famous shaman, the priest-wizard Gray Snake. For long weeks, now, they had lived here in the cliff above the sea, and they were content. Bright Sky's sister stole away to visit them occasionally; and if the hatred of Gray Snake pursued them, it caused no worry. For soon they were going farther, across the shining water toward the unknown; and a new life was stirring within the lissom figure of Bright Sky, a new heart soon to beat beneath her heart. Together they were heading for the blue peaks beyond this sea, and a new home.

Red Stone paused at the boat, and ran his hand affectionately, proudly, along its side. Fire had blackened and eaten out its heart, to be scraped away by stone knives; the shell was nearly ready for use.

"Not a bad job," he declared. "At a pinch, we could start now; but we'll do it right. No hurry, with plenty of meat in the larder. And Little Flower wants to go with us."

"Yes," said Bright Sky. "She too wants to get away from this place of horror, from the clutch of Gray Snake, from everything here!" Her gaze went to the western sky, where clouds were mounting. "But why hasn't she come? Perhaps Gray Snake found she was coming here and killed her. His power is unlimited. He was able to drive us away. He tried to kill you."

"And could not," Red Stone laughed. He pointed to a huge boulder just beyond, which a dozen straining men could not have moved.

"You see this stone? It's like the one at the village, which he moves a dozen feet away by his magic; he says the Great Spirit does it for him. That old rat, my dear, is no more a wizard than you are! Influence with the Great Spirit? All in my eye! I've been figuring a few things out for myself.

"Now, suppose you take that deer up to the cave, and block the entrance well; then we'll spend the rest of the day taking a look along the swamp trail for Little Flower," he went on. "And before you go, Bright Sky, take a squint at that boulder. By the

time you get back, I'll have the Great Spirit move it for me over
to those fire ashes. Just to prove that I'm as good a magician as
Gray Snake. Get going!"

SHE STARED at him, fright and perplexity and admiration
mingled in her face, then went back to where the deer had been
left. Stooping, she shouldered it without effort, and started up
the face of the cliff toward the cave.

Red Stone, chuckling, looked among the rocks and produced
a massive staff cut from a hardwood branch. With this he went
to the boulder, adjusted his staff, and heaved. The boulder moved.
Grunting, he heaved again and again; the boulder shifted position and was at length a dozen feet away, above the ashes of the
fire. Red Stone flung away the staff and stood upright: the principle of the lever had been discovered in man's world....

Bright Sky appeared now with spear in hand. Her gaze went
to the boulder; a sharp cry of amazement broke from her.

"It's nothing, nothing at all," said Red Stone, with a grin of
delight at her astonishment. "I'm a magician too—a shaman of
the Great Spirit! I have influence with heaven, as Gray Snake
says. Some day I'll show you how it's done."

"Don't joke about the Great Spirit," she said warningly.

"Right." He nodded, gravely. "I'm joking about that rat, Gray
Snake. It suits you and me, my dear, to be chucked out of the
village, to live our own lives, to depend on ourselves; all the same,
one of these days, I'll kill that charlatan. That is, unless we load
our things into the boat and go, first."

He picked up a bit of charred wood, and with it scrawled on
the boulder he had moved. The scrawl was shapeless; frowning,
he tried again. In his concentration, his features took on odd
lines, the eyes slanting, the firm lips twisting. Watching him,
Bright Sky remembered the tales of people with yellow skins
from far in the west, who had come generations ago, and were
lost to sight.

"THERE!" HE stepped back and dropped the charred wood. The scrawl had become a queer creature with long looped tail and wings. "The Thunderbird! How do you like him?"

She laughed, uneasily. "How do you know what it looks like? No one has ever seen it. Besides, Gray Snake makes the thunder, and in answer comes the Thing from the swamp. I don't like it at all; we should not have anything to do with it. Besides, I'm worried about Little Flower, so let's be off."

Red Stone grunted something more profane than polite, and they started off together at an easy lope—she with her spear, he with bow and shafts. Each had a long knife of flaked stone as well.

The western sky was banking heavily with cloud by the time they were past the redwoods and heading downward for the edge of the huge swamp beyond. The miles fled behind fast; the sea vanished. At length they were skirting the edge of the great fen, which held more mud and quicksand than water.

A grisly place it was, and threatening. Stagnant, dark, thick with ancient dead trees, no man could penetrate it, or dared; for slimy things lived there, and above all, the Thunderbird, a creature of horror, like none other known to man, that winged in the air yet did not fly. Rumored to come forth only at night, and when thunder swept the air, it had been glimpsed only once or twice, by old men who told the tale and shivered. Always, far back as the tale of generations went, the tale of this swooping death was the same; its appearance was uncertain, for those who met it died. And always in the same fashion.

Some of the people, afar, worshiped it; all feared it. Gray Snake claimed that it, like all other living things, embodied the breath of the Great Spirit; and he had evolved a strong medicine, a mysterious charm, to protect one against its ravages. None the less, few took chances on his familiarity with the Great Spirit.

Bright Sky and Red Stone pursued their way swiftly, silently, watchfully. By day there was little to fear from the swamp, but alertness was second nature.

Suddenly, abruptly, Bright Sky froze in her tracks, sniffing; the scent of blood was on the air, and with it a queer fishy odor. Red Stone, with a gesture for caution, melted into the shrubbery and disappeared from sight like a shadow.

She stole on, until at length she came to the verge of an open space ahead. Then she froze again and stood staring, and gripped her spear, pallor growing across her face; for there was death, and all she had feared, and more. Her sister, a cold stark thing, face down; killed as she fled, killed after the manner of the Thing from the swamp. Always, the Thunder-

"So you walked into the trap, even as my dream said you would do!"

bird killed in this fashion: terrible pecks with his long beak, shattering the spine of his fleeing victim.

BUT MORE—A cloud stole across the sun, and the bright day was darkened ominously, both literally and figuratively. Squatted beside the corpse was Gray Snake the shaman, the priest-wizard, clad in his robe of reptile-skins. His powerful body was crippled by one withered leg. His face was like a mask of stone, impenetrable and unchanging.

He had made a tiny fire, and beside it a tiny bark lodge. He was quite alone, and was just concluding the simple ritual for the dead—blowing the smoke of the fire through the little lodge, then setting it afire and fanning the blaze to each of the four quarters of the horizon.

Silently, Red Stone appeared and came forward. Bright Sky trembled a little, then quieted. The shaman did not look up until his work was done; he scattered dust over the embers, and his glittering eyes struck up at the warrior.

"She who was, is returned to the Great Spirit," he said, in the tranquil phrase that expressed death.

"By whose doing?" demanded Red Stone harshly, and sniffed the air. "I smell fish oil!"

"No; the sacred fluid of protection, the great medicine to avert harm." Gray Snake pointed to the dead girl. "She came to me last night and I anointed her with it."

Red Stone jeered. "A lot of good it did!"

"The Great Spirit sent for her; not even the strongest medicine could prevent." The shaman glanced up at the massing clouds, as a mutter of thunder sounded afar. "Who can avert the will of the Great Spirit? When your mother gave you birth, she glanced around, and her gaze fell upon a red stone; that became your name. Into your body entered a tiny part of the Great Spirit that is in all things. When you die, it returns whence it came."

Red Stone sneered. But the watching Bright Sky listened uneasily. This calm speech on the part of the shaman was unnatural; he had adopted his best professional manner, instead of venting his real hatred for the warrior. Why? The girl was suddenly afraid.

"When we kill for food," went on Gray Snake, "or in self-defense, we ask the pardon of the Great Spirit for what we do; he hears us and is content. This girl did wrong, because she came to see you and her sister, as was forbidden. Therefore she died."

"I THINK you had some hand in it," said Red Stone bluntly.

"I? Do not be absurd. I did not leave my lodge all afternoon or evening; all night long I was there, making medicine." The response was placid, assured. Another growl of thunder, as though in assent, came from the darkening skies. Even Red Stone glanced up, startled, then eyed the wizard uncertainly. He too felt the oddity of this poise and self-control.

"Gray Snake, why should I not kill you now, as I've sworn to do?" he demanded. The other looked up with a grim, tight-lipped smile.

"For two good reasons, Red Stone; but speak of them later. Through my magic I have learned that you and Bright Sky are living in a cliff above the sea, a cliff with a square, angular top, and halfway up a huge jutting rounded mass of black stone. The Great Spirit showed me the place in a dream. There you live, with the woman who was cast forth because of her ugliness."

"You mean her beauty," Red Stone said scornfully. "And because she would not look twice at you. Well, what of it?"

"You and she must die," the shaman said in his calm way. "So the Great Spirit has told me."

"Also, he has told me to kill you," said Red Stone. "A dream, eh? I suppose you had the dream in broad daylight, and tracked us from afar, and found us." He shifted his spear and held it poised. "Well, speak up before I kill you; what is to prevent me doing it?"

"Two things," said Gray Snake, and made a gesture.

THE BUSHES opposite parted; two warriors appeared, shafts notched and bows bent, ready to let fly the arrows of death. Red Stone saw that he was caught, and stood unmoving. Half a dozen more warriors leaped into sight, and with excited yelps closed in around him. They took his weapons, and swiftly bound his wrists.

The shaman cackled with laughter that held no mirth.

"So you walked into the trap, even as my dream said you would do!" With this, he rose and struck Red Stone across the face. "And where is Bright Sky? Answer!"

Knowing that she must be watching the scene, Red Stone shrugged.

"Look! The Old One! The Thunderbird!"

"How do I know? At home, perhaps."

Gray Snake gave swift orders. Three of the warriors darted off to watch the approaches lest Bright Sky should come; others dragged Red Stone to a small tree at the edge of the clearing. They lopped the branches from the tree with their stone knives and hatchets, and tied the prisoner against the tree. Then they fell away and stood at a distance.

But Gray Snake, exultant, came close to the prisoner and spoke, low-voiced.

"You chose to fight me instead of helping me; you mocked, you jeered—and now you are where you are. This very night while the Thunderbird is working his will upon you, I'll go to the cliff by the great water, the cliff with the big black stone halfway up its face, and Bright Sky will make me welcome. Now shout aloud your hatred, your scoffs, your jeers!"

Now Red Stone remained silent, aloof, dignified, as though he had not heard. He was mortified at the way he had been tricked and taken, without a chance to strike a blow; yet the knowledge that Bright Sky's presence was unknown and unsuspected, held him steady.

She, motionless as the tree against which she leaned, watched and listened with aching, fluttering heart; but the hand that gripped her spear was firm. One of the guards had passed within a dozen feet, seeing her not. It was not for herself that she feared, but for the man yonder lashed to the sapling.

A jagged streak of lightning split the sky; the crash of a thunderbolt reverberated; and she quivered helplessly. Night was coming; already the darkness of the storm-clouds had banished the daylight. Men from the village had gathered now, watching the captive, taunting him, but hanging off. Gray Snake had removed his mantle of reptile-skins, had flung it over his head, and was crouched beneath it, a shapeless hulk, making medicine. The purpose of his calm talk about the Great Spirit was obvious now; it had been meant to impress the lurking, hidden warriors, and had served its end.

She saw the body of her sister carried away for burial. She heard her own name bandied about as the gloom increased; ugly she might be, by the standards of the tribe, but more than one of those men had desired her mightily, and hated Red Stone because he had won her.

ABRUPTLY, GRAY Snake stood erect, whipped the snake-skin mantle around him, and spoke in a mingling of words and sign-talk:

"This man Red Stone was put out of the village because he had offended the Great Spirit. Now his offense is deeper; we caught him coming armed to seek us. Yet, since he has killed no one of us, it is against the law of the Great Spirit to take his blood. In fact, I will anoint him with the sacred medicine to protect him against harm; thus, if he dies, it will show that the Great Spirit would not pardon him."

He gave quick orders. Men ran in and clumped about Red Stone, who was set free and then faced against the sapling. His arms were put around it and his wrists bound; he was helpless to resist. Gray Snake came to him, and produced a small gourd; over his naked back, the medicine was smeared.

Red Stone's voice lifted in mockery.

"Fish-oil, shaman! I can make that same kind of magic medicine, just as I can move great rocks unaided, and do other things you do."

Indeed, the powerful and penetrating odor reached the watching girl; it had the same fishy smell that had clung to the body of her sister.

"Perhaps you can," said the shaman, and laughed harshly. "But your medicine will not save you, your magic will give you no help; it is false, false! When the Old One comes out of the swamp, when the Thunderbird comes at the bidding of the Great Spirit, let your magic save you if it can!"

There was an instant of silence, as the men fell away from the captive. Then Red Stone cried out with sudden comprehension and fear:

"Ah—now I understand everything! Flee from this place, all you who hear me! It's the smell of this medicine which brings the Thunderbird! Flee, flee! This accursed shaman anoints with his fish-oil, not to save but to kill! He caused the death of Little Flower by it, as he will cause mine. Flee, all those who love me, and leave me to my fate!"

"Poor man!" exclaimed Gray Snake with compassion. "The Great Spirit has touched his brain; he utters wild words! Call in the guards."

The others muttered assent, and sent for the guards. Some of the men had already slipped away, for they were far from home and at the very edge of the swamp, and darkness was deepening.

BRIGHT SKY, however, knew too well the ring of fearful despair in the voice of Red Stone; she knew those words were meant for her ear, to warn her, to reveal the deviltry of the shaman, to save her. The truth flashed upon her in full force— with this gloom, with the thunder that muttered unceasingly and the occasional flashes that rent the sky asunder, the Thunderbird, the Old One, the nameless horror, might come at any time. An eddy of the still, storm-tensed air bore from the swamp a fearful breath of sickening, rotted odors.

"Three of you remain here." Gray Snake selected three warriors. "The rest of you, go back to the village!"

They melted away, gladly enough. Gray Snake took his three aside, and with great solemnity gave each of them a little medicine-sack as protection against all harm; what was more to the point, he instructed them to remain in hiding at the edge of the clear space. Their sole duty was to make sure that Red Stone did not work free of his bonds or get away.

"I myself will remain within call," he assured them. "But I must seek a retired spot to make further medicine and pray to the Great Spirit."

He took the bow and quiver of Red Stone, and vanished in the greenery. The three warriors clumped together and took counsel; they were not twenty feet from where Bright Sky stood motionless, and their voices carried clearly to her. She was dismayed to find that they trusted implicitly to the shaman's assurances, for she had hoped they would steal away and give her a chance to release Red Stone. Better to stay in company than to separate was the gist of their talk, for the night was coming, and already one could scarce see clearly across the open space. So, weapons ready, they plunged into the brush and were lost to sight.

At the sapling, Red Stone stood silent, waiting. The fishy odor expanded on the air. Bright Sky relaxed, trembling.

Wait for full night to come? She dared not risk it. Now, at any time, might come swooping the Old One, the Thunderbird. Better the risk from those three men, than from the ancient horror which went back beyond human memory!

She stirred. Spear a-trail, she left her covert and started straight for Red Stone, whose back was toward her. He had begun to sing his death-chant, accounting himself lost; he sang of his deeds, his battles, of Bright Sky and the babe to come that would share her beauty, and his own renown. A wild, fierce pride and joy filled her heart as she stole on toward him.

SUDDENLY A splitting peal rent the heavens, a glare of light filled earth and sky. With a leap, the girl darted toward the tree, knowing that if the three watchers were alert, they must have seen her. So they had; in the stillness after that thunder-peal, yells rose faintly shrill. An arrow whipped past her.

She jerked out her flaked-flint knife as she came to the sapling. The chant of Red Stone ended in a gulp of amazed recognition. She caught at his bound wrists and sawed desperately at the thongs; the knife was slow to bite. In the obscurity, she sighted three dim figures bounding forward.

Frantically she redoubled her efforts. One rawhide strip parted, then the other.

At the same instant her voice rose in a shrill scream of terror: "Look! The Old One! The Thunderbird!"

The three, already within striking distance, checked their rush, cast startled glances at the lightning-rent sky. She pressed her knife into the half-useless hand of Red Stone, snatched at her spear, and struck.

The ruse had served her well. To the spear-thrust, one warrior cried out and plunged sidewise, but took the spear with him as he fell. Clinging to the shaft, Bright Sky went sprawling with him, trying ineffectually to wrench the spear-flint loose; his dying arms caught her, pinned her to him; his hands struck out

Yells arose shrilly and an arrow whipped past her as she jerked out her flint knife.

at her, but death was already in his heart, and he could do her little hurt.

Meantime the other two warriors leaped upon Red Stone.

The jagged but keen leaf of flint split one coppery throat and brought a bubbling gush of crimson. Ducking an ax-blow, Red Stone grappled the second warrior, and they went rolling together.

When Bright Sky wrenched clear of that deathly embrace, Red Stone was springing up, a fierce and exultant whoop bursting from his lips.

"Not hurt?" He caught at her, drew her to him eagerly. "Ah, what a woman you are! And I thought, I hoped, you had gone!"

"Don't be silly," she panted. "Of course I didn't go. This is no time for love-making—let's get away from here, quickly! Gray Snake may come at any minute."

"Not he," said the man, with a laugh. "He's gone to find you, at the cave. Somehow he knows about it; he told me so, when he spoke softly to me. We'll give him a surprise. Here, see if you can scrape that accursed fish-oil from my back."

He visited each of the three warriors, gathered their weapons, tore loose the spear, and came back to her. She rubbed and scoured his back with grass, but only succeeded in making the odor more powerful. He checked her and straightened up.

"All right; let it wait till we get home. You're right. We'd better get gone. I can wash it off when we reach the sea." An oath of angry dismay escaped him. "Gray Snake will find that deer and gorge himself! Well, there'll be some left; we'll have enough to load everything into the boat and get away from this accursed place—"

"And meantime you smell like a dead whale," she interrupted with impatience. "Come on, come on! Every moment you stay here is dangerous!"

With a grunt, he complied, having looted the three dead men of everything from fire-bags to knives.

THERE WAS no rain; that would come later. It was full night, pitch-black, illumined now and again by distant lightning. Red Stone gave all his attention to following the trail by which they had come; but Bright Sky, with each lucent coruscation, darted anxious glances behind them. So powerful was the fish-scent, so impressed was she by the appalling cleverness of Gray Snake in using it, that fear rested heavy upon her, even after they had left the swamp behind and were climbing toward the giant redwood forest.

"Faster, faster!" she kept urging her husband, though they were loping steadily along. An agony of impatience was upon her. "It'll be safer, once we reach the tall trees—"

A vivid flash swept across the whole sky. She looked back; at her gasp of palsied terror, Red Stone swung around. He caught a glimpse of the dread Thing, far above. Gripping her arm, he drew her headlong into a little clump of pines.

They hugged the earth together; she was venting gasped sobs of sheer panic. They heard that monstrous, incredible shape hurtle through the air, close above their protection, and heard it return, seeking passage through the pines. Red Stone leaped up and shouted aloud, and the sounds ceased. But the death-smell of the creature, the same smell that had come out of the swamp, lingered.

"Quick!" he ordered, pressing a firebag upon her. "A fire, and hurry! We must go on, and there's just one way to go—with torches! I'll find a dead tree, while you build the blaze."

With trembling fingers she adjusted the fire-stick and spun it in its groove, until the spark came and caught, and a flickering light lifted on the pine-needles and twigs.

In the air above them, there sounded furious squeakings and metallic clashings. Another flash of lightning showed the creature itself—huge wings, a good twenty-five feet in span, a grotesque head five feet long, tipped by an enormous beak and a feathered crest. It hung in the air, hovering, waiting.

Red Stone had ripped loose a number of resinous dead pine branches.

"Here's enough to last us home," he said. "Get two torches alight, while I take a shot at the Thing."

Bow strung, arrows ready, he made his way to the edge of the trees and waited. Another lightning-flash, the twang of the string, a muttered oath, a swirl in the air and a crash of branches. Red Stone was back, breathing hard.

"The Thing has scales!" he ejaculated unsteadily. "The arrow went true, and just bounced. Give me that light! You take the other; bring the rest ready for use. No wild animal, devil or bird or reptile, can stand fire. All set?"

She assented and crept forth.

FOR A moment, her heart utterly failed her; it seemed they were both gone out to certain destruction. The vast, half-seen Thing swooped at them. Red Stone shouted again and waved his torch; her own smoky, blazing brand circled in air. Into the very flame came that long incredible beak as though to drive at them—then a squawk, a scream that fairly lifted their spines, and it was gone.

"Come on!" shouted Red Stone, and she was leaping after him, clutching spear and unlit torches in one arm, firebrand in the other.

They had beaten off the Thunderbird, but this was brief triumph. For they had not beaten him afar; the putrescent odor lingered; the swooping shape followed them, hung poised so closely that at times the torch-glow touched the Thing that floated there. And always the glow was reflected by those great round orbs up above.

They hurried on. Not to watch the death overhead was hard; yet they must watch the trail as well, and the torches. When one burned down, Red Stone lighted another and flung the blazing stump of the first high in air—so high that it gave them a glimpse of the hanging horror, the huge beak a spear-length long that carried death.

On and on through the darkness; the giant redwoods gave no protection, for the Thing swept under the towering branches, pursuing them with eerie and malignant persistence. Rain was boding in the air, but had not come. Lightning had ceased entirely, though now and again a mutter of distant thunder resounded.

"The Thing kills, but does not eat!" exclaimed Red Stone, as they hastened on. "It did not eat Little Flower—it killed, as it killed others, and let her lie. Why? Perhaps it eats only fish. Perhaps that devil Gray Snake knew this; the scent of fish draws the Thing. That was why he put the fish-oil on my back—"

He tripped, went floundering, and his torch was extinguished. Instantly the creature swooped, though it had no wing-beat; it floated down, silent and horrible, until Bright Sky sent up a shower of sparks from her own torch, and got another alight for Red Stone.

IT WAS an ugly moment, but it passed. They were getting toward home now, and the salt breath of the sea reached them. Red Stone slackened his pace to speak of the shaman.

"He'll be at the cave; let me go ahead," said he.

"No! Don't leave me!" she cried hurriedly, panic-stricken. He, with confidence regained, laughed and quickened pace. They were nearly at the cliff now.

"You have your fire; you'll be safe enough, Bright Sky! Wait down below, by the boat."

A passionate fury seized him, as he turned the corner of the cliffs and caught the gleam of a tiny cooking-fire on the ledge outside the cave. He forgot all else; reassured now as regarded the Thunderbird, carried out of restraint by the thought of Gray Snake up there, gorging on the deer he himself had brought in, Red Stone hurled his torch into the water and leaped at the cliffpath, disappearing from the girl's sight.

If he thought all danger past, she knew better. A terrible cry burst from her, as the light from her own torch caught a vast

*Red Stone swung around, caught a
glimpse of the dread Thing.*

shape wheeling close, wheeling silently and flitting toward the cliff. She followed, desperately plunging at the well-known path.

She looked up. By the light of the tiny fire on the ledge outside the cavemouth, she saw the figure of Gray Snake; he had expected her, but not Red Stone. She glimpsed, for one instant, the two shapes. She saw them moving, striking; saw Gray Snake dart for the cave and dive headlong into it, with the figure of Red Stone at his heels, grappling him—and then something blotted them out.

A cry of horror burst from her. The instant or two that she spent climbing that path seemed ages. Whirling her torch, she reached the ledge before the cave. A fetid odor assailed her.

*The creature hung
in the air above—
hovering, waiting.*

Shriek upon shriek came from the cave itself. Spear ready, she
held up the torch and slid in.

Something blocked the way. Beneath it, protruding, she saw
the moccasins of Red Stone. She seized his foot, tore him out
bodily, found him hurt and senseless. In spasmodic rage and
frantic terror she plunged her spear into the shapeless Thing
beyond that blocked the way—again and again, setting the torch

against it, wrenching the spear loose, driving it home afresh. The yells of Gray Snake were mingled with the frantic twittering, chirping cries of the inhuman creature; against the frightful odor of it, fought the crisping stench of feathers burning.

The entrance was narrowed still further by the stone they had placed there. She dropped her spear, darted to the stone, and put her weight on it. As it moved, a tide of blood came rushing forth, dark and noisome, around her feet. The stone blocked the entrance in part; she shoved it with frenetic strength, stumbled back into the darkness, caught up the body of Red Stone and carried him down the path.

SHE PAUSED at the bottom, gasping, to examine him. Gray Snake must have struck him down, for he had two wounds on the head, but he breathed. She lugged him on among the dark rocks to where the nearly finished boat lay, and left him. Horror still hot upon her, she stole back up the path to where the embers of the little fire still afforded light, and the blazing torch she had dropped on the ledge. The deer lay there; Gray Snake had just begun to cut it up. She looked at the welling tide of blood, listened to the dread silence—and hastily snatched up the meat and fled. Whether she had killed the Thunderbird, she knew not, nor cared. The Thing was there safe; and escape beckoned. Nothing else mattered.

Into the dugout she flung the rudely fashioned paddles, dragged the boat to the water, and returned to Red Stone. He was groaning faintly. She got him to the boat, lifted him in, and shoved it forth on the black waters.

A distant flash of lightning from the lessening storm lit up the shore, the rolling water, the boat, the cliff above with its ominous black boss of rock—then everything faded and was gone as she struck out, and a rush of rain filled the darkness.

THE RUSH and patter of rain, and darkness.... It filled the room around us, then was gone as Norman Fletcher switched on the lights. He leaned back in his chair; and what he saw in our faces must have gratified him, for he smiled as he reached for a fresh cigar and passed around the humidor.

I relaxed, stole a glance at Wallach, and saw that he was frowning, puzzled, intent. Professor Smythe's face caught my eye; he was stammering, trying to speak, unable to find words in the grip of some excitement that shook him. Some one else spoke up sharply.

"Look here, Mr. Fletcher! That thing wasn't any dragon! It was a Pteranodon, a giant member of the pterodactyl family— its fossil remains have been found in Kansas and other places. And it didn't have any tail."

"Others did." Fletcher laughed softly. "I've given you the result of my experiments; obviously, this was one instance of survival. It shows how the dragon-myth persisted, how the extinct flying reptile lingers in man's racial consciousness. Now, which one of you gentlemen desires to propose a subject for our next meeting?"

"I would," I said quickly. Norman Fletcher gave me a nod.

"Very well. What's it to be?"

Professor Smythe let out a squawk. Then Wallach chipped in ahead of him.

"Wait, please! One thing I'd like explained. We've just seen what's alleged to be an actual scene from the lives of prehistoric American Indians. I can vouch that it was no motion picture; I don't know what the devil it was—*but how did they speak English?*"

A dead silence fell. The Professor, purple in the face, restrained himself. Norman Fletcher gave Wallach a quizzical glance.

"Did you watch the moving lips of those who spoke?"

"I did; the words didn't correspond."

"No; they were dubbed in." Our host sighed. "My friends, no one has been able to translate what was said; I had to have words supplied, just as they're supplied on a sound-track in a movie—"

"Wait, wait!" Professor Smythe bobbed up, waving something. "You don't know—you can't guess—by heavens, it's absolutely incredible!" He paused to get his breath. "Here's that photograph from Utah you haven't seen yet. Well, look at it! These amateur bone-hunters turned up the greatest thing that's ever been discovered, and let it go to ruin! Human bones mixed with prehistoric bones—the peculiar air-spaced bones of the Pteranodon—like no others! But look at it, look at it!"

The photographs were passed around. When Norman Fletcher saw them, he let out a gasp; and no wonder. I saw the reason when they came to me. For jutting out above what had been the bed of an ancient sea, and now was desert, they showed a cliff: exactly the same cliff we had just seen, with that peculiar black basalt mass halfway up, and beside it the mouth of a cave!

It positively flabbergasted all of us. It drove everything else out of our heads.

A S W E drove homeward, Wallach said: "If we're to believe all this—Smythe bobs up with a photograph of the very place we saw in Norman Fletcher's trick picture, and a yarn about the bones of that guy Gray Snake and the Thunderbird having been found! Either it's the most damnable coincidence that ever happened—or it's sheer collusion."

"Smythe isn't that kind," I protested. "Norman Fletcher's too big a man for such a thing to be suspected. Look how he owned up to your question about the language!"

Wallach swore heartily. "Nobody's too big to fall for a good show like that; trouble is, it was too darned good. Coincidence? Not much. Me, I'll put my money on a frame-up! By the way, what subject did you propose for next week? You said you had a good one."

"My, Lord! I forgot all about it!" I exclaimed blankly. "I'll telephone Fletcher in the morning. Yes, it's a good one!" And I told him what it was.

Wallach chuckled. "I'll say it's good! This time, we've got that old fraud on the run, if he accepts your challenge!"

And Fletcher did accept it.

THE SINGING SANDS
OF PRESTER JOHN

THE FOURTH STORY OF "TRUMPETS FROM OBLIVION"—A
BRILLIANT SERIES WHICH MAKES REAL AND REASONABLE
THE STRANGE LEGENDS THAT HAVE COME DOWN TO US.

"**N**ORMAN FLETCHER,**" I stated, "has a theory
that the race of men aren't fools; that the myths and
fables of old have a basis of fact."

"Something to that!" Parker kindled. "Fletcher! Do you mean
that Yankee scientist who's accomplished such wonders with
ultrasonic waves? Why, he's one of the world's most famous
men!"

"Well, he's got our local Inventors' Club about gaga," I said
wryly. "He's been giving us weekly demonstrations of a sort of
wrong-way television; he claims that it recaptures and brings
back scenes and sounds of the past, on the principle that light
and sound never die. He's promised some day to bring back
Caesar's dying voice, and so forth. Just now, he's been recreating
the origin of old myths. I don't know, none of us know, whether
he's having fun with us, tricking us with some illusion, or really
showing a marvelous instrument of the future."

IN HIS own way, Parker is as famous as Norman Fletcher
is in electrical wizardry. He has traveled everywhere, chiefly
in Asia. Mention any obscure spot in the middle of the Gobi
Desert and he's been there. It was Parker who brought back that
wild story, later proved to be fact, about the grave of Genghis
Khan.

As we discussed Norman Fletcher's remarkable feats, my
friend's interest kindled. He scoffed at my skepticism; Fletcher,
said he, was too famous a man to indulge in any childish illu-

sion or trickery. Especially as Fletcher allowed us to give him, each week, a subject for the next week's demonstration. Rather shamefacedly, I admitted that tonight we were to witness a subject I myself had suggested.

"You see, I wanted to obviate any chance for trickery," I said. "A week wouldn't give him time to get a movie faked up— though we're fairly certain that what we see isn't a motion picture. We have some good technical brains in the Inventors' Club. I suggested the old explorers' yarn, reported by Marco Polo and even as far back as Herodotus, about desert sands that sing. In fact, I did more: I quoted a line from some old poem, and he took it for this week's subject—the Singing Sands of Prester John. Of course, there's no connection between singing sands and the mythical Prester John—"

"St. George! Send help against these spirits of evil! St. Michael! To the rescue of good Christian folk!"

PARKER HAD been looking at me with an amazed expression.

"But there is! My Lord, man, there is!" he broke in. "The singing sands—I've heard 'em, just as Marco Polo did! They're open to scientific explanation. Like the famous singing Memnon—when Lord Curzon was in Egypt, he investigated the statue of Memnon and proved just how it had happened to sing."

"But Prester John was in Abyssinia!" I exclaimed.

He shook his head.

"No; it goes farther back, as far as the Crusades. Prester John was in Asia. These yarns about him, and about the singing sands of the Lopnor desert, date back to the time when that desert was the garden of the world and the richest province in China. But deforestation, changing streams and lakes, ruined it and the desert moved in. Why, Sven Hedin found an entire city scooped bare by the sand, a whole forest! And next week it was covered from sight again. Even now, travelers there make fires from sand-buried poplar trees that died a thousand years ago! Look here, I'd give a good deal to attend your seance tonight!"

Easily arranged: I phoned Norman Fletcher; he had heard of Parker, and was delighted to include him in the invitation. So there we were.

OLD FLETCHER, white-haired, affable, perhaps a bit lonely, had come to cherish these weekly meetings. He loved to make each meeting the occasion of a bang-up dinner; and tonight was no exception. When at length we rose from the table and followed into his laboratory, where stood an open humidor of cigars, we knew we had dined well.

Norman Fletcher took his seat at his switchboard, the only piece of apparatus in sight. The entire house was of cut stone; we sat facing a bare granite wall. I felt a trifle guilty over bringing Parker, for if there were anything amiss with what we saw, he would know it; yet Norman Fletcher seemed unperturbed.

He switched the room lights low, and turned to us.

"While the tubes are warming up, my friends, let me say that to tune in tonight's subject has been extremely difficult; why, I cannot determine. Not until late this afternoon did the results become good."

Wallach, our technical genius of the screen, spoke up dryly.

"Then I presume you've not changed the sound effects that you've recovered from oblivion? The characters won't speak in English, but in some forgotten tongue?"

Norman Fletcher gave him a twinkling glance.

"They'll speak in English, Mr. Wallach; that's been arranged—the words have been fairly well synchronized. Indeed, it's highly necessary! You're about to witness a scene from Central Asia of a thousand years ago; the language recovered is today unintelligible. I suppose you gentlemen are aware that in the Seventh and Eighth Centuries Christianity, in the form of the Nestorian Church, had spread far over the Eastern world? From China south to Sumatra, it was so widespread that there were more Christians in Asia than in Europe. According to legend, they were ruled by a king named Prester John."

"Didn't the Pope send an embassy to him?" asked some one.

Fletcher nodded.

"More than once, but too late. In the Twelfth Century Pope Alexander III sent an envoy and a letter; the monk Sergius went—and was never heard from again. The Crusaders hoped that while they attacked the Holy Land from the west, Prester John would attack from the east, as their ally. Remember, it was a day of simple faith, of credulous beliefs, when men fought terribly, sang lustily and reached for the stars in childish confidence! What you're about to see and hear, is a trumpet from oblivion, a sweet-toned trumpet—it happened three years after the monk Sergius started east to find Prester John, in the year 1180. For two years he traveled; then he died and his letter was taken on by another—"

Norman Fletcher checked himself abruptly; there was a crackling sound from his unseen tubes, and the blank, solid stone wall before us showed a faint drifting light that gradually became stronger. Now, I had examined this wall with the greatest attention. It formed the exterior house wall, was unplastered, and was composed of large granite stones. Yet now, as previously, it dissolved before our eyes as the light increased!

Fletcher played with his switches. A queer, thin sound grew and grew, yet remained very faint; it was something like the sound of wind in a pine tree, but sharper, more definite, like distant singing on two notes only. The light grew stronger and the wall dissolved—we were looking through it now, as though through some window. I heard Parker, beside me, utter a low gasp.

SAND WAS flying amid jagged, scattered rocks; a desert scene, the wind blowing hard, the sun shining bright and strong, and more and more definite came the uncertain song of the blowing sand—but always upon those two notes, until one fancied in it a distinct motive, a cadenced rise and fall, like that of a singing voice.

A horse dashed from behind the rocks, then another. Two riders, whipping, spurring hard, so muffled in strange garments that to see anything of them was impossible. One caught peals of laughter as the horses leaped away. They plunged through the sand, came upon a long, low shoulder of rock, and crossed it. The sound of singing ceased entirely, as the horses raced across sand and rock to a double line of huge green poplars.

Past the trees, in upon cultivated lands. More trees ahead. A river valley grew to the eye, and a road, trodden deep and wide—the great Silk Road, with a glimpse of lakes shimmering far southward, and high Himalayan peaks and glaciers across the sky. The Silk Road of China, one of the great arteries of the world, on which silk and woven stuffs and paper and printing were flowing into the western parts of the earth, as they had been flowing these thousand years and more.

A city grew in the river valley or rather gorge—a city walled and guarded. The great road passed on the uplands beside and behind it, where a second little city of caravanserais and shops arose; but the city itself lay within walls, and the two horses raced on to its gates, where armed guards halted them. The first rider showed a signet of jade and both were passed with respectful salutes.

NOW, THREADING the narrow streets to the palace, also walled and gated, the riders threw back their wraps. The first was a girl, beautiful, of Chinese cast. The second was a man, with short curling golden hair, blue eyes and white bronzed skin. At

*"Why," demanded suddenly,
"do you say it means death to
visit the palace of Ung Khan?"*

the palace gate they entered, unquestioned by the guards, and drew rein before separating.

"You have an hour," she said. "Then, remember, my father wants to hear more about the western lands. When the feast is finished and the lamps are low, come to the Pavilion of the Western Fairies; I'll be waiting."

"Listen, Lady San-kao!" he exclaimed, his brows knotting a little. His words were not fluent; he spoke slowly, carefully. "You've promised day after day to tell me what no one else will or can tell me; the way to the realm of Prester John, him whom you call Ung Khan! What's the mystery? What's the secret?"

She leaned over, her eyes laughing. "Tonight, T'ie Kia! I swear it!"

Then she was gone with a leap of her horse; but he, frowning, sought the quarters that had been assigned him, turned over his horse to the battered old half-Tartar servant who had come with him out of the west, and sought his own chamber.

There he removed his outer garments, took off the flexible mail-shirt that had given him his Chinese name of Iron Armor, and sank down to munch a huge peach from the salver of fruit the Khan had sent him. For he was an honored guest in this city of Taklamakhan, Great Palace of the Khan, at the edge of China; he had been here some weeks, awaiting some response from the Emperor of China as to whether he might be admitted to the country. And he might be more weeks or months ere the response came. The Khan loved to hear his tales of the west, of Byzantium and other lands; he was accounted a good liar and a right merry fellow.

But not a soul would, or could, tell him anything about Ung Khan, or Prester John.

His servant came in and squatted respectfully. This old Tartar had been the servant and guide of Friar Sergius, when the monk lay dying in a town at the verge of the Indian mountains. Walter of Sicily, young and filled with the breath of adventure, had come upon them there, abandoned the traders with whom he traveled, and took up the glorious task of carrying on the dying monk's errand.

And now, a year later, he was T'ie Kia, or Iron Armor, waiting at the door of China, with the letter from the Pope in his baggage, and Prester John as far away as ever.

"Have you learned anything, Hung?" he asked.

The Tartar shook his head.

"Nothing more than we knew already, Lord. Somewhere in this land was the realm of Ung Khan, but his name is unknown today. I met an ancient man this morning, a Buddhist pilgrim bound for India. He said there had been such a ruler, but the Mongol tribes had stamped him out and his whole people with him, long ago."

Walter's keen, vigorous features were despondent; his wide-shouldered, powerful body drooped, and he spat out the peach-stone with a muttered oath.

"If I had not sworn on my honor to deliver this letter from the Pope, I'd quit now; but an oath to a dying monk—well, slow oaths are best kept! I'll find out something tonight, after I leave the Khan. The Lady San-kao knows, and promised to tell me."

THE OLD Tartar wrinkled up his face. He had traveled far to the west, had seen many men and women of all races; he eyed women with a warrior's disdain—an old warrior's.

"There is some talk of your friendship with that lady," he said sourly. "She is the Khan's sister. This is not China, where the position of great ladies is circumscribed; but all the same, I've heard talk. You'd better leave her alone."

Walter laughed, his eyes kindling. "Ah, what a girl she is! And you've taught me enough of the language so I can get on with her; but never fear, the Khan and I are friends. Look here! If Prester John is dead, if there's no Christian kingdom in these parts, then I'm free of my oath to Friar Sergius!"

The Tartar grunted, caring nothing about oaths as long as he got his pay regularly. Fired by this thought, Walter rose, took a walk to stretch his legs, left the palace and sauntered out into the city bazaars. Behind, at some distance, followed a palace official who was charged with his safety. Some of these Tartar, Mongol or Tungan tribesmen might be tempted by this white stranger's glittering gold chain to try rough jokes.

AND SUCH a city! Even to one who had seen Byzantium and palaces of Ind, this place held a blaze of glamorous color. The golden stupas or domes of shrines and temples mingled with the tender apricot and peach orchards; soldiers thronged the streets, wild tribesmen, Chinese regulars in gayly lacquered armor;

patches of mulberry trees along the turbulent little river at the bottom of the gorge, and the sheds of silkworkers, flanked the bazaars where all manner of tradesmen and merchants thronged.

"There is talk of your friendship with the Khan's sister," he said. "You'd better leave her alone."

Chariots and huge winter-shaggy camels, horsemen, fishermen from the lakes, red and yellow lamas from monasteries, jugglers, musicians—a wild thronging medley of life. Over all, and everywhere, lifted the *tinkle-tinkle* of camel bells, coming from these patiently plodding beasts who threaded the great Silk Road from the Jade Gate in the east to western Samarkand.

Searching the bazaars, Walter chanced upon a curious red coral necklace, highly carved, and bought it as a gift for Lady San-kao. He paid with links hewed from his golden chain; a chain that was rapidly shortening, since funds were running low. Then back to the palace, in time to change for dinner.

A long and interminable meal, this, broken by jugglers and by dancing-girls; the hall with its enormous carven pillars and gay lanterns and fantastic costumes—Tibetans, monks, soldiers, diplomats, with the Khan himself at the head. A morose man, not old yet older than his sister, the Khan honored his guest from the western regions with the same passive air with which he would kill him if orders to do so came from China. He was a vassal of China, of the Kin dynasty which ruled in Peking, the fabulously wealthy and corrupt imperial line soon to be stamped out of existence by the Mongol hordes.

When the feast degenerated into a wild carouse, with the tiny cups of hot wine coming thick and fast, Walter quietly took his leave unobserved. He picked his way, alone, across the wide palace gardens. A spring moon hung in the sky, red and angry with the desert dust that blew afar; from the lower gardens came the turbulent sound of the river, whose waters were high but confined within the walls of the gorge, and the mill-wheels were running full blast. It was because of the water-power here that the city lay in the gorge itself.

Curious weather, he reflected; the river was full, the lakes were overflowing, yet there was no rain. These torrential waters came in hurtling masses from the snow-covered mountains above.

SOFT VOICES greeted him; the two slave-girls of Lady San-kao were watching, and led him to the little summer-house where she awaited him. A curious dim lantern of fish-skin lighted the soft pillows, the sweetmeat box of many trays, the rich rugs, the rustling silken garments—strange luxury for a girl who could ride and think and act like a soldier!

Girl? No; woman, alluring and lovely, touched with Oriental mystery and yet frank and open-hearted as a child. She smiled as Walter sank down beside her, and reaching out, touched the strings of a queer, long lute stretched across the floor, and sang, almost under her breath, a song of unknown words and barbaric rhythms. It struck him with an odd sense of familiarity.

"What song is that?" he demanded, as her voice ceased.

"You do not recognize it, Lord T'ie Kia? It is your own song, the song of your quest here, your long travels; it is a song which will never cease nor have an end; the song of death and its terror, and of life that has no end."

"I'm in no mood for riddles," he said, with a touch of irritation. "Death has no terror; we all die, and why fear it?"

"Ah, rough soldier! But who wants to die young?" her soft voice chided him. "Do you know what that song said? A queer, simple song of the camelmen:

> *The wind blows and the stars twinkle above the hill,*
> *As they did when we, like you, rode this way;*
> *But now we know all that you have yet to learn.*

Walter frowned.

"More riddles, eh? There's nothing about me or my travels in that song!"

"You'll see, Lord T'ie Kia! Perhaps you'll understand it tomorrow, when I take you to the palace of Ung Khan. We'll ride there together, you and I, as we rode today."

"What?" He thrilled to the name. "You mean that Prester John is near here?"

She assented softly. "In two hours we can reach his palace."

"By the saints! Then why haven't I learned it before now? Why has everyone shrugged and denied knowledge of him or his realm? Why is his very name apparently unknown?"

She stirred, and spoke earnestly, her voice tender and melancholy as the voices of the wood doves in the peach orchards by the river.

"Here is the answer, Lord; to mention that name, to discuss it or the things concerning it, is bad luck, for it is accursed. You know where we were riding today, out beyond the long ridge of rock? That was once all lovely country and beautiful gardens, stretching over the horizon; now it is desert. Few of our people have ever heard the name of Ung Khan. We care nothing about the past, and know little of it; we live our own day, which will soon be gone, for the desert comes drifting slowly upon us and nothing can hinder it. That ridge of rocks holds it off, and the dikes and irrigation walls; but some day these will burst, and there will be no people to rebuild them, and the desert will be lord of all."

"Then," demanded Walter quickly, "is Prester John, whom you call Ung Khan, dead?"

"He and all his people are dead, yet they are not dead; they are accursed and can never die. They prey on the caravans. Men are lured from the road by voices that call to them; they follow, and die. Sometimes whole caravans perish, for camel bells lure the beasts off the track. Only last month, Ung Khan himself and a party of his horsemen were seen, marching with drums and trumpets; they attacked a small caravan and it perished. One man was picked up, dying—and he told of it before he died."

"And you know where his palace lies?"

She smiled rather sadly.

"Yes. I'll take you there tomorrow, even though it means death to do so; for I know, Lord, that to you the fulfillment of your vow means more than life—or love."

"That is true," said Walter abstractedly.

He was plunged in thought. That she herself believed this fantastically strange and impossible story, was quite obvious; along the caravan route, he had heard much of these evil spirits and ghostly attackers. Never, though, had anyone previously mentioned the name of Ung Khan in connection with them.

What to believe? He crossed himself furtively and struggled with the facts. He was well assured that evil spirits existed; this was easiest of all to credit, for everyone knew that devils inhabited the desert. What puzzled him was that Prester John and his folk, who had certainly been good Christians, should now be devils and spirits of evil. Well, no use trying to understand; he might learn much more tomorrow. So, like many a better man, he consigned theological riddles to limbo, and turned his mind to the woman beside him.

She stirred him, as she would have stirred any man; he was well aware of her liking for him; yet, in his simple way, he regarded her as a pagan, a worshiper of idols, and forced himself to fight against her charm.

"Why," he demanded suddenly, "do you say that it means death to visit the palace of Ung Khan?"

"I don't know," she rejoined. "So it is said; people have gone there and have not come back, so it must be true. Perhaps the evil spirits live there."

"Ah! That must be it. Well, they'll not hurt us!" he exclaimed vigorously. "I'll take the letter of the Pope with us; besides, the sign of the Cross will banish any devils. So have no fear."

She laughed softly, sadly. "I have none, Lord T'ie Kia, if you are with me!" Her hand went to the lute again, and she gently repeated the refrain of the queer little song. Once more Walter frowned at its haunting familiarity, but could not place it.

He gave her the coral, which was rare in this heart of Asia; she was delighted as a child. They sat, talking, till the lantern flickered out, and talked on while the moon mounted the sky, still ominously tinged by the sand-dust floating on the eternal wind that blew from the high peaks. Outside, the two slave-girls twittered and laughed, and from the Khan's great hall the thin sound of music and dancing and drunken song drifted faintly across the garden.

WHEN THE party there broke up, and flitting lights showed the guests being assisted away, Walter stirred; he found himself with Lady San-kao practically in his arms, and in his heart such a joyous bliss as he had never felt. Therefore, he reasoned, it must be wicked, since she was a pagan, and he lost no time in departing, after arranging to meet her on the morrow.

But, as he went his way into the darkness, it was with a strange mingling of happiness and of regret, and the Words of the singular little song followed him in farewell, with the inexplicable sense of familiarity in its tinkling refrain:

The wind blows and the stars twinkle above the hill,
As they did when we, like you, rode this way;

But now we know all that you have yet to learn.

He went to his own chamber, where the Tartar servant snored, got out his long straight sword and wiped it well, wiped his mail-shirt, produced the crucifix that Friar Sergius had bequeathed to him, plumped down on his knees and prayed, and tumbled into bed. But, despite the crucifix still clutched in his hands, he dreamed of the lovely, vivacious pagan features of Lady San-kao, and heard her gentle, mournfully cadenced voice pronouncing his Chinese name; and when he wakened, staring into the moon-glow with startled eyes, it was all in vain that he invoked the blessed saints to banish the thought of her. So, sensibly, he ceased trying.

HE WAS oddly worried by her premonition about the morrow; the very inflection of her voice showed how deeply she was convinced that it meant death to guide him to the palace of Prester John. Absurd! Such pagan superstitions were not for him. Still, he knew in his heart that she would do it wholly for his sake; this was at once disturbing and heartwarming.

He recalled his vow to the dying Sergius, his undertaking to deliver the papal letter at the palace of Prester John. His eyes widened. Why, sure enough! The morrow would see his errand accomplished, his vow fulfilled! Whether Ung Khan lived or was dead, no matter; here was the way out, and no evasion either! Upon this pleasant reflection, he slept again....

With the morrow, then, he was up and about very early, in high spirits. To the astonished old Tartar, Hung, he confided the surprising news that they were not going on to China at all; that, in fact, they were probably returning westward in a day or two; and that he himself was sallying forth this day to do battle with all the evil spirits and devils of the desert. He was only half serious in this, but the battered old Tartar peered at him anxiously.

"And if you do not return, Lord?"

"Why, then go back and bear word of me to any priest or monk you find, and go your way!" said Walter, laughing.

He got out the papal letter, with its huge lead seals, all

enclosed in a water-tight cylinder; rubbed up his hauberk afresh and polished his steel cap; and dressed himself with care, when he had scraped his face clean. Mid-morning found him ready, and he sent Hung for his horse. A keen wind was blowing as usual, but the sun shone brightly.

He girded on the long, straight sword, hung the crucifix about his neck, and donned the muffling skin coat and hood that concealed all except the aquiline lines of his face. Passing outside, he found the horse waiting, and at the saddle-bow hung the letter-cylinder by its carrying-strap. He was just mounting when Lady San-kao appeared, clattering up to join him with a gay greeting.

She parted her fur to show him the coral necklace at her throat. Laughing, he leaned far over in the saddle, caught her hand, and pressed his lips to her slim fingers. A party of Chinese, passing, looked with horrified incredulity at these actions; the sister of the Khan thus conducting herself, and riding alone with a barbarian! Still, these people of Taklamakhan were more than half barbarians anyway, and unversed in rules of conduct.

Laughing, jesting, in huge joy that the end of his labor and travels was now in sight, Walter rode out beside her. Here in the gorge along the water, built half on former islets of the stream, the town was sheltered from the keen wind; but once they had left it and mounted to the height above, where the Silk Road ran, the snowy wind hit hard. A huge caravan had come to rest near the caravanserais, eastward bound; seeing the two riders setting forth alone, a number of the camelmen ran toward them with shouts of warning. They drew rein.

The fur-muffled men surrounded them, all talking at once. The caravan, which had just come in, had encountered peril not twenty miles from town. Evil spirits had assailed them, ghostly parties of horsemen had killed some of the guards; these ghosts had worn ancient armor and had made wild music with drums and trumpets. And, when the caravan closed up and made firm head of resistance, they had vanished in a puff of sand.

Laughing, Walter jested heartily when the two rode on, leaving behind the well-meant warnings.

"Ghosts or devils, we're safe from them!" he cried, indicating his crucifix. "Besides, when have ghostly weapons prevailed against steel and iron? No danger!"

"That remains to be seen, Lord T'ie Kia. Those ghostly riders, evidently, were Ung Khan and his company."

"More likely, imagination," he scoffed. "If you're right, then we're doubly safe; do I not bear this letter to Ung Khan himself?"

This was a reassuring thought.

THE TWO of them rode hard and far, and saw no living thing. Noon came, and Lady San-kao pointed to a huge expanse of jutting rocks and twisted dead trees ahead.

"There!" she exclaimed. "The palace of Ung Khan!"

So Walter comprehended that there was no palace after all, but the ruins of one, amid the ruins of a vanished civilization and forest. It made no difference, he reflected; his vow would be fulfilled just the same.

Devils? Evil spirits? Looking back in the direction of the ancient, lonely Silk Road, Walter of Sicily could well believe anything possible in this eerie land. All the desert seemed on the move, now in puffs and flurries that hid half the landscape, again in high invisible swarms of sand that turned the blue sky to brazen yellow, and dulled the sun. Not hard to imagine anything happening in such a country. He crossed himself and rode on.

The two of them came in among the long-dead, twisted poplars, only half uncovered by the sand. A cry of astonishment broke from Lady San-kao as they headed among the rocks.

"Look! It's all uncovered! And when I was here before, almost nothing showed!"

"So you've been here before this, eh?" And Walter uttered a loud, joyous laugh. "Ha, curiosity! Ho, Ung Khan!" His voice lifted in resounding tones upon the emptiness. "Visitors for you, Prester John! An errand from afar!"

BEFORE THEM the palace lay silent, swept for the moment almost bare of sand. A palace once, perhaps, and a city stretching for miles, blurred by whirls of drifting sand-eddies. A palace of dry stark timbers, huge, cavernous, roofless. They rode up, dismounted, and tethered the horses.

From his saddle, Walter took the precious cylinder that had come so far, and walked beside his companion into the dead palace. He could not doubt it was the place he sought; those massive, eroded beams showed deep carvings, among them the Cross and other religious emblems. They came to what had been a hall and stepped on a mosaic stone pavement bare in spots of its sandy covering. Walter faced the upper part, halted, flung up his hand.

"A message, Ung Khan!" roared his voice. "Greetings from him who sits in Rome, and a letter! Is it your will to receive it?"

As it chanced, a scurry of wind lifted the sand at the far end, lifted and whirled it up in an eddying shape. From Lady San-kao broke a cry of terror; to her eyes it seemed like a response to the challenge. But Walter saw it for what it was, and with a laugh strode forward into the whirling sand, and laid down the cylinder.

"The vow is accomplished!" he declared, and made the sign of the Cross. "Now, in the name of God, accept my charge!"

He faced about, and halted in astonishment. Here in the ancient building, and among the near-by masses of rock, all the sand began to be moved and stirred by the wind. It rustled against the dry, glass-brittle wood, and then a singing sound arose, strident, thin, and far-off.

Walter recognized it instantly; he had heard the same sound among the rocks on the previous day, the sound of singing sands. But he recognized something else, and stood staring at the girl in sudden comprehension. This music of the sand was an oddly monotonous sound, yet definite, like a song that had only two notes.

"The song, Lady San-kao!" he burst out. "Your song! There it is!"

She nodded, though fearfully.

"Yes," she answered. "Now you understand why I said it was your song—this song of the singing sands that the camelmen sometimes chant as they walk along! If— Ah! Listen!"

She went white to the lips. From somewhere came a new and distant sound; the rolling beat of Mongol drums, the thin clash of cymbals, the blare of trumpets. It was so real, so distinct, that for an instant Walter felt fear clutch at him, but, with an abrupt oath, he strode past her, came hastily out to the entrance, and looked.

A cloud of sand was sweeping down upon the lost city and palace. Horsemen with it, two-score and more, wearing strange ancient armor, carrying strange weapons. They had sighted the tethered horses, and now began to spread out. Something whirred in the air, whirred and whistled and sang shrill. Lady San-kao caught at him.

"Arrows! Singing arrows!"

"Then, by God, they're real!" Walter whipped out his sword. "Real or false, pagan or devil, flesh or spirit—look on this!" He held up the cross-hilt, high. "St. George! Send help against these spirits of evil! St. Michael! To the rescue of good Christian folk! One of them, at least, a good Christian," he added hastily.

The words were still on his lips when the girl beside him cried out again, and caught him, turning him around. He looked, and his jaw fell. There among the rocks above appeared other figures of men, strangely dressed and armed. More arrows flew, arrows with pierced heads that whistled and shrilled high as they passed through the air. But the shafts, from one side and the other, were not directed at the two who stood here.

SUDDENLY THE scales fell from Walter's eyes; superstition left him, in a blaze of comprehension.

"Ha! By the saints, I have it!" he cried, catching the girl in a wild and joyous hug in his eagerness. "Look! No devils at all, no evil spirits; this explains everything! Desert men, Huns or Tungans or Mongols—caravan raiders! They fear to attack the caravans direct, but sweep down with sandstorm or night, luring the guards, killing a camel here and one there in the lagging file—ha! Devils? All nonsense! Here are two bands of them, enemies! They care nothing about us—"

She too understood, and shared his laughing exultation as all

"A message, Ung Kahn! Greetings from him who sits in Rome, and a letter! Is it your will to receive it?"

thought of the supernatural passed in prosaic, reasoned explanation. His words were true. Here in the bared old ruins, perhaps, each of the raiding bands were seeking shelter from the sandstorm. As the two figures watched, the opposing parties circled out, swept away, and were lost amid a clash of arms and a roll of drums as the sand hid them.

Walter sheathed his sword, turned to Lady San-kao, and caught hold of her.

"So let all idle fancies perish!" he exclaimed. "You are mine, I am yours; by the saints, I'll make a good Christian of you yet! Do you understand? Will you go with me into the west?"

"Yes," she whispered, lifting her face to his. "Yes, oh, yes! But I think we had better be quick about it—the sandstorm promises to be a bad one!"

Roaring with laughter, he put her into the saddle; they headed away, with the storm sweeping and hissing behind them and the sky there a dull yellow.

IT WAS a supreme moment, a wildly joyous moment, with life swept clear and all paths straightened, and ahead the road of life opening before them, as the great Silk Road opened when they won back to it and headed for the city again. Yet it lasted for only this little while, as the horses galloped.

Sand clouded everything ahead of them, as behind—and this was a strange thing. They came to the rocks where they had been on the previous day, where the long rocky ledge barred the desert from the fields and groves and town. There Walter drew rein suddenly.

"Listen! This is where we heard the singing sands first. Ah! God's love!"

His sudden startled ejaculation rang high. Higher still rang the burst of voices from beyond the rocky height; no singing sands now, but a wild tumultuous screaming of folk, both men and women, in utter mad panic. It surged up and up. People appeared on the rocks, running and staggering and shrieking, women holding babes, men wild-eyed, soldiers, tradesmen. At sight of the two on horseback, the wild sobbing cries became shrieks of rage.

"What is it? What has happened?" demanded Lady San-kao.

A howl of fury answered her.

"The dikes have burst! A wall of water and gravel higher than the city has swept it away—all are dead—the city is gone! It's your doing, you who have betrayed the gods and companied with the foreign devil—"

It was fearfully sudden and terrible. Arrows flew, a spear darted, weapons flashed. One low cry burst from Lady San-kao as a barbed shaft thudded; a wilder, more passionate shout of grief and fury from Walter, and his long sword whirled. His horse leaped into the throng and he struck to right and left. They fled away from before him and were gone, all save the dead, and he spurred back to where Lady San-kao still sat her steed among the rocks, her head drooping.

He saw the feathered shaft protruding from between her breasts, and tore at her with frantic fingers to bare the wound; one glance told him all was useless, and a bitter groan came from him.

Her eyes opened, mistily. Her fingers went to his, twined about them, and a smile touched her wan lips.

"Dear—dear T'ie Kia!" she murmured. "It does not matter; nothing matters. I am happy. And listen, listen to what the sands are singing—"

To him came the odd little two-note whisper of the sand among the rocks, as the yellow waves beat down upon them and muffled out the whole world, and her voice repeated, faintly and more faintly:

> *The wind blows and the stars twinkle above the hill,*
> *As they did when we, like you, rode this way;*
> *But now we know all—all that you—that you have yet—to*
> *learn—*

Her voice died out, her hand fell, the yellow sandswirls beat down upon them and the dim figures vanished completely.

Vanished in darkness; only the faint sound lingering, the distant, thin sound of the singing sands. And this too ended. In the silence, Norman Fletcher switched on the room-lights.

Fletcher reached for a cigar, then turned and looked at us. Not a man of us moved or even spoke, for a long moment, Then somebody sighed, and the tension broke.

"By gad!" burst forth Wallach, his eyes shining. "Fletcher, you have something there! A logical, simple explanation of Marco Polo's remarks; more, reality and human interest—why, those people were living people!"

"Of course." Norman Fletcher smiled at his enthusiasm, and glanced at me. "I trust you found it satisfactory?"

Unable to find words, I merely nodded; but my friend Parker spoke for me. He leaned forward in his intent way.

"I COULD add a touch or so to that story," he said quietly. "But first, may I ask what subject you're going to take up next week?"

"Perhaps you have a suggestion?" our host asked courteously.

"Well," said Parker, with hesitation, "I'm bound for North Africa, but I'd stay over if you'd undertake to look into a pet hobby of mine—the old myth about the Amazons, the country of fighting ladies, you know. There are many theories about it; but I'd give a week of my time to learn where it really started!"

"I'll be very glad to attempt it, Mr. Parker. And just what is the touch you could add to this story from a thousand years ago?"

"Well, I've been to that very place we just saw, for one thing," rejoined Parker. "I've heard those singing sands, have written about them. But the queer part of it is that the city in question was actually buried by a flood, as related at the close of the story—and was uncovered a few years ago by the wind! Sven Hedin the explorer passed by and saw it."

Then he became silent. Our meeting broke up, and I don't think Parker said another word; he seemed preoccupied. But, as I was driving him back to the city, he touched my arm and spoke.

"Funny thing; do you know, the camelmen up in the Lopnor country still chant that apparently meaningless song as they stride along with the camels? Fact. And, until tonight, I never understood it." He quoted the words softly: *"But now we know all that you have yet to learn."*

AMAZON WOMAN

A VALIANT FIGURE, THIS WARRIOR OF A GIRL WHO DOMINATES
THE FIFTH STORY IN "TRUMPETS FROM OBLIVION," A
SERIES WHICH MAKES REAL AND REASONABLE THE AGE-
OLD LEGENDS WHICH HAVE COME DOWN TO US.

LAMBERT, WHO though a famous physicist, was a stodgy Briton, pursed up his lips.

"What you say is impossible," he declared in his flat, somewhat pompous manner. "Radio waves travel at the speed of light; we first discovered that in England. But sound is much slower. Therefore your statement is impossible."

"Norman Fletcher has made it possible," I rejoined. He waved his hand.

"He may be a great scientist here in America; we never heard of him in England. You say he recaptures sound and light from the past, and recreates scenes, such as the death of Cleopatra. That may be theoretically possible, or to recreate her voice; but not both at once. No, my dear fellow. It's impossible."

So was Lambert; but he was a famous man just the same, and an honored guest in our city. I abandoned the argument.

"What," I asked, "is your theory regarding the origin of the Amazon myth? You know, the fighting women who had nothing to do with men. The Amazon River got its name because a tribe of some such females was supposed to inhabit its territory."

Lambert regarded me with his steady, slightly unpleasant look.

"I have no theory," he said placidly. "No one could have any theory. The myth of the Amazons goes back beyond known history. Doubtless there was such a tribe of women in ancient Greece or Asia Minor."

"Norman Fletcher," I said (and he frowned at the name), "believes that all these legends are founded upon fact of some sort. With his apparatus, which has something to do with his ultrasonic wave experiments, he has succeeded in bringing back scenes from the dim past, showing the origin of such beliefs and myths. A sort of television,—though he denies it is that,—from thousands of years ago."

Lambert smiled tolerantly. "My word, you Americans are gullible! Any such trickery can be readily exposed and explained, you know."

"Wait," I exclaimed. "Whether you know of his work or not, Fletcher is famous for his electrical and radio discoveries. He's no trickster, but a modern wizard of the first water. An old man, wealthy. For years his laboratories have been maintained by the Pan-American Electric Corporation; he's the genius behind their remarkable innovations."

Cleon handled his sword fast and well.
Behind, the axe of Telamon crunched
savagely.... They were thorough.

"And he performs the impossible?" queried Lambert, with a sniff.

"You came here," I said, "to address our Inventors' Club tomorrow. Fletcher has done our same group the honor to demonstrate his discoveries, week by week. Tonight, as it happens, he's invited us to witness his demonstration of how the Amazon myth originated. He gives no explanation of his process or apparatus; he merely demonstrates. I have his permission to bring a guest at any time. Will you go?"

Lambert was stubborn, but no fool. He knew about the Pan-American Electric, though he had not known that Norman

Fletcher was the amazing genius behind that corporation. When he found I was serious, he accepted the invitation eagerly.

WE WERE to assemble at Fletcher's house, or rather his laboratory and estate outside town, after dinner. Our Inventors' Club contained a number of really remarkable men, in various lines. Yet none of us had fully decided whether Norman Fletcher was displaying to us some marvelous scientific apparatus of the future, or putting something over on us in the way of illusion.

I did not tell Lambert this, of course. I never tell a cocksure man anything more than I must. And I had a sneaking idea that perhaps he, who was Fletcher's superior as a recognized scientist, might somehow pierce to the secret of those amazing demonstrations.

I motored out with my guest, and the other members of the club met us at Fletcher's big stone mansion. The butler explained that Norman Fletcher had not yet returned from dinner with friends; meantime, we were to make ourselves comfortable in the laboratory. So, with his excellent cigars and easy chairs, we did.

Lambert was, of course, the lion of our little hour. One or two of my friends got me aside, found that our host was unaware of his presence, and grinned delightedly. They had the same thought I did. If there was really any trickery, Lambert would see through it; and he was not the kind to yield to illusion.

Still, these suspicions appeared ungenerous and unworthy, when old Norman Fletcher did walk in. His erect, white-haired presence was magnetic. He met Lambert with unfeigned delight; he had, he said, arranged to meet Lambert next day and take him over the laboratories, but this prior arrival was unexpected. His warmth thawed even the cold Briton.

LIGHTING A cigar, Fletcher took his seat at the controls, which resembled the manual of an organ. He touched a key or two, the room-lights sank low, and he smiled at us as he said:

"Gentlemen, our subject for tonight is the Amazon myth; and while the tubes are warming, I might say that this is one of the most consistently patterned of all myths. It is always the same:

A country of warrior women, who expose one breast, who avoid all men, and are hostile to strangers. We find it alike in Asia, Africa, South America, elsewhere. The queen of the Amazons appears in the Iliad. What is remarkable about it?"

"The very consistency you just mentioned," said some one.

"Right," agreed Norman Fletcher, smiling. "Alike everywhere. This might well argue a single remote origin of the legend, perhaps about the year 2000 B.C., to venture a guess. Handed on by one race or nation to another, the legend remained within its fixed grooves—why? Because it was logical, true, and lay so far in the past that it had no cause to change. New Amazon countries were discovered or imagined, and they kept the same attributes of the old myth."

"Which began—where?" I demanded.

"In Asia Minor. In the empire of the Hittites, that Mongolian race whose rule extended from the Aegean to the Euphrates, at the close of the Bronze Age. The race that fought Egypt bitterly. Only within recent years has its story been exhumed from the dead past, by Sayce or other scholars—"

Norman Fletcher paused, and became attentive to his controls, as the light came.

Now, our chairs were placed facing a perfectly blank wall of stone. There was no apparatus visible here; it was all out of the way. This was an outside wall of the laboratory, running straight to the roof twenty feet above; and it was solid stone. I, aware of what was coming, had chosen a seat that gave me a view of Lambert.

THE LIGHT, which came apparently from nowhere at all, played on that stone wall. It was no projected ray or beam; it just took shape and grew. As it grew, the solid stone was dissolved.

No other words can express it. Where had been stone, was now a window upon the past. Not an actual opening, for outside was black night; yet through this wall we were looking upon sunlight and blue sea, and a rocky coast. Now came Norman Fletcher's voice again.

"The coast of Asiatic Turkey, on the Black Sea, near the ancient ruins of a forgotten city that the Turks call Boghaz Keui—"

His voice died away, drowned out by the steady monotonous slapping of waves under a boat's prow. The light increased; the coast grew, and became plainer. A river-mouth opened, a settlement and wharves clustered about it, and looming above it a hill, with more hills beyond. This one was topped by buildings, groves, shrines, until it was a thing of gleaming beauty in the sunlight.

The boat was a long, low Greek galley, thrusting ahead with its one square sail. The crew clustered in the benches or astern. Two men stood in the bow, one old, one young, staring at the hill and the wharves and settlement ahead.

"So that is it!" said the younger man.

"So that's it!" said the younger man.

The older laughed.

"No, far from it, Cleon! Merely the outpost, the sentinel to keep off intruders. This way your brother passed, five years ago. He stood with me as you stand now, and swore he would enter this land or die. He did not die—that I know; yet he vanished."

"And I'll learn his fate, or rescue him. Five years! He must be dead, Dion; yet I'll follow him. To me, he was all the world—a demigod and more. I've waited these five years to get here with you; I've crossed the seas; I've worked up with the trading-company; now I'm here."

"And your ambition will prove a hollow mockery. You'll learn nothing."

Cleon's brows drew down. For so young a man, he had a heavy, straight, intent look, such as comes to one who has a long while followed a single purpose and one ambition.

"We'll see about that. Here comes a boat out to meet us.— Ho, men! In sail!"

They were just off the river mouth, with its miserable collection of huts and makeshift dwellings, wharves and sheds. Only the hill, with its groves and temples, hinted that the tales of a glorious city back from the shore might be true, and a more glorious country beyond, a country of which minstrels sang, but which no man of Greece had seen.

To the old shipmaster Dion, to all these other Greeks, this was no more than a trading-voyage, on company business. To Cleon, it was merely a means to an end. Here was the land of mystery and terror, the land ruled by fighting women, the empire that had planted colonies at Ephesus and elsewhere: and to enter it was death! To pass the limits allotted to traders, was death. But his brother had passed; and Cleon meant to pass.

A small-boat put out from shore, ran alongside, and two men came aboard. One was an olive-skinned, slant-eyed man with long hair twisted in a tail; the other acted as interpreter. Where from? Corinth. The Island Trading Company. Pass and papers? Dion produced them. Good. Take the wharf straight ahead; when the galley is empty, draw her up on the shore for calking and scraping.

The small-boat saw them in to the wharf. The sun was low; business could await the morrow. Here in the hamlet, most of the people were Greeks, or of Greek descent. Wineshops beckoned; girls were waiting with flower-garlands. A watch remaining aboard, all hands leaped ashore and thanked the gods for dry land underfoot again.

Cleon looked farther—beyond the fence outside the hamlet, and the guard station where the little slant-eyed men stood watch—on to half a dozen horsemen coming at a gallop. He caught his breath. Horsemen? No! The women famed in song and story, the Amazons!

He recognized them instantly, by the descriptions. Short kilts, one breast bare, a curled cap, a half-moon shield, a bow and quiver. They were there, in the life! They were real, reining in their horses to stare at the ship, to stare at him. He walked on out to the fence, and stared back—chiefly at the flame-haired girl.

She stood out from the rest instantly. Her shield flashed gold. Her red-gold hair, her superb white steed, her white kilt, all made a glowing spot of color—but less glowing than her eyes and her eager face, as she urged her horse closer.

"Do you speak our tongue?" he asked.

A laugh lit up her face.

"Why not? Did you come on the ship? From far Crete?"

"Not quite so far," said he. "Ah, goddess! You are very beautiful; I think your beauty must come from heaven! Where will you be at moonrise tonight?"

"At moonrise?" Surprised, she gestured toward the hill. "I'm on guard until then, serving the goddess. We go back to the city after moonrise."

"Good! An hour after moonrise, come along the road that leads up the river—say, a mile from here," he blurted out impulsively. "I want to talk with you. I want to know you, and—"

She shrank. "You fool! You madman! They'll kill you! Do no such thing. Why, you must be insane!"

All this poured out of her in one hot breath. Then her companions urged their horses around, laughing, and the whole group went tearing off at a wild gallop. Cleon stared after them, until Dion and others dragged him away.

Now everyone crowded into the wineshops, eating, drinking, bragging and brawling as pockets emptied; but he, the yellow-haired Greek, drank alone; and ate and drank again. He was first officer of the galley and looked it, wide in shoulder and jaw, with command in his eye, a reckless kill-devil twist to his lips, and corded muscles in arms and wrists.

As he sat, queer thoughts rioted in him. His driving ambition suddenly had two objectives instead of one. He had heard much of the Amazons, who ruled all this empire of mystery in the east; those glorious fighting women, under whom the queer slant-eyed men were said to be slaves and serfs. Other seamen had heard of them, had seen them in the flesh, and around them had grown up many fantastic legends. Cleon was inclined to doubt many of these yarns.

Now he had visioned one who transcended all the others. In his heart he felt that she had been drawn to him; in her eyes had leaped a kindling eager welcome. Despite the dismay and shrinking and hot words, she would keep the rendezvous tonight; he was sure of it. But would he? There lay the question. It startled him, wakened him, put his brain to work. He began to ask questions of those around, to listen, to observe.

"Carelessness is the thief of success," his idolized brother had been wont to say. He remembered this. He was careful, now, most careful. He did not let even Dion guess what he intended to do this night.

THE MOON was behind a cloud-bank when he quietly slipped out of the wineshop. He had his bronze Cretan sword, a long, leaf-shaped weapon, razor keen; his helmet, sandals, purple robe, a pouch with money. Nothing else, for the conquest of a realm of mystery, except the head so proudly and masterfully set between his shoulders.

In the open he paused. From the hamlet, he knew, a road disappeared up the valley beside the river; a road rumored to go to the enchanted, unknown city of mystery somewhere close among the hills. But at the village barrier the squat, ugly guards watched by day and night. Cleon turned his back on the road and the barrier, and went down to the shore and the fishing craft, where there were no guards.

Hittites, these slant-eyed warriors with double-faced axes. In their eyes it was unthinkable that any stranger should deliberately court death by passing inland; they were posted to keep back fools and drunken men. So, as Cleon waded out into the water, there was none to see or care.

He progressed quietly down the shore past the hamlet to where black rocks arose. With some difficulty he landed on the rocks, circled well around hamlet and barrier, and came dripping into the road. Thus simply, the first obstacle was passed. There were, luckily, no dogs about.

The cold water brought reality; to think that the Amazon would keep the rendezvous struck him as absurd and fantastic. Still, the look in her face, her eyes! He trudged along the cart-track, and found that it curved in under the very side of the templed hill. He halted, and looked up at the groves and shrines. He was now on the side away from the sea. He had plenty of time; the moon was still hidden. Why not take a closer look? The thought persisted.

From the hill was coming music, the clash of bells and cymbals, the sound of women's voices singing in chorus. Guards, in service of the goddess, she had said. What goddess? Cleon was curious; these heathen probably had queer uncivilized deities. He eyed the dark slopes in the starlight, eyed the flaring torches in the upper groves, and abruptly went at the climb. No guards on this side, perhaps.

He encountered no danger, except from thorns; he mounted swiftly, silently, and was surprised by the height which he attained. The brush and trees were thick. Above him loomed a wall. He reached it, found a stout vine, and gained the top. There he crouched, daring no farther, fascinated by the spectacle in the torchlight beyond.

To Greek eyes, accustomed to rude buildings and primitive architecture, the shrines here seemed like veritable homes of the gods—graceful structures, wide porticos, ornaments and columns innumerable. The grove of trees was alight from urns of ruddy fire, showing figures dancing and singing, the music swirling wilder and madder—all women, apparently, with armored figures of Amazons here and there.

Suddenly Cleon became aware that the moon was coming out from behind the clouds. He turned, then halted, staring.

The moon was now in golden flood. And off where he had seen only solid hills, he now beheld something else pricked out by the mellow radiance—something seeming visible only from this very hill. It was the city of mystery, the city that poets named Themiscyra.

NOT FAR distant, though farther by the roundabout road up the cañon, it stood out distinct and clear like an actual vision of enchantment. Cleon caught his breath; then he understood that those buildings surrounded by hills must be lit up by fires or illuminations; this day, no doubt, was some festival of the unknown goddess. A cluster of magic beauty, dimmed by distance, the white structures rose in lofty grandeur.

Abruptly, he remembered his rendezvous, and started his descent. At once the city was lost to sight, but the memory of it lingered. He realized that sheer good luck had led him to this vision of unseen things, beheld by no other Greek eyes, at a moment and a spot which alone would reveal it.

DOWN IN the rough road again, he trudged on until he came to a clump of trees, with clear spaces ahead and behind. Here he waited for a while, listening. Presently he caught the click of a horse's hoofs. Peering forth from shelter, he saw the white steed. She had come! And she was alone.

He stepped out into the moonlight. The horse snorted; the Amazon drew rein for a startled instant, staring. Then she slipped from the saddle, holding her reins.

"So—you were not joking or boasting!" she said in a low, tense voice.

"After I saw you, no," Cleon rejoined. "Surely you must be the queen of these warrior women, these Amazons!"

"Queen? Warrior women?" She looked bewildered, then broke out at him earnestly: "You must go back, now, at once, while there's time! If you go farther, it means death, and worse than death. Go back, do you hear?"

Cleon laughed a little. "I've been too long seeking this road, to go back now. Especially since finding you."

"Oh! You must be daft!" she said with impatient anger. Then she leaned forward, peering intently at him. "Is it possible that you are Cleon?" she asked. "Cleon, the son of Agias?"

Amazement leaped within him.

"Ah!" he exclaimed joyfully. "Then you are indeed some goddess, to know me!"

"Don't be absurd; I'm nothing of the kind," she said sharply. "However, suppose you tell me why you came here and why you're so determined to risk death!"

Puzzled, bewildered, Cleon answered:

"Five years ago my brother came here, and disappeared seeking the wondrous city that lies beyond the hills, and the Amazons. I have come to find him."

"Ah! I knew it must be so!" she murmured. "You have his look. Even had he never told us about you, I would have known—"

"Then you know him!" Cleon, with sudden comprehension, came close to her, breaking into eager words. "He is alive and well!"

"He is alive," she said, giving him a strange look. "Are you absolutely determined to find him, even if it means death? Think well!"

"I've thought for five years." Cleon laughed softly as he spoke. "Yes."

"Very well." She threw the reins over her arm and turned. "Come along, in among the trees. It's dangerous here; others will be coming. Wait a little, and talk; then we may go ahead safely."

HE ASSENTED without question. They threaded their way into the copse; the horse was tied; with a sigh of relief she put off quiver and half-moon shield, and sat beside him, tossing back her long red-gold hair.

"Ah! I've been on duty ten hours; it's good to relax. Well, start at the beginning. My name's Maia; I'm captain of the temple

guards, and it's a dog's life. Your brother Telamon is overseer of the slaves in the quarries. He had an eye burned out, a hand and a foot struck off, and went into slavery, when they picked him up exploring the country. We have supervision over the quarries. That is how I know him. It's very simple."

Cleon chilled. His brother, mutilated!

"At least, he's alive."

"It's more than you'll be."

"No matter. I can help him, see him, talk to him. Then, if death comes, what of it! At least, I'll buy it dear: with sight of new things, unknown wonders, the enchanted city of Themiscyra that no man has seen, yet is sung by minstrels afar! To pierce mystery and terror, and then die—well, fate might be worse,"

"You're a strange man, but I like you," said Maia. "You can't do these things you talk about, without help. Where will you get it?"

"From you," he said. "I could see that in your eyes, Maia. Ah! Quiet!"

He caught hold of her suddenly, warningly. Voices drifted along the road, with the sounding hoofs of horses. A little company of Amazons appeared and passed by, laughing and

She broke out earnestly: "You must go back now, at once, while there's time! If you go farther, it means death. Go back!"

jesting. Cleon relaxed, loosed her, and lifted her hand to his lips. She spoke angrily.

"I suppose you think I'm fair game for any foreign seaman?"

"No, my dear, no," Cleon rejoined. "You are a goddess."

She laughed, but her laugh had a harsh and wondering ring.

"Cleon, your head is certainly full of queer ideas! Amazons, for example. Where did you hear such nonsense?"

"Everyone knows it," he said in surprise. "You fighting women, whose queen rules all this country! Seamen have seen you frequently. It's no secret."

She sighed. "Yes, I remember your brother had the same odd fancies. I was doing my first guard service, when they brought him to the quarries. And this enchanted city you mentioned— well, it's real enough. But no Amazons, no queen, no fighting women!"

"What?" He touched her bow and shield. "Why, then, these arms?"

"Cleon, the Hittites rule all this land," she said earnestly. "It's their empire; they have their own rulers—a cruel people. Now, only women may serve the goddess; other gods have priests, but she has only priestesses, temple servants, guards—all women."

"What goddess are you talking about?" he demanded.

The girl gestured impatiently.

"She has many names. The great earth-goddess. Your brother says that in your country she is known as Cybele or Demeter."

"Oh, I see!" murmured Cleon. "And here only women serve her?"

"Precisely. At most times no men are allowed in the groves or temples. Every temple has hundreds of us guards, and after our period of service, we become priestesses. Our duty is to keep out all men. But seamen or foreigners have often seen us on duty. They have taken for granted that we're fighting women, Amazons, that the country all belongs to us. But far from it, far from it!"

Her voice took on bitter accents.

"Ours is no pleasant destiny. Next week, I myself become a temple priestess; we have no choice. It's a high honor to be a priestess, yes. But for some of us who regard virtue and purity as sacred things, it's a frightful, a horrible honor! I can't make you comprehend it all, but I'd prefer death, a thousand times!" Her voice was impassioned, athrob with emotion. "Better death, than such honor!"

"Well, I don't quite understand, but let it pass for the moment," said Cleon. "How can I reach my brother Telamon?"

SHE REACHED out and took hold of his hand.

"With my help, as you said. With my help, you can aid him to escape, and get away safely with him. I'll give my help—on one condition!"

Cleon kissed her fingers again.

"Granted. Name it."

"That you take me with you, away from this land of blood and terror!"

"Done," said he; and his heart sang for joy, and he caught her to him quickly. "Ah, goddess or woman, or both, we belong to each other! I knew it at the first sight of you; my heart told me everything—yes, it's a bargain!"

She kissed him, briefly, and drew back. "Will your men at the ship miss you?"

"They'll say nothing."

"Very well. Tomorrow you'll hide, with your brother. Tomorrow night, you and he and I will seek the seashore again. Come; it's safe now; the moon is sinking."

CLEON UNDERSTOOD that behind this attitude of hers was something he did not yet grasp, some background he did not comprehend; but he was content to seek reasons later. Clean with youth and the salt sea air and vigorous heritages, he was far from guessing what depths of Oriental abomination were reached in the worship of the "great goddess" of the Hittite

*Cleon had heard of
Amazons; now he
had met one who
transcended all others.*

people, a bacchanalian routine destined to plague and debase
the world for thousands of years.

The moon was dying in the west. They walked, leading the
white horse, gradually climbing along the roadway that followed
the river. Ahead, Cleon caught glimpses of the city on the cliffs.

"We go not there, but to the right," said Maia, and spoke
bitterly. "We of the temple guards, destined to be priestesses, are
barracked separately, near the quarry slaves. We ourselves are no

better than serfs; a life of honor and ease and shame, for we are chosen to serve the base appetites of men."

"Yes? I've heard rumors of queer things that take place in these parts," said Cleon. "But I thought men were banished from your temples?"

"Except once a year, at the great feast; but there are other temples." She turned suddenly to him. "Will that sword at your hip cut?"

"It is sharp."

"Good. Cut my leg, here.... Cut, I say! I need an excuse to get off duty tomorrow and tomorrow night. I'll say that I fell on a spear-point. Cut!"

He bared the bronze sword, and slashed at her thigh, with a groan. She refused to let him touch the hurt, but mounted and went on, the blood streaming over leg and foot and horse's belly.

Not far at all. The valley showed buildings to the left; these were the barracks of the guards of Amazons, and the stables. She guided him to the right, to the very edge of a great gulf in the rock, and dismounted by a stout pillar that stood alone. In the pillar was a huge metal ring.

"The quarries are here; the slaves are here; your brother is here," she said. "You can reach the quarries only by descending a long ladder. The first length of the ladder is taken up at night, to prevent escape, although all the slaves are mutilated besides. Tear your robe into two strips, and it will be long enough. I can let you down by it. Tomorrow night, I'll let down a rope-ladder. But think well! You can still turn back safely!"

With a laugh, he caught her, kissed her, and faced the gulf....

The robe ripped apart and knotted, he let himself over the edge while she held the makeshift line. Below, he found the rungs of a ladder set in the rock.

"All's well! Until tomorrow night," he said. From above, he heard her call the name of Telamon, repeating it softly, until a reply came from below.

He was on his way down. Voices floated up from the pits in

the rock. The noisome odors of unwashed and untended slaves rose rank to spoil the night. Cleon kept on, finding that other ladders joined the first. He came at last to the bottom. Chains clanked dismally, and a hoarse voice said in Greek:

"Who is it? Who are you?"

Cleon turned his face to the moonlight. A gasp, a wild sobbing cry, and fingers gripped him.

"You, you! Cleon, my brother—it can't be true—"

"True, Telamon, true."

They embraced and then went and sat in darkness, torn by emotion, trying to find coherent words; for each of them, talk was hard. Cleon, despite the preparation given him, had found his brother a stranger—a rough, shaggy man who walked with a rude crutch, and who had only one hand, which was fastened by a chain to his one foot. Only the voice was the same as of old.

PRESENTLY TEARS were past, and cool sanity returned. Cleon related his story by snatches; they consumed bread and wine together and the crippled man fell into soft, wild laughter.

"So you had the same crazy notions, Cleon—aye, all the outside world has them, I know! Amazons. A queen, a city of mystery and enchantment. Bah! The Amazons are temple guards. The city is a hell of cruelty and luxury. These olive-skinned Hittites are a fierce, inhuman people. Wait till you see how the slaves are treated! But I know this girl Maia. You were lucky to have met her. A noble and glorious woman—"

His voice halted, then went on:

"The noblest woman in all this accursed country. No wonder she shrinks before the fate in store for her, a fate welcomed by most of them as a high honor! It's a rich land, Cleon, wealthy past belief. The cities are filled with riches, crammed with luxury, with vice, with abomination of all kinds…. But I see you're worn out. Sleep here, in my own hut; remain here, and be safe. If she comes tomorrow night, there's a good chance after all. By the gods, it seems incredible! If we get a boat, and get away—ha!

The very idea makes the brain burst! It's all impossible; but the gods may favor us; and after all, it's best to die trying."

So Cleon slept in the overseer's hut, and wakened not until morning.

With daylight, Cleon remained close hidden, but received shock upon shock, for all was in plain sight. First, his brother, a shaggy crippled monster; then the slaves, from all races, hideously crippled like his brother; then, occasional Hittites who came and went. Fierce men, olive-hued, slant of eye, cruel of hand; he saw cruelties that day to leave him cringing and shaken.

And on the rock of the fringing cliffs, fronting his refuge, he saw cut and carved the figures of temple guards, Amazons, with their kilts and half-moon shields—looking down, and laughing. Symbols, these, of tyranny, oppression and inhumanity past all credence. He heard men talking; and the talk he heard, the mention of things in camp and city, opened his eyes to the Orient.

Adventure, mystery, enchantment, were stripped away; harsh realities remained, to burn the soul and sear the free Greek spirit. Cleon had not known that such things could be; it was his first meeting with the Eastern world, the first encounter of Nordic and Mongol-Asiatic. The Turanian hordes whose empire had gripped all this eastern-stretching land appalled him. The luxury, the vice, the mass abomination, was devastating.

He now saw all that Maia had not been able to tell him—at least, he perceived enough to understand. He saw why she had welcomed his advent, his help, why she chose to risk death with him rather than life here. And when sunset came and his brother Telamon came stumping in with rations of bread and wine, he looked up and shivered.

"Ha!" said Telamon. "I see you've absorbed a thing or two. You look ten years older. Still greedy for what lies over the horizon—adventure, the lure of the unknown?"

"No," broke in Cleon harshly. "Why haven't you escaped before this? Are there guards?"

"None are needed. Where to go, and how? A leg off, or a hand off—the mark of a slave. It means torture if caught. Who'd risk it?"

"Somewhere to go now," said Cleon. And the other nodded.

"Thanks to you. So old Dion's still shipmaster? Will he take us aboard?"

"Can't hope for that," Cleon replied. "The trading-company has an agent aboard; the men will be scattered, the cargo half unloaded. No; we must take some fishing-boat. I saw plenty on the shore, there at the river mouth. Follow the coast to the straits, and go on through to the farther sea—our own sea. Agreed?"

"Aye; then tell our story everywhere!" Telamon grimly exclaimed. "Bring a few ships of our Greeks over here to land and raid, burn, slay—ha! All this silly tale about Amazons has frightened us long enough. We've seen temples with their guardian women by the hundred; we've imagined things, and the yarns have grown to fantastic dimensions. Now that's all ended. These women can't fight. Now we'll go back and tell the truth to the world!"

"And then avenge what they've done to you," added Cleon, kindling to the thought. "What fools we've been! We've always thought that this was the end of the world; now we know better. It goes farther. Even the Cretans, with their navies, never pierced to the truth of these matters. They too believed in the Amazon country.... Well, enough of dreams. We must get away before we can do anything. It's time that Maia was here. Can you climb those ladders?"

"With one foot and one hand gone? Not easily."

"Then you can mount on my shoulders.... Let's see your chains."

These presented no great difficulty. The hardened Cretan sword hacked through the links, and Telamon was free.

In the darkness they came to the mounting-ladders. Slaves lacking hands or feet could at a pinch rove such paths; but with an entire length of ladder removed from above, escape was impossible.

Cleon mounted a little way and called. Maia's voice floated down. Satisfied that all was prepared, he descended and got Telamon mounted pickaback, then tackled the climb. It was well that his shoulders were powerful; long before the top was reached, he was gasping under the burden. The final ascent up the loosely swaying rope ladder was pure torture. At the top, he somehow staggered over and came down with a crash, aching and exhausted.

"All's well that ends well," said Telamon, picking himself up with a laugh. "Ha, Maia! Greetings, girl."

SHE JOINED them in the obscurity, and Cleon clasped her hands. Horses were waiting, and moonrise was quivering in the eastern sky. Only two horses; there must be double riding this night, but Telamon could have one beast to himself.

Then, seeing Telamon unwind a coil of light, strong line from about his waist, Cleon exclaimed sharply:

"So that's why you were so cursed heavy! What's it for?"

Telamon grunted. "Do you think those slaves down below didn't know what was afoot? I had to buy their silence. All they want is to die fighting and killing. I promised to let down this line. It'll help 'em up the ladders, and particularly the rope ladder."

"You know what it means?" broke in the girl, sharply.

"Aye. If a couple of hundred of those poor devils get up, your wondrous city of Themiscyra will taste a little blood and fire this night! It'll distract attention from us, however."

"Well, tie it to the pillar-ring," said Cleon impatiently. "Then I'll give you a boost into the saddle, and we'll be off."

Telamon, who had made fast his line, let it slip down the ladder's length, and Cleon helped him to mount. Then he was up behind the girl, with joyous greeting.

"Bad news," she said, deftly stringing her bow and thrumming the taut gut string. "Some of your drunken seamen had a row with the Hittite guards at the hamlet today. More guards have been sent down; also a guard-post has been established at the narrow bend of the road, above the river. We can't get past them."

"We'll get through them," said Cleon, but his heart sank. With a woman and a helpless cripple, what chance? "Have they horses?"

"No; they're all from the infantry detachments."

"We'll lead. Telamon, you follow. Maia, can you swim?"

"Of course; it's part of our training."

"Then the gods favor us! Lead ahead."

The horses moved on. The moon lifted, and Cleon suppressed a groan. This was the culminating peril, for darkness was their best ally—but there was no help for it....

As they went, he plied Maia with questions about herself, the country, the Hittites. These Turanians were terrible as fighters, but they hated and feared the sea. Their trading cities,

Chains clanked; a hoarse voice said: "Who is it? Who are you?"

down the coast, were strictly warded against all foreigners. Sometimes this duty was left to the female temple guards, the Amazons; it was easy to see how the legend of warrior-women had originated.

Of herself, Maia spoke briefly. She was of the royal race that had ruled here before the Hittites came; she, like all others of that race, was devoted from infancy to the temple service. Another way, as she said bitterly, of obliterating that race.

So, as they talked, they came toward the narrows. From its grip at her saddle, Maia took the double-bladed axe, which was, with the bow, the particular weapon of the Amazons, and a symbol of the two-headed eagle of the Hittites. She passed it to Telamon.

"Every blow may count," she said briefly. He uttered his harsh laugh.

"Thanks, Maia! Now I'm a man again, as I may prove before the night's out."

"Careful! There they are—"

One look showed Cleon there was no hope of evasion. Cliff on one side, river on the other; in the center of the roadway a score of men camped, on watch, stirring. An officer was striding out to meet the horses.

"Give him your arrow and ride through them," he said to the girl.

THE ANIMALS quickened pace. The officer called out angrily. The bowstring twanged; the shaft tumbled him out of the way, a yell went up. Straight in the mass of men plunged the horses, but the Hittites gave no inch. They leaped, stabbed, hurled themselves like madmen at the two beasts.

Cleon handled his sword fast and well. He cut down a man who came leaping in from the side, slashing at another clinging to the horse's neck. Behind Cleon, the axe of Telamon crunched savagely, crunched again as armor gave to his blows…. Then they were through, and speeding from the yelling soldiery.

"Hurt?" cried Cleon.

"No; only the cut you gave me last night." Maia gave a laugh, and glanced back. "They're running after us. We've only a couple of miles more to the shore. What then?"

"Avoid the hamlet and make for the rocks north of it," said he promptly. "You and I must swim around for a boat and leave Telamon. We must go softly, quietly, and get off unobserved."

"You expect a lot," she said dryly. Behind them, Telamon grunted approval of the double-bladed axe. They rode on, at speed, until they had to slow the horses lest the Hittite guard ahead take warning. Behind, far outdistanced, the pursuit was still in place, grimly following.

MAIA DREW rein abruptly, as another track crossed the road. She slid down. "Loose the horses here, and they may throw off the pursuit."

"I've no crutch, girl," growled Telamon.

"Use me," she panted, with her eager, vibrant laugh.

The horses were stung to headlong gallop down the cross track. The three went on, Cleon and Maia supporting Telamon. They skirted the hamlet, as yet unalarmed, and gained the rocks where Cleon and landed the previous night. In the clear moonlight, the jagged granite was black, the water was black.

"Wait here, brother," said Cleon. "Take care of Maia's bow and shafts. I'll keep my sword. Quick, Maia! No time to waste."

He led the way into the water, and she followed.

The hamlet was asleep. They swam down, turned in, found the sloping beach beneath their feet, and headed for the boats pulled up. Then the shouts of the pursuers alarmed the guard-post at the barrier. Men began to turn out; voices rose; arms clashed. Luckily, their attention was not directed to the beach, but landward.

Cleon flung himself at a stout fishing craft pulled up less far than the others. Maia joined him. Together they tugged and shoved; the boat moved, slid, took the water. The voices rose more fiercely; a shout pealed up, then another, deeper and hoarser, in the voice of Telamon.

"They've found him!" gasped the girl.

"Hurry—oh, hurry!"

A clang of metal, a death-yell, lent force to her words. The whole hamlet was by this time in turmoil and alarm. Cleon was in the boat now, dragging Maia after him, getting out an oar; the mast was still stepped, the sail furled, but there was no time for that now. The boat moved, moved faster, heading for the point of rocks.

Clash and clang of metal again, the deep hoarse shout of defiance, the yelp of dying men, told of the double-bladed axe at work. As they neared the rocks, the clear moonlight made everything mercilessly distinct. Another gasp came from the girl.

"The bow—I forgot! He can't use it!"

He was there, in between two of the jutting rocks where they could get at him only from the front. The axe swung; the harsh voice blared; clash upon clash, as the crowding figures heaved up at him and fell away again under those smashing blows. The boat touched, and Maia, with a leap, was ashore.

Cleon cursed as her leap sent the boat out. Then he had it in again, and followed. Telamon had gained momentary respite. The Hittites had drawn back. A new yell arose from them, a yell of dismay and anger, as the figure of Maia appeared, snatching up bow and quiver. Cleon, sword ready, showed beside her.

"To the boat, brother!" he said sharply, and took the half-moon shield Maia shoved at him. "Quickly!"

Telamon went scrambling, hobbling away. With a new yell and a rush, the Hittites surged forward at the gap in the rocks.

CLEON MET them, sword and shield, as they trampled the dead men in the way and came at him. The bronze blade flashed and bit deep; the shield warded off thirsting weapons. They pressed in; a spear-point slid under his shield, but he evaded it and smote the holder where head and shoulders came together. Another slash, a thrust into a darkly evil face, a scream. The dying man caught his leg and pulled him down.

Then, behind him, the bowstring twanged and twanged again. With a ringing thud, the shaft sped home. Screams sounded; the wave of dark figures was broken. Cleon came to his feet again, meeting the rush of a man who slid in from one side, crashing shield into axe, stabbing with the keen bronze. That man plunged like a diver, but his dive was into the arms of death.

Cleon leaped back beside Maia. "No use!" he panted. "Too many—look!"

Too many, indeed. They were flooding along, weapons glittering in the moonlight. Arrows were flicking around the pair, clashing on the rocks. The bowstring twanged again and yet again, striking death into the massed throng. But next rush would overcome them; already the ring of Hittites was shoving forward.

"Be ready! Run for the boat!" exclaimed Maia, and then lifted her voice in a great shout: "Look! Men of Themiscyra, look at your city! The enemy are in it—look!"

Some turned, looking up the valley. Cries of consternation and fury burst from them; others turned and saw. Every arm was palsied, as they became aware of the lurid light in the sky, the flames leaping from the high doomed city as from some great funeral pyre, lighting the hills and the silvery sky in red ruin.

Maia beside him, Cleon was scrambling for the boat. She was aboard now; Telamon had an oar out in his one hand; with a shove and a leap, Cleon followed the girl and laid hold of another oar.

A Hittite came leaping in pursuit. Maia's bowstring twanged, and he went headlong into the water. Then the boat was sweeping out and out in the moonlight, urged ever farther by the two oars, until she was floating at safe distance on the tideless sea, and Cleon was fumbling at the brown sail.

The canvas rose and filled. Telamon's oar steered her out; the shouting men, the rocks, the hamlet lights, died and merged and were gone. Only the spurting flare of fire from the inland hills told of how these loosed slaves had sought vengeance and found it. Cleon stood beside the girl, his arm around her, their heads etched in the moonlight like the heads on some ancient coin.

THE MOONLIGHT faded. The boat vanished; the two heads, the two faces aglow with exultation and high emotion, lingered and then died. The room lights flashed on, and Norman Fletcher, turning to us once more, picked up his forgotten cigar.

"Well, gentlemen?" he said urbanely. "I think we all know, now, how the legend of Amazons originated?"

I THINK most of us had the same thought. Damn the legend! The whole thing was a contradiction. Some one put it into anxious, irritated words.

"But they got away, Mr. Fletcher! And if they did, then they told the truth about all this mythical country. And that would explode the whole Amazon legend!"

"But they didn't get away, and the legend persisted," said Norman Fletcher, slowly. "That is perfectly obvious, gentlemen. We saw them escape, yes. What became of them? I don't know. I can't tell. They never reached Greece; that is certain, for the legend was never exploded. The Hittite empire disintegrated. By that time, customs had changed; the temple women were no longer armed and attired like the mythical Amazons, and the origin of the legend never became known. We have seen it tonight, actually; unfortunately, we have no proof of it."

"I beg to differ."

My friend Parker, the explorer, who has been everywhere in Asia, stood up.

"I've seen the ruins of that city," he said. "Some day it will be dug up. But I've seen more. On the cliffs flanking those hill-ruins, are ancient carvings, showing women in Amazon garb, with two-headed axes and all. Amazons. Now, that's sober fact. How it got into your story, I don't know. But the carvings are there, and are recorded."

As we filed out, I turned to my guest Lambert, got him into a corner, and put the matter to him.

"Come, let's have it!" I exclaimed. "You saw what happened. If it's some illusion, you'd know it. If the whole thing is the scientific marvel it seems, you'd know that, too. What do you think of it?"

By his look, I saw that the Briton was profoundly disturbed. He gave me a sharp glance, and his firm lips compressed. Then he drew himself up.

"The answer, sir, is very simple," he said in his slightly pompous way. "The whole thing is rankly, utterly impossible! That's all."

Which was, perhaps, as good an answer as any—that he could make.

FIVE MILES TO YOUTH

THE ANCIENT FABLE OF THE FOUNTAIN OF YOUTH FORMS
THE BASIS OF THIS DRAMATIC STORY—THE SIXTH IN THE
MUCH-DISCUSSED SERIES "TRUMPETS FROM OBLIVION."

TRUMPETS FROM oblivion! What on earth does that mean?"

"Glimpses from the past, messages from departed ages," I said, trying to explain the phrase to Viola Conway, our visiting celebrity. She was a wary, determined young woman lawyer, specializing in patent rights, who was addressing our Inventors Club on the subject. "You've heard of Norman Fletcher?"

"Mercy! *The* Norman Fletcher? The electrical wizard? Does he belong to your club?"

"No," I said. "But the laboratories that the Pan-American Electric Corporation built for him are just outside the city. He's been demonstrating some of his discoveries with high-frequency and ultrasonic waves. He can bring back scenes from the past."

"I don't believe it," she said flatly.

"Neither do I; but he does it, Miss Conway. Trumpets from Oblivion, he calls them. He's been working on myths and legends, showing how they originated in past ages."

"Wait! Let me get it straight. He actually brings back scenes and voices?"

"Yes; but the voices have to be translated and dubbed in, somehow. He says it's not television; that's the only thing I can compare it all to. For example, tonight he's going to show some of us, after your lecture, how the Fountain of Youth idea originated. You see, he claims that all the myths and legends of mankind are founded somehow on fact."

"Tonight? A real Fountain of Youth?" she exclaimed. "I'm going with you. Arrange it, please. I must go!"

I demurred hastily. Some of Norman Fletcher's demonstrations were a bit on the strong side, even for a woman lawyer. But Viola Conway set her jaw and had her way.

That's how she came to walk in with us, that evening, when we assembled at the huge granite structure that was Fletcher's home and personal laboratory. Fletcher, charming old Yankee that he was, made her welcome; his white-haired, powerful features gave no indication of the dismay he must have felt, for he seldom admitted women to the place. I fancy he regretted the open leave he had given me to bring any guests I liked.

Viola Conway took hold; she was that kind. She gave no one else a chance. She talked a blue streak all the way into the gaunt, stone-walled laboratory. When we took our easy chairs and cigars, she hauled out some Turkish cigarettes and kept on talking; she had a line of chatter that got on one's nerves. Finally I gave her a nudge and gesture, and she shut up.

Our chairs were set facing a perfectly blank, solid stone wall. There was no apparatus that we could see. Fletcher sat at his controls; the outfit looked like an old-fashioned melodeon, had no apparent wires or connections with anything; yet when he touched a switch the lights in the room dimmed.

"Takes a little time for the tubes to warm," he said genially. "You know, it's a very odd thing about the subject before us tonight, the Fountain of Youth, in that it takes us back to very definite persons and times."

"I don't see how you can expect to get any origin for that legend," said some one. "It's a craving of the human heart, really, that goes back to the first man."

Fletcher rumpled up his white hair and laughed. "Or the first woman! True. But remember, we're dealing here with a very definite legend, even with maps and guides; a supposed fact that set the whole world afire four hundred years ago and caused explo-

rations which very largely opened up the world's knowledge of America. That's our subject—the actual Fountain of Youth!"

"Oh! Then there really was one!" chirped Viola Conway.

Fletcher bent a cautious eye upon her.

"I didn't say that, Miss Conway. The story is very curious; I've had the Spanish put into English, so you'll hear English words spoken. Ponce de Leon, you'll remember, got the story and the map when he was in Porto Rico; although he was sixty, he set out with three ships. Later, he brought over a colony from Spain—"

"Oh, I know that name! He discovered Florida!" exclaimed Viola Conway.

I nudged her more violently.

"Watch the wall!" I said in her ear. "And for heaven's sake, keep your trap shut."

She colored, gave me a furious look; but before she could speak her mind, she caught sight of the light playing on the stone wall. And after that, she just forgot all about me or what she had to say.

Even to me, who had seen it many times, the miracle of that light was fresh and astonishing past belief. It gathered from nowhere on the solid stone wall, and it dissolved the stone before our eyes; and then it continued. We saw through that granite wall as through a window, but not into the outside darkness—rather, we continued with the light, and there before us were waving trees and sunlight, and a gaunt gray man with fanatic eyes and a stiff jaw under his ragged gray beard—and facing him was a girl.

A N   O L D   man, straight as a ramrod, stalwart, uncompromising and terrible; he wore steel breastplate and back-piece, was girded with a long sword, and looked as though he could use it. The girl spoke, with a defiant flash of her eyes.

"Think twice, Ponce de Leon!" she said, deep in her lovely throat. "*Adelantado* you may be, governor of all these lands, ruler of Florida and Bimini for the King; but I am no common street wench to be given like a Carib slave to any of your colonists. I came out from Spain to marry Don Diego de Sotomayor; and I have changed my mind; and that's the flat of it."

"I think there is a devil in you," said old Leon with a growl. "You charm and you defy, Estrella of San Jacinto! You make light of all laws and bargains. You agree to marry a man, then throw him over when you see him, and set your heart upon another. Because you come of good family, you defy me. But take care! Greater than you have gone back from the New World to Spain in heavy chains."

The girl laughed lightly. "Why not meet me halfway, Don Ponce? Look. I did not know Don Diego was a cruel and somber tyrant, wasted by years of debauchery, accustomed to treat women as he does his Indian slaves! No. Instead, look at the scholar Christoval, compare him—"

"Peace, rebellious tongue!" old Ponce de Leon suddenly burst forth in anger. "Go to your quarters, attend to your work, let this matter await later judgment! And keep your mouth shut. Make any more trouble for honest men, and I swear by the nails of God, I'll pack you off in chains by the next ship!"

When the old *conquistador* used that oath, he meant business.

"Very well," said Estrella. "If by honest men you mean your old comrade Don Diego, tell him to keep his tongue and his hands off me, or I'll put a dagger into his swollen midriff! I obey, Your Excellency; meekly and humbly I obey Your Gracious Majesty."

With light and mocking words she departed, a neat baggage, a glorious gaudy baggage, all high spirit and red cheeks and black passionate eyes; a baggage filled with fire and laughter and eagerness, who feared no one and made the fact evident.

Leon sank back into his seat beneath the stretched canvas sunshade, swore most heartily, and beckoned a slave to bring him drink. Others approached; officers and assistants, traders, builders. With an effort, he flung himself into the work again.

Here in the bright Florida sunlight, his colony had come to earth. The ships lay anchored, and their lading was coming ashore. Hasty dwellings were being erected; the lines of a fort were traced; a camp was formed; and the royal flag of Spain waved from a stripped tree.

Nearly thirty years had passed, since the New World had been opened up, they had been years of continual conquest, of blood and tears and gold; and it was nearly ten years since Ponce de Leon, governor of Porto Rico, left his hard-won repose, donned his armor, and set forth to find the land of promise and perpetual youth. Now he had located it, he had brought a fleet to conquer and colonize it, and the magic waters of the fountain were being searched out and tracked down. For, unhappily, the actual fountain itself was elusive.

But getting a colony established in a subtropical forest land, where the Indians were bitterly hostile, was difficult. So the old *adelantado* found it. Even the bright mail of Spain, and the arquebus and cannon, helped but little.

THE AFTERNOON sun wore on; the details ironed themselves out, and presently came Don Diego de Sotomayor, a vivid man, though somewhat burned out by his vices, which were many. He had a cruel eye and a cruel mouth and a tongue touched with gall; but he and the chief were old comrades, *conquistadores* of the ancient breed. Leon gave up business for the day, sent some of the many Carib slaves for wine, and sat with his friend in the tent that served until a headquarters house was built. On the morrow, Sotomayor was going in search of the blessed fountain, which could not be far away.

"I've picked the best fifty men, but even the best is staggering with scurvy," said Don Diego, warmed by the good Xeres wine. "Ten arquebuses, twenty crossbows, as many pikes. And ten Caribs to scout the forests. Provisions for three days."

"Well done," approved Leon. "We know it's close; due north of Cuba, by the map, and this is the spot. The Indians have told of it."

"You're hopeful," growled the other, "I'm not. Remember, when Ortubia found the Isle of Bimini, his men were like mad, bathing in every spring. This island of Florida may bring the same ill luck. Besides, that damned university scholar you brought along for secretary has been hinting the search is useless. The men are discouraged."

"Eh? Christoval?" The bushy gray brows of Leon masked angry eyes. *"Por Dios!* This passes all bounds, Diego!"

"I think so myself; but he's your man, not mine. What luck with Estrella?"

"Impudence." Old Leon sighed. "She's all fire, Diego; it might be better to set your eye on a kindlier wench. That is, unless you find the fountain."

"IN WHICH case,"—and Sotomayor laughed,—"you and I will be giving the young fellows a long start and then raising new families, eh? No, no; I hold the lass to her bargain. It's my right, and I demand it."

"You shall have her," said Leon. "Look you! I've brought all the books from Spain that deal with the matter— Vespucci, Pedro Martyr, and the rest. Maps as well. I've set Christoval to drawing up an accurate brief covering the whole question of the fountain of youth. He'll be finished in another day or so. Then I'll clap him into chains and send him back to Cuba with the ships."

"Good. The Caribs report Indians all about. Any use to conciliate them?"

"Those heathen? Kill them on sight," said Ponce de Leon with disdain. "Capture a few women if you can; make them talk. Send me back word with a guide in two days, and I'll move out to support you—eh?"

"Not bad. It'll give more time for the search. And it might not be bad to bring the lass Estrella along. Easier to break her will, out in the forest," said Sotomayor callously. "Too many people here around the

camp. We might settle things more readily with your secretary, as well. Bring him. Why waste good chains on the rascal?"

The two grinned, one at another.

"But mind this," Leon said earnestly, pawing his ragged beard. "Mind, Diego! Don't take any advantage. When you find the spring, send a messenger at once. You might take a plunge yourself, just one to try it; but keep the men out of the water."

"Right," said the other. "Why not move up your headquarters as soon as I find the spot? Place the colony there and use this as a base of operations."

"An admirable idea, Diego! It'll take care of our difficulty with those two, the lass and Christoval, also. You're taking along that Indian woman who claims to know just where the fountain is?"

"Naturally; she's kept chained day and night. Bimini—she recognized the name at once, remember?" Sotomayor's cruel eyes gleamed avidly. "Ah, Ponce, we have it, we have it! I feel that we're close upon it this time!"

"I'm certain of it, comrade." With the wine, with rising hopes, old Leon flushed eagerly. The two of them, worn and wasted by illness and debauchery far beyond their age, thinned by hurts in savage battle, pushed to shadows of men by tropical ardors and disease and dissipated energies, flamed up to the thoughts that mounted in their brains.

"Think of it, man!" cried the *adelantado*. "Ten years off at one dip, they say! We have reports from Indians who have seen the effects!"

"Aye, but perhaps they were talking to please us, as their habit is," Sotomayor rejoined. "However, this time there's no doubt we're hard upon it. I'll send you back good news, as soon as we strike any!"

Leon lifted his winecup. "Think of it—to be twenty again, with our brains, our knowledge of the world, our experience! Here's luck to you, comrade!"

The flagons clinked; the sun went down upon the Florida

swamps; and the voices of the outflung guards and Carib allies reported all well.

ALL WELL indeed, and better than well, for next afternoon came back a messenger from the column with word that caused wide rejoicing. A large Indian village located and burned, the naked savages cut down, their women and children captured in part, with all hell let loose upon the red heathen. More, the fountain of Bimini was reported five miles farther on, five miles at the most! The location was sure and certain this time. Five miles to youth!

Through all the camp and the ships ran a flame that night, an ardent, blazing madness that coruscated in every brain and kindled every tongue. The famed spring of Indian legend, Bimini! The fount of eternal youth itself! Those who had book-learning repeated the words of Pedro Martyr—*fonte perenni*—to the others. Here was the island written about, reported, mapped; found at last! Here was the island so long sought; for there was no doubt that Florida was the island mapped north of Cuba.

The credulous, tottering sick men, half dead with scurvy, went wild as the stories passed around. No wonder was too great to come out of this New World, the home of all wonders. Sickness ended, age wiped away, the tales of Indians proven true; health, youth, gold for all! Fires blazed; cannon thundered; lilting Spanish songs and drunken voices drifted across the water.

TWO OF that ecstatic company alone remained untouched by the contagion.

They had met among the palmettos behind the foundations of the new fort. They stood in the starlight, hand in hand. Estrella de San Jacinto, all mental bars down, voiced the anxious, fear-inspired thought that she would have denied by proud daylight.

"Christoval, what's to become of us? It's all hopeless, so hopeless! I've kept a brave front, but it's no use. Here in this savage land we can't run away, we have no refuge. Yet we can't face the power that will destroy us. Ponce de Leon is governor; Don

Diego is royal commissioner; they're both merciless, hard as iron."

"So will I be, if needs must," said the young man, his voice low and deep, his thoughtful features composed. "Little Star, take heart! I have one bold stroke to play, but I can't see yet how it will help us. Never mind what it is—trust me to find a way, some way."

"Ah, Christoval, stop dreaming!" she said sadly. "For you, chains and death; for me, a living death in some Cuban convent. Can't you see it?"

"Clearly, my love," he assented. "Two evil old men, bitter of heart, who between them rule our little world. The old can be so terrible! Ponce de Leon, the *adelantado,* I can strike to the heart, I can wound where the hurt will go deepest; Sotomayor, his evil genius, remains. To him I must find a way, by help of destiny."

She stared at him in the starlight, so young, so grave, so confident.

"How can you be calm, Christoval?"

"Because, Little Star, I love you, and must win you. Sotomayor, the soldier! Well, perhaps I must meet him on that ground; I, the despised student, the scholar of Salamanca, may yet surprise him. With those two old men cleared from our path, who remains?"

"Here, you mean? In charge of the colony? Oh!" She started suddenly. "You mean Don Juan Castelzar! Your friend—"

"Who remains in charge of the ships." Christoval jerked his head toward the lights of the galleons. "He can't help us now; he could if he were ashore. He, the second in command now, might be all-powerful if Leon and Sotomayor were removed."

"What do you plan?" She came close to him, her voice filled with alarm, with anxiety. "No, no, Christoval! You can't mean—murder! I love you for what you are, my dear; because you're better, finer than all the rest. Don't talk of murder. Don't bring yourself down to that level. We could never enjoy life if—"

He laughed and drew her to him, joyously.

"Silly! I'm not talking of murder. Sotomayor—well, it may come to killing there. Not to murder, I swear it! But we're fighting for life, and more than life; remember that, Little Star. The odds are heavy, but we'll best them."

They clung together, wordless, mute in the despair of love that had scant hope.

A sound of voices roused them, startled them. Christoval drew away.

"They're calling me—the governor must want me. Farewell!"

A last kiss, and he hurried away.

I T W A S as he thought; Ponce de Leon had sent for him, and he hastened to the headquarters tent. The *adelantado*, shaking and yellowed with fever, was sitting at the table and eyed him grimly.

"Ha, Christoval! Finished with the brief, yet?"

"Just finished, Excellency."

"Good. I'll inspect it tomorrow. Now, sit, and write. Orders and requisitions."

Christoval sat, trimmed a quill, and looked at the gaunt aquiline features, so ridden by illness.

"Excellency," he protested gently, "can the orders not wait until morning?"

"No. Tomorrow we must march to meet Don Diego, leave the work here to be finished later, and establish main headquarters farther on. First, requisitions to be set ashore in the morning from the ships by Don Juan Castelzar."

The secretary wrote. With meticulous attention to detail, Leon forced himself to cover every point, his iron will surmounting all physical handicap and suffering. The long-sought spring had been found, and he himself was pushing inland to join Sotomayor and establish headquarters there, as a spearhead for the colony which would push back the savages and make this coastal base secure.

Christoval wrote on, his features giving no hint of the pity, fury and awful futility that warred in his mind. Twice he started to speak, but forced back the words; it was not time. He knew more about this fountain of youth than did the old governor; in fact, he knew all.

BUT LEON forged on with burning zeal, a fervent enthusiasm fed by fever. He listed those who were to accompany him; he named Estrella and other women of the company. Christoval looked up from his paper, wide-eyed.

"But—your Excellency! Women, on such an expedition—"

"Silence, fool! We move headquarters to the wondrous spring. Don Diego has put all the heathen to flight. On with your work!"

Christoval compressed his lips and obeyed. At length it was done, the orders and requisitions signed by the trembling fingers of the old governor.

"If it please you, Excellency," said Christoval, "I have made certain discoveries in regard to the fountain of youth which should come to your attention."

"Tomorrow." Leon relaxed and stifled a groan. "I can do no more tonight; I must sleep. Tomorrow, before we march. And you march with us!"…

Morning rose with alarm. Two sentries attacked, wounded by arrows. The Carib scouts were sent out, and alarm died; a few vagrant redskins, no more, who refused fight.

The *adelantado* was an organizer. The brief alarm over and scouts sent out, he retired to his tent and sent for his secretary. Under his lieutenants, packs were being made up and the details of the march were moving like clockwork. Soon the advance would be under way.

Christoval, laden with books and documents, came into the big tent, and Leon sent out everyone else.

"Your brief, your memoir on the *fonte perenni?*"

"It is here, Excellency."

"Last night, you spoke of certain discoveries. They are written down?"

"They are for verbal report to you alone."

Ponce de Leon eyed the younger man with bitter searching gaze and frowned at the calm, resolute features fronting him. Victim as he was of wild credulous dreams and hopes, such masterful youth as this irritated him to the quick, reminding him of all he had lost and was seeking so determinedly to regain.

"More wild rumors, I suppose, such as the Indians tell?"

"No, Excellency. Definite fact this time, and thoroughly documented."

"What?" A tinge of color rose in the gray cheeks. "Then we must have it at once! You have the writings of Pedro Martyr there? And the map that goes with them, showing the island and fountain? There's definite location; are your discoveries as certain?"

"Even more certain, Excellency."

The old man warmed. "And you stand there unmoved—bah! What are you made of, that the greatest wonder in the world leaves you so calm? But I forgot. You're in love, or think you are. Well, if you've spoken the truth, it may save you from the punishment you merit for sowing dissension among the men. Prove your words!"

CHRISTOVAL TOOK the opposite stool, rid himself of the papers and books, and opened the latter to marked pages. He did not share the eagerness of his chief; he was coldly inflexible, assured.

"Very well, Excellency. You are aware that nearly thirty years ago, in 1493, the Pope assigned these newly discovered lands to Spain, on condition that the natives be baptized?"

"Are you speaking to a fool?" snapped Leon. "Of course I know it."

"Here,"—and Christoval displayed one of his texts,—"is the work of Amerigo Vespucci. He reports that in compliance with the will of His Holiness, a font for baptism had been established on an island in the Gulf of Mexico."

"I know, I know," said the governor, frowning. "A false report—rather, made in error. We've been too busy killing the heathen to start baptizing them as yet."

"Quite true." And the secretary smiled thinly. He was on tremendous tension, knowing full well what he was about and what it would mean, but giving no indication of his strung nerves. "However, the statement of Vespucci is an important link in the chain of evidence that I'm about to reveal. A most important link. You'll notice that he uses the word *'fonte'* in speaking of the font for baptism."

"Certainly, certainly," said Leon with some asperity. "What other word would he use? Do you call this a discovery?"

"I'm coming to it, Excellency. Now, here is the work of Pedro Martyr, the 'Decade of 1511.' He does not mention the Fountain of Youth—"

"But," declared the governor excitedly, "it is the map in his work which does mention it by name, which shows it here! The Isle of Bimini!"

"Precisely; in his exact words, *'isla de beimeni parte.'* Or, to use the original Latin again, *'fonte perenni.'* Pedro Martyr speaks of this baptismal spring or fountain. His cartographer misread the Latin, misunderstood it completely, and imagined that the *'perennial fonte'* meant the Fountain of Youth. It is quite clear from the text—"

"But Pedro Martyr speaks definitely of the Fountain of Youth!" exclaimed the old *adelantado.* "Look! Here is the passage—here—"

His voice died, and he swallowed hard.

"Precisely; there it is," said Christoval. "Merely repeating the words of Amerigo Vespucci. Not an eternal fountain of life; but a perennial or fixed, established spring for the baptism of savages. You and others have never carefully dissected these texts. You have jumped at hasty conclusions, perhaps from ignorance of Latin, just as did the man who made the map."

PONCE DE Leon stared, his deep-set eyes outraged, rebellious, dismayed.

"But," he cried angrily, "if what you say were true, then there is no mention at all of the Fountain of Youth!"

"Exactly the case; such a place exists only in the imagination," Christoval replied steadily, inflexibly. "In effect, there is no Fountain of Youth at all, Excellency, except in the legends of Indians. The Spanish word *'beimeni'* on the map refers to washing, to baptism; it has nothing to do with the legendary name of Bimini—"

"Impossible! You are utterly mad!" burst forth Ponce de Leon, the veins standing out on his forehead, his face gray and terrible.

"Not at all," said Christoval calmly. "You certainly know enough Latin to see for yourself that I'm right. If not, call in Fray Hernan to translate this for you. Through the absurd mistake of supposing that *'fonte perenni'* refers to some fountain of eternal youth, arose this whole wild and fantastic legend. When the Indians are questioned about it, they endeavor to please you—"

"A lie! A damned outrageous lie! There's no truth in anything you say!" screamed out the *adelantado* hoarsely. An excess of fury shook him; for a moment he seemed on the verge of apoplexy. Then, with a smothered groan, he sank back into his chair, drawing the map and book with him and staring at it with distended eyes.

After all, delusion and credulity aside, Ponce de Leon had a whiplike brain, a sure grasp of detail; in a word, intelligence. The awful realization of years wasted on a fool's errand, thanks to this map, and hastily assimilated Latin, and the tales of Indians, smote him to the very quick; he struggled against it, but it grew upon him none the less.

Christoval could read how it grew, in that gray and tortured face, seared with evil torment, with the sudden crash of avid, longing hopes and dreams before the hard touch of reality. Upon this insecure foundation had been erected, not only the frantic hopes of that old heart, but a physical structure—these ships, this colony, this grant from the king of the lands here, title and honors! A deeper and more terrible groan shook the man. Abruptly he was years older.

Then his head jerked up. A flood of passionate color ran through his cheeks; his eyes bit into the secretary with blazing rage. He came up out of his chair.

"You accursed scoundrel!" he spat out. "You, at least, shall tell no one else this fantastic story! No one would believe it—"

He stiffened, listening, and swung around. Christoval, startled, turned and glanced through the opening of the raised flap, at the clearing.

A swift and growing outbreak of voices was heard; a Carib yelled, then another. A woman screamed. Movement of men, morions and breastplates flashing in the sunlight. An arquebus exploded, then a second, and the entire camp was in writhing turmoil. A soldier came running, feet pounding the sand hard, and panted into the tent, his face ashen, his eyes wide with dismay.

"Excellency! It is Don Diego de Sotomayor!"

"Where? What?" demanded Leon. "A messenger?"

"He himself, with half a dozen men. No more. *Los Indios!* Indians by the hundred in the forest, everywhere—there! Look!"

THE INCREDIBLE sight was plain—Sotomayor indeed, sword in hand, bare of head, armor splashed with blood and mud; behind him, half a dozen staggering men with arquebuses, most of them bandaged and hurt. No more. The men sank down. Don Diego came striding across the clearing, indomitable, iron-hard, defiant of all the world.

Hurriedly, Ponce de Leon poured wine and extended the cup. Don Diego seized it, emptied it, grunted hoarsely.

"What does it mean?" demanded the governor. "What has happened? Where are your men?"

"Dead," said Don Diego. "They attacked us last night. We cut through them. Men dropped all the time. We came on. More died. We are here—what's left of us. And the savages are upon you by the hundred!"

Ponce de Leon gripped at him. "But—but—the spring—"

"Water like all other water. The stories all a vast lie, Ponce. A lie!"

The governor stepped back, his face ghastly. "God forgive me! Yes, I know it now. Christoval showed me—a horrible mistake. The text misread, misunderstood—there is no Fountain of Youth, Diego. All a lie."

He slumped for a moment. Then more shots roused him—shots, yells, wild shouts, the resounding twang of loosed crossbows, frantic calls of alarm, calls for the governor. Attack! Attack on all sides—arrows in the air, Spaniards dying there in the clearing, a rift of powder-smoke as more guns were loosed.

Then indeed old Leon awoke, caught up his sword, and was gone at a run. Don Diego stepped to the table, poured more

Don Diego found himself fighting for his very life.

wine, and swigged it. His eyes fell upon the forgotten secretary.
A tide of passionate fury leaped into his eyes.

"You!" he rasped out, with an oath. "You damned dog of a
clerk, a scholar, who dared to obstruct me! You accursed rascal,
who have spread stories among the men, who have fed Ponce
your damned lies and broken him—by the saints, he looked like
a man in the torments of hell! And all because of you."

Outside, a cry rose: "Los Indios!"

Christoval smiled easily, but his eyes were very alert and quick. "You seem disappointed, good Señor Don; youth has eluded you, and love, and victory," he said with edged words that drove deep home. All the while the noise of battle grew more furious outside. Men were working around the one cannon that had been landed and mounted; trumpets were blowing; Indian yells were ringing.

"But," went on Christoval in his calm way, "that should not drive you to rage. After all, you're lucky to be alive, at your age. You have seen your thousands die under whips and torments; the Indian slaves granted you for their wellbeing have been worked to death. And now, what? Is there anything so terrible as evil old men like you and Don Ponce—except it be futile old men?"

D O N D I E G O bit his lip savagely. He fairly trembled with acute fury.

"You dog! Do you dare to jeer at me?"

"Ah! I am not a *rico hombre* or a great man," said the secretary, "but at least I am a gentleman of good blood, and I wear a sword. That, I think, was all you started with when you came to the New World, Don Diego. And it is all you're ending with as well."

"You'll not see the ending," gasped Sotomayor.

Swift as light, he moved with his naked blade—moved swift and sharp and cruelly, so that the rapid lunge was unexpected as death itself. Wary and alert as he was, the secretary could not quite evade. As he writhed aside, the point of the blade slashed at his chest but missed his throat.

A step, two steps, and he swung around to meet the intent and lustful rush of Don Diego, this time his own sword out and ready. Outside, the cannon roared, an arquebus volley echoed the roar feebly. Don Diego, pushing his rabid attack, cursed in hearty surprise as the blades clashed and slithered, as the calm features of Christoval leaped into flushed anger, as the younger man beat him back and back until he found himself at bay against the tent wall, fighting for his very life. Then outside—

"*Los Indios! Los Indios!*" a cry rose.

A F E A R F U L panic cry, a medley of screams and women's voices close at hand. The two men separated, glanced aside. Across the open flitted naked savage figures—they had poured in upon the defenses from the rear. Women's voices again; with a hot shout of alarm, Christoval leaped away and was gone.

Don Diego panted after him, halted, saw a swirl of figures at one side. The redskins were being stormed and flung back, outside the camp lines. With the old battle-cry of *"Santiago!"* Don Diego charged for the spot where the *adelantado* and half a dozen men were knotted against a savage press.

He struck no blow. As he came up, the cannon roared again, the crossbow bolts whirred and clanged. The naked throng, riddled with death, broke and fled. From the moss-hung trees, from the palmettos, a rain of farewell shafts poured at the clearing.

"Jesu! Maria!" gasped Don Diego, as one, then another, smote him—and he died at the feet of his old comrade.

A gray shadow of a man, Ponce de Leon straightened up, took two steps, and the men running to him caught him as he staggered. A feathered shaft protruded from his side.

"Tell—Don Juan—command—take command—" he faltered, and went down.

They carried him into his tent, and the shaft was cut out. The wound was not mortal, but something more than mere blood had gone out of that gaunt iron *conquistador.* Hope had gone, and the will to live, with his lost belief in the Fountain of Youth. When they carried him aboard ship and set sail for Cuba, he neither moved nor spoke nor cared, but lay with closed eyes and gray waxen features and stricken soul, as the pennons of Spain retreated....

The light upon the stone wall faded out, and the stones of granite grew solid once more; Norman Fletcher touched a switch, and the room lights flashed on.

Stroking back his white hair, our host picked up his cigar and turned to us with his genial smile. The smile died, as the yawp of Viola Conway broke the silence.

"Oh, I think it's wonderful!" she broke out. "Whatever it is, Mr. Fletcher, it's wonderful! But tell me quickly—what became of that young man and the pretty Spanish girl? It was all their story, wasn't it?"

"No, it was not," said Fletcher.

"But what became of them?"

"You know as much as I do," he rejoined. "Presumably, they married and lived happily ever after."

"Oh, but I wanted so much to make sure of it!" she rejoined, blissfully ignoring his sarcasm and the helpless looks the rest of us were exchanging. "And was what he said the real story of the mistake? Wasn't there any Fountain of Youth after all?"

Fletcher gave me one murderous look, and I knew that if I ever again brought a female to his laboratory, something would happen to me. But he regained his composure.

"No, Miss Conway, there was not," he said affably. "You've heard how the story actually arose, put in words of one syllable; there's more to it, but to crystallize the growth of a legend in a few words is rather difficult."

"I see," she rejoined vaguely. And then she did a frightful thing, quite innocently; but innocence is no excuse.

"There were some striking lines, and one in particular," she chattered breezily on. "Especially that one about old men. Is there anything more terrible than old men? No, that wasn't it. What was it he said? Oh, yes! I remember. The old can be so terrible! That's true, frightfully true, isn't it? The old can be so terrible!"

IT WAS a tribute to Norman Fletcher, of course, that she never thought of him, never realized that he was actually an old man, as she gushed out the question.

He gave her one glance, and then beamed. His eyes twinkled, and with the greatest kindliness and courtesy he let her have both barrels.

"Well, Miss Conway, I don't know, to tell the truth. Perhaps you will, some day."

And she never got it until, when we were halfway back to the city, I heard her give a gasp of indignant realization.

THE TREE THAT WAS NO TREE

THIS SEVENTH IMPRESSIVE STORY IN A SERIES DESIGNED
TO MAKE ANCIENT LEGENDS REAL AND UNDERSTANDABLE
TAKES YOU BACK TO THE VIKING AGE.

A STORY OF grim deeds, of heroic simplicity, of strange wisdom—a shadow against the moon. It began in the quiet study of Norman Fletcher, the white-haired old Yankee scientist, whose fame as a wizard of electricity made him sought by the many famous men who came to our city.

Sir John Broughm was such a man. When I interviewed him and he found I knew Fletcher, he insisted I take him out to the great estate that was one vast laboratory for the Pan-American Electric Corporation. Not that Broughm needed taking. He would have been welcomed without any introduction other than his name, being the most noted astronomer and mathematician in Europe—an old, frail man, looking as though any strong wind would blow him away.... Gentle, wise, but very steady and serene.

So they sat talking, and I listened. Broughm was a strange contrast to the forceful and energetic Norman Fletcher, whose age seemed to increase his powers. We were speaking of Fletcher's pet belief that any myth or legend could be traced back to an actual cause, and Sir John Broughm nodded his head.

"Superstition, Fletcher, is only another name for faith, belief in something! Yet none of man's wonders or marvels is half so marvelous as the wonders of astronomy."

Fletcher looked up sharply, gave me a glance, frowned uneasily.

"Wrong, Sir John. I could point you an example, if you have time."

"I always have time to be proven wrong," said Broughm with his gentle smile, "but the effort is not invariably successful."

"Mine is apt to be. Excuse me; I'll be back very shortly." Norman Fletcher rose, and gave me a word: "Tell Sir John about

my demonstrations before your Inventors' Club, like a good chap."

He left the room.

I TOLD Broughm about our weekly meetings with Norman Fletcher, who had undertaken to trace for us the origin of various legends and superstitions. He did this by means of apparatus which, in an earlier time, would have got him burned as a wizard—apparatus which overtook and brought back light and sound, scenes and happenings of past ages.

"At least, he says it does," I went on rather lamely. "None of us quite believe in it. He refuses to explain his inventions or apparatus. I'm not sure that it's not some sort of illusion or television. He claims it's a by-product of ultrasonic wave experiments."

"Startling and extraordinary, if true!" said Broughm. "Yet he's famed for his work with short waves, for his discoveries in this almost untouched field. Science has only attained the edge of such discoveries. You say the voices are recreated?"

"They can be," I rejoined. "He has to dub in voices somehow, to make it intelligible to us."

Here befell sharp work and fierce... as the axe hewed at Hall, twice he cut Erick and missed.

NORMAN FLETCHER returned, smiling, and set forth his excellent cigars.

"Talking about my demonstrations, eh? Well, I had a queer thing happen. I was fishing in the ether, the other day, and caught something. I'm still tuned in to it. It's the example I mentioned, Sir John. You're acquainted with the name of Yggdrasill?"

Old Broughm lit his cigar with care, and nodded.

"Yes. The mystical ash tree of Norse mythology—its roots in hell and eternity, its great stem supporting the world, its branches reaching into the heavens. A singular conception. The ash, of course, has always been linked with magic and necromance and wizardry."

"But," asked Fletcher, "how would you explain such a legend or myth?"

Broughm waved his cigar. "Oh, very simply! The tree of life, of knowledge, of time and space; a tree has always symbolized these vague abstract things to primitive races."

"Indeed? You think a rough, rude, bloody race like the early Norsemen could even conceive so fantastically beautiful a thing? Trees meant little to them, remember."

Broughm looked startled. "I hadn't thought of that. Perhaps—er—have you reached some other conclusion?"

"I have. I know exactly how the Yggdrasill legend originated," said Norman Fletcher. "Through my apparatus? Yes, of course. I couldn't make a public demonstration with this story; it—well, it wouldn't do, that's all. A story of grim deeds, of heroic simplicity, of strange wisdom… a shadow against the moon. People might not understand—"

He finished vaguely, a disturbed look in his face as his voice trailed off. But the old astronomer laughed and came out of his chair, eagerly.

"But I will. The moon, at least, is in my province! Where do we go for the tale?"

"We go," said Fletcher, "into Norway of about the Fourth Century A.D. Come along to the laboratory, both of you."

His manner was strange, his usual affability had departed. He wore the air of a man who has decided against his better judgment, but goes on to the end.

We entered his private laboratory. The walls, solid granite like the rest of the house, rose twenty feet to the roof. Three walls were occupied with apparatus. The fourth was blank and empty. Before it were ranged the easy chairs usually occupied by Norman Fletcher's guests, grouped about his own chair and control stand, which resembled the front of an organ. This showed no connections or wiring of any kind, yet from it he controlled his remarkable demonstrations.

He seated himself, touched a switch, and the room lights dimmed.

"The tubes require a little time to warm," he said apologetically. "And I should tell you, Sir John, that the voices you will hear come in translation; you will appreciate the necessity. The actual language of past ages and peoples would be gibberish to us. Of course, if I were to pick up, for example, the intimate conversations of Lord Nelson and Lady Hamilton, their speech would be intelligible to us—"

"God forbid!" exclaimed Sir John with a shocked expression. "If you can really do such things, what secret of history, of life, of human contact, is safe from your prying?"

Norman Fletcher gave him a queer, straight look, a one-word answer:

"None."

Sir John Broughm produced a handkerchief and wiped his brow nervously.

BUT NOW the light began to grow, and talk ceased. A pale yellow light appeared on the blank stone wall in front of us. It deepened, strengthened, became whiter. Fletcher touched a switch, and a section of the wall disappeared. Rather, the stones seemed to dissolve; the light pierced them, banished them.

Then we were looking through the wall, as through a window, at an upland countryside, at an old-fashioned farm spring-house where women were at work. Byres for cattle and grain and a lofty, rudely massive building showed aside. The women here were churning milk. One of them, obviously in charge, was tall, nobly made. A gold ring clasped her arm, where the sleeve of her woolen tunic ended. She had yellow hair in huge braids that fell over her shoulders to her ankles, and she was older than the rest. Thirty-odd or so.

Helga, the others called her. Despite their laughing chatter, they paid her respect, but not in fear. Her features showed grave tenderness; her deep eyes were warm.

"Oh, news, news!" Another girl came running and panting, to join the work. "Biorn Bareleg just went by on his way home! What do you think, Helga? Who do you think has come home again? Do you remember Hall Grimson, who was carried off by rovers years ago? All of fifteen years ago. I've heard my father tell of it."

Helga's face lost its ruddy color for a moment. "Hall Grimson!" she echoed. "Yes, yes. I knew him. He was given up for dead long ago. You say he's back?"

"Yes. I heard Biorn telling the thralls about it at the horse-trough."

Helga stepped outside and approached the horse-trough, where two thralls were caring for the horses. The air was keen and fine with the autumn frosts, the trees on the hills were riotous with color. And, against the coming long winter, the thralls and farmers were bringing in wood from the hills, huge piles of it.

"What's this story that Biorn Bareleg was telling you?" Helga demanded. "Is Hall Grimson really home again?"

"Yes, lady." The thralls nodded, and one went on speaking. "Though it will do Grim no good, for he died two years back, and his woman last year, after selling the stead."

"What of Hall?" Helga asked sharply. "Where is he?"

"Down there." The thrall pointed toward the distant fiord. "Landed from a trading-ship. A great man now, a wizard, wealthy—oh, strange stories, says Biorn! But if Hall seeks to sit in his own house, he'll wait long. Erik the Priest bought it, and Erik keeps what he has."

Helga turned away and went to the house. One thrall winked at the other.

"And Erik will get what he has not, one of these days, eh? She'd bear him strong sons; she's not too old. He wants her, and these lands of hers, now her man's dead."

"May Odin avert the day!" said the other thrall. "Remember, you fool, how Erik flayed that thrall of his alive, last winter? Hope not to fall into such hands!"

Slaves, indeed, had a hard life and a hard death, in those days.

HELGA WENT into the long house and hall, and opened a chest in her own room, at the head of the common hall. Ere long, Hall Grimson would come here. His father's property, now part of the wide lands of Erik, the priest of Odin, adjoined this farm; Helga had known Hall in other years, had known him well. That was before he disappeared, carried off by raiding vikings; before she had married Gorm the Red. The years had flown; Gorm was dead, she was mistress of these lands, and widely courted....

When Hall Grimson came, that evening, she was wearing her new gown of white wool, the gold ring on her arm, and about her throat a necklace of little seashells such as children make. She sat at the head of the board; her farmers and women, her thralls, two visiting chapmen with goods to trade, and Olaf, brother of Erik the Priest, made up the company. Hall Grimson strode in at the doorway and halted.

"The gods be good to all here!" he called in greeting. "Is there welcome and guesting for a homeless man?"

"A seat beside me is waiting for you, Hall Grimson," said Helga, and stood up to meet him, a glow in her face, her eyes shining. "You have been long coming."

"A late comer takes what's left, as the saying goes," he said, and strode up the hall, and put out his hand to hers. A flush

While men murmured at Hall's discourtesy, Helga asked: "A tree more fair than any woman?"

rose in her cheeks, and he took the bench at her side, while all present stared at him.

"Where have you been since I saw you last?" she asked, smiling. He looked at her, looked at the necklace of seashells, and laughed.

"To the end of the world. To Micklegarth, the city of the Romans, and beyond.... Ill talk, though, on an empty stomach, Helga of Gormsdale."

Food was brought in, steaming meat and fish, and beer in plenty. There was scant talk for a while; all eyes were still upon Hall Grimson.

He was stark and tall, heavy in the shoulders, smooth of face and rugged as rough stone; he wore a shirt of glittering links, and a sword that glittered also. Until now, iron was little known in Norway, being a rare thing. But Olaf, brother of Erik, spoke up with his crafty and slithering tongue.

"You have traveled far, Hall Grimson. But in all your travels have you seen a more wondrous thing than the sun shining on Norway hills, and the beauty of Lady Helga there?"

"Aye," said Hall, and emptied the beer-horn while men murmured at his discourtesy. "Aye. A tree."

"A tree?" repeated Helga. "More fair than a woman, any woman?"

"More fair than all the world, more wondrous than all the world!" exclaimed Hall with a certain fierce ecstasy. "It is Yggdrasill, the mystic ash."

Some laughed, some frowned, but he eyed them with arrogant high gaze and went on:

"The tree grows at the world's end, and it supports the whole world. Its roots go down into hell and emptiness, its branches extend up into the heavens. There is no tree so great as Yggdrasill. I came home to tell you of it."

They regarded him uncertainly, for he spoke in grave earnest. But Helga, from the side, saw something white within the mass of his dark hair; it was a white scar that ran half across his head.

"Is that the only reason you came home, Hall?" she asked.

"I do not know—I do not know," he said almost vaguely. "There was a fight; my head was split; I have forgotten many things, Helga." He threw out his hands with a helpless gesture. "I had so much to say, and now it is gone! I came to tell of the tree, and brought a sword for those who refuse to hear of it."

OLAF, WHO sat across the board, laughed softly, sneeringly.

"We have swords also; why another, Hall? None are much good, for the edges turn and the blades bend. Even this sword of mine," and he hauled it forth, "would bend on a skull like yours—if you think to make trouble for any here."

So he sat, half threatening, bronze blade extended across the board. Hall Grimson laughed, and moved suddenly. His sword came out; one swift, clanging stroke, and it smote the bronze blade clean asunder.

"Answer enough!" said he. "You never saw a sword like this, Olaf Flatnose!"

True; the gleaming, glittering blade went the rounds and was examined by all men with envious admiration. This was before the day when peace-bands were worn upon weapons, and men said Hall had done well not to slay Olaf where he sat, for the threat.

"I learned to make such swords, in Micklegarth," he said. "I intended to do great things here in Norway; but most of them went flittering when my head was hurt."

"The curse of Thor, most like," suggested Olaf.

"Thor?" Hall roared out a laugh. "Thor and Odin and all the old gods are dead! The shadow of Yggdrasill fell upon them, and they died."

At this blasphemy, Olaf and the two chapmen and others departed in anger, refusing to hear such words. But Helga rose, and taking Hall's hand led him outside into the starlight, and sat with him on the bench outside the door, still holding his hand.

"Dear Hall," she said softly, "that was a great wound on your head, and it has done you great hurt. Greater hurt lay in your departure. I waited, until I had to marry Gorm; now he is dead. Have you come back to me, Hall?"

"I have not, I have not," he rejoined, and groaned. "I thought you were lost to me forever, and I gave you up. I wandered here by chance, Helga. What was my purpose in coming? I cannot say. It had something to do with the tree; I know I meant to tell all men about the wondrous tree. But nearly everything that happened while I was gone, is forgotten."

"And you did not come back to me?"

"I took oaths; what they were, I cannot remember, except that I gave up all women," he said brokenly. "Nor would you want me, Helga. I live from day to day, everything a blur to my mind. I have riches—for what? Whence came they? I do not know. Ah, the necklace of shells that I made for you on the shore! You have kept them."

Hall Grimson

"And your image, Hall," she said, very gently. "Yes, I'd want you, if you came to me. I've always wanted you, always will. An oath forgotten cannot hold—"

"Don't tempt me!" He stood up abruptly, and groaned again. "Oaths, solemn oaths! I dare not break them! Yet I know only that I came to tell Norway of the tree. Why? That I cannot say, Helga. The gods are dead; only the tree matters... the tree—"

He plunged at his waiting horse, disregarded her frantic words, and rode off like a madman, into the night....

Helga of Gormsdale resumed her quiet, serene sway over the

stead and its farms. She put away the necklace of shells, she put away her white woolen gown, and worked hard getting the beer brewed, the meat and fish smoked, the wood in and other tasks against the long winter.

She perceived the truth, sadly. Hall Grimson held all the world's wonders in his head, and could have no good of them; that white scar told how the blow had sealed them away, spoiling his memory. Men said the gods had punished him thus.

TALK OF him drifted in, as the autumn waned and the first snows boded the winter. The whole land talked of him, indeed. He drifted hither and yon, guesting with one man, then another, driven on by fears and quarrels as he spoke against the gods. His tales of the Yggdrasill tree waxed more wonderful and were repeated afar, and were half believed, for he was most furiously earnest about it.

Its roots went down into the realms of death, and were nourished by the fountains of all wisdom; whoever found this tree and had a piece of its mystic wood, could not die. Its trunk embraced the whole earth and upheld it firmly against all assaults of the giants and of the dragon Nidhug, the creatures of evil. From its branches, reaching into the topmost heaven, fell eternally a divine dew of honey that brought peace and happiness to men, and security against evil and strife.

Security to Hall Grimson, it brought none. Tales of killings drifted in, until Helga sat wide-eyed and fearful whenever news came. A chief in Thrandheim was slain; another over the fells in Markland; fifteen angered men waylaid Hall under Thorsness and attacked him, but five fell there and the others fled. Matters went worse. He was outlawed at the autumn Thing, and fled into the uplands, to the high crags of Eaglefells, and there built himself a lair.

From Gormsdale, Helga could look up to those rocky heights, could fancy that she saw him there, now and again. Once he came down, when Erik the Priest was sacrificing a horse to Odin, and he braved Erik at the gathering and spoke again of the tree that obsessed him. Words led to blows, and he killed four men there and wounded Erik, and went away.

He came by Gormsdale that same night, strode into the hall, and asked for food. It was given him; none knew as yet of the doings at Erik's stead. Now he had a shield of bronze plates, and on the outside he had bound two ash twigs, one across the other. Helga asked him what this meant, but he did not know.

"It is a sign," he said; he had become gaunt and terrible, but when his eyes touched on Helga, they became warm and pitifully entreating. "A sign. I have forgotten the rest. A sign of the tree, Yggdrasill."

"Stay with us," she said. "You are welcome here, Hall. Stay, and tell us more of your wondrous tree—"

"I cannot," he broke in. "There was a fight at Erik's place tonight; snow is coming down and I must be away so it will cover my tracks. Battle, battle! Why must it always be so, when I seek only peace and a chance to tell of the tree that conquers all evil? But I cannot remember. However, Helga, I remember one thing. When we were children, and I made you that necklace of shells, I said some day I would bring you a glorious golden necklace from afar, one fit for a queen! Here it is."

He put something in her hand, went out to his horse, mounted, and rode off. When Erik's men came in pursuit, snow had covered over his trail. But Erik, what with his wound and the insult to the gods, and the killings, swore bitter vengeance, and fell to gathering his men.

HELGA WORE the necklace Hall had given her, and from this came trouble. There could be no hiding its source; it was said to be the greatest jewel in all Norway. A necklace of massy golden links; and hanging from it was a golden cross, upon which was worked the figure of a man with outstretched arms. A curious thing, and what it meant was unknown to any.

She was wearing it the night Erik came so suddenly. There had been heavy snows, and now they had crusted well so men could travel on skis. Most of Helga's people had scattered to their own steads; this night, she sat in the hall spinning, with two women and her thralls, when Erik strode in. And, from outside, came the murmur of voices tokening many men there.

"Greetings, Helga of Gormsdale!" said he, and came forward—a tall, powerful man with yellow hair falling over his shoulders, and his huge war-axe dangling from his wrist. He ignored her startled greeting, and halted before her, eyes flaming.

"I am not given to halfway measures, Helga," said he. "It is told me that this accursed Hall Grimson has given you gifts— aye, I can see his gift on your throat now. You know well that I have sought you in marriage."

"Me or the lands of Gormsdale?" asked Helga, looking at him unafraid.

"Both," he said bluntly. "I have many sons, but none born in wedlock. I want you to be mistress of all these lands, and of my hall. I have come to take you and send you to my stead, while I go to destroy this Hall Grimson."

A thrall, a brave man, caught up a knife from the board and sprang to defend his mistress. Erik snarled and struck out quickly with the axe; the thrall dropped, with his head crushed, and the women screamed.

Erik the Priest laughed at them.

"No halfway measures!" said he. "I've courted you with fair words long enough, Helga; now I'm taking you in my own way—"

She came to her feet in a flame of anger and struck him across the face; then Erik tapped her skull with the axe-haft, and she collapsed, senseless. He bound her hands with a strip torn from her own kirtle, and called in his men—two score of them, with his brother Olaf, heavy laden and armed. They could not reach Hall's lair until the second night; the climb was hard, and they could travel only at night, for Erik hoped to surprise him. Now he signaled out Olaf and another man.

"Wrap her well and tie her on one of the sleds," said he, "and take her home. Guard her well until I come."

"What about this place?" said Olaf Flatnose, looking at the comfortable stead, and the women. "It is a fine place."

"It shall be yours," said Erik, "provided you keep her safe for me."

So Olaf Flatnose was well pleased, Gormsdale being a wealthy valley.

He and the other man bundled Helga and tied her on a small sled, and set forth along the trail, deeply broken through the snow by the company. Reach Erik's stead they did not, however, for where the trail curved in Eriksvale, the sled suddenly went off sideways, flinging itself and them into the deepest snow. Floundering, they loosed the lashings and drew Helga out, and in the moonlight Olaf saw that her hands were free.

"You threw off the sled!" he cried. "That was ill done——"

"This is better done," said she, and snatched his spear, and drove it through him.

The second man fled from her; in her wrath and despair, she was like a Valkyr maiden dealing death. Before he could get his feet planted in the ski-straps, the spear smote him, and this was his bane. Then, taking the skis and weapons of those two, and their packs of food, she set forth.

NEXT AFTERNOON, Hall saw her coming, though he knew her not. He sat at the mouth of his cave high on Eaglefells, at the sharp summit of the pass called Axefirth, being like an axe-blade against the sky. From here he could see all the lower country, even down to the fiords and the sea beyond. He saw her figure coming straight along the snow-slopes, but could not see Erik and his men, since these kept from sight.

Late in the afternoon she came up the last climb, following the path Hall himself had broken. When she came close and he saw her face, he knew her and leaped up in amazement. With her burden, and the extra pair of skis over her back, she needed all her powerful build to make the climb.

"Helga! I thought it some peasant from the other side of the hills. You?"

"Not I alone," she said, flinging off her burden and standing erect. "But life and death, and perhaps the end of many a man to boot. Look!"

She pointed. Far below, appeared many tiny dots: Erik and his men, beholding her figure climbing ahead, knew that Hall was warned and had thrown off secrecy.

"Erik the Priest and his men," she said.

Hall smiled grimly.

"They'll not be here before moonrise; time waits. Come into the cave and start a fire. You're blue with cold."

BY THE blaze they shared the food she had brought, while she told him all that had happened down below. He listened, lips tight and eyes angry.

"For that, Erik shall die!"

"Not so," she returned calmly. "You seek peace, you say; well, prove your words! I brought skis and food. Go now, down the eastern slopes into the inland country. Fear not for me. I can hold up my own end. With Olaf dead, Erik will think twice ere he lays hold of me again; besides, I have many friends."

He looked at her and his jaw set hard; then he shook his head.

"Go I will not. I am not minded to run from a few men, least of all Erik."

"Then I stay with you, Hall; I have waited long to share things with you."

"The tree endures, though I perish," said
Hall. "It is greater than any man."

"Stay if you must," he said stubbornly, "and learn the worst."

"Agreed, then. The moon is at full, and rises early. But suppose I were to go with you over the hills?"

"You could not," said he. "I have sworn oaths against all women."

"Many oaths make much ruth." And she laughed mirthlessly as she spoke.

They sat through the sunset into the darkness, while Hall talked of the wondrous tree as she had never heard him, with magic in his voice and earnest air, making up words and phrases as a skald makes poetry, until all his talk fairly sang and shimmered. She knew then why word had gone afar about him, for it was a marvel to hear him speak in this fashion. What the tree meant, however, he could not say.

Just before darkness came, he went outside and looked; Erik and his men were coming steadily, though still a long way off. He came back and heaped wood on the fire.

"Best burn it all now," he said. "Tomorrow it won't warm us."

Later, he put on his shirt of links, and a fur above it, and wiped sword and shield. Helga took the sword and spear of Olaf Flatnose. The moon was just rising, but the rocky approach to the lair was in darkness, being on the western side.

"I hear feet crunching," said Hall. "They have put off their skis. Here, stand on the ledge before the cave; that way, only one at a time can come at us."

Feet crunching the snow and scrambling among the rocks came closer.

Presently Hall lifted his voice.

"Ho, Erik! What seek you here?"

"I seek nothing, but the gods seek vengeance," came the voice of Erik. "Who is that standing behind you?"

"You shall find out, when you come closer," answered Helga.

They knew her voice, and were astonished. In the obscurity below, the massed figures became visible, and the moonlight

reached them by
degrees. Erik the
Priest stood forth,
his long axe in
hand. Before the
ledge where stood
the two were
strewn boulders,
so it was difficult
for more than one
man at a time to
get at the place.

"Now, Hall,"
said Erik, "there
is an end to your
footless talk
about your tree."

"The tree
endures, though I
perish," said Hall
Grimson. "It is
greater than any
man; all the wide
empire of Rome
has bowed to it."

Erik laughed harshly. "I will answer your silly lies, Hall.
You say that the branches of this wondrous tree reach up into
heaven?"

"And higher," said Hall. Erik laughed again and swung up his
axe, pointing to the full disc of the moon.

"Then how does it happen, Hall Grimson, that these branches
you prate about cast no shadow on the stars or the moon? There's
answer enough for you. At him! At him—and Odin further the
work!"

The men yelled acclaim. Bowstrings twanged; the shafts flew, but Hall warded his head with his shield, and the arrows that struck his body glanced from the chain shirt.

"With wizards, spear and sword have more luck than arrows," snarled Erik. "Take him!"

Two men came scrambling up the approach, eagerly. They came running at Hall with weapons glittering. The foremost stood hewing with a sword, the second shoved in a spear. Hall thrust forward his shield, his white sword swung and fell, and sheared off the hand and arm of the first man, who turned and ran, shrieking. Then Hall caught the spear and drew it to him, and the second man with it, and smote him to death.

"Your gods choose poor workmen, Erik," said he, with his harsh laugh.

Erik foamed at his men, but they bade him earn his own keep, and with his broad axe swinging, he came striding on. The moon was lighting all clearly now.

HERE BEFELL sharp work and fierce. Erik the Priest was heavy on his feet, but very long in the arm; it was hard to get within sword-reach of him. Hall leaped about as the axe hewed at him; twice he cut at Erik, and missed. The shield was shattered and smashed from the blows, and he threw it clear, blood running down his arm.

He cut in again, and this time slashed Erik in the thigh, though not deeply. Now, both men had worked around until they stood almost over the dead man, whose blood had run out thinly and far over the rocks and was half-frozen already, for it was a cold night. Hall recovered and slashed in again, but his foot slipped in the blood and he came to one knee.

Erik struck quickly at him, but slipped also. Instead of striking fair, the axe hit Hall over the head with its flat side. That was enough to send Hall down flat upon his face. Erik, recovering, stepped back and swung the axe.

"A gift for you from Odin!" said he.

"A gift for you from Olaf Flatnose," said Helga, and loosed the spear she held. It struck Erik and went straight through

The disc of the moon was no longer round. "Kill the wizard!" went up a roar.

him; as he staggered, the axe fell clanging, and clutching at the spear with both hands, he backed away. His men came around him and made shift to pull out the spear, but he had his death from that hurt.

And then, suddenly, as Hall Grimson tried hard to gain his feet again, a wild shrill cry broke from Helga.

"Look!" she cried. "Look! There is the answer, Erik! Look at the moon—the tree is overshadowing it! Look!"

One and all looked, and terror fell upon them. The clear round disc of the moon was no longer round; a shadow was against it. A dread silence fell; then a harsh mutter of amazed voices babbled up. And here, Hall Grimson came staggering upright, with a cry.

"I remember, I remember everything!" rose his voice. "Listen to me, all of you! The tree Yggdrasill is the tree of life, the tree of the cross! I was sent into these lands to tell—"

"Kill the wizard!" went up a roar. Bowstrings twanged. A spear slanted athwart the moonlight. One and all turned suddenly, rushing forward in panic fury. "Kill the wizard! Slay them both!"

A shaft searched out Helga where she stood, and another; she sobbed a little and leaned back against the rock, drooping. A spear struck Hall and glanced from his chain shirt; an arrow thudded through his neck above the protection. They surrounded him like wolves around a stag, striking and tearing.

His sword glittered. Men died there around him as the steel hacked and stabbed. There was less light now; half the moon's face was hidden.

"Helga, Helga!" The voice of Hall Grimson lifted again, for the last time. She made answer, but faintly, and with the effort, collapsed. A cry of grief and pain burst from him; as they pulled him down, he fell forward on the spear that thrust him through.

His voice was stilled, his tale untold, a tale for which this northern world was as yet unprepared. But as word of this night's work went abroad, men remembered other shadows against the moon, and against the sun; and so they discovered that the story of the wondrous tree Yggdrasill was not fancy, but sober fact—there was the proof of it in the heavens! What else could shadow sun or moon?

THE CLASH of weapons faded, the darkened moonlight died away. To a touch of Norman Fletcher's finger, the room lights brightened; before us was only bare stone wall again.

"Most remarkable! Most remarkable, Fletcher!" Sir John Broughm leaned back and gazed wide-eyed at our host. Fletcher, puffing his cigar alight, nodded.

"I think so myself," he said judiciously. "Reduced to essentials, we have the story of a man carried away into slavery as a youth; winding up in Byzantium, after the Eastern Empire had adopted Christianity; and no doubt becoming a monk and setting forth to convert his native land. Fighting on the way, a hurt head, a loss of memory in large part—nothing remained with him except the symbolic story of the Christian emblem— the tree, as it was so often called. Imagination did the rest."

"Pardon me, gentlemen." I cleared my throat uneasily. "But, Mr. Fletcher, I was looking up subjects to talk over with you for future demonstrations, the other day, and I came upon this Norse myth of Yggdrasill. The queer thing is that scholars say it actually had its origin in some half-understood story about the Cross!"

"Nothing queer about that," said Norman Fletcher, smiling. "You've just seen how the myth did originate. Incidentally, Sir John, I think it makes my point. Just what was your remark on the subject of astronomy?"

SIR JOHN Broughm's white brows drew down.

"Ah! I remember. None of man's wonders or marvels is half so marvelous as the wonders of astronomy—hm!"

"Proven by the tree of Yggdrasill," said Fletcher, "to be wrong. Is there anything in astronomy half so marvelous as the dimensions of the Christian tree? In its embrace of the world, its extent up into heaven and—"

"Tut, tut! I concede no such thing, sir!" exclaimed Broughm. "I did not come here to argue religion. I refuse to argue it! On the contrary, if it were not for astronomy the demonstration you have just shown us might be called illusion, trickery, anything!"

"What has astronomy to do with it?" demanded Norman Fletcher.

"Just this, sir. Presumably, the date of your story of Hall Grimson was about the end of the Fourth Century, A.D. Am I correct?"

"Roughly, yes," agreed Fletcher. "As nearly as I can assign it."

"And about that time, sir, there was a total eclipse of the moon visible in Norway; the exact date I cannot recall at the moment."

Fletcher stared at him. "Why—upon my word, Sir John! Why, that would prove—"

"It would prove nothing, sir,"—and Broughm rose to his feet,—"except matters which I do not care to discuss, or even to think about. I still maintain, sir, that no figment of man's imagination can equal the wonders of astronomy!"

Fletcher regarded him fixedly for a moment, then smiled.

"I get your meaning. After all, was the tree of Yggdrasill a figment of man's imagination? Or was it a divine—"

"I refuse to discuss the matter," Sir John said hurriedly. "Good night, sir!"

And on this, we parted.

THIS EIGHTH STORY IN THE TRUMPETS FROM OBLIVION
SERIES EXPLAINS THE STRANGE AND DRAMATIC
ORIGIN OF THE FAMOUS UNICORN MYTH.

ALL THAT matters about Morphy is that he was a utilities millionaire who collected art and knew it all; a fat, pursy, opinionated man who would give a hundred dollars to charity as quickly as he would his right arm. He had finer instincts, as his art-collecting showed, but they had been thickly overlaid with gross materialism.

As we talked business, I mentioned Norman Fletcher's experiments. At this, Morphy showed interest and asked for more. He knew who Fletcher was, naturally; the wizard of Pan-American Electric was one of the most famous scientists in the country. I described some of the experiments Fletcher had allowed our local Inventors' Club to witness, and then Morphy exploded.

"The man must be insane!" he exclaimed violently. "He must have gone off at an insane tangent, rather. He may be the greatest electrical genius in the world today; but all the same, I say he's a madman.... No, I don't know him. What of it?"

I merely smiled, and he actually purpled with anger.

"Now see here," he said, transfixing me with his fiery little eyes, "since you know him so well, go and ask him to perform his blasted tricks for me. I'll be in the city two days. Make an engagement with him for me, and I'll give my time to see his show. Tell him to trace the origin of the unicorn and virgin legend, and I'll pay whatever he likes—if he can do it. But he'd better not try any trickery with me."

It was like that—brutal, domineering, insulting, typical of

*Rishya caught a wave of
the arm from Thutmose.
"There's the signal!" he
exclaimed. "Hang on now!"*

the man. He cut me short—and I was so furious that I drove straight out of town to the Pan-American laboratories where Norman Fletcher was established, and poured out the whole thing, insults and all.

But Fletcher, white-haired and kindly, heard me out, and then chuckled.

"What you need, my friend, is to hear the third movement of the Seventh Symphony; it's a great restorer for frayed nerves," he observed. "Hm! Morphy is a big man in his way. He's on the board of directors of the Pan-American, too. Where can I reach him in town?"

I told him, and he scooped up the telephone and presently got Morphy.

"This is Norman Fletcher," he said affably. "I just received your message—or should I say your orders? Yes, of course I can do it. But why should I do it?"

He listened, and tipped me a wink.

"My dear sir, your desires and your money are matters of utter indifference to me," he rejoined. "Certainly, I can show you how the whole unicorn legend originated, and the basic truth behind it.—Pay me, you say? You can't pay me, Mr. Morphy. I'll gladly put my invention at your service tomorrow evening, on one condition. There are suffering, starving people in the world, victims of oppression, injustice, hatred; I'd like your check for five thousand dollars toward a relief fund."

I could hear Morphy bellowing over the wire. Presently he calmed down, accepted the offer on condition that the performance was satisfactory, and rang off.

"Why on earth did you give him an out?" I demanded. "Now you'll not get his money."

Fletcher, a shrewd old Yankee if there ever was one, ruffled up his white hair and smiled again.

"Blustering, domineering, stingy, Morphy may be; but he's a big man in his way and does know art," he said. "A man doesn't grow big in the world by being petty at heart. Artistic appreciation, also, points to concealed qualities. Be here at eight tomorrow night."

I WAS prompt. There were just the three of us; the elephantine, suspicious Morphy, the urbane and beaming Fletcher, and I. Fletcher took us into his private laboratory, with the massive granite walls, the easy-chairs, and the keyboard that was like a small organ. I lit one of his cigars and listened, as he briefly sketched his ideas and work.

He believed that all the old legends and myths of mankind had a foundation in fact. To discover this fact, he reached back into the past with his marvelous inventions, which put into play all the wizardry of ultrasonic waves and other discoveries for which, as Fletcher frankly said, the world was as yet unprepared.

"If I can recapture light and sound from the past, recreate scenes and voices from thousands of years ago, find again the lost moments of the human race—is that any more incredible, or more difficult to explain, than the color in a rose-leaf?" he said calmly. "It is not television, though I do use certain principles of television. My chief difficulty is picking up voices, turning them into English, and synchronizing them properly. But tell me, Mr. Morphy, how you happened to pick the subject of the unicorn."

Morphy, who looked rather sullen, chewed at his unlighted cigar.

"Because the story of the unicorn has entered into the ancient art and mythology of the world. I've got Fifteenth Century tapestries depicting it. I've got cups of unicorn's horn, supposed to detect poison in any liquid and save the owner from it. The world believed in such an animal for thousands of years."

"Even fifty years ago, explorers announced that they had come upon its traces," assented Norman Fletcher. "It's usually supposed that people confused the unicorn with the rhinoceros, but that isn't so."

"Ah! You do know something about it!" Morphy brightened. "Right. In China, long before a rhinoceros was known, the unicorn story was in existence. In Egypt and elsewhere, the same. Marco Polo thought the rhino was the fabled unicorn, and started the confusion that exists today. The original yarn goes back to the Greeks—the story that the unicorn could only be captured by a pure virgin; and the unicorn was a kind of deer with a single horn."

"Which, as the naturalist Cuvier pointed out, is physically impossible," said Fletcher. "Because its frontal bone must have been divided, and therefore could not have a horn.... One moment, while I start the tubes heating."

He reached out to the keyboard before him. The room lights dimmed and faded. On the blank stone wall facing us, gradually became more effulgent the peculiar light which indicated that his apparatus was at work.

Morphy, becoming animated, went on speaking.

"The unicorn was an heraldic emblem in Scotland, and James I put it into the royal arms of England; but as I said, the story started with the Greeks. And Pliny distinctly says it is the Egyptian oryx, a kind of antelope. So the story came from Egypt, no doubt."

"ANCIENT EGYPT," assented Norman Fletcher. "And until the French Revolution, food at the French court was tested for poison by means of a unicorn's horn, or what passed for it. The unicorn of Herodotus and Pliny, however, is the oryx of Egypt—today known as the gemsbok. On the other hand, the legend of the unicorn and the virgin princess has definitely been traced to ancient India. How can these conflicting theories be reconciled?"

"They can't," Morphy asserted dogmatically. "That's the devil of it! We'll never know the facts, if there were any. We'll never know how—how— Good Lord!"

His voice failed. His eyes bulged as they stared at the wall; his jaw dropped. And no wonder. In front of us, that wall of solid granite was apparently dissolving beneath the play of light. Where that light fell upon them, the stones actually thinned

*"In you," said Akhenaton, "I have confided my city,
my palace, myself and those I love. That is now ended.
I shall confide the City of the Horizon to another."*

and vanished, until we were looking through them, as through a window opening.

Not upon the outside night, however. Instead, a scene of sun and sky and sand grew before us.

A low word came from Fletcher.

"Egypt! I'd recognize those cliffs anywhere!"

EGYPT AND the Nile bank, indeed. Two figures took shape there; a man on horseback, armored, stern, harsh of eye, speaking with another man—some official, by his gorgeous robes and collar of rank—who stood beside him.

"Yet it is beautiful, Horemheb!" said the latter, staring at a far scene.

"To you, Senefer, Chamberlain of the Palace, it may be beautiful," dryly replied the soldier Horemheb. Sarcasm filled his voice. "The City of the Horizon! The glorious capital of the heretic Pharaoh, Akhenaton—the scoundrel who has turned his back on the old gods of Egypt and founded a new religion of peace and beauty—*arrgh!*"

He spat in scorn. The chamberlain sniffed slightly.

"Aye. He proclaims that God is a spirit, forsooth!"

"A spirit! Who ever heard such nonsense?" snapped Horemheb hotly. "All the old gods, the old customs, banned; the royal family lives without dignity or formality. The Pharaoh talks to common folk in the streets. He invites foreigners to the palace itself; he gathers so-called wise men from the whole world. A prince from India arrives and is made a guest in the palace. Egypt is going to the dogs, I tell you!"

"True, Horemheb. But I'm in charge of preparing this place for the princess and that same prince from India. I see the sail of their boat coming. Do we meet tonight?"

Horemheb turned his horse. "Yes. The meeting is at my house. Tutankhamen will be there, and the others. I can count on you?"

"Assuredly," replied the chamberlain.

Horemheb kicked in his spurs and was gone at speed. The scene widened. Here along the western bank of the Nile, slaves were at work putting up tents and gay pavilions; behind these, a broken ridge of sand cut off the view of the desert.

Senefer, the palace chamberlain, returned to the neglected work, hurrying the slaves. Coming slowly up the river was a gorgeous palace barge, and he eyed it with a sneer.

"Pharaoh's daughter, who scoffs at the gods!" he muttered. "Tonight will see the end of you and your heretic father alike, and a new king sits in Egypt tomorrow!"

Here, obviously, was disaffection, discontent, treachery. But, with bland features, the chamberlain lifted his voice. A figure appeared on the sand ridge, a dark, shaggy desert man, the chief hunter.

"They're coming!" called the chamberlain. "Bring the horses."

Over the ridge came more desert hunters, bringing loose but saddled horses, and two light chariots superbly teamed. Their leader came to the chamberlain and saluted him.

"All ready as ordered, Lord. Who hunts?"

"The Princess Meryt, or Merytaton if we must be formal," snapped Senefer. "Thutmose, chief sculptor and artist of the city yonder. Lastly, the prince from India who's a guest in the palace. *Arrgh!* If old Amenophis were Pharaoh now, the rascal would have been flayed alive at the frontier instead of being a guest under the royal roof!"

THE CHIEF hunter glanced at the approaching barge, then downriver at the scene there.

"It's beautiful, beautiful!" he murmured in awe. "Loveliest of all the world's cities!"

He spoke the truth. Here on the west bank of the Nile was open desert; opposite lay the city in distant view, where the huge limestone cliffs drew back in a semicircle and enclosed the City of the Horizon.

Quays bordered the river. A verdant stretch of cultivated land was cool to the eye. Behind lifted the palace and temples and other buildings, dotted by lakes and pools, shaded by giant tamarisks and trees of Asia and Syria. The Pharaoh had abandoned imperial Thebes for this city of his own building. Heretic he might be, but in his heresy was embodied an ineffable beauty.

IT WAS still very early in the morning; the sun was barely up.

Now the palace barge slid in at the bank, and slaves held the gangplank. A number of the palace attendants came ashore, taking possession of the tents. The Princess Meryt followed; a radiant, tender girl, in years a mere child, but budding into womanhood with the precocious development of youth under burning skies. With her was the prince from distant India,

Rishya, the traveler and scholar, a young man gravely golden whose Sanscrit tongue stumbled heavily over Egyptian speech. He was one of the numberless foreigners brought from all lands to appease the thirst of the Pharaoh for knowledge.

Last came Thutmose the sculptor, a young man who loved hunting and celebrated it in his sculpture, which had cast aside all the stodgy formality of the past. Youth was building a new Egypt these days, to the bitter resentment of the older generation.

"We'll go at once," said the princess to Senefer. "We can return here for shelter in the heat of the day. Get the archers mounted."

The chamberlain strode off, as archers of the guard came ashore. The three were alone for the moment; Princess Meryt turned to the other two.

"I'm afraid," she said simply. "We can't manage it, Thutmose."

"Nonsense!" exclaimed the sculptor, a flashing laugh in his bold eyes. "You two made appeal to me; an hour or two of privacy, away from all the world! I'm arranging it, so don't lose heart. You can't back out now."

"Oh, I'm not backing out!" The girl's eyes sparkled, an excited flush in her cheeks. "I'm just afraid, that's all!"

The two men laughed. Thutmose gave the Indian prince a glance.

"Can you handle your team, once I strike out at full pace?"

Rishya nodded. "Trust me. I've handled horses all my life. But if the Lady Meryt fears for her safety—"

The princess whipped around angrily.

"My safety? It's yours I'm thinking about, Rishya! I've schemed this thing; Thutmose has undertaken to manage it at this end. This is our one and only chance to get away for an hour or two, and be alone. I told my father, and he laughed. Just the same, if anything should go wrong, you'd be the one to get blamed."

Rishya's white teeth flashed in a hearty laugh. He made no

reply, for now the chamberlain returned, the chief hunter came up, the two chariots were brought. Light, graceful cars they were, with blooded horses from the royal stables.

Thutmose dismissed the charioteers. He mounted into one car and took the reins and started his horses off in the lead. Rishya mounted into the second car, a tall and sinewy figure; his flowing robes, his close-wound turban with jeweled aigret, were regal. The slaves muttered that he looked like some god, rather than a foreign prince. When Princess Meryt scrambled in beside him, the chamberlain protested that the regular palace driver should be at the reins, rather than a foreigner.

The princess silenced him with an angry word, and they were off. Mounted archers and the hunters rode on either flank. Firmly lashed inside the chariots were bows, shafts, sun-parasols, and baskets of food and wine. Rishya, as they topped the rise, flung the girl beside him a smiling glance.

"You can still change your mind," he said warningly.

She laughed, clinging to the handgrips as the car swayed. She wore a thin golden gossamer gown, such as the palace ladies used in summer, a cloak over it, and a tightly fitting cloth cap.

"Not for the world, Rishya. I don't turn back. Besides, this is our only chance."

A chance to be alone together! These Egyptians were queer, thought Rishya; privacy was the one thing they could not command. Informal as was the court of Akhenaton, he had found it stiff and rigid and terrible. Things were different in India, thank the gods!

YET WITH all his heart he desired a little time alone with the princess; and by help of Thutmose, it was possible, for the artist and sculptor was himself a lover, and was willing to risk much in serving these two. Thutmose alone knew just where they were going, and how to find the ancient shrine of Hathor, and its tiny oasis far out in the desert. They had come, on this pretext of hunting; it was the only way.

Straight out into the desert swept the horsemen, westward toward infinity, the sun at their backs.

RISHYA, MANAGING the team superbly, was conscious of the girl's presence, of her kindling beauty, of the singular quickening spirit within her, so like that of Akhenaton himself. There were no sons in the royal house, and Meryt was the eldest daughter of the doomed line.

Doomed it was, as Rishya had already conjectured; for Akhenaton was sickly. He would die young, hated by his people because he had turned from the old gods. They could not understand the strange faith he had invented—belief in a Heavenly Father, a god who was an intangible spirit, present always in the sunlight that renewed the life of all things.

"Are you content?" Rishya asked, as the horses settled down to the pull. She looked up at him with radiant eyes.

"With you, yes. Here in the desert—ah, it's wonderful! If it could be like this forever!"

"Only for a day," he said gravely. "A day, to dream of afar in after years—a day, one day, to enter in my book of memories! I shall tell all India about you, Princess."

"That's no consolation," she rejoined. "Give up India and stay here!"

"And die of heat and hatred? No, thanks! Your people don't like foreigners."

Both had the same thought, and the truth was bitter. Egypt had no place for Rishya, and for Meryt was no escape from the destiny of a king's daughter. Suddenly, she caught at his arm, with a low word.

"Look! Look what Thutmose is doing—another man in his chariot!"

The sculptor, indeed, had slowed his horses. A rider had swung in beside his car, with a few low words; then, swinging from the stirrup, dropped into the chariot. Another hunter took charge of the riderless horse. What it all meant, Rishya did not understand, but a moment later, caught a wave of the arm from Thutmose.

"There's the signal!" he exclaimed. "Hang on, now—hang on!"

Until now, they had all been plowing through soft, wind-blown sand in which the horses sank fetlock-deep. But ahead rose a stretch of higher ground, more graveled and dotted with brush. Toward this, Thutmose directed his car, and Rishya followed suit with a swirl of the lash.

The horses leaped, with the light cars bounding and careening after, and both teams burst into mad and furious speed. Yells of consternation and dismay arose from the guards and from the desert hunters, whose shaggy mounts were no match for the superbly blooded palace horses. Meryt, clinging desperately, saw the others falling behind and behind, and her voice rose in shrill encouragement. Then she sank down on the cushions and gave all her attention to keeping her grip on the hand-rail, while Rishya balanced like a seaman as the chariot rocked and swayed.

Thutmose had picked his ground well. Once across the graveled stretch, the two chariots were half a mile ahead of the others; now they plunged into broken ground, following a long wadi of soft sand that turned and twisted. A couple of miles of this, and they emerged suddenly on more gravel, where the wheels left no traces, only to dive anew into a maze of dry washes.

An hour later, the horses foam-lathered and spent, both chariots drew up at a little group of trees, sunk in a depression amid the sand. Here was a tiny spring of water; amid the trees was a ruined shrine of Hathor, goddess of love, erected by some forgotten ruler; nothing else, save the tracks of wild beasts. The ruse had succeeded. The hunters and guards were lost. The three

A snort, a pawing of the sand, and the oryx was gone.

were now alone—with the fourth. This was a dark, lithe man who took charge of the horses, while Thutmose approached the princess and Rishya.

"Who is he?" said the sculptor, to their questions. "One of my slaves—a spy, who took this way to get speech with me. He has full details regarding a conspiracy. I'm going to wander off with him and get the story. You, my children, shall have the place to yourselves. And keep your weapons handy, Rishya; there are beasts about."

Conspiracy? Little they cared, either of them. Here was solitude; cushions, food and wine from the cars, bows and quivers close to hand, the horses watered and tethered—and each other. Nothing else really mattered.

"I'm leaving tomorrow, leaving Egypt and you," said Rishya.

"Our first day and our last day together, Meryt; let it be beautiful as yourself!"

"Why?" She looked at him, desperately calm. "Why must it be beautiful—when it hurts?"

"Because I'm going to tell all India about you, about this day, about my love!"

This, for some reason, amused her; she was between tears and laughter. She spread out her cloak on the cushions, and Rishya lay at her feet. In her gossamer-woven gown, all her loveliness was but half-hidden; beauty, in those days, delighted the eye and took no shame. She was child and woman at once, wise with her father's wisdom, heart-heavy with her own hopelessness, and there was love between them....

Akhenaton, meantime, sat in the courtyard of his palace in the City of the Horizon, where fountains plashed and lotus-flowers floated on the pools—and his scribes sat with him. Before him came men from all countries, black Nubians, Syrians, Hittites and people from the ends of the earth, relating to him their wisdom and stories of their gods, so that he might dictate what he willed to the scribes, and his reflections thereon.

Little he dreamed, as he sat there, that his wisdom and empire and religion and dynasty would die and be forgotten of men, while the adventure of his daughter, out in the desert this same day, would become a legend immortal.

IN THE desert by the shrine of Hathor, in the solitude denied to princes, was love; and with it were tears and laughter, sighs and smiles—heart-hunger satisfied, in the hours that could never come again. The sun climbed to the zenith and onward, and Rishya, suddenly mindful of the sculptor, sprang to his feet and looked around. No sign of Thutmose. He turned to Meryt.

"I must find him. We dare not linger too long!"

"Find him, then, and call before you return. I'll take a little dip in the pool."

Rishya swung away, his heart full to overflowing. They must

leave, they must part; the perfect memory would remain through life, but the moment of parting was bitter.

Presently he found Thutmose, sitting with the slave under the shadow of a high rock, talking, eating, drinking. The sculptor greeted him with a laugh.

"A wonderful tale, this, for the ears of Akhenaton! I forgot all about you two. Where's the Princess Meryt?"

"Taking a dip in the spring. Ah! Give me a drop of that wine!"

He finished off the leathern bottle. Thutmose scrambled up.

"We'll have to get started. Best not leave her alone, either. Come along! I'll go back with you; then you can have ten minutes to make your last pretty speeches, while we get the horses harnessed."

They walked back among the little grove of trees. Rishya called aloud, and the voice of Princess Meryt answered:

Approaching was the mother of the baby oryx—head lowered, deadly and savage.

"It's all right—but be careful, careful! Come and look. Don't frighten the darling."

Wondering, they stole forward and came upon amazement.

NEAR THE pool of the well, Meryt was seated, playing delightedly with a tiny, knock-kneed baby antelope. The little beast nuzzled her; she stroked it, caressed it, and the picture was one of such grace and charm that it held all three men motionless and silent.

Then, abruptly, the hand of Thutmose, clamped on Rishya's arm, and a low breath like a suppressed groan escaped the Egyptian.

"Don't move—don't speak! Too late now to reach the weapons. That's the most savage of animals—ah, ah! We can't help her—"

Rishya looked, and his heart stopped. Approaching the princess was the mother of the baby antelope—an oryx, head half lowered, and eyes fastened upon the girl. The two long, straight horns were deadly. The beast itself was deadly, savage, moving with grim swiftness.

All was motion; there was no time to think, to act, to move. To Rishya came the horrible thought of the girl impaled on those frightful horns—but even as he froze, the princess looked up, saw the oryx, and a cry of delight escaped her. She stretched out her hands, with no more fear than if the beast were one of the tame palace animals.

Rishya comprehended the frigid silence of his two companions. A cry, a move, might startle the beast into fury; otherwise, there was just the chance. And, as they stared, the chance won. The baby oryx escaped from the girl and came uncertainly to its mother. The mother, absorbed in its safety and in the sight of the princess, halted.

The girl's outstretched hands stroked the inquiring muzzle, touched the horns, patted the long head. Astoundingly, the oryx moved forward a little, sniffing; the perfumes with which Meryt was anointed had caught the keen sense of smell. The eager voice of the girl, and her unafraid hands, were friendly. The oryx actually thrust forward her head, nuzzling the princess as the baby oryx had done, with an unmistakable evidence of affection.

In the twinkling of an eye, everything changed. The baby oryx went unsteadily away. The mother followed; then halted, as the three men broke into motion. A snort, a pawing of the sand, and she was gone with her offspring in the lead—gone among the trees, over the first sand-rise.

"We have seen one of the most beautiful things in this world," said Thutmose, in an awed voice. "Fear inspires fear; beauty and affection inspire affection—away, away, for I have work to do before night comes!"

And, in a frenzy of haste, he rushed them away on their return drive.

WITHIN THE hour, however, grim reality fell upon them all. Merytaton was the eldest princess of the royal house; her disappearance had caused swarms of cavalry and chariots to be sent out, scouring the desert. The first company of searchers who encountered the two chariots wasted no words; the princess was whisked away, and Thutmose and Rishya, bound, were taken in as prisoners. The enormity of their offense was terrible, in Egyptian eyes. Impalement or flaying alive were the least of the anticipated punishments.

Back in the city, Rishya sat alone in the cell assigned him. He cared little what might happen; this one day had left life-memories with him. Love, and loveliness beyond compare! That picture of Meryt and the oryx was graven in his heart. He put it into a stately Sanscrit poem—the king's daughter and the horned beast, savagery conquered by love and beauty. He was still occupied by this when they came for him, and took him to the palace for sentence by the king.

It was sunset, the thrilling and incomparable sunset of Egypt, the vista of the Nile and the western deserts all touched with green and gold. The scene awaiting him, however, was scarcely what either he or his guards had anticipated.

The Courtyard, gay with tiles and frescoes of bird and beast, held only Akhenaton and the queen whom he cherished above all the world, Nefert the beautiful. Pale, thin, delicate in feature, the king was not yet thirty; Nefert had borne their first child at twelve, for marriage came early in this land. He smiled, and ordered the guards away, and told Rishya to be seated, and the eyes of the queen rested on the stranger with tender sympathy.

"My guest and friend," said Akhenaton, "you have been guilty of a great crime. In the eyes of the world, love is the greatest of all crimes; in the eyes of Egypt, the beauty and affection of the royal house is not for strangers. The Princess Merytaton is to marry a noble of the land, in order that heirs to the throne may be found. You cannot see her again. This night you leave the City of the Horizon, for you are banished."

Rishya looked from Akhenaton to the sweet queen, and drew a deep breath.

"I do not desire to see her again," he replied quietly. "I have nothing to deny, since you know all. Today I have seen her more lovely, more exquisite, than she will ever again be seen. I have put her into a poem; I shall tell all India of her beauty!"

"Let us hear your poem," said Akhenaton, who had been very curious in regard to Sanscrit and the customs and beliefs of India, whose Vedic hymns were so like the religious hymns he himself had composed.

Rishya recited the sonorous Sanscrit lines he had composed, and explained their meaning. As he did so, Thutmose was brought in between guards, and stood waiting. Akhenaton beckoned him forward and dismissed the guards.

"A strange story," he said thoughtfully. "A symbolic and beautiful story—you say the oryx actually treated her with affection? The spirit of the Lord was evidently with her; the Aton, the ruler of heaven and earth, the Father of all! And you saw this thing, Thutmose?"

THE SCULPTOR saluted the king, and extended a scroll.

"Lord, I saw it, and made this drawing, a design for a stele—a sculpture in which the occurrence shall be commemorated forever!"

Akhenaton unrolled the scroll. The queen leaned over his shoulder, looking at it. He uttered an admiring word, and showed it to Rishya. There, in the new style of art which discarded the old formality, appeared the figure of Meryt in profile, sitting and caressing the oryx.

"Admirable!" exclaimed Akhenaton. "You shall do this stele for the temple, and make copies to send to every city of Egypt! But I forgot; you must be punished for your crime, Thutmose. We'll settle that in a moment. First, Rishya, while I do not understand the words of your poem, they stir me; and I do understand you. What reward can I give you, as a poet? I, who am a poet also, appreciate such things. Name your reward."

"That scroll in your hand, lord of Egypt," said Rishya quickly. "And the picture it holds. Give me this, and I shall bless you."

Akhenaton smiled, and removed the golden gorget or collar he wore.

"The Lord forbid that I disdain the blessing of any man as noble as yourself! Take the scroll, and this collar with it, my friend. In an hour, a chariot will be ready to take you to the frontier. Letters to my governor in Syria and beyond, are being written. Until you depart, remain with us, I command you. And now, Thutmose!"

He turned to the sculptor. "You have this day offended Egypt. I must punish you."

"The will of the King is my pleasure," said Thutmose calmly. "It is true; I have no defence. But I offer reparation."

Akhenaton's brows lifted. "Reparation?" he repeated.

"Yes, Lord. Even now, as we speak, a plot is being formed against you at the house of Lord Horemheb, commander of the city garrison. Besides Horemheb, certain captains of the army and some of the priests of Ra are concerned in it. Also, the noble Tutankhamen is to succeed you on the throne—he is to marry the Princess Merytaton tomorrow."

"Tomorrow!" echoed Akhenaton, incredulous. "He is to succeed me?"

"You are to be killed this night."

The sun had dropped below the horizon. A chill stole across the courtyard; a dread, silent chill that gripped them all. Nefert watched the sculptor with eyes big in a livid face, one hand at her heart. Akhenaton seemed unable to believe what he heard.

"Tutankhamen? A young man, one of the greatest nobles in Egypt…. Horemheb? The first soldier in Egypt. And they wish to kill me! How do you know all this? If we know it, there is time to prevent."

"There is none," said Thutmose quietly. "One of my slaves has entered into the plot, has learned all its details. You cannot count upon the loyalty of the troops here; only your palace guards are faithful."

"And you," said the king.

"And I," repeated the sculptor.

Queen Nefert leaned forward.

"Akhenaton! You must act, act!" she exclaimed impulsively. "Send for the regiments of Nubian archers downriver, at the concentration camp. You can trust them—"

"They could not get here before dawn," said Akhenaton. "Let me think."

"At least, send the guards and seize these traitors!"

"Let me think," repeated the king, and she sank back with a helpless gesture, her face tragic.

Thutmose spoke briefly, answering her demand.

"If you send to seize them, they'll know they're under suspicion; and they'll strike at once."

"Precisely," murmured Akhenaton, smiling a little, and fingering his lower lip in a way he had.

A DRIFT of perfume wafted across the courtyard. The laughter of children came from the royal apartments; the little princesses were at play. At last Akhenaton's head lifted, and he glanced at Rishya with a gentle smile.

"My poet from afar, we have talked much of beauty and peace, and the Father of all things, Aton, the Lord," he said slowly. "And today's happenings—what were they, if not a sign from the Lord? The savage heart yields to affection; the eyes and hand that know no fear, conquer the beast of terror. Why not?" He beckoned to one of the guards, and ordered a chamberlain to come, and presently the official stood before him.

"Go to the house of the Lord Horemheb," he said, "and ask him to come here at once, for I would speak with him. Take the same message to the Lord Tutankhamen; if you find him at the house of Horemheb, so much the better. Wait! Take a collar of honor to Horemheb—Nefert, give me the collar you wear."

The queen took the golden ornament from about her neck, and the chamberlain departed with it. Akhenaton looked at the sculptor.

"The others who are in the conspiracy—the captains. Name them."

Thutmose did so. The king nodded, fingering his lip, and presently sent for a scribe. Queen Nefert leaned toward him, with eager breath.

"I see! You're going to seize those two when they come, unsuspecting!"

"My dear, there's one thing you should have learned by this time," said Akhenaton, drawing her to him and embracing her, as he often did in public—to the huge scandal of the court officials. "That is, your husband is not a liar, and has no fear. Only fear leads to tragedies, my dear. Therefore, tomorrow morning Tutankhamen will not wear the royal uraeus of Upper and Lower Egypt—not yet awhile, at least!"

He released her, looked at the scribe who had appeared, and told him to wait. Lights were brought,—for now the swift darkness of the desert was falling,—alabaster lamps, whose soft glow filled the place with a tender radiance. A guard came in, saluted, and announced Horemheb.

"Let him enter," directed Akhenaton. "Luckily, his house is close by."

D O U R A N D truculent, the soldier marched in, casting a wary eye around and then saluting the king with obvious relief and assurance.

"My friend," said Akhenaton, "you served my father Amenophis faithfully, as you have served me. I am no warrior, as you know; to me, war and strife and blood are abhorrent. Yet Egypt must have soldiers, and you are the first soldier of Egypt. In you I have confided my new city, my palace, myself and those whom I love."

He paused. Horemheb saluted him again, but across the dark, stern features passed a slight quiver of alarm; to his conscience, those words must have been ominous.

"That is now ended," went on Akhenaton. "I shall confide my palace and the City of the Horizon to another." Again he paused, and in the warrior's eyes the alarm deepened. Then he went on, smiling: "In you, Horemheb, I am placing a greater trust—I confide all Egypt to you. The court orders for tomorrow will announce that you are captain-general of my armies and minister for war, responsible only to me; the post will carry with it the rank of prince, and such treasury grants as may be necessary to sustain that rank. That is all. Come to me in the morning, and we'll discuss the measures to be taken on the frontiers."

THE PALLOR of his face succeeded by a dark flush of joy, Horemheb saluted again, expressed his thanks in a few words, and withdrew. As he went, he passed Tutankhamen, who was just entering. The king beckoned the latter forward—a pale, handsome young noble, richly attired, who saluted the king and queen and stood waiting uneasily.

"My friend," said Akhenaton, smiling, "as you know, I have no heirs of the body. Today I was discussing with the council the marriage of my eldest daughter to the noble Saakareh, and it was suggested that her sister, Ankhsenpaaton, should also be married to a man suitable in birth and qualities to succeed to the throne in due course. At the council meeting tomorrow I desire to propose your name, but we thought best to mention the matter first to you, tonight. If for any reason this marriage, with the rank and estates involved, be not to your taste, speak freely."

The young noble was utterly overcome. He was not the type to make a bold bid for a throne, though he might serve as pawn in the hands of others. Here, unexpectedly, he saw himself given princely rank, a daughter of the Pharaoh, a future assured and solid without the least risk, with possibly succession, ultimately, to the throne itself.

He stammered out his joy, saluted the queen in gratitude and delight, and Akhenaton turned to the scribe. He gave the names of the captains whom Thutmose had mentioned.

"To this, estates in Lower Egypt," he said. "To that, command over ten regiments. To another, commander of a thousand horse, the rank of general of cavalry. Make out the letters and affix my seal."

Tutankhamen withdrew. Queen Nefert looked at her husband, swallowed hard, and shook her head in silent wonder. The king laughed heartily, as he met the gaze of Rishya.

"You, at least, understand me," he exclaimed. "Even if Thutmose fails to comprehend, and the queen thinks I have lost my mind—you, I believe, understand."

Rishya bowed. "Yes, Lord; 'twas well done," he said gravely. "They will know that you've learned something; they'll abandon the whole plot. Each man for himself now. Your lack of fear has conquered them; your affection has checked their savagery."

"Exactly," said Akhenaton, with a nod. "The lesson which I learned today. And now, my friend, say farewell. Your chariot and escort are waiting. Go, and tell India and the lands beyond, how Egypt is ruled by the Lord of Peace, the Father of all things!"

So Rishya took his departure. Thutmose the sculptor walked out with him to where the chariot waited, and before the great gates of the palace, said farewell.

"It was very noble and beautiful," said Thutmose. "Just the same, it's not a bit practical. Beautiful theories don't work in Egypt; only bloodshed brings obedience. If Akhenaton carries his theories to extremes—well, you'll hear of others ruling the land of Egypt, that's all!"

"I'm afraid you're right," said Rishya sadly, and stepped into the chariot.

LIKE AN echo the words lingered. The scene was enfolded in darkness; then it was swept away, melted, dissolved into nothing. Before us rose the gaunt naked stone wall, with the light dying upon it, and the room-lights went on suddenly. Yet the words still lingered in the air.

"And, by heavens, he was right!" burst out the voice of Morphy, thick with excitement. "That's exactly what did happen! The heretic king and his religion were swept away! Look here, I've studied the art and history of Egypt—how does it happen that every damned detail in this picture was correct? Even about Tutankhamen, King Tut, you know—his marriage to the second daughter and how he eventually got the throne—how on earth did you do it, Fletcher?"

Norman Fletcher sighed, leaned back in his huge easy-chair, and reached for a cigar.

"Morphy, *I* didn't do it. This wasn't a picture. You saw what actually happened three thousand years and more ago. More, you saw how the unicorn story started—how it went from Egypt to India."

I leaned forward with quick objection.

"Hold on! You're wrong there, Mr. Fletcher. Nothing about a unicorn in that story. It was about an oryx—the original of the unicorn, perhaps, but it explained nothing about a single horn."

FLETCHER LOOKED at me and smiled. Morphy uttered an explosive oath.

"I've got it! I see it now—by heavens, Fletcher, you're dead right about it! That picture Rishya carried with him to India, eh?"

"Just so," said Norman Fletcher.

"But," I exclaimed, exasperated, "what about that picture? What about a unicorn?"

Morphy chuckled, and turning to me, he explained:

"In Egyptian art there was no perspective at all. They didn't understand it. They made a profile picture of an oryx—and only one horn showed. Get it? There's your unicorn in a nutshell! That's how the story got to India; that's how Greek travelers learned about it from the monuments of Egypt. No perspective!"

"Then," said Fletcher quietly, "I take it you're satisfied with the experiment?"

Morphy stared at him.

"Satisfied? Man, it was wonderful! Illusion or reality, I don't care which; it brought every detail of that period to life! Do you know that Akhenaton was probably the first ruler in the world to preach a religion of peace and purity—a god who was a spirit? Do you know that some of the hymns he wrote were the originals of some of the Hebrew psalms? That's a fact! Ask any Egyptologist! The Hebrew literature owes a lot to that old Pharaoh!"

"In that case," Fletcher rejoined, "the oppressed peoples of the Old World will owe a lot to you, I'm happy to say."

Morphy stared at him blankly, uttered an exclamation—and promptly drew out his checkbook.

LADY AND THE EVIL EYE

THE NINTH DRAMATIC TALE IN "TRUMPETS FROM OBLIVION"—
STORIES BASED ON THE REALITY OF OLD LEGENDS.

THE DAY that I shared in one of Norman Fletcher's experiments, or rather watched him at work, gave me a brutally shocking experience that I have no desire to repeat.

Our Inventors' Club, before which Fletcher had been demonstrating what he termed his "Trumpets from Oblivion," had disbanded for the summer. That day I drove out to the Pan-American laboratories on a business errand. Some one mentioned that Fletcher had been ill, and I looked him up. I found him at work in his private office, and he received me with hearty acclaim.

"Come in, come in! Make yourself comfortable; I'm glad to see you. I've had a touch of flu but it's over now, and I'm taking things easy."

"If you're busy—"

"I'm not! In fact, I'm about to play around with my pet invention, so you're just in time to sit in on an experiment and name the subject. Half a minute, now, till I finish these notes, then we'll go at it."

As I waited, it was with a self-conscious feeling. Here was a famous man, hailed by the world as an electrical genius, heir to the wizardry of Steinmetz and of Marconi, placing himself and his time and skill at my service! His affability, his friendship, were genuine. My heart warmed to the old Yankee, with his bushy snow-white hair, his ruddy features, his shrewdly twinkling eyes.

*Gervase, marked for death, meant
to take full toll before dying.*

My thoughts flickered back over his odd theory, that all the old myths and legends of the world invariably had a basis of fact. He had proven this theory, too, with the astonishing apparatus he had invented, comprising his researches in ultrasonic waves, light waves, and other little-known and untrodden paths of physics. In recalling light and sound, which never die, in bringing back scenes from the past with what I can only describe as a sort of backfiring television, he had amazed everyone. Unperfected though his invention was, it was none the less a thing of rank magic to me.

"Ready? Come along to the laboratory," he exclaimed cheerfully. "Now I can relax for the day. Have you thought of some subject you'd like to probe?"

"Along the line of your myth theory?"

He chuckled. "Trumpets from oblivion, eh? Yes."

"Well," I said, "do you suppose we could learn anything about the origin of the evil-eye notion?"

"The evil eye?" He ruffled a hand through his white hair. "You've certainly picked something there! That belief is actually as old as the human race. Archaeology has turned it up even in prehistoric days. Excellent! We'll see what we can get."

And, thought I with a thrill, I would settle a few doubts of my own. I had always half suspected that Norman Fletcher's experiments were part trickery or illusion, that his demonstrations were somehow made up beforehand. No chance for that here.

"Remember," he said, as we came into his gaunt laboratory with naked granite walls, "you'll have the language problem to cope with. We can't understand the words used in the dim far past; I'll have no opportunity to translate them into English and synchronize the speech. Now, make yourself at home and we'll get to work."

I dropped into one of the easy chairs, and took a cigar from the box on the table. Fletcher seated himself before the keyboard, no larger than an organ manual and not unlike one in appearance, from which he controlled all his apparatus; there was none in sight, but I knew it must be somewhere about the place.

Under the touch of his finger, the room lights dimmed. Fletcher had never explained his invention, had never discussed how it worked. Now he gave a mere hint, which was quite incredible had it not been justified by results.

"We never know what we'll pick up, while fishing for the subject." He took a cigar, bit at it, and lighted it in his careful way. With it, he pointed to metal plates under his feet. "Conductors. I must obtain results by sending thought impulses into time and space—a difficult thing to explain, yet quite simple. You know, we're on the threshold of vast discoveries in the field of light, sound, invisible waves and impulses of all kinds. The little I've learned leaves me terrified and awed, I assure you."

"You can't mean that you produce these—these visions—with mental telepathy?" I blurted out. He smiled, then broke into a hearty laugh.

"No, and yes; the radiations of the brain, amplified and controlled—who knows how far they reach? Not I. It was by accident that I stumbled on this one manifestation. For years, bacteriologists have been at work on much the same thing: One well-known scientist has made some surprising discoveries in the field of human radiation and in ultrasonic-wave phenomena; then there are the Russian and German investigations into ultra-violet and other invisible radiations of wave-lengths shorter than visible light, and so on. Such human radiations have been measured at two thousand angstrom units—"

He broke off abruptly, and I learned no more.

On the stone wall before us, where a golden glow of light was growing, a huge and shapeless something now was crawling, palpitating, moving. Fletcher leaned forward to his controls, his fingers moving swiftly. The shapeless thing disappeared, the stone wall began to disappear and dissolve. I heard Fletcher catch his breath.

"Too damned close!" he muttered. "That's the first time it's materialized on this side of the wall—careless of me! By the way,"—he turned his head, speaking casually to me,—"I should add that human blood possesses this power of radiation, to a marked degree."

Where the light rested on the wall, the stones had vanished. As through a wide-open doorway, we looked upon another room. I knew that outside it was a mid-afternoon of bright sunlight; yet this room before us was in night, lighted by a massive candelabrum on a table, and beside the table sat a veiled woman working at embroidery.

She was richly attired, jewels sparkled on her fingers, everything about the room conveyed an impression of luxury, of

Oriental richness. Tapestries of Bagdad weave hung on the walls, the stone floor was thick with rugs, and above the empty fireplace were a pair of gold-damascened Arab scimitars, with an emblazoned Arab shield. One vaguely recalled that heraldry had started in the Orient and been brought to Europe by the Crusaders.

The veiled woman looked up. A door opened and an old serving-man appeared. At first his speech was without meaning; then it became intelligible. For he was speaking French—not the French of today, but old Norman-French. While to the eye this differs vastly from the present-day language, to the ear it was otherwise; not by any means clear and distinct, but not difficult to comprehend.

"LADY ALIXE," said the old servitor, "a knight has arrived at the castle—an English knight, Sir Gervase of Cliffden. He landed at Acre three days ago and is on his way to Jerusalem. He has two Arab guides, and a letter to your father."

"Did you tell him," asked the lady, in a low, controlled voice, "that my father was killed by the Saracens last week?"

"I did, lady. He asks shelter for the night, and an interview with you."

"Did you tell him," her voice came more bitterly now, "that this is an evil place, that Lady Alixe of Beltran is an evil, murderous woman accursed by God?"

"God forbid, lady!" exclaimed the old man hastily. "Those things are not true. We know that you are the most beautiful and good—"

"Never mind," she broke in wearily. "Send the man here, when he has eaten. And send us wine."

The old servitor departed. The veiled woman resumed her embroidery. Her hair was massed in vivid gold; nothing of her face could be seen, but her fingers plying the needle were slim and young and lovely to see.

*"Mansur," she
said, "see that Sir
Gervase, leaving,
has competent
guides."
"I am not leaving,"
said Gervase.*

SUDDENLY ALL became clear, with these words, with
the hints of the Orient all about. This Beltran was one of the
numerous castles scattered about the Holy Land, held by the
Crusaders or their descendants, before the Saracens expelled
them. Lady Alixe was one of these transplanted offshoots
of chivalry, fighting and dying in a far land for their faith,
surrounded by a half-Arab environment. Her father slain, she
held the castle in his place. But why the veil? Why was she not
married? Was she young or old?

The door opened again. Into the room strode a man young,
yet not young; he was ablaze with virility, a strapping, power-

ful figure in leather surcoat and chain shirt. His face, framed
in shaggy black hair, was eager, dominant, masterful, its youth
belied by harshness of sun and wind and suffering. To gain the
Holy Land, in those days, one suffered much.

He fell on one knee before Lady Alixe and kissed her hand,
and spoke.

"Lady, my father and yours were old comrades in arms; it
grieves me to hear that your father, good Count Beltran, is no
more. Here,"—and he produced a folded, sealed vellum,—"is a

letter the learned monks at Cliffden wrote for my father, introducing me."

"I thank you, Sir Gervase," she replied, taking the document and laying it aside. "Sit down, I beseech you; what little hospitality we have, is yours."

A servant brought in wine; he was a dark Arab who saluted the lady silently.

Gervase took a seat, gave her gossamer veil a curious glance, and spoke out impulsively.

"Let me remain here and serve you. No doubt you have need of a soldier, with things as they are, and more need of a friend. I'm in no haste to reach Jerusalem. No protests, I insist! We're old friends, or should be."

She glanced aside, startled, as a sound came at the door, a scratching sound. Gervase laughed and swung to his feet.

"That's my friend Molitor—I picked him up at Venice, and he won't let me out of his sight. A stout fellow, and intelligent as the devil. You'll like him."

He jerked open the door as he spoke. A dog leaped in, a lean hunting shape of greyhound blood, who sprang on him with avid joy. "Down!" commanded Gervase, and went back to his seat. The dog stood looking around, and a change came over him.

His hackles rose, his eyes glared; he crouched to the floor and then came to Gervase and crouched again, fear and a fierce angry terror upon him. Gervase touched his head and he relaxed.

"What's got into you, Molitor? Nothing to fear here, old fellow."

"But there is," said Lady Alixe.

Gervase jerked up his head. "Eh?"

"The dog knows, what you do not know," she went on, sadness in her voice. "The dog knows what all the peasants know, what people all around me know, what is whispered through the whole land. God knows it is no fault of mine, but the lords of the kingdom at Jerusalem have threatened to burn me for a witch, and now that my father is gone, they may do it."

Gervase drained his flagon.

"Nonsense or madness, which?" said he angrily. "Are you jesting with me?"

"This veil is no jest," she said. "This is why I cannot accept your friendship or your offer of service, though I thank you with all my heart. This is why you must leave here in the morning."

"I will not," he rejoined curtly. "What's the reason, in God's name?"

"Ask Mansur, the Arab castellan who will take you to your room." She touched a bell. "And before he comes, let me give you an earnest of what he'll tell you. Here, Molitor!"

THE DOG looked up, rose, came to her outstretched hand, sniffing. She lifted her veil so that he could look up into her face. Gervase, from one side, caught a glimpse of loveliness—but the dog suddenly shivered and sank down. Terror came upon him; an acute shiver seized him, and pitiful whines, until Lady Alixe leaned back again, and hid her face. Gervase looked on frowningly, perplexed, and the door opened to admit the Arab.

"Mansur, take Sir Gervase to the best chamber, give him all he desires, tell him all he wishes to know," she said. "When he leaves in the morning, see that he has food and competent guides."

"I am not leaving," said Gervase, and stalked out of the room with the dog at heel, following closely.

MANSUR TOOK him to a room in the tower, overlooking the countryside and the Arab village and the palm groves. When they were alone, Gervase turned to the dark man.

"Why does Lady Alixe wear a veil?" he demanded. "What is this mystery about her?"

"Lord, I will tell you," said the Arab. "But first, I pray you, give us aid; there's no time to lose. Sergeant Giles commands the garrison, for all the officers were killed with the Count, and he's a fool; no one knows what to do. You must take charge."

"What the devil are you talking about?" snapped Gervase, staring. "Your whole castle is at sixes and sevens—that's easy to see, and a worse-looking garrison I never beheld; but what's so urgent?"

Mansur dropped his voice. "We have not told Lady Alixe, my lord, but two men arrived just before you, knights from Jerusalem, seeking her. We've given them food and wine in a room apart and put them off with lies—for we fear they have come to kill her."

Sir Gervase crossed himself. "Before God, such madness I never heard! You're all mad here! You suspect noble knights of dastardly actions—"

"Lord, come and meet them yourself, but keep your sword-belt on," said the Arab. "All we ask is a man to lead us, in her service!"

Gervase, who had loosened his belt, buckled it again. "Show the way."

Molitor at his heels, he followed the Arab to another chamber, and strode in upon two knights at table, being served by their squires. They gaped at him. One, a stern scowling man, wore the mantle of a Hospitaler; the other was beefy, ponderous, sinister of eye.

"Who the devil are you?" demanded the latter.

"Sir Gervase of Cliffden, an English knight, in acting command of this castle," said Gervase. "I've just learned of your arrival, gentlemen. And you?"

"Sir Hubert Montjoy," the Hospitaler rejoined. "This is my companion, Sir Balthasar, a very worthy knight of Provence. We have orders from the King at Jerusalem; but whence came you? We knew of no knight left alive here."

"Live and learn," Gervase said curtly. "Your business here?"

"Is with Lady Alixe of Beltran. Is she ready to receive us and hear our errand?"

"Let me hear it first."

Sir Balthasar came out of his chair, angrily.

"Ha! Some damned English adventurer just arrived!" His French was difficult to understand. "Out of this, rascal! We bear orders under the royal seal to take over command of this castle and send Lady Alixe to Jerusalem."

"Let's see your orders," said Gervase, stonily, and advanced to the table.

Montjoy drew a sealed packet from his pocket, and showed the dangling ribbon and seal.

"Does this satisfy your worship?" he said with a sneer. "Or have you fallen under the spell of her basilisk eye?"

"I fear, Sir Hubert, that I don't comprehend," Gervase replied. "Did you say 'basilisk eye'?"

"Certainly. All the world knows that Lady Alixe is accursed, that she possesses the Evil Eye which casts death and misfortune on all around. That's why she's to be burned at Jerusalem— after fair trial, understand."

"Oh!" said Gervase. "And you're eating her food and drinking her wine! You, who should be patterns of chivalry; you who have sworn to serve womanhood and protect it!"

"Young sir, apparently you have high ideals," sneered the Hospitaler.

The long arm of Gervase went to a wine-flagon; he shot the contents into Sir Hubert's face. Swinging around, he gave the Provencal a buffet that knocked him back into his chair.

"Is my meaning plain?" he demanded. "You are recreant, traitor knights—"

"You damned fool, I'll have you flayed alive for this!" Montjoy, sputtering, hauled out his sword and stalked around the table. "You've resisted the royal authority—at him, men!"

THE TWO squires leaped up. Sir Balthasar was out of his chair again, roaring oaths. Gervase scraped his long steel out of the scabbard and perceived that the Arab had fled.

"Up, Molitor!" said he, and leaned forward to meet the sweeping, vicious attack of Sir Hubert. What followed, was sudden and terrible beyond words; for, with death all around him, the English knight could waste neither time nor motion.

*Lady Alixe lifter her veil—and the dog suddenly
shivered and sank down, terror upon him.*

He ducked low under Montjoy's blade, his sword swept out
low and far. A squire came in with dagger drawn to stab him
from the side, and his point ripped that man's throat open, even
before Montjoy came to the floor, screaming, with a leg gashed
off. Sir Balthasar was almost upon him, swinging a sword as
ponderous as himself, and the other squire was darting forward
with a hunting-spear in hand.

Molitor took this squire, leaping in upon him, gripping his
throat and dragging him down with worrying growls. Gervase
gave the point to the Provencal before the latter could strike a
blow—gave it to him full and deep, piercing from midriff to back
and jerking his blade loose again. Ludicrous anguished surprise
swept into the man's fat face, his sword dropped, he clutched at
himself and fell atop the cursing, groaning Hospitaler, whose
life was running out with his bloodstream.

"Off, Molitor!" shouted Gervase, but was too late to save the
hapless squire, for the long jaws had torn out his jugular.

Gervase, leaning on his sword, stood shaking his head sadly
at the ghastly scene. Sir Hubert cursed him and sank down in
death. The Provencal was groaning his last.

"God rest them!" said Gervase, and wiped his sword. He was not callous at all, but death was very common in this day, life was cheap, and the man who could not kill quickly did not live long himself, except in servitude. Gervase had learned to kill, and so had lived.

He took the parchment from the table, opened it and eyed it curiously, being unable to read. He held it to a candleflame, and was watching it burn when the door was burst open and Mansur came into the room, followed by a number of men-at-arms. Gervase turned to the silent, staring group.

"To my room with me, Mansur. You others, give these men burial and clean the room, and say nothing to the Lady Alixe."

Mansur accompanied him back to his own chamber. There he began to stammer something.

"Never mind about the dead men," cut in Gervase. "What's all this nonsense about Lady Alixe and the Evil Eye? Out with the truth, on your life!"

"Lord, it is no nonsense." The Arab shrugged and spoke resignedly. "As the wise men of my race know well, once in many generations is born a person whose gaze holds the power of evil influence. Such a person is the Lady Alixe, not of her own will but by the will of Allah; who is man, to avert his destiny? Upon all who endure her gaze, falls misfortune or death. Animals of all kinds perish; children die or fall ill if she caresses them. The monk who served the castle took care of her last year when she was ill; he sickened and died. Many of those who served her have likewise died. Now she wears a veil, which lessens the power of the Evil Eye. Mind you, there is no harm in her! She is a sweet and gentle lady, and grieves bitterly for the harm she has done."

"So that's the explanation!" said Gervase. "Who is the over-lord of this place?"

"It is held in fief direct from the King, at Jerusalem."

"Good; then no one will bother about those two knights, for a while at least. Waken me early. At sunrise, I want every man in this castle assembled in the courtyard. How many men-at-arms have you?"

"Barely thirty remain, Lord."

GERVASE FLUNG himself down in the darkness, but not to sleep for a while. He was superstitious; the whole world was ridden by superstition. Yet he refused to accept this story of Lady Alixe and the Evil Eye. There might be some basis for it, yes, but it had been enlarged and aided by ill luck and evil mischance. So he dismissed it, resolving to test the matter for himself. Nor would he accept the testimony of Molitor, snorting in uneasy slumber beside him.

That he had come at the right moment to save Lady Alixe from harsh destiny, he saw quite clearly. His own destiny had been abruptly altered; this killing of the two knights had changed everything for him. No Jerusalem now, no service with the King there!

"We'll think about the future when the time comes," he resolved, and fell asleep.

SUNRISE FOUND him at work in the courtyard, inspect-ing, ordering, arranging, with a blaze of vigorous energy that swept everything before it. He was, in fact, appalled at what he found. Thirty men-at-arms, mostly French or of French descent, and fifty Greek mercenaries, in the main a slovenly lot. The castle was well supplied with food and wine, but arms lacked and defenses were slight. Below stretched a rich and fertile valley, with a large village and clumps of palms three miles distant; the villages and farmers were chiefly Arab and Syrian, he learned. Of horses, barely a dozen. The raid on which Count Beltran had perished had been disastrous in the extreme; the castle was an easy prey for the first band of Saracens to come this way.

Gervase took what measures he might. In the midst, he became aware of a veiled figure and the voice of his hostess.

"What, Sir Gervase, still here? I ordered you to depart this morning."

"Destiny ordered otherwise," said he. "I want you to ride with me to the village, yonder, and a bit farther."

She stiffened a little. "You talk as though you were master here!"

"I am," he said, regarding her steadily, trying vainly to pierce the thin veil. "It's my belief that I was sent here by God to save a very gentle lady from evil fortune; and I mean to do it. I've no patience with fools or rascals or silly childish nonsense. Suffer me to have my way, lady, since it's for your own good. I've found a mission in life, and intend to see it through."

His voice was resolute; so powerful was his air, that he dominated the whole place. As she hesitated, sudden interruption came.

Villagers had been streaming in at the open gates, bringing produce and fruits.

A wagon laden with oil-casks creaked across the stone, for the olives were in fruit and were being pressed. A man came to Lady Alixe and dropped on his knee before her, averting his face as he, in barbarous French he said:

"Lady, there is sickness in the house of Mar Obed. Two children and the woman."

"Mar Obed has no children!" she exclaimed in surprise. "What woman?"

"A wandering Arab woman with two children, who came

to the village yesterday on a dying horse. Mar Obed sheltered them; the woman was weak and ill, and is in no great peril, but the two children are dying."

"What does he say?" asked Gervase, and she repeated the words.

"We'll stop in and look at them," he said. "I have some skill with wounds and sickness. It's part of the knightly training; and God knows I've practiced it on many a poor soul since leaving England! Go and dress for the ride, Lady Alixe; I'll have out the horses."

With a gesture of helpless assent, she departed.

A little later they were riding down the cart-track toward the village, the two of them, with Molitor gamboling joyously around and ahead. Gervase wore his chain mail and a light steel cap; the sunlight well became his alert, strong features, saved from arrogance by the humorous wrinkles about his swift eyes.

"You're a very foolish man," she said softly, as they headed away from the castle. "Didn't Mansur tell you about me?"

"We'll discuss that later," he answered curtly.

"And the terrible thing you did last night. I heard the sounds as those men were being buried, and made Mansur tell me all about it. At least, all he knew."

DISMAYED, HE checked his horse for a moment. His gaze went to her, keenly. In this instant he cursed the veil that hid her face.

"Then you know!" he exclaimed. "They had come to take over the castle, to send you to be burned as a witch. They tried to murder me. And you call it a terrible thing to defend my life?"

"I did not know," she said gently.

"Well, you do now. This land is no longer safe for me, or for you; now it's a matter of saving ourselves. If we had money, we could do it; money is power. But I've so cursed little. You probably have none."

She laughed. "Plenty, Gervase! My father has ransomed more

than one Saracen. I have money and jewels at the castle; more is on deposit with a Genoese banker in Acre. What good is it to me? A woman alone is helpless."

"Ha!" His eye kindled. "You're not alone nor helpless, my lady."

"Hopeless, rather." Her hands made a fluttering gesture of futility, mournful as her voice. "What can I do? Nothing, accursed as I am! Better to let them take me, and end my life."

"Bosh!" he said roughly "I've got the thing through my head by this time. I'll make it plain later. There's a woman at home, in England, near Cliffden; she lives in a hut in the woods. Goody Toad, they call her; she has the Evil Eye and is a witch. My father saved her from being burned, and she has told me all about it."

"About what?" she asked, as he paused.

"The Evil Eye. Something inside of her—a kind of power. If she stares at weak or sick animals, they die. But if she shuts her eyes and touches them, something goes out of her that cures them. People don't know this; they think she's wicked and accursed and can do only bad. Well, here we are at the village! Who's the man we seek?"

"Mar Obed. He's not an Arab but a Syrian. This is his house on the right."

They were among the houses, and Gervase noted a scattering on every hand. Mothers caught up their children and vanished hurriedly. Men drew back, although they saluted Lady Alixe humbly enough. One man hurriedly daubed his face and breast with a white powder. A girl, staring in fright, jerked a little box from her gown and scattered more white powder on her head and breast.

They dismounted at the door of Mar Obed. The Syrian, a bearded, bronzed man, saluted them, and Gervase noted that his bearded countenance, also, had been hurriedly strewn with the white powder. Lady Alixe talked with him, and turned to Gervase.

"He says the wandering Arab woman has been taken to another house, but the children are here; young children, fevered and dying. Go and see, if you like. I cannot. They would say that I looked on them and killed them."

"No, you're coming with me," Gervase replied. "Remember, your destiny is in my hands. I want you. Do as I say, lady, and trust me."

She moaned a little, but obeyed.

INSIDE THE house, two children, dark-skinned and obviously Arab, lay on a pallet. The wife of Mar Obed, a kindly woman of middle age, was hurriedly dusting them with white powder, dusting her own face as well; she regarded Lady Alixe in abject terror.

The children, their little bodies drawn and emaciated, were muttering and tossing, looking about with fever-bright, uncomprehending eyes. Gervase examined them attentively, then asked for wine. Lady Alixe translated, and Mar Obed brought a cup of wine. Into it, Gervase put a few drops of liquid from a tiny phial.

"A fever remedy I got from a leech in Marseilles," he said. "Tell them to give it to the children later, a few drops at a time. Now lean over the bed and place a hand on each child."

She drew away. "No, no! You don't understand—"

"I understand better than you," he said gravely, compellingly. "Do as I say! Put a hand on each child, and close your eyes, Remain quietly until I give the word. If old Goody Toad had the right of it, we'll scotch this Evil Eye nonsense once and for all. Obey me!"

She was trembling violently, but yielded, and he placed one of her hands on the head of each child. A groan of fear came from the watching Mar Obed.

GERVASE, REGARDING the two little ones keenly, saw a change come over them, and his heart leaped. The feverish tossing gradually ceased. The racing pulses quieted, the bright eyes closed. Presently they fell into peaceful slumber, breathing gently and easily.

"Enough." Gervase caught the hands of Alixe away. She staggered, and he supported her within his arm. "Ask them what this white powder is."

She did so. Mar Obed responded at length and showed a small box of the powder.

"He says," she translated, "that it's a powder used everywhere in the Arab countries, here and in Egypt and in Persia, as a protection against the Evil Eye. The greatest Arab wizards and doctors make use of it."

"Hm! Those Arab doctors are wise men," he rejoined thoughtfully. "I heard of them in Sicily; they positively work wonders. Ask him to give me some of the stuff."

Mar Obed complied readily.

Gervase tasted the powder, made a wry grimace, and tucked it carefully away. Then he strode out, handed Lady Alixe to her saddle, and mounted. Instead of heading back, he gestured toward the desert.

"Ride past the palms, out into the wilderness a way. I want to talk with you."

She assented in silence, and they rode on, with Molitor keeping company. The village and the palms dropped away. Amid untrodden sand, they came into a little hollow, a bowl whose edges rimmed the sky. Gervase drew rein, dismounted, and gave her his hand. As she came from the saddle, he caught swiftly at her veil and ripped it away.

TEARS SPARKLED on her cheeks, tears filled her eyes; she had been weeping as they rode. Despite the anger that now came into her face, it was very lovely. Her eyes were a bright and vivid blue. A proud face, touched with sadness and beauty ineffable.

"How dare you! How dare you!" she gasped. Gervase came to one knee, seized her hand, and brought it to his lips.

"Pardon, lady! But I had to see you as you are; your voice told me, last night, how beautiful you were. Your voice has filled my soul. The touch of your hand has been singing in my heart. Dear lady, don't you see the truth? It's like Goody Toad said—a power for good, not a thing accursed!"

"Oh, if I could believe it!" Her anger vanished, and anguished emotion filled her eyes. "Those children—they slept, they slept! My touch did them no harm! Yet it can't be true. If my eyes are accursed—"

"They're the most beautiful eyes in the world," broke in Gervase. "Listen! It's very simple, dear lady, just as old Goody Toad said. There's a certain power, yes; it can exert harm sometimes. That happened to you, perhaps once or twice, in little things; just as your vivid, bright eyes frightened Molitor last night. Then came exaggeration. Everything that happened was laid at your door. Tales spread and spread more wildly; fear lent wings to thought. You came to believe what was said. Others believed it. But now—you're looking at me, looking into my face. Does it harm me? No, by the saints! I ask no more than to meet the kindness and tenderness of your dear eyes all my life long!"

"Gervase! You are insane, mad!" she murmured. He laughed a little and once more pressed his lips to her fingers.

"Not at all; I'm utterly happy," he said, and rose, looking into her eyes. His sternly chiseled features were no longer harsh, but very gentle. "Look, dear lady! You've seen how this same power can heal, can do good. Here, let me prove it, Molitor! Here, you rascal!"

The dog came bounding to his side, caught sight of Lady Alixe, and shrank, stiffening.

"Close your eyes. Stoop down, touch his head," said Gervase, smiling. "Dogs read the eyes of humans, dear lady; it's a fact few people know. Do it, do it!"

She complied. Molitor shivered slightly at her touch, then quieted. As she stroked his neck, he lost his cowering air; after a moment, his head came around and he nuzzled her hand and

*Gervase gave the point to the Provençal—full
and deep, piercing from midriff to back.*

licked it affectionately. She drew erect with a swift and startled word.

"True! It's true—oh, Gervase!"

Color swept into her cheeks, a rush of tears came into her eyes. She put out her hands to him, and Gervase upheld her, pressed her head against his shoulder, and his lips brushed the golden mass of her hair.

"What did you do to him—ah, the powder!" She shrank away, lifting her face in sharp conjecture. "Did you put that white powder on Molitor? Is that why he feared me not?"

Gervase broke into a laugh, but checked it thoughtfully.

"Heaven forbid! That powder, by the taste, is nothing but alum. Hm! There may be something to that powder, after all; these Arab wise men possess many secrets. This powder, that puckers the skin—hm! It might possibly fend off any such influences, in some queer way we don't understand. Bah! Sweep all that nonsense out of your head, my dear! From now on, we go up the world together. We'll abandon your castle and leave this land."

A S S H E listened, she yielded and drew against him, sobbing softly and happily, her face against his shoulder.

"We'll go to Acre," he went on, kindling to the thought. "There we'll take ship for Venice or Byzantium—perhaps to England; why not? The weight is off your heart and mind together. Here between sky and sand, you've come awake, you've learned the truth, you've cast off the darkness of your life, And I'll make the truth clearer to you, God helping me, through the years—"

His voice died away upon silence. A growl came from Molitor, a yapping angry bark; at the voice of Gervase, the dog subsided at his feet. Lady Alixe lifted her head and looked up, following the gaze of Gervase.

The rim of sand against the sky, above them, was broken by the shape of a horseman in glittering mail, who sat looking down at them. One low, incredulous gasp escaped the woman.

"Khalid! The Emir himself—Khalid of Damascus!"

As they looked, the rim of the bowl was broken all around. Men came into view, outlined against the blue sky, checking their horses silently; dark, bearded men in Arab chain mail, bows strung and shafts notched. Gervase relaxed. Caught, beyond escape! Caught, by swift savage raiders of the Saracen!

Lady Alixe moved swiftly. "I know him," she breathed. "He speaks French, he has often been a guest at our castle—Emir Khalid!" She lifted her voice in a clear, ringing call. "I'm the lady of Beltran! This knight is a friend—"

"It matters not who you are," broke in the Emir, a darkly indomitable, impassive shape. "I have sworn death to all Franks. It was I who slew your father Count Beltran. I shall kill every Frank I meet, for the injury that was done me last month, when my wife and children were carried off by Franks. Yield, both of you! Yield or die!"

Gervase scraped out sword. "Die like a man, then," he said grimly. White to the lips, Alixe tried once again.

"Khalid! We've done you no harm—"

"Take the woman alive," said the impassive Emir, "Kill the man. Shoot, Ali, and may Allah further your shaft!"

Alixe, who understood the Arabic words, flung herself before Gervase.

"No, no!" she cried fiercely. "They give no mercy—rather death, than a harem! Those infidel dogs shall not take me!"

Her long dagger flashed out in her hand. The Emir lifted his hand.

"Four of you, dismount and seize her. Ali, kill the man for me!"

Four of the Arabs dismounted; and of a sudden everything was happening at once. The bowman beside the Emir drew back his shaft. The four Arabs were plunging ankle-deep down the sandy slope. Gervase quickly stepped aside and put Alixe away from him with a shove. The bowstring twanged, and the shaft flew like a flicker of light.

LIGHTLY THE sword of Gervase swung. It struck the arrow in mid-air and knocked it aside. The Arabs gasped; to them, it was magic. To Gervase, it was nothing; mere child's play, the everyday training of the straight-sworded Northmen and Normans.

Another twang, another flying shaft. He struck—and missed, losing balance in the sand. The arrow hammered on his mail-shirt. It broke, but the shock bore him back, overbalanced as he was, and he came down. To those who looked, it seemed that he was dead.

"Allah!"

With the shrill pealing yell, the other men dismounted and came rushing down the slope. The first four were already closing in upon Alixe, wolfishly.

She evaded one; her dagger struck out at another, but the man caught her in his grip. Molitor came up in one terrific leap and caught the Arab by the throat; but another, curved scimitar swinging, struck at the dog and killed him.

FOR THAT man, it was an evil moment.

Gervase was already coming to his feet; a cry of grief and fury burst from him as he struck. His blade clove through helmet and skull of the warrior, who pitched forward across the dead hound.

Alixe poniarded the man who held her. Then, smitten across the head by a mailed fist, she slipped down sidewise and lay quiet, senseless. The man who had struck her died, as the point of the long straight sword sheared across his belly; a spring, and Gervase was above her, bestriding her figure, feet planted firmly in the sand. He wasted no breath on battlecries; he was marked for death and knew it, and meant to take full toll before dying.

They were flooding all around him now; they had left their bows with the horses, but steel was out and whanging at him. The first tried to rush him off his feet, but he met them halfway in this. He struck at their faces, swift and hard and fast; screams rang and blood spurted, for it was a ghastly business. The lithe curved blades were swept aside by the heavy sword; men staggered or reeled away from before him.

He leaped suddenly, turned about, caught those striking at him from behind. With point and edge he drove death into them, his tall figure towering above their lesser build. They pressed in for a moment. A Toledo blade slashed across his breast, piercing the chain-mail and bringing blood; another scimitar clanged on his steel cap, so that blood streaked down his cheek. Then they rolled back, as the smiting heavy sword struck down man after man, and blood spurted in the sunlight, and hurt men crawled, and screamed to Allah.

It could not last. He knew it most desperately; they were too many. Two came plunging at him, from either side. He cut down one, but his sword stuck there, and the other was in upon him, bearing him down. His sword was lost. His naked hands broke that man's neck, but already others were in, and he went down, down, slipping in the bloody sand, and they piled up above him.

"Back! Back, I say! Away from him!" The clarion voice of the Emir Khalid reached into them. The pile broke away. One warrior, poised to stab Gervase in the throat, was dragged off by his fellows. They scrambled clear, looking up in amazement to their leader. Gervase came to one elbow and reached out for his lost sword, but they did not move.

"Touch him not!" roared the Emir, swinging out of the saddle.

A man had come up to him, panting, gasping out eager words. In hot haste, the Emir turned and came down the slope in long leaps, and halted before Gervase. The latter came to one knee, sword ready, thinking it was the end, but the Emir checked him.

"Is this true?" The dark face was all ablaze, the eyes wildly alight. "Was it you, and this woman, who healed those children in the village? Answer, answer!"

"Aye," panted Gervase. "What of it?"

"My children, my children!" Reaching out, the Arab caught him in a wild embrace. "My wife, escaped from her captors with the two children! Allah bless you! Allah reward you, my friend and brother—"

THE HOT gasping voices died out; the sunlight faded, the red gouts of blood were gone. The stones of the wall became visible once more. Then the experiment went wrong.

A cry broke from Norman Fletcher. Against the wall something moved. A wild bloody figure, holding a long ax, moved in front of us, came rushing at us—no picture, no vision, but some actual thing from the past. I saw Fletcher plunge at his keyboard, as the ax swung. It fell, missed him, struck a chair beside him—then it faded and was gone, with the crash of the blow still in our ears.

It was gone. The light was over, and died away. Fletcher came to his feet and looked at me; he was very pale and shaken. I looked at the chair. It was rent and splintered by a tremendous blow; but the room was very quiet.

"Good Lord!" I cried. "Did I dream that thing—that ax?"

FLETCHER EXHALED a deep breath, laughed shakily, and pointed to the chair. "There's your answer," he said. "Those controls went screwy on me—confound it! Well, well, all's right that ends right. Here, have a fresh cigar. Anyhow, you got the answer to your request for the Evil Eye material, eh?"

"More or less," I said, biting at the cigar. Right then, I needed a drink. "But I'm afraid I didn't get much of it. That alum stuff, for example."

He gave me a shrewd glance.

"No? To me, that was the most interesting detail of all," he observed reflectively. "We've just been told, flatly and unqualifiedly, that at the time of the Crusades, and presumably later, alum was used all over the Moslem world to avert the Evil Eye. Suppose we look this up and find it true,—and mind you, I've no doubt whatever that it will be substantiated in fact,—then what?"

"Well?" I said. "I'll bite. What?"

He shook his head. "There may be something in it from a scientific standpoint, that's all, directly in line with my own experiments. Alum, a powerful astringent, puckering the skin and membranes—yes, yes, it might have some such effect as we've been told. I've learned something today, let me tell you! Certain persons do emanate magnetic power, or invisible rays; science has proven that the Evil Eye is no mere fancy, but founded on sober reality. Once in generations, a person may show up whose radiations are extremely strong—for good or for evil. Hm! I'm going to experiment with the alum idea. Those old Arab physicians had something on the ball!"

Looking at the smashed and broken chair, I could not repress a shiver.

"So has your damned machinery, whatever it is!"

Fletcher took my arm, his shrewd eyes twinkling. "My friend," he said impressively, "come along to the library, where I'll lay before you the kindest words of tongue or pen."

"What are they?" I asked suspiciously.

" 'Scotch or Bourbon?'" he rejoined, smiling.

"For once you're dead right," I said. "And the quicker the better!"

THE WOLF WOMAN

THE STRANGE WERE-WOLF LEGEND COLORS THIS BRILLIANT
STORY—THE TENTH OF THE "TRUMPETS FROM OBLIVION."

NORMAN FLETCHER phoned me one morning. Even though one may know Fletcher well, to get a call from so distinguished a scientist,—one of the great men of the earth,—is to get a thrill.

"Hello!" came his cheerful tones. "Have you a stenographer in your office?"

"Yes," I replied in some astonishment.

He chuckled. "Have you a particular young woman there named Stephens?"

"Oh! Sure. Why?"

"I have a letter here from her."

"You have what?"

"I got a letter from her the other day, asking if I could reveal the origin of the werewolf myth. If you're not busy, will you bring her out this evening?"

"Of course!" I promised. "I've been meaning to get in touch with you. The Inventors' Club want to know whether you'll be good enough to give any more demonstrations—"

"No!" he barked, with an unwonted brusqueness. "Sorry; I've undertaken a lot of Government work and may leave for Washington soon. Besides, something's gone wrong with my apparatus. Apparently it's getting out of control; I'll explain tonight."

I hung up, thinking uneasily of the recent occasion when something had gone wrong with his infernal invention. Then I

called Miss Stephens and she flushed when I told her of Fletcher's words.

"Perhaps it was terribly impertinent," she confessed. "But you
had said so much about those experiments—and I did a thesis
at college on the werewolf—and—"

"And all that remains is for you to drive out there with me
tonight," I said cheerfully. "You'll have the last word—or the
first word—on the werewolf subject."

She was demure enough as I ushered her into Norman
Fletcher's laboratory that evening and performed the introduc-
tions; but her demure quality had solid subsurface foundations.
In no time at all, she had Fletcher interested, for she knew her

subject; everything that had been written about werewolves, or humans who took wolf form at night, was in her head.

"But where's your apparatus?" she exclaimed, looking around.

"Working with ultrasonic and high-frequency waves, with electricity of all sorts—and nothing in sight!"

It is true that about this grim stone-walled laboratory was little to suggest the home of the most advanced electrical scientist in the country. Easy-chairs were grouped about his instrument-board, or controls; this, looking like the triple manual of an organ, gave forth a faint hum of tubes at heat, but seemed unconnected with any other apparatus.

FLETCHER SETTLED himself before it and dimmed the room lights. To my displeasure, Miss Stephens accepted a cigarette and smoked with an air of enjoyment. She knows very well that I discourage cigarettes about the office, but she disregarded me entirely and seemed absorbed in Fletcher and his theories.

"Reduced to its essentials," Fletcher said, "the myth is that a person dons a girdle of wolfskin and turns into a wolf, to prowl at night; a woman is usually the subject, and as a rule it makes a grisly and horrible story. It goes back to the earliest of the Greek writers, even back to the Assyrians, and the belief still lingers in Europe today."

"Yes," said Miss Stephens. "I have Vetlugin's book on the Russian legends about it."

"Oddly enough," pursued old Fletcher, "the werewolves of the Christian dispensation were usually beneficent creatures, even touching and pitiful. While attempting yesterday to discover the origin of the legend, I chanced upon the story I'm going to show you. It concerns St. Odo, abbot of Cluny."

THAT HIS singular genius actually brought back scenes and sounds of the past, that the tremendous power of his ultrasonic mechanism could recapture, by a sort of backward television, real incidents from across the ages, we already knew. There was much about his process, however, that he had never revealed to anyone.

"Then," I said, "the characters tonight will talk old French, I presume?"

"No," said Fletcher hurriedly, for already the yellowish light was beginning to play upon the stone wall facing us. "My apparatus is somehow out of kilter; it does unexpected things, I regret to say, and I've no time to work on it now. Something about those new tubes and the iridium I've been using."

"What's that got to do with the language employed?" I asked.

"Everything. I can now get the sound alone, or the scenes alone. Yesterday I made a recording of the sound on this story and rushed it up to the university. Professor Hartmetz translated it into English and had the words recorded anew, rushed it back to me by dinnertime tonight, and I now switch the recording in on my sound-track. Ah! Pardon me."

A telephone was buzzing insistently. He reached out to the instrument and spoke. I watched the yellowish light dissolving the stones of the wall; the solid granite melted and began to disappear before our eyes. Suddenly Fletcher's voice sounded sharply.

"What?" he ejaculated. "What's that, Hartmetz? A horrible thing? Impossible! It was a lovely story, about St. Odo and the wolves—what? It was not?" Agitation suddenly thrilled in his tones. "Good Lord, man! Then there must be something wrong! Well, let it go. Thanks for calling me. I've got the thing on now. Good night."

I vaguely realized that something in his program had gone decidedly amiss; in the reflected radiance I saw him mop his brow and dart an anxious look at Miss Stephens, but she did not notice. She was staring at the wall. Those solid stones had now almost vanished, and as through a window, we were gazing out upon a scene that was no picture, but reality in every dimension. I caught a dazed mutter from Norman Fletcher.

"Sanscrit, he says—Sanscrit! The old Aryan race, thousands of years ago; no, no, it's impossible...."

A woman's laughter drowned out the mutter.

The scene before us blurred and moved, blurred and took shape anew—a vista of hills and forests, of squat, massive towers.

Again everything blurred; the apparatus was certainly not functioning aright. The woman's laughter rose louder; it was no ringing musical peal of mirth, but the bitter laughter of hysteria. Suddenly the scene came clearly.

She was standing in a courtyard, laughing; a glorious figure against the background of rough stone and ancient thick trees, a woman laughing wildly, torn between grief and furious anger. The group of men regarded her with fear and awe. Her laughter died out and she put both hands to her face, as though to shut out some frightful vision.

This whole scene conveyed an impression of indescribable savage majesty; one sensed it, felt it in every detail. In this place was no delicacy or grace. The courtyard, the walls and buildings, were of enormous ill-fitted stone blocks; the trees were nobly massive; an air of spacious power pervaded everything, as in some dwelling of the gods.

The very doors, the stone seat, the beam-ends under the eaves, were gigantic and heavy-hewed. The weapons of the men bulked crudely large; spears with great bronze blades, huge splay-bladed axes of bronze, swords like beams of metal. The men themselves were built to match—figures of muscled strength and power. Outstretched at the woman's feet, red tongue lolling, was a tamed wolf of tremendous size, eying her sharply.

The woman lifted her head and bared her face. She was in white, a golden torque about her neck. Her radiant loveliness struck forth like sun through dark clouds; it was a regal beauty, a richly glowing force instinct with energy. There was nothing passive about her. Into her stark blue eyes came a flame that shook her whole body, and her voice leaped forth like a clarion.

"Fight, Shatra! I'll lead, with you and the warriors following."

"Very well, but you know what it means, Indra," said the stalwart warrior, Shatra. "You know how they kill us; all day long we slay the little dark men, and at the end when we're exhausted, they overwhelm us. They're in countless numbers like ants. That's how your husband the king died; that's how most of our warriors

*"Take the track,
Vic," said Indra,
when the gate
clanged shut.*

have died. We are few, and they are like the forest leaves. Barbarians, rude and uncouth and swart—but they fight!

"That," he went on sadly, "is how our Aryan people have vanished. They slew in vain, and were overwhelmed. They drifted away and migrated, their civilization is lost; these little dark men have swarmed over the whole land. We alone remain, and now it is our time to die, if so you command."

THE FLAME died from Indra's face.

"You have sworn to obey me and my son to the death," she said quietly.

"Our oaths stand; order it, and we fight and die—you and your son with us."

She caught her breath. "I see, I see! What are their terms?"

"They will not attack; behind our walls we can stand and laugh at them, killing them as they come. Their king gives a choice. Go forth freely and migrate, unharmed, seek another land as most of our people have done. Or else remain here in our stronghold; they'll send us what we need of food, but every man of us who leaves the walls, will be slain; women and children taken for slaves. We are the last of our people, Indra; the choice is yours to make and we abide by it."

She listened, wide-eyed. "Clever, these people! Let us remain here—and any who go forth, die! They're not anxious for any fight to the death. Come."

She beckoned imperiously and started across the courtyard. They followed her, mounting by the stairs to the stone tower over the gateway.

This was the donjon or central keep, the palace quarters of the dead king of a vanished people. From the squat tower, Indra could look down into the courtyard of the crudely massive castle itself, whose walls stretched afar over the hill. Within these walls was a small town. Outside was a vast camp stretching afar by hill and forest. And, from this camp, a score of the besiegers had come into the great courtyard of the castle, and waited there.

Indra looked at them. Hardy, swarthy men, different from her own people; smaller in stature, armed only with sword and bow. No stalwart hunters, like her powerful race, but numberless as the sea sands in that vast camp, an ocean of men who had flooded down over the snowy peaks and had driven her people out of their land. Small men, these Dravidians, yet they had conquered the mighty Aryan people and driven them into migration and exile afar.

"Perhaps it were better to go, like the rest," she murmured.

"We could take nothing, Indra," said one of her chiefs. "We must leave all arms and all treasure."

Her lips firmed. Her eyes flashed.

"No, then!" she exclaimed. "No! Keep our arms and our city; we, the last of our race!"

The chieftains assented and went to tell the Dravidian envoys.

Indra, looking out upon the hills, perceived the deep cunning of these small people.

On the hills and slopes all about the town and castle, were palaces and châteaux. The Aryan princes and nobles had used these, for coolness in summer, for hunting in the winter; now the Dravidians occupied them, and the owners were dead. She perceived that the swarthy warriors thus held the place in a cordon. Their main host could go its ways and they would wait, grimly.

The summer had ended, autumn was whistling over the mountains, the first snow would fall any day now. Indra lifted unseeing eyes to the southward. There, over the vast lands that stretched to the sea and the ends of earth, the dark people had moved in. The Aryans had gone, scattered in migration after migration to the west and north, over the horizon to destiny unknown. Here among the mountains were the final remnant.

HER HUSBAND had fallen, the princes and great men had fallen. They had slain until they were borne down by sheer weight of numbers, like a man defying the tide to cover him. She, and the last of her people, and the boy who should some day be a king—her son; these were left. A king? Over what? There was no longer a kingdom. There would be no more a people over which he could rule, when he reached manhood.

An old councilor came to her, and pointed to the courtyard below.

"Come, Lady Indra! The king of these people comes; you must meet him before the gates and swear the oath."

"Eh? What oath?" she demanded.

"To observe the treaty; that none of our people shall war against his or leave these walls. Otherwise they die. He swears to let provisions enter freely, even to supply them, and to carry no fight to us. A great oath, with all the gods to witness!"

IT WAS so accomplished before the gates, in sight of all men, and with sacrifices to the gods. This King Savastri drew the eye

*"Lady, we have kept the peace; but
your people have come slaying."*

of Indra. He was a man of thirty, proud of eye and bearded, very active and light on his feet despite his armor; his features held a certain humor, and men said he was merry and as a warrior unequaled. He was grave today, however, and Indra thought his dark eyes were hungry as he looked upon her.

So she swore that she would permit none of her people to make war or leave the castle. And he to his own oaths, and the people and the host bearing witness. It was published that anyone leaving the castle might be slain by the dark folk, without redress.

"Leave now, if ye like—your whole people," said King Savastri, white teeth flashing in a laugh. "Leave, and die! The quicker it's done, the sooner we'll have your women."

His eye touched upon Indra as he spoke, but she turned away in contempt and made no reply to the taunt. Thus was the doom of the last Aryans sealed. They obeyed Indra to the letter, as they had sworn to do. Being a fierce people, they might have preferred to sally forth and die fighting, but she thought of the boy, and decided to temporize; so they obeyed, though it meant slow death for them all, cut away from the whole world.

But Indra sat in the great courtyard, as the days passed, with the huge tamed wolf, Vic, at her feet; and her blue eyes flamed as reports came to her. The Dravidian host had flowed away over the hills like an ocean wave. Plenty of them remained; their leaders dwelt in the little castles and châteaux, the dark folk made villages around each one, and their king, Savastri, occupied the massive hunting-lodge built by Indra's husband, three miles away. From here, he ruled his dark people, who had taken over the whole land. The autumn rains came down, and the first touches of snow, but little frost as yet.

It was said that everywhere in the country the civilization of the Aryan people was lost and ruined, for these Dravidians were an uncouth and ignorant race.

Indra listened to all and said little, toying now with the boy, now with the wolf. The prince was a child of four; he and the wolf were friends. A grim and fierce thing was Vic, trained to obey Indra and to defend her; the greatest of wolves, he had been captured as a pup and tamed, but his heart was savage. So large was he that the boy Shiva rode about on his back, though this did not please Vic overmuch.

On the afternoon of the first snow, with a gale sweeping over the hills and forests, Indra sent for her old councilor Ran, and for the chief warrior who remained, the stalwart Shatra. To the latter, she spoke briefly.

"Tell whatever officer commands the guard at the little postern gate in the east wall tonight, that he is to let me go out and watch for my return, without question."

"You, Indra?" exclaimed the warrior, astonished. "Who accompanies you?"

"Vic," she said. At his name, the wolf lifted head and eyed her, unwinking.

UPON SHATRA fell fear and dismay. "Lady, think twice!" he said. "In the whole country, none of our people remain except women who are enslaved. If you're found abroad and taken or killed—"

"Prince Shiva will then be in your care," she said, and dismissed him. When he had gone, she turned to the old councilor.

"Would you break the oaths you swore to the gods?" he demanded, eying her keenly.

"I swore much for my people; nothing for myself," she said, and this was true. "I alone can make war upon these dark folk; I alone can avenge my dead husband and our lost cities and country, our scattered people. I know secrets none other lives to know, and ways of doing this. Let's have no argument, Ran. Are they sending us cattle tomorrow?"

"It was so promised," said Ran. "A hundred head."

"Good. See to it, then, that those who bring the cattle, are told a certain story they may carry back with them. The story you used to tell me, about our ancestors who changed their shape at night and became ravening wolves."

"As ordered, I will obey," said the old man. "But what drives you to such extremes of vengeance and hatred? Why cannot you live like the rest of us—"

"Live until you die behind walls, or go forth to be killed?" she said in disdain. "If you must know, I shall bring about the death of that man who rules them."

"So?" Old Ran fingered his white beard. "Because of his look and his words, when the oath was sworn—eh? I hear he is better than his nobles and leaders; in fact, a wise ruler, a king with brains—"

Indra flushed. "A king who shall taste the vengeance of the conquered! See that the story is told them. I intend to make that man Savastri suffer before he dies. No other can kill him, but I can. The wind howling upon the thick trees howls death this night!"

"He lives in the castle your husband built, with guards and warriors—"

"And I, who helped build that castle, know its secrets," she said, smiling terribly.

THAT NIGHT, respecting her signet ring, though they could not see her face, the guards at the little east gate let her out. She was clad in a robe of wolfskins, and the head was drawn over her head after the manner of hunters, with a flap down to conceal her face. She carried a hunting-spear, and the huge wolf Vic was at her heels. They saw her vanish into the trees where the storm tossed and the first snowflakes were drifting and sifting; and so closed the gate again, looking one at another with affrighted eyes.

Toward dawn, her voice summoned them, and the throaty howl of Vic. A torch was brought, and recognizing her, they let her in, but not as she had gone. Red was her spear, and the cruel jaws of Vic slavered blood.

"Do no talking," she ordered the guards, and went her way.

With morning, Dravidian warriors drove cattle into the great castle, as promised, and told a strange tale. Wolves had broken into the king's lodge, none knew how; one of their princes, and two of the bodyguard of the king, had been slain. The wolves had vanished again.

These men were told the legends of the royal house, and how certain of its princes could take the shape of wolves,

"I'll lay that ghost, if ghost it be!"

at will. Undoubtedly, the ghost of the dead king had acted thus, taking vengeance upon his conquerors. With this cold comfort, the Dravidians were sent whence they had come.

Three days later, King Savastri and six of his chieftains came demanding speech with Indra. She had them brought up to the courtyard of the keep, and sent Vic away to the kennel he occupied; he was licking his jaws and his fur, this frosty morning.

Word spread that there had been more killing in the king's lodge, last night. Indra appeared, with Ran and others of the council behind her, and greeted the king. He saluted her, his bold, eager eyes never leaving her face.

"Lady, there is peace between my people and yours, for so you have chosen," he said abruptly. "We have kept the peace; but your people have come upon us in the night, slaying."

"That is untrue," Indra replied, and beckoned Ran. "Go and discover if any man left the gates last night or yesterday. If so, he shall die here and now for disobedience."

The old man departed, and she looked again at Savastri, unsmiling and serene.

"You are no liar," he said impulsively.

"I am no liar," she rejoined. "Now tell me what has happened."

"This is the second time," he said, while his chieftains assented. "Last night two of my captains were slain—mangled as though by wolves. A guard thought he saw a wolf-shape slinking through the rooms. Evidently your people are doing this."

"If so, they shall die; I swear it," she rejoined. "Is it possible you don't know the legends of our royal house? The ghosts of the dead are visiting you, great king; the ghost of my husband, whom your warriors slew, takes a wolf-shape in the night and kills. This is the old story, for my people are hunters and forest people."

"I have heard some such story being noised abroad," said Savastri. "All nonsense! One of those captains was killed with a spear, last night. Wolves don't use spears."

"S O ?" S H E regarded him steadily, a cool smile of contempt in her eyes. "Great king, let me advise you to change your dwelling. Seek safety elsewhere. Let your warriors occupy the royal lodge and risk the vengeance of dead men; you can hide safely in another place."

The cool mockery of her words was bitter to bear, and Savastri flushed.

"I'm not that sort, lady. By the god Shiva! I'll lay that ghost, if ghost it be!"

"Shiva?" She started slightly. "Who is he?"

"One of our gods."

"Aye? It's the name of my son—there he is, now."

The boy appeared crossing the courtyard. Savastri and his chiefs regarded him, and their stern dark faces changed and lightened with swift admiration. The boy was like a radiant sunbeam. Savastri turned quickly to Indra.

"Lady, marry me!" he said abruptly. "Marry me, and your people shall go free!"

Her eyes chilled. "When I marry you, barbarian, it will be upon the couch of death!"

So barbed with disdain were her words that the Dravidian chieftains growled angrily, but Savastri only looked into her face and a smile leaped in his quick eyes.

"You'll be worth the having," said he. Before her fury could find response, old Ran came back and made report.

No man had left the city or passed the walls since the peace had been sworn.

"My warriors are not liars," said Indra. "Further, King Savastri, I swear that if any man leaves the city, I'll inform you of it; if any of my people undertake any action against your people, they break my oath and their own, and shall die. Go back, and hide from the ghosts of the dead!"

There the matter ended, and she had the last word; but something in the way she said it drew a speculative, searching look from Savastri. Perhaps he suspected her from this moment.

WHEN SHE heard the talk of her council and leaders, however, she went white with fury. To all of them it seemed that Savastri was the kingliest of men, and wise withal. That same night she went from the little postern gate with Vic, and returned long ere dawn; word came next day that four Dravidian chiefs, drinking together at an outpost, had been slain by a wolf—who left human tracks in the snow.

"My husband," said Indra to old Ran, "is having company on the ghost-path!"

"What good will it do you, or your people?" he asked.

Her face clouded.

"I don't know—yet. Only one thing matters to me, Ran; one

person. Somehow, I shall assure his future; I shall find some way!"

"Prince Shiva was born to be a king, true," said Ran, scratching his white beard. "But the Aryan people have gone forth across the world, vanishing as a cloud in the sky; they are gone. They may found other empires afar, other races and peoples may spring from them, but they are gone. And we who remain here are doomed. Better a swineherd in safety, than a king without a kingdom or a people!"

Her blue eyes flashed. "King's blood will have king's name," said she curtly. "Three nights from now, my husband will be avenged."

Old Ran looked after her as she departed, and wagged his head sagely.

"A husband under the ground is best left there," he grumbled, "as many a woman has found to her cost ere this."

THREE DAYS passed swiftly; evening of the third day brought snow blowing through the forest trees and a keen wind whistling over the roof of the world. In this bitter night, only a beast could find his way abroad.

"Take the track, Vic," said Indra, when the gate clanged shut behind them. Obedient to her word, knowing her voice and speech, the wolf trotted ahead as she released him.

She followed close, muffled in her wolfskins, with furred leggings, the hunting-spear in her hand. The snow now falling thicker, swirled about them, but the big wolf kept straight on, well knowing what way they went. They came at last to a thicket of trees; half a bowshot distant was the king's lodge, where a flaring cresset flickered in the storm.

Among the trees, they approached the building still more closely. Vic halted, beside a jagged rock that was rapidly piling high with snow. Indra put out her hand to it, and the mass of rock slid smoothly. Into an opening thus revealed Vic darted, but Indra called him back to heel. He obeyed, with a whine of repressed eagerness; the killer was aroused.

She passed down steps, along a tunnel, and to steps again; mounting these rapidly in the pitch blackness, she paused at a tiny gleam of light. She was now in the king's lodge, by a secret passage installed for emergencies; the others who knew of it, were dead.

She touched a panel and it slid aside, letting her look into the main room, where a huge fire was dying down on the hearth. The firelight showed a number of dim figures at the door; and a voice reached her, the voice of Savastri the king.

"No, no! I remain here with two guards, and the dogs. The rest of you, out to the huts and keep watch on the grounds! I'll have no woman taunting me, even if she were the most glorious woman on earth, with skulking in safety while my captains run risks. I remain here, to meet the man-wolf if it comes. You others, stand watch outside. Go!"

They went, grumbling and protesting. One of them made some laughing remark.

"Aye," replied the king, a curiously vibrant ring in his voice. "From my first sight of that woman, my heart went out to her. I'll have no other, I tell you! There's no other in the world her equal, no other for me, and that ends it. Goodnight!"

Indra, listening, caught her breath in quick anger. Vic began a growl; she reached down and silenced him with a touch and a word, then looked into the room.

"The dogs are uneasy, they smell something," said a voice. She saw a guard, and two large wolfhounds, though they were somewhat smaller than Vic.

"That may be," said the king. "Both of you take the outer room, with the dogs. I'll sleep in the room beyond. Keep a light burning in your room."

An alabaster lamp was taken away, and the place was empty except for red fireglow.

PRESENTLY INDRA put her weight upon the secret door, and it swung aside. About the neck of Vic was a heavy collar of wolfskin like his own; she gripped it, and he emerged with her into the dimly lit chamber.

She did not hesitate. She was alone in the lodge with three men; two of them, and the dogs, must be killed before she could kill Savastri as she intended. She knew where lay the rooms in question; and, since she disdained to attack sleeping men, she went straight to them now—two sleeping-rooms at the end of the hall.

As she neared them, she halted, crouching. The door of the first was somewhat ajar, a light shone across the hall, a man spoke.

"I tell you, the dogs smell something—look at them! Bring the light. Let's take a turn around the place. I'll take the dogs on leash."

The dogs growled and whined; Vic's fur lifted under her hand, a savage throaty sound came from him. One of the men came out, bearing the lamp. He checked himself and put it on a stand.

"Forgot my bow," he said. "Go ahead. I'll come with the lamp."

He withdrew. The other came out, the two dogs straining on leash. They gave sudden wild tongue, sensing the presence of Vic. Indra knew it was the moment.

"Take them, Vic!" she said, and loosed him.

The great shape went hurtling for the dogs. From the guard burst a terrible cry; he frantically loosed his dogs. He had held them an instant too long. Vic was into them with the kill-growl, murderous jaws slashing too fast for eye to follow. The three shapes mingled into one—a shapeless scramble of ferocity, from which flew fur and bright drops of blood.

Indra was darting forward. The guard, long sword sweeping out, struck at the battling animals. One dog was dead, the other down. The guard sighted Indra's figure, and slashed at her as he swung around. Her spear went through him, and she tugged it free as he fell. The second dog was quivering in death and Vic was up and whirling, with fiery eyes and blood-slavering muzzle.

OUT INTO the open came stumbling the second guard, bow bent and shaft notched. Seeing Indra, he started back. Vic went for him, and his bowstring twanged; he snatched a second shaft and shot. Both arrows thudded through the throat of the gaunt wolf, through throat to brain. The wolf's rush, however, took him at the man, leaping even as he died—leaping and slashing with cruel teeth. The guard was borne backward, and the teeth of the dying beast ripped open his throat and chest.

"Vic! *Vic!*"

A sharp cry, as Indra darted forward. She knelt in the pool of blood. The head of the wolf lifted slightly. His eyes rolled upon her in the lamplight; then his head fell and his eyes rolled no more. He was dead. Silence, and the gusty odor of hot blood, settled upon the place.

"So men and beasts keep company down the path of ghosts!" said a voice, amused, calm, poised: the voice of King Savastri.

Indra was up, spear ready—up and flinging forward. Savastri stood in the doorway, a dagger in his left hand, a long coiled whip in his right. He wore a crimson robe and was bareheaded.

She was at him like a flash of fury. The spear drove straight for his heart, a death-blow; but it slid away from armor beneath the robe. Across her face, half masked by the flap of wolfskin, lashed the heavy whip. Blinded, she staggered but struck again with the spear. The whip coiled about the weapon and jerked it out of her hand. The spear fell with a clatter. The lash burned across her arms and body, burned again. Savastri was striking with cool, deliberate intent, but striking swiftly.

A scream burst from her. She threw herself upon him with savage ferocity.

He evaded her spring, caught the wolf-head above her head, and tore it away. The fair glory of her golden hair burst forth; and the loaded whip-butt thudded down.

She crumpled without a word and lay in a huddled, inert heap.

"So!" said King Savastri, gazing at her face. "I suspected as much. Ha! Now to see where she and the beast came from."

He caught up the lamp, picked his way across the blood-spattered floor, and in the main room found the secret door ajar.

Going back quickly, he dragged the great body of Vic down the hall and to that secret door; even for his sinewy strength, it was no light task. He cut the collar from the dead wolf's neck and kept it. The beast's carcass he shoved into the hidden passage, and closed the door again.

Returning to the frightful scene of death, he picked up Indra and carried her into the farther room; she was breathing heavily, and would be unconscious a long while.

PRESENTLY KING Savastri opened the door of the lodge and blew a blast on his horn. Guards came running; picking out some of the captains, he took them with him to the grisly hall, and showed them what had happened.

"The wolf came, and the wolf went," said he, showing them the collar. "You see this? Now come, and see who wore it. The stories that we heard were true."

He took them into the farther room. There upon the bed lay Indra, senseless; now she was clad in a long white robe that Savastri had put upon her, after hiding the wolfskins. He beckoned his staring captains outside and closed the door.

"Here is the girdle." He gave it to one of them. "Throw it into the fire; she will never again be able to play wolf. Rather, she remains queen!"

INDRA OPENED her eyes to daylight and snow drifting in at the window. She lay in her own bed, in what had been her room in the royal lodge, and warm skins covered her. At her side sat King Savastri; he had been bathing her bruised head and face with a wet cloth. Now he leaned back, regarding her.

She stared at him. With a rush, memory returned; yet she was held spellbound by finding herself here and thus. She tried to speak, and could not. He smiled, leaned forward, and touched her forehead with the cloth again; his fingers were deft and very gentle.

"Apparently you had a bad dream," he said casually. "You've been talking about wolves ever since my guards found you wandering among the trees."

Her eyes dilated upon him. "Wolves?" she whispered. "Wandering? You devil! What jest is this? You know well—"

"Be quiet," broke in the king. "Be quiet and let me speak, for a little space. Here; if this will make you feel better, play with it," and he thrust a long dagger into her hand, then came to his feet and went to the window-opening.

She gripped the dagger and watched him, a flame in her eyes.

"Whatever you may think," said the king calmly, "you were picked up among the trees and brought here, by my guards. How you came there, how you left your castle, does not matter. If you're tempted to remember anything else, dear lady, it was all an evil dream. Let it be forgotten. I'm glad you're here, for I've something to say to you."

She lay like a trapped beast, wary and tense.

"Say it," she said in a low, hard voice.

He came toward her, smiling. "Indra, these people of mine are a crude, savage lot of barbarians; I'm one myself. But I have sense enough to know that all the civilization, all the fine things, of your Aryan race are perishing in the hands of my people; this whole glorious land of yours is going back to the jungle. I want to save it. You can save it. You esteem it an insult if I speak of loving you, of wedding you because you're the only woman I know who is fit to be a queen, and my wife. But there's another reason. Our people, and your son—Prince Shiva."

The name drove into her, quieted her, held her intent upon him.

"Marry me," he went on in that calm voice. "Let your people mingle with my people, let them keep all they have and more, let them teach my people your Vedic Hymns, your gods, your ways of life and art and work. The remnant of your people can grow great again, among mine; they may be a sect, a caste, apart. A superior caste, not slaves!

"I have no sons to follow me, Indra," he went on. "But with you for wife, I'd have a son, and one whom my people would worship and revere. Your boy; let me adopt him, as the future king of this people. It was not I who slew his father, but one of my captains whom your wolf killed."

"My wolf!" Her eyes widened upon him, her voice came with a catch. "Ah! Then your sorry jest is ended!"

"By the gods, I'm not jesting!" Suddenly impetuous, he came swiftly to the bed and looked down at her, and he was all ablaze. "You're no liar, Indra; you swore oaths for your people, but there was no mention of yourself in them. That gave me the clue. And what was it you said—that you would marry me only upon the couch of death? Well, you're lying upon it now; death for you and your son and your whole people, if you make that choice."

HE DROPPED on the edge of the bed beside her, and threw out his hands.

"You have the knife; use it!" he said, hoarsely earnest. "The choice is yours. Here is my throat; kill me, if you like, if that will satisfy you! For I worship you, Indra; I worship you with my whole heart. I offer you myself, to kill or to take...."

"And with myself, your son's life," he went on swiftly, seeing her hand move and the knife flash. "Instead of death and ignominy, he shall have honor and a crown. Your people shall have life instead of death; this nation shall rise again—if you so choose! I offer a glorious future, worthy of you, and the name of Prince Shiva shall be enshrined among our gods. But kill me if you so desire. There is no one to interfere."

With one hand, he drew the edge of his robe over his face, and waited.

The silence of the room was stirred only by the rustle of the wintry branches outside. He could hear her quick, hard breathing, but no word came from her. Suddenly she moved and caught her breath, as though to plunge the knife into him; but he did not stir.

The knife clattered on the floor. Her hand touched his.

THE SCENE blurred and vanished. The stone wall came back into sight, the yellow light died away, the room-lights flickered on. Norman Fletcher turned to us, awe and amazement in his eyes.

"I'll be hanged!" he broke out. "This isn't what I expected to show you at all. It's not the same thing. This apparatus is playing tricks! But, my word! Did you get the meaning of what we just saw—the allusions to historic and ethnologic fact?"

"Rather!" Miss Stephens nodded, a tinge of excitement in her cheeks. "A scene from the dispersal of the great Aryan race, somewhere on the uplands of Asia, back before history began! And the legend of the werewolf, which curiously enough seems to be a purely Aryan legend, a sort of race-myth!"

Fletcher stared at her.

"Well, it might have been worse," he said slowly. "I see now why Hartmetz said the language was a form of Sanscrit. And damned bloody it was, too. I'm sorry you saw it."

Miss Stephens tossed her head slightly. "Why?" she rejoined coolly. "If you ask me, I thought it was fascinating, positively fascinating! All of it."

When we were driving home, I asked what she had honestly thought about it.

"Oh!" she said in her demure way, which I now realized was not really demure at all, but rather blasé, "he didn't fool me for a minute. I think he was just trying to shock me."

"Really!" I said, not without sarcasm. "And did he?"

"I'm afraid," she drawled, "that poor Mr. Fletcher is behind the times."

I let it go at that.

THE HEAVENLY BIRD

"THE HEAVENLY BIRD"—THE ELEVENTH STORY IN A SERIES
DESIGNED TO MAKE REAL AND REASONABLE CERTAIN ANCIENT
LEGENDS—IS CONCERNED WITH THE FABLED PHOENIX
AND ITS ORIGIN IN THE MIND OF AN ARRANT RASCAL.

WHEN NORMAN Fletcher entered the office and invited me to lunch, I was amazed. The old Yankee inventor, greatest electrical genius of the age, almost never came into town.

"Well, I've got a whole day off," he said, laughing. He was the picture of health, with his ruddy cheeks and mane of white hair. "Looks like Washington for me, with this war-defense work—"

Brill, the senior partner of my outfit, burst in upon us in a rage; he had been to a lecture the previous evening, and had been fairly seething, all morning. He quite disregarded Fletcher.

"I'm telling you," he roared at me, "we ought to give some of these birds what we'd get in their place! Suppose I went over to Germany and told the Nazis they were full of prunes, and talked about our glorious country and how much better it was—what'd they do to me?"

"Ship you back," I said, laughing.

"In a wooden overcoat!" he barked. "You're damned right. That's what—who's this?"

He saw Fletcher and checked himself. I introduced them, and Fletcher smiled.

"You seem all excited, Mr. Brill. Join us for luncheon and cool off, won't you?"

"Delighted," said Brill, and bristled again. "Still, it makes me hot under the collar! 'Risen like a phoenix from its ashes,' says he, talking about Germany. Phoenix! Oratorical bombast! There never was any such thing."

"But there was," said Fletcher.

"Eh?" Brill gawked at him. "You mean there was? That mythological bird of some kind who died in blazing fire and was reborn again by the flames—or some such hooey? I've forgotten the exact details. You're not serious?"

Fletcher nodded. "Quite. It's my belief, Mr. Brill, that all the legends and fables of mankind are founded on fact of some sort. The case of the phoenix is not a haphazard legend occurring all over the world, as so many myths are. It goes back to a

In rapid dialect, Abdallah said: "Trust all to me; I'll have you out of here in five days."

definite source which we know: An Egyptian priest told Herodotus about it, and the Greek traveler wrote it down; that was the beginning of the legend. The phoenix came from Arabia to Egypt, said the priest."

"And how did the Egyptian priest know?" demanded Brill challengingly.

Fletcher laughed.

"If you've time, I'll tell you over the luncheon-table."

I had never realized what a magnetic personality Fletcher had, until I heard him talking there at luncheon. His quiet manner concealed the most startling information, the most abstruse knowledge; there was some intangible force in him.

"It happened in ancient Egypt," said Fletcher musingly. "It is, I fear, a gory yarn; human life was cheap in those days, and particularly so in Heliopolis, the City of the Sun."

He paused, to pass cigars—his Havanas—the most fragrant cigars I ever tasted.

"Abdallah, or the Slave of God, as the name signifies," he went on, "had come from the interior of Arabia with an enormous caravan of trade-goods, gold-dust, and slaves, owned by the rich

and powerful trader Hassan. Abdallah was a man of parts, an unconscionable liar, a merry rascal who looked like a fool and was not. He left home with nothing. On the way, pretending he could write, he became secretary and factor to Hassan; he could not write a stroke, but he had a magnificent memory.

"We find him in Heliopolis, alone. The caravan had been sold, the camels had been sent back to the frontier; Hassan and his secretary remained in Heliopolis to collect the moneys due. Hassan, out on a party with some other merchants, drank too much, blasphemed the gods of Egypt, and made some insulting remarks about the Pharaoh; he was straightway clapped into jail by the priests of Ra, who were all-powerful in the city. This left Abdallah sitting in a rented room of a tavern, with nothing to his name except the clothes he stood in, a bird in a hooded cage, and what few effects of his master he had been able to save. There was just one word to describe that young man—impudence!"

IMPUDENCE WAS the word for it, no doubt about that. His face, which could be blank and witless on occasion, in repose was merry, with flashing impudent eyes, a wide pleasant mouth, and a saucy tilted nose. He had a way of flinging up his head in a bright, quick motion, which was a delight to see.

Just now he was morose, and kicked unkindly at the wicker cage in the corner, with a muttered oath. He drew aside the cloth cover of the cage and looked at the bird within—an enormous fighting-cock of weird coloring and shape, like no other. Some merchant in Arabia had brought the cock from farther east, and Abdallah had brought him to Egypt, only to find that Egyptians had other and more normal uses for such birds than cock-fighting.

"You blasted nothing!" he growled dismally. "You're worth too much money to eat, but I've nothing else. Stranded! Beached in a foreign city, like a pearl-fisher whose boat has sunk and leaves him perched on a reef! I'll have to wring your neck and eat you yet. Fool that I was to bring you to a land where they never heard of fighting-cocks! My credit's stopped, I can get no grain to feed you, no bread to feed myself, no money to help poor old Hassan. Nothing but bills payable—ha! Bills payable! And here's Hassan's seal. Ha!"

He stopped short in sudden thought. Then he made a dive for the plain cotton robe he had washed and hung up to dry. Slipping it over his head, he tied his sandal-strings tight, dabbed some water on his face, wiped it, and pocketed the silver ring bearing Hassan's seal. From one corner he took a pile of papyrus slips, on which were scrawled some quite meaningless characters—his own writing, for he brazenly pretended that he could write—and with one of these in his pocket, he strode out.

Ten minutes later, he was closeted with Minos the Cretan, chief of his master's creditors; the office of Minos was close to the temple of Ra, and shaded by gorgeous plane trees.

"Good day, Minos," said Abdallah briskly. "In the matter of what you owe my master Hassan, as here inventoried—"

"Save your breath," said the Cretan, grinning. "Hassan's in jail and will probably die there. We'll talk of that little debt when he's out."

"Little debt!" Abdallah's eyes enlarged. "For the gold dust and the precious weaves and the girl slaves—well, well, let it be as you say, Honest Minos. May I borrow your pen for a moment?"

He leaned forward, took the reed pen from the table, and made marks on the slip of papyrus. The Cretan eyed him curiously.

"Do you call that writing? You Arabians are fools. What are you doing?"

"Doubling the amount of your debt, good Minos." Abdallah looked up innocently. "You see, I've been ordered to visit the high priest of Ra immediately—in fact, I'm on my way there now—and bring the accounts of Hassan and his seal with me. It seems that the priests have levied an enormous fine against my master, and are going to collect all the accounts payable. So, to help Hassan, I'm doubling the amount you owe him."

Minos came up out of his chair with a bound. When the

priests of Ra, with all the troops of the Pharaoh behind them, started out to collect anything, they either got it or got somebody's head.

"You're doubling the amount!" cried Minos. "Idiot! I'll pay the actual sum on the spot, since that's the case."

"Oh! Very well, if this is your pleasure," rejoined Abdallah. "But, since the amount is a large one, I beg of you to make three parcels of it."

"For which you'll give me a receipt over your master's seal."

"Of course! But my Arabian writing cannot be read by you; have your scribe write in Egyptian, and I'll sign and seal it."

Which was duly done. Abdallah's hentrack was accepted as a signature, unquestioned....

Well aware that he might be watched, and having in mind the likelihood of collecting the other bills payable by somewhat similar methods, Abdallah left the merchant's office and went straight on to the big imposing temple, whose massive surroundings housed many hundreds of priests. Second only to the royal governor was the high priest of Ra in Heliopolis, and like all these priests of Egypt, Abdallah knew him to be a shrewd and subtle man. When it came to duping, these priests of Ra were adepts.

"If you've a sword to sell, sell it to the man who has one, as the proverb says," reflected Abdallah, entering the vast portals. An idea had come to him on the way over, and his eyes twinkled. Then, assuming his blandest and blankest air, he asked one of the guards where the high priest might be found.

"What, you rascal? Who are you, to seek the high priest of Ra?"

"I am the high priest of the great god of Arabia, El or Allah," said Abdallah in his simple way. "I bear messages from my god, and gifts, to the high priest of Ra."

The guards gathered, not sure whether they dealt with a madman or a real desert priest. One of the priests of Ra happened by, heard the argument, and took charge of Abdallah.

"Two of you follow, with weapons ready," said he grimly. "You may have use for them."

He led Abdallah through the temple precincts to the magnificent chambers of the high priest, who was an imposing person, even majestic, and came of royal blood; his name was Ra-enfer, and at his mere word, men were slain without question. The priest saluted him humbly.

"Lord, this man, obviously an Arabian, sought speech with you, telling the guards that he was high priest of some desert god, and had messages and gifts for you. But—"He came closer to the high priest and spoke softly, under his breath. Watching the eyes of Ra-enfer, Abdallah began to conjecture what this whisper could mean, and guessed at the worst. He knew the priests had an admirable spy-system.

NOW, THE money of Egypt was not in coins, but in rings of gold and silver. Abdallah let one of his three packets drop to the stone floor, clumsily; the cloth wrapping it came away, and the rings of gold were displayed.

The high priest leaned forward.

"Who are you, Arabian?" he demanded.

"Me? Why, lord, I'm Abdallah, the secretary of the merchant Hassan."

"What? You confess it?" cried the high priest, but his eyes flitted to the money.

"Certainly," said Abdallah innocently. He had guessed aright, and now breathed freely. "I had to take such a position; I could not spend the money of Allah to travel here, as I was ordered by the god. So I took a secretary's place. We are poor people, in Arabia; even the high priest of Allah does not disdain labor. Now that Hassan is in prison, I am free to obey the orders of Allah. So I have come to speak with you, in private."

"This is an honest simpleton," said the high priest, and motioned his subordinate. "You may go. Let the guards wait at the door, out of earshot, in case I need them."

Thus alone with Ra-enfer, Abdallah took a chair, made

*"You tell of a great wonder, if true," said
the high priest, repressing a smile.*

himself comfortable, accepted a cup of wine gratefully, and
smacked his lips over it.

"Lord Ra-enfer," he said, round-eyed and trusting, "I received
a revelation from Allah, whom I serve, and who is the same you
call Ra. I was ordered to come here with a certain gift, and to
tell you that the phoenix will arrive in Heliopolis, in token that
the gods favor your city and bless it, beneath your rule."

"Indeed!" said the high priest complacently. "And what, may
I ask, is the phoenix?"

"A bird; the bird of heaven. There is only one phoenix, my lord. No other exists. He looks somewhat like a cock, somewhat like a pheasant, somewhat like an ostrich; his plumage is most glorious, being of divers hues, but the tail is yellow and red. He may be known by his beak, which is of a blue like the sky."

"He sounds not unlike the sacred bird we call *benu,*" mused the high priest. Then his eyes sharpened on Abdallah. "Only one in the world, you say—eh? Only one? What manner of tale is this?"

"Lord, it is known to all priests in Arabia!" said Abdallah with glib simplicity. "Only one such bird exists. When he is old and comes to die, he seeks some sacred place where a nest of cassia twigs and frankincense must be made ready; he is laid upon it at sunset, and fire is set to it; this fire must be great enough to consume him utterly. While it burns, he sings his own dirge and praises the sun-god, though his voice is not over-musical. From his own ashes he rises again with the sun, young and glorious to behold, with a hood over his eyes. When a priest removes this hood, he flies back to heaven."

Ra-enfer listened to all this nonsense, gravely appraising the man and the tale. His suspicion could not linger before the earnest conviction of Abdallah, who was obviously fool enough to believe every word he uttered.

"You tell of a great wonder, if true," said the high priest, repressing a smile. "How often does such a miracle take place?"

"Every hundred years," said Abdallah promptly. "This is the hundredth year, lord; the occasion is only four days away. It was revealed to me that the phoenix has chosen this temple for his rejuvenation, and henceforth will accomplish this in Heliopolis every hundredth year. In token whereof, I have been ordered by Allah to make you an offering," and he touched the packet of gold rings, "which will pay for the burning-nest."

"Ha! By Isis and Osiris!" muttered the high priest, and his eyes glowed.

Here was a simpleton from the desert with a new idea, which

was rare in Egypt. The fool believed all his own tale; so much the better. Magic was part of the religion in Egypt; every priest was a master of the art. Of course it was all nonsense about the wondrous bird; but it would be a spectacle marvelous beyond belief, and if the phoenix never showed up—well, that could be arranged. The gravely piercing eyes of Ra-enfer narrowed as he envisaged the possibilities from all angles.

BUT ABDALLAH, sipping his wine, read the thoughts behind those eyes. He had planted them deliberately; and he could scarcely repress a chuckle of impish delight.

"Four days, you say?" demanded the high priest suddenly.

"Counting tomorrow the first, the evening of the fourth day," said Abdallah. "Such was the revelation; it was repeated to me last night in a dream. There can be no doubt."

"Evidently not." Ra-enfer beamed upon him. "My son, I welcome the prodigy! You must let me put you up here in the temple in apartments befitting your rank; I'll furnish you with priestly robes—"

"No, no!" exclaimed Abdallah. "Thanks, my lord, but that cannot be. The priests of Allah are sworn to simple living and poverty. A single robe of cloth, and a turban for the head, is all the garment allowed us. True, this cotton robe of mine is somewhat frayed."

"Let me replace it with a robe of the finest linen," said Ra-enfer eagerly. This answer had banished his last suspicion. The man was certainly a fool. "And new sandals."

"If such be your desire, it would please me," Abdallah replied with simplicity. "Here is the offering I was commanded to bring. The nest, I repeat, must be of great size and sufficient to consume the phoenix to ashes."

He laid the packet of gold rings on the table. No doubt that they were genuine; the priests were bankers of all precious metals, and these bore the stamp of the Memphis temple of Maat. The high priest summoned a guard.

"Go to the treasury, and ask the treasurer for a robe of the finest mixed wool and linen, and sandals of the best quality, edged with gold. At once."

"Wait!" exclaimed Abdallah hurriedly, and slipped one horny bare brown foot from its sandal. "Take this to get the size right. Good. Now, my lord, will you have a writing given me, a receipt for this offering, which I may lay up in my temple at home as evidence that my mission was accomplished?"

"Gladly," agreed Ra-enfer. "But you must give me more details about the phoenix—at what hour he will appear, and where. How he must be treated and so forth."

Abdallah veiled his eyes and his confusion together; this was getting serious, and he had not yet accomplished his prime object.

"Tomorrow at this time, my lord, I'll come and inform you," he said, lifting to the high priest a gaze of childish trust. "You see, I must ask the god for a revelation on those matters, tonight. It will come; Allah never fails to answer."

"A remarkable god," observed Ra-enfer, not without irony.

"And there is one favor I must ask you," went on Abdallah. "Technically, I am still in service to the merchant Hassan. I must be released from it, must fast and pray and make my ablutions, before asking Allah for a further vision."

"Easily done," said Ra-enfer. "I will have the fellow empaled at once."

"No, no!" cried Abdallah in real agitation. "My lord, this would anger the god, my god, and the phoenix, the wondrous bird of Allah! Instead, I pray you, give me an order to visit this Hassan in his prison, that he may release me from his service by word of mouth. And, I pray you, send a guide with me, because this vast city bewilders me."

Ra-enfer regarded this simple fool from the desert with tolerance, and affably assented to his desires.

SO PRESENTLY Abdallah went forth from the fine house of Ra, wearing one of the rare temple robes, with golden-edged sandals on his feet, and preceded by the temple chamberlain

Abdallah was working hard upon an
extremely annoyed, struggling hawk.

who cleared the way with imperious voice and whip. Word of
the honors done this ragged desert fellow spread abroad widely.

Twice or thrice, in passing the offices of merchants who owed
Hassan money, Abdallah halted the chamberlain and entered
the offices, very briefly. Merely a word in passing—he would
return presently to see about the payments due. Then on his way
again, leaving consternation behind him.

The city prison, near the barracks, was a grim and loathsome
place of dour granite. The entry, known as the Gate of Death,
was spattered with blood, and was hung with heads of those
lately executed. Floggings and tortures were daily matters here.

The order of Ra-enfer opened all doors. In the foul depths of
the prison, with guards and the temple chamberlain to hold off
the hapless wretches crowding around, Abdallah found Hassan.
He saluted the amazed merchant with a kiss of respect, and

spoke in a rapid Arabic dialect that none other could understand.

"I am working for you, master; trust all to me. I'll have you out of here in five days. When any come questioning you, say I am the high priest of Allah and took service with you; that's all you know. Say it's not unusual in Arabia. Now release me from your service, loudly, that all may hear."

Hassan had not become the richest merchant of Arabia from any lack of brains. He did as he was told, and asked no questions. So the chamberlain was enabled to make report, as Abdallah desired, to the high priest of Ra.

By sunset Abdallah had visited nearly all the creditors of Hassan; and without exception, made collections in full. So great was the sum, indeed, that he took half of it all to a merchant whom he could trust, and obtained bills of exchange on a house in Pelusium, a city of the frontier, for the amount.

With the setting sun he returned to his tavern, paid his bill to date and a week in advance, and ordered the best dinner to be had. Then he went to his room and removed the cover from his caged bird, and inspected the strange creature.

"You certainly look old and droopy, and no wonder," said he, with twinkling eyes. "And you'll look worse, four days from now! And it's certain that no fighting-cock of your queer breed has ever been seen in this land of marvels. So rest in peace! I'll feed you later."

O N T H E morrow, Abdallah came limping to the temple of Ra, complaining that the thongs of the new sandals were too tight. He was greeted like a royal prince this time, and could have had a dozen pairs of sandals for the asking, and solid gold at that.

Now, he had spent the morning wandering about through the bazars, which were open in the morning and until late at night, being closed during the heat of the day. To his very real alarm, he perceived that he was being followed by an expert shadower, or possibly two. He had spotted one man, and suspected another. It was clear that everything he did was noted and reported to the temple, the more so as he was now a conspicuous figure in the city. Any suspicion would have unpleasant consequences; the kindest fate he could expect would be flaying alive, a regrettably common occurrence in Egypt.

S O H E made no secret of his work in clearing up the affairs of Hassan; indeed, he bragged complacently of it, to the priests conducting him to Ra-enfer.

The latter received him promptly and graciously, introducing him to a number of the chief priests, and inquired after the promised revelation. Had it come?

"Of course," said Abdallah in his most simple and matter-of-fact way. "The phoenix will arrive in the course of the third night, and will be found in the temple gardens at dawn. Capture him without fear; he is old and sick, and seeks to avoid his destiny, but the gods compel him to it. Give him water to drink, but no food. At sunset, tie his legs and place him on the fragrant nest. Light it as the sun touches the horizon, and then place guards and forbid any man to approach the spot until daybreak. He will then be found in his rejuvenated guise, ready to fly to heaven when you have loosed his hood."

The priests looked one at another, with a certain admiration. This was too good to be true; it was perfection. It had all the ingredients of an old legend of the gods brought to life. A simple man from the far desert, a perfectly incredible tale of an incredible bird, revelations and divine messages—and it could be made a tremendous public demonstration, to impress the populace and heighten the power of Ra and his priests.

"Oh! I forgot to say," added Abdallah, "that the word of Allah indicated a certain spot for the ceremony. This spot is on the front terrace of the temple, between the two great statues there."

A spot in full view of the whole city, where the populace could gather by thousands to watch the miracle! Ra-enfer could not conceal his satisfaction.

"Also," Abdallah went on, scratching his head, "there was something, about a message: The bird would leave a message in the morning amid the ashes. I do not know what it means myself. That is, provided the conditions were faithfully met, and the guards posted well away from the spot to keep all people away."

The priests began to think that there might possibly be something really miraculous about this business.

Abdallah, refusing gifts and honors, took his departure. He eyed the two statues as he went, and was himself rather well satisfied with the whole business. He had previously examined them with the greatest attention. They were colossal figures, full thirty feet high, of the great Pharaoh Rameses, the Conqueror; seated figures, hands on knees, set out a little space before the temple entrance.

But, as he made his way home, he realized that the same man was shadowing him, a fellow deft and agile, marked by sloping shoulders and a heavy face. He took his course through the bazars, stopping here and there, buying a trifle of this and a trifle of that—all in small quantities. Like all Bedouins, he wore a sheathed knife slung about his neck, under his robe.

When he came back to the tavern, where he was now an honored guest, he fed and watered the fighting-cock in its wicker basket, then sat himself down and pondered. He went over each detail of his project with the greatest care, and regretfully decided that if he were to live, another must die—at the proper moment.

This arranged in his mind, he went to work playing with his purchases—odds and ends of feathers, dyes, wax and needles and thread, glue and such like. Being a deft man of his fingers, he found his experiments successful; and this pleased his rather devious mind.

H E   W A S not astonished, next morning, to find the whole town in a ferment. Heliopolis, while not one of Egypt's largest cities, was the city of the sun, and not unused to miraculous events; but this was something new. The bird from Arabia, the wondrous phoenix, which would come and rejuvenate itself in sight of all men, would be something worth the seeing! Not the least wonderful point was the schedule of the whole thing. To be produced by the priests of Ra before sunset; to be burned alive, burned to ashes; and from those ashes, with the sunrise, a new bird would arise and wing his way to heaven—eh? A great spectacle, if true!

If true! Ra-enfer the high priest, took particular pains in his proclamations to avoid the least suspicion of trickery. From the moment that the funeral pyre of the phoenix was lighted, a space two hundred feet square about the spot, which would include the colossi of Rameses, would be under constant guard all night. Not a soul would be allowed to set foot within this space. The people were at liberty to remain outside the line of guards, and to make the night an occasion of celebration or prayer to the gods, if they so desired; but none, public or priest, could intrude upon that guarded square in front of the temple.

Abdallah the Bedouin, hearing all this, chuckled softly, and perfected his plans.

THE THIRD day of his prediction to Ra-enfer wound to its close. Abdallah, alone, drew the gamecock from his cage and inspected the gorgeous bird critically. What with travel, heat and confinement, the bird was in sorry state.

Abdallah carefully clipped his wings so he could not fly. Having found a gum that would serve his purpose, he anointed the head and crest of the bird, dusting it with gold. The result was gorgeous in the extreme, and would last the necessary time. He then, with the proper dye, turned the bird's beak to a brilliant blue. This done, he returned the cock to the basket, donned his temple robe and his golden sandals, and sallied forth.

As he left the tavern, openly, the accustomed shadow took up his trail. Abdallah did not go far; being close to the wharves and river, he sought an unfrequented spot where the stone-ships from the quarries far upriver landed their freight. Here he strode along rapidly; then suddenly turned on his heel and strode back. The trailer, unable to find cover, affected indifference; and

There was a surprised squawk of fear; then
the cord whipped about throat and neck.

Abdallah, in passing the starlit figure, swiftly turned and came
to grips. His knife was deadly and he knew his business.

Without a shout or an alarm, the spy collapsed, stabbed twice
through the heart.

Abdallah dragged the limp lifeless form to the water's edge,
and thrust it in for Father Nile to sweep away downstream, then

hurried home. He now had much to do, and not too much time in which to manage it all.

In his room, he doffed robe and sandals, and donned a tattered old blue robe belonging to Hassan—which, with a dark camel's-hair burnous, were still here. Thus attired, he slipped out of the tavern unobserved, money jingling pleasantly in his hand. He trotted along to the Street of Scribes, found a scribe at work with reed and brush and papyrus, and squatted down to bargain. Here was the one weak point in all his scheme.

To detail the fantastic and devious lie with which he regaled the scribe, would require a volume; the one thing, however, which makes any lie seem true, Abdallah had in plenty. The jingle of gold backed up his story to the hilt, and Abdallah was not niggardly. An hour later, he carefully tucked away the writing in hieroglyphics which the scribe gave him. The scribe, having indited another letter at his bidding, made ready to depart in haste and catch the upriver boat that left at midnight; for the scribe was to deliver this epistle himself in Memphis, being well paid for the whole thing.

It would be days before that scribe found no such person in Memphis, days more before he returned; thus, he would be in no position to cry that he himself had written the message on papyrus, the sacred message left for the priests of Ra by the wondrous phoenix! However, he would profit well by the journey, reflected Abdallah cynically, and bent his steps to the shop of a certain dealer in falcons and other birds used in hunting.

When he departed, he carried a basket in which reposed an enormous hawk, trained like most hawks to fly the instant his hood was removed; and until then, to remain motionless.

HOME TO the tavern he brought the hawk. Here he donned the dark burnous of Hassan; its hood would cover his face and head at need. With a wicker basket in each hand, he slipped quietly out of the tavern again and sought a boat-landing near by, where light craft could be hired.

He hired a tiny boat, and according to custom paid for it in full, to insure the owner against non-return. He put his two baskets in the boat, seated himself with the paddle, and let the current float him away. The Temple of Ra was downstream from here, well downstream; and the magnificent gardens of the temple ran down to the very edge of the water. As the Nile was high, Abdallah had nothing to worry about. The gardens ended in wide marble steps, where the priests and temple folk were wont to bathe.

A few were splashing here and there in groups, as Abdallah's craft drifted down, for the water was pleasant at night. Avoiding the groups, he drew in and came alongside the steps, briefly; long enough to reach the gawky gamecock out of the basket, dip him hastily into the sacred Nile and toss him ashore. Scandalized and outraged, the bird shook himself and scuttled away hastily from the water, up into the gardens.

"And if ever the priests saw anything like you, then I'm a liar!" murmured Abdallah, as he sent the little craft out into the current.

He now considered that the worst was over, that ahead was nothing but wearisome though necessary detail, with all danger past. In this he was wrong.

He spent two hours in a riverside tavern, renting a room and presumably sleeping. In reality, he was working hard by lamplight upon an extremely annoyed, struggling hawk, whose plumage and tail he augmented freely with gum and previously dyed feathers. He even managed to add a crest of variegated hues. A sprinkling of gold dust on undried gum provided the final touch.

IT WAS just before dawn, the darkest and dreariest hour of night, when, basket in hand, he approached the right-hand colossal statue of Rameses, before the temple of Ra. Through the top ring of the basket ran a long double cord, so long as to be bothersome, the end of which was attached to his left wrist.

Not a soul was about, not a soul was in sight. A dim light burned inside the temple entrance, and the guard was in there. The stone platform, facing the east, was deserted, and Abdal-

lah's bare feet
made no sound.
Cloaked in the
brown burnous,
he was invisible
in the darkness,
for the haze of
dawn covered
the stars.

At the foot
of the tower-
ing statue, he
slipped out of
the burnous
and made it
fast about the
basket; this job
was going to
need a trifle of
agility. Leav-
ing basket and
burnous below,
to follow by
means of the
cord, he got up
the pedestal,
up to the enor-
mous foot of the
Pharaoh, and reached up for the knee high above. His hands,
slipping over the polished granite, came upon a projection; by
means of this, he started up. Then, with a sudden sweat of cold
fear, he froze motionless.

"You damned rascal!" muttered a voice, a man's voice, above
him. Above!

Abdallah clung, terror shooting through him like a hot knife.

Fear of the supernatural leaped in him for an instant, of the gods whom he mocked. Then the voice went on:

"May Typhon curse you, blasted bird of hell! Bite my hand again, and I'll wring your neck, miracle or no miracle!"

Still Abdallah clung there; comprehension came to him, his brain cleared, he fought to check back the almost hysteric laughter that rose in him. A man was up there, indeed; some priest or servant of the temple. Up there, on his own identical errand!

"I should feel flattered," he reflected. "Those priests are clever; they've adopted my own private scheme! Therefore, it's bound to succeed. They're not taking chances on having no phoenix appear with miraculous qualities. They've provided the bird of miracle here; if the phoenix doesn't show up in the garden, they'll provide one at that end. Hm! This might save me a lot of time and trouble. Unfortunately, they're aiming at a mere miracle, but I have another end in view."

He hung poised against the leg of Rameses, weighing the possibilities.

To let the priests of Ra go ahead with their own miracle, was out of the question. This would destroy the whole point of his scheming, which lay in the papyrus he had obtained. He must, therefore, go ahead as planned—which meant that he must remove the man hidden in the lap of Rameses above. His knife? He shrank from this. If anything went amiss, if he were detected, it would involve flaying alive; to spill blood in the temple precincts meant being nailed to boards and having the skin stripped off.

To spill blood—ah! He took a fresh grip, and reached up. Here was the means to his hand, quite literally. Hesitating no longer, he thrust himself up, up and over the granite edge. There was a surprised squawk of fear and consternation; then he had the man gripped. The double cord whipped about throat and neck, and sank in.

It was a silent, scuffling play of life against life, muscle against muscle; and the iron-hard Bedouin had the soft city man down

and throttled in no time. Throttled, beating out with futile flail-
ing hands, and sinking into death. The cord was anchored in the
soft dead throat.

Abdallah explored. As he had anticipated, the lap of Rameses
was not shallow but deep and ample; three or four men could
hide here. He was further gratified to find that his mind and
those of the priests had run alike, in that this hidden fellow
was provided with a soft dark covering, for the same reason
he himself had brought the burnous. Then, lucky happening,
there was a small basket of food and wine—something he had
overlooked!

THE BIRD, some sort of gyrfalcon, was nothing like his
own splendid one; he wrung its neck, and shoved it and the dead
man together far back in the recessed lap. There was plenty of
room. Over them he put their own robe; when found, eventually,
the priests might smell the ruse, but it would be too late. And if
anything went wrong now, no blood had been shed.

"Decidedly, I should have been a priest of Ra myself!" thought
Abdallah cheerfully, as he hauled in the line and secured his
basket. Dawn was just lightening in the east.

His hawk he left hungry and thirsty this day; he himself
feasted. The brown burnous, spread widely over him, kept off
the sun, concealed him from sight of anyone on the roof-tops or
temple roof, and blended with the granite. It would catch no eye,
and from the ground below, this deep hollow was quite invisible.

The day passed; Abdallah ate, drank, dozed, ignored the heat.
He could hear the feet and the voices of thousands, he heard the
resounding news that the phoenix had arrived as the prophecies
foretold; and lifting up a corner of the burnous, he was able to
see the spot below where the pyre for the wondrous bird was
built, as the afternoon waned.

Thence, too, with sunset, he glimpsed the ceremony in that
guarded open space. The priests, hundreds of them, in full panoply; the chants, the music, the prayers to Ra. The figure of Ra-enfer, holding that luckless gamecock from somewhere beyond

Arabia, and laying the bird with legs bound on the pyre of sticks and twigs. Amid a deep silence of awe, the pyre was lighted.

It was no small nest; the flames rose, the wretched cock flapped his gaudy wings as though fanning the flames, and sank down. From the awed crowd, massing the square and the streets, arose murmurs as the sunset died and the pyre smoked out into embers. Night came.

Within that square of guards, no man dared set foot, as the night drew on.

Outside the square, the crowd sang, danced, feasted, were gay; at midnight, came an end to the lights and the noise. Priests were chanting somewhere, solemnly. Abdallah waited, biding his time.

Not until the mist from the river, before morning, went floating across the stars, did he move. Then he fed and watered the hawk, abundantly; hooded the bird, put him in the basket, lowered the basket carefully, and followed. He was wrapped in the brown burnous, and the descent was awkward, but he made it. In the obscurity, a vague shadow, he drifted across to the ashes of the pyre, on its platform, and presently drifted back.

The dawn grew in the sky. Murmurs arose from the waiting, watching thousands, from the priests; awe deepened as increasing daylight revealed the thing there. A bird like no bird ever seen before, resplendent with gay hues, queerly feathered—the phoenix! The miracle was accomplished!

The sun appeared. The morning hymn to Ra was echoing from the great temple, as Ra-enfer the high priest approached that silent, motionless, hooded bird. He prostrated himself before the pedestal, then came close, reached out, and removed the hood with trembling hand.

The phoenix glanced around, blinked around, moved a little. Suddenly he took wing and lifted. At first he flew awkwardly, darting hither and thither; a feather fell and fluttered down. (It was preserved for generations as a precious relic.) Then he soared up and up, and was gone in the heavens. Amid roars of applause and delight from the crowd, the high priest picked from the ashes a roll of papyrus, and opened it. The roars fell into dead silence. Ra-enfer, giving plain indications of his own awed wonder, read aloud a greeting from the phoenix of Arabia to the priests of Ra. Then his voice faltered, as though he misliked what he read, but he had to go on with it. After due thanks for the care and attention given by the priests, the message read:

"Let your noble work, I pray you, be completed by the release of the Arabian Hassan. Let him, who blasphemed the gods, be set at liberty by the gods, that he may hereafter fear and respect them; and that all the gods may bless you, good priests!"

Roars of acclamation arose from the crowded thousands. And Abdallah, from his safe high perch, peeped down and chuckled in gratification.

FLETCHER'S VOICE fell silent. The scene he had painted was gone; we were back at the luncheon-table, and Brill was frowning as he lit a fresh cigar.

"So it was all a rank fraud?" he exclaimed.

"Apparently," said Fletcher, smiling. He also took a fresh cigar and lit it with becoming care.

"Well," broke out Brill, scowling, "that bears out what I hold. There's no sense in all this mythological tommyrot!"

"There must be sense in anything that has passed into the speech of the world, as has the similitude of the phoenix rising from its own ashes," Fletcher said gravely. "We see the symbol of the phoenix all around us, in every phase of life, under our eyes every day—"

"What?" interrupted Brill, scornfully. "Where, for example, here and now?"

Fletcher reached out to the ash-tray, which held cigar ashes, dead matches, the butts of three or four cigars. These last, he touched lightly.

"There," he said. "If I were a cigarmaker, I could take those unfinished bits of cigars, unwind them, and make a whole cigar again. From the ashes of themselves. You see?"

He rose, shook hands with us, and departed, laughing to himself. Brill scowled at the ash-tray, and finally spoke.

"Something wrong. Something screwy with that cigar business. It's one of those things that sound fine at first, until you look into 'em more closely. Cigars from ashes! From dead butts, he should have said."

"I think Fletcher was having a bit of fun with us," I observed. "Anyhow, we know the origin of the phoenix legend; and hanged if it didn't sound plausible!"

Brill started to his feet.

"He never told us how he knew it!" he exclaimed, with a startled air. "He never told us— Why, say! He put it over on us all the way! Where'd he get that yarn, I ask you?"

"Don't ask me," I rejoined, chuckling. "Ask Norman Fletcher."

WOMAN OF THE SEA

THIS TWELFTH STORY OF THE "TRUMPETS FROM OBLIVION" SERIES
IS BASED UPON THE WORLD-WIDE TRADITION OF MERMEN AND
MERMAIDS—QUASI-HUMAN INHABITANTS OF REMOTE DEEP SEAS.

HOW THE mermaid argument began, I don't know. It raged all over the golf-course that summer afternoon, and at the nineteenth hole it settled into a hot debate. Heise, the banker, contended it was all piffle, all delusion. The Padre said the legend had been traced back to the manatee or dugong, a Caribbean creature resembling a woman when swimming. Briggs argued with his legal mind that since mermaid legends were old as history and were found all over the world, even among American Indians, they must have some basis of prehistoric fact.

My argument was that many towns and seacoasts have been swallowed up by the sea, and it was natural for ignorant peoples to imagine mermen and mermaids existing as survivors of the lost population.

Heise said this was nonsense.

"Most of the old mermaid legends," he affirmed, "deal with lakes or rivers, not with the sea: the very name of mermaid—meer-maid or lake-woman—shows this."

"That's European legend only," argued the Padre. "What about the Assyrian fable, thousands of years ago? As a matter of fact, no man knows definitely about the derivation."

"One man does," I said. "One man can tell us, can even show us, where this mermaid belief came from! That man is Norman Fletcher."

"Hello!" The Padre eyed me. "You mean the electrical genius?

The wizard of the Pan-American Corporation? I've often wanted to meet that man; he's famous all over the world; yet we hardly know him here in the city where he lives."

"He lives mostly at his laboratories outside town," I rejoined.

"I've heard a lot about Norman Fletcher," said Briggs, with interest. "They say he's greater than Marconi or Steinmetz; that his investigations into ultrasonic waves have revolutionized television and radio. Do you know him?"

I nodded. "Rather well. During the spring, he gave weekly demonstrations to our Inventors' Club. He believes that all myths and legends have a factual basis, and proved it to us. His general theory is that sound and light never die, and can be brought back—that, for instance, he can reconstruct past events. It's some sort of television with reverse English—though he denies it; I can describe it in no other way. He could show us where the mermaid myth arose, if he took the notion. Shall I give him a ring?"

There was immediate acclaim, though nobody believed Fletcher had any such powers. I got the inventor on the telephone and told him of our argument.

He laughed.

"Bring your friends out tomorrow evening, if you like. Mermaids? Well, I guarantee nothing, but we'll see what happens if we go fishing in the seas of antiquity! I'll get the apparatus shaped up today and see what I can find.... Tomorrow evening, then."

So it was arranged. Knowing from experience what we would see, I tried to tell the others, and prepare them, especially the Padre. I need not have worried; he was as curious and eager to see Twentieth Century magic as any of us.

NEXT EVENING we drove out. The Pan-American laboratories were impressive, a small city in themselves, elaborately walled and guarded. A good deal of war work was going on in connection with the national defense program, and Fletcher

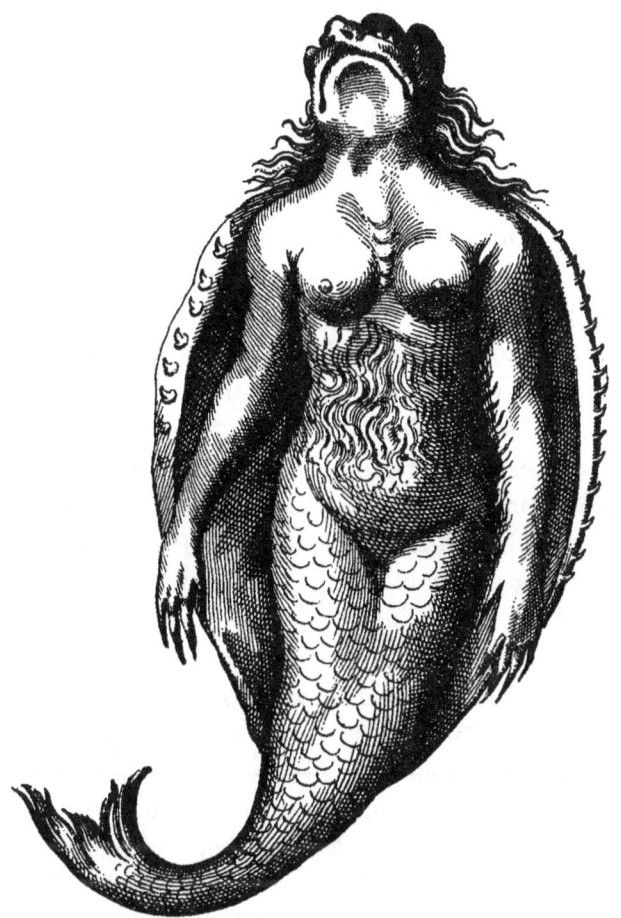

was said to have perfected some marvels in this regard. Yankee ingenuity is far from dead.

Our host received us beamingly. He too was impressive, with his mane of white hair, his ruddy ageless countenance, his personal charm. He took us into his private laboratory with the stone walls, where little of anything was to be seen.

Before the blank end wall of solid granite were ranged comfortable chairs; a cigar humidor stood open, and we made ourselves comfortable. Norman Fletcher seated himself before his controls, the only piece of apparatus in sight; this looked like a triple-manual organ, and was apparently unconnected with any other apparatus. He lit a cigar and regarded us genially.

"I suppose you know that you're now in a house of rank magic," he observed lightly, "where everything's done by electricity or by wave-force! Seriously, I've looked into this mermaid question, with interesting results. I've had to make a special sound-track for the voices, in modern language; while I can create, or re-create, scenes from the past, the language offers difficulty."

"Do I understand," asked the Padre, "that we're about to see what actually took place at some past time?"

"Correct," replied Norman Fletcher. "I don't wish to explain the process, except that it involves new discoveries in ultrasonic waves. Within the past few weeks I've evolved some new tubes, but they require a little time to warm, so there's no hurry. Now for the mermaid myth! It's as old and universal as the hills; the fact that it has fascinating variants would indicate it to be founded on truth.

"I've chanced on one of those variants," he continued, puffing easily at his cigar, "which may serve as a general type or example of how the legend evolved in all ages. Among the early Portuguese explorers arose a singular tale of mermaids who grew on their backs a long hairy mantle which they could hook together in front, or leave open, at will. This passed into Italian, then into French and Dutch narratives and books."

"Quite true," said the Padre eagerly. "It arose from stories of seamen who had seen the dugong or sea-cow swimming about the South American shores."

Fletcher, smiling, shook his head and exhaled a thin cloud of cigar-smoke.

"I'm sorry to contradict, but it did not. We find it in the narratives of early Portuguese voyages down the coast of Africa, before the Americas were discovered." He took a paper, an old and yellowed map, from the top of his instrument-board and handed it to me. It was a map of the West African or Congo coast, of 1731. "Look at this; the legend, you see, persisted to comparatively recent years. Look at the top left corner. Inside Cape Lobo, or Lopez as it is today—see those islands? That's the spot. The squadron of Argelho touched there briefly in the Fifteenth Century, getting fresh water from the river-mouth. It was a grand place for wrecks, since—"

HE CEASED speaking; the room lights dimmed; upon the stone wall before us, a yellowish light began to play, gradually becoming more intense; it came from nowhere—there was no projection, no ray in the air. It just grew, and as it grew, the stones dissolved.

I heard startled exclamations. The Padre caught his breath. To me it was no novelty, yet the wizardry of the thing gripped me now as always. The wall had disappeared, and we were looking through it, as through a window, upon a sunny sandy beach under blue skies. It was a wide river-mouth. Outside the bar were anchored three Portuguese caravels, Fifteenth Century ships. Beyond them showed the bluff outlines of Cape Lopez; inside the cape were patches of green, islands thick with trees, a good two miles from the shore.

Here on the sandy beach where boats were drawn up, were men white and black. A group of Portuguese in armor, with watchful guards; other men filling casks of water. Talking with them were savage blacks—a chief, seated, while a warrior held a shade of leaves above him, and other warriors clustered around. An interpreter spoke. All was peaceful; trinkets had been exchanged, gifts made, and files of blacks were bringing fruits and palm-nuts down to the boats.

"It's an amazing thing!" exclaimed Dom Luis Argelho, bearded and gaunt. "Tell him to send his men and bring us back one of these gods. We'll pay well."

THE INTERPRETER spoke. The black chief and his men broke into dismayed words; a fetish wizard shook his rattle and howled in negation. The interpreter turned.

"They say no; the gods of the islands must not be disturbed.

They have the shape of women, with tails like fish. From their backs grow hairy mantles, which they can close in front. Sometimes they come here to the shore, where offerings are left for them at certain seasons—piles of fruit. It is forbidden for anyone to approach them or injure them, since they bring good luck. This is very certain, the wizard says. They have brought the tribe great good luck and much wealth. If you disturb their gods, they'll attack us."

Young Carvalho laughed and mouthed a jest about mermaids and seamen. He was young and bold of eye, nor did the eye lie: he was reckless of life, ever ready to dare anything on these African shores, for behind him in Portugal lay ruin. War had swept away all he had or was, war and drink and dissipation. Now, hardened by the voyage south, he looked the bold spirit he was. The commander glanced at him and frowned.

"Tell him to send his men and bring back one of these gods," said Dom Luis Argelho to the interpreter. "We'll pay well."

"Carvalho! I ordered that every man ashore should be armed. Where's your armor?"

Carvalho's bold eyes twinkled. "Excellency, I lost it at the dice last night. I think Diego de Senza wears the breastplate; I see the morion on the head of Dom Joao yonder—"

A laugh went up, and the Admiral bit his lip. It was impossible to be angry with Carvalho. At this instant a shouting arose among the blacks; their voices rose in clamor, and they began to point with their spears.

The interpreter exclaimed suddenly:

"Excellency! They say one of the gods is coming now—look, *look!*"

The Portuguese turned. And Carvalho, staring with the rest, saw what he had never thought to see in life.

An object, a person, was swimming in toward the beach. It avoided the three ships, off to the right; along this shore, in shelter of the cape, was almost no surf at all. It was heading straight for the group, and man after man crossed himself furtively or gasped low oaths.

"A woman!" exclaimed one. "Look!" The swimming thing paused, as though in alarm at so many folk, and swung up on a high wave-crest. A woman—no doubt of it. A woman, white and shimmering, with a queer high something humped on her back. She plunged with the wave and was gone, then came up again, but no longer a woman.

Amazement seized Carvalho and the others. They could see her plainly, now a great hairy beastlike shape. One of the men aboard the ships had fired an arquebus. The shot hit close to her; the smoke bellowed; the report echoed. No longer a woman, but a swimming beast, the thing turned about and headed out and away for the island.

"After her with a boat!" cried Carvalho. The interpreter exclaimed quickly, and Argelho issued prompt denial.

"No! These blacks would attack in a moment. They're angry now, because of that shot. Mermaid or monster, let the creature go, and have no trouble. We'll be out of this accursed place in a day or two, but we must keep these tribes friendly. This is a splendid spot in which to found a settlement and trading-post.... Eh? What's that?"

The black chief was speaking earnestly and showing something at his neck; a gold coin, strung on a chain of cowrie shells. According to the interpreter, a gift long ago from those gods of the island. Argelho examined the coin.

"A golden ducat of Venice, apparently, but much worn," said he. "No others like that? Then let it pass. Curious! The monster is gone from sight. Well, to work, to work! Ask him what price he will take for that high ground along the river. Tell him we may come to help him against his enemies and make trade, and open a station here."

LET IT pass, a golden ducat of Venice? Not easily, at least for Carvalho; gods who could provide one such broad gold-piece, might provide more. He played with this thought; and it set his brain afire....

Shrewd Fray Marcos hit the nail on the head, that night, as he talked with the commander. From discussing the marvel and making sketches of it, the good friar went on to the subject of Carvalho, who had lost at dice everything he owned except sword and dagger.

"There's grand stuff in him, but he's found life too easy," said the friar. "Now he's well on the road toward hell, and has missed the turning."

"What turning?" asked the blunt Argelho, frowning over this symbolic speech.

"The road called Incentive," replied Fray Marcos. "He knows nothing better in life than riotous living. He's totally ruined, financially; he borrowed money in Lisbon to pay for his equipment on this voyage. The steel in him has never been tempered; the manhood in him has never been wakened."

"He can fight like Satan himself!" growled the commander.

The friar smiled sadly.

"Aye, like Satan, more's the pity! Over a wench, an insult, a bottle of wine. That's the limit of his horizon. Now he'll become desperate, reckless of life, and reach hell fast. I'll have a talk with him in the morning."

The good friar was a pessimist; his appraisal wronged

Carvalho somewhat. When with morning he sought the latter, to admonish him, no Carvalho was found. He was not aboard. He had stood watch until midnight, but not a soul knew anything about him after that.

Carvalho had vanished. At this, panic seized the men; in view of the prodigy they had witnessed, all of them, they believed this to be a place of devils. Even Argelho flew into a passion, to hide his own uneasiness.

"The tide's just past flood," said he. "Up anchor, and off with the ebb! Away from this accursed spot! Straight out to sea—give that cape a wide berth."

SO THEY did, leaving Carvalho sound asleep—on the sun-warmed sand of the island of the gods. Letting himself overboard by a trailing line, unseen of any, he had struck out in the dawn-darkness. Sword and dagger, shirt and jerkin—nothing else to hamper him. The water was warm; he was ignorant of sharks. He came to the island shore exhausted, staggered up under the nearest greenery, and dropped in the sand.

He wakened with morning well along, to look for the ships. They were gone. He saw them at last, bearing far out to sea to round the cape. He gaped at them, felt a quick spasm of panic, then rallied and laughed.

"Alone!" he exclaimed. "Alone in Africa! Alone with the gods—and mermaids! Well, the ducats of Venice won't do me much good now."

It was nothing to be merry about. His heart sank most damnably when he realized that the ships were gone, and not returning. He could not understand it. He had thought they would be here for another day or two, and that he could spend a few hours exploring the island of the gods—and the Venetian gold.

He sat down to watch the sails out of sight and to think it over. Occasional ships came along here, Portugals and others; very occasional Moors came at times, for slaves and gold-dust, and from them he could expect only slavery; the Moors were

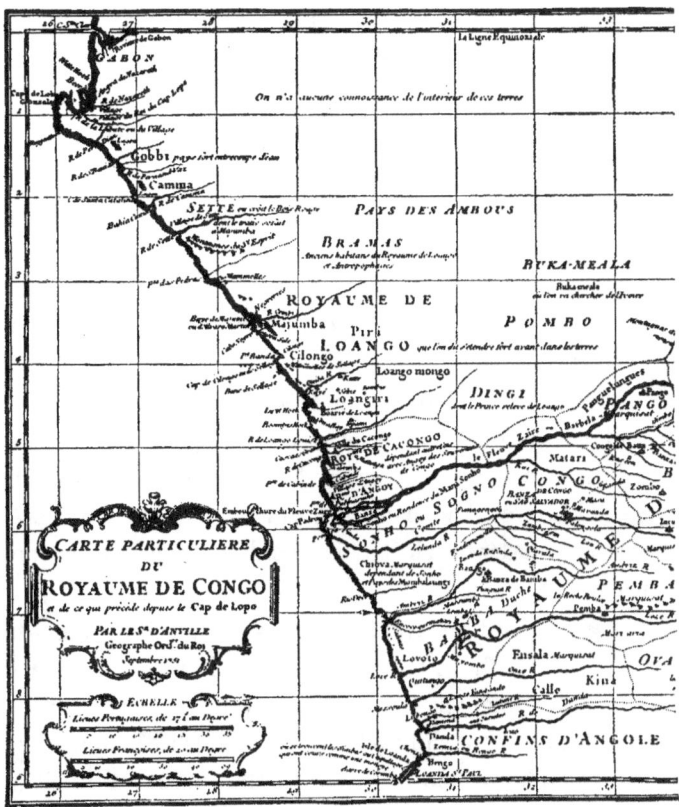

the terror of the world. Until the caravels returned, which might not be for months, he was marooned.

From the blacks on the mainland he might or might not get welcome; safety was not so certain either. However, the blacks did not come here to the islands. Their boats were mere dugout canoes for river use and they seldom or never ventured offshore.

"There remain only the gods—or monsters—to consider." Carvalho came up to his feet. He gazed around, looked toward the river and the mainland, and laughed again; this time with more of a ring to the laugh.

"The unknown gods, and this new land of Africa!" he said, and put hand to sword. He loosed the blade, and his dirk, from the scabbards; both had been greased against the water, and he wiped the polished steel clean and dry. "If the gods are only women, why worry? On, then, and probe destiny!"

Sound of his own voice lent him heart; let courage be what it may, Africa is a land of monsters, and to him was a world unknown.

He surveyed the greenery close at hand, essayed it, and recoiled with a shake of the head. Trees and brush and thorns grew in a tangled mass, and he could discover no path by which entry might be had. After all, the shore offered the easiest way, and he turned to it.

He kept close to the trees, mindful that the blacks might see him, otherwise, and come over with their spears and bows to defend their gods. He was thankful when at last a curve of the shore hid him from the mainland, and he could leave the loose sand for the harder beach. To his naked feet, the sun-hot sand was torture.

He kept on and on. The island was some miles in length. Twice he saw paths entering the brush, but decided not to risk them; the open felt safer. Insensibly, he turned the end of the island, and out of sight fell the rivermouth. The long cape, toward which he was now facing, was shut out from his vision by other islands, none of any size but all thickly grown. Islands and reefs, a maze of them, and sandspits.

O N O N E of those islets Carvalho saw something move and leap; stopping dead, he stared, and then a chuckle escaped him. A goat, several goats; probably wild ones. Curious! How had they come to be on the islet yonder? There were no tracks hereabouts. He had seen no tracks at all, in fact—

As this thought occurred to him, he was again on his way, only to come again to a dead halt. Speak of the devil, and he appears! There was a track now; the tide was high and it showed only in the dry sand, but it seemed to be made by footprints, curving back into the water again. Did the swimming gods, then, walk like humans?

A little unnerved amid the morning silence, he went on.

Sunlight and silence and the multitudinous noise of the water amid the reefs. He went on, until his pace slowed and his dark eyes widened on the scene that opened.

The beach curved inward among rocks, and from the island's heart issued a sparkling rill of water to be lost in the sea. The brook vanished under a green tangle of fronds and high palms, but along it ran an obvious beaten trail. On the sand lay drawn up a queer shapeless little boat of skins stretched on a framework, and beside it were two rude paddles; with these were heaped several hairy skins. One, by itself, was outstretched, and the amazed Carvalho beheld on its larger end a huge painted mouth and eyes.

Fear shook him. Mermaids came out of the sea, and shed these queer mantles—ah! Mermaids used no boat like this, no paddles! Something stirred and moved among the trees; he swung around. A flitting object whirred past his head and splashed in the sea. With it came a sound he recognized, a twanging, clanging sound—a crossbow had been fired, the quarrel had missed him.

INSTANTLY HE was himself again. That crossbow was reality! Joyously he laughed, and to play safe, crossed himself swiftly, then spread out his hands.

"A friend!" he cried aloud. "Whether you be gods, monsters or devils, I'm a man alone and a friend."

"A friend!" The trees seemed to echo the words, but it was a human voice. "A friend, Felicia! And he signed himself! Moors don't do that!"

"Quiet, Melusine!" sounded another voice, in Spanish like the first.

"Felicia! Name of fair omen!" said Carvalho gayly. "A goddess, by your voice; and by your name a creature of happiness and beauty! Appear, divinity, and assure yourself that I'm no enemy!"

He advanced to the brook, knelt beside it, and drank with a sigh of relief. He had begun to dread the tortures of thirst. When he rose, Felicia was approaching from the shelter of the trees.

He swallowed hard. His laughter died. Here was a woman bent, gnarled, stooped, and not a little mustached; an old woman, clad in rags and tatters. She glared at him.

"You are no Portuguese!" she cried accusingly. "We knew you were a Moor. Those were Moorish ships here yesterday!"

"Portuguese, honest Christian caravels of Lisbon," said Carvalho, and gave his name. His astonishment at her Spanish speech was extreme. Still, she was swarthy, like some Spaniards. "Where are you from, *senhora?*"

The old woman laughed, cackling harshly, but her shrill mirth was wild and witless.

"Liar! You're a Moor, an infidel, a pagan!" She shook a skinny fist at him. "You don't fool me, you scoundrel! I know what you're here for, curse you, curse you, curse you—"

She fell into a screaming, raging fury. In the midst of it, she cried out upon God and toppled forward, blood running from her mouth. Carvalho knelt and lifted her head; she was dead before he touched her.

Bewildered, dismayed, aghast, he set her down and rose. Startled, he found a girl at his side, silent-footed, her gaze driving into him. He crossed himself and took a step backward. She was all white and black and scarlet—black hair and eyes, white skin, scarlet lips and ruddy cheeks, wearing a loose white gown. Under his look, her face changed, her eyes became gentle with grief. She stooped, touched the old woman.

"Poor Felicia! She has suffered so much that it feebled her mind," said she gravely. "Carvalho, you said? I am Melusine Sarmiento, of Burgos in Castile. Are your ships here?"

"They have gone. I'm alone," he stammered.

She gestured and turned.

"Bring her. Madness had grown upon her; she said they were Moorish ships. None the less, she was a true friend. Bring her, and leave her with me and my grief. I'll talk with you later."

Carvalho saw that, beneath her impassive exterior, emotion was struggling. He picked up the skin-and-bone corpse

*Where are the gods of this island?"
Carvalho demanded.*

and followed Melusine along the trail. It took them among thick trees, into shadowy recesses. He saw goats staked out on tethers; two thatched huts; a wide clearing where yams were growing, and behind this a grave marked with a wooden slab.

Melusine pointed to this slab.

"Put her down. Leave her with me; it is my affair, not yours. Wait on the shore."

He obeyed, awed by her beauty, her authority, her cool self-possession. Of the reputed gods or monsters he saw no sign.

Out on the white beach again, he lay stretched out comfortably, still puzzled, but making the best of it. A sound of sobbing came from the trees; afterward all was silent. And then, when the sun was high, she came in her fleet silent way, and dropped beside him.

"She is buried," said she simply. "Here—I have brought you fruit to eat."

"Where are the gods of this island?" he demanded.

She gestured scornfully. "I remain; the other two are dead. There are no gods, Carvalho."

IT TOOK him a long while to understand. They moved into the shade and remained there talking, while comprehension came to him; her story did not come forth all at once, but by degrees. It was a grim tale; life was grim for many a woman then, and she was but a girl.

Two years she had dwelt on this island, with the old woman and a man, now also dead.

Raiding Moors in Spain had captured her; little more than a child, they had sent her as a gift to the sultan in Marrakech, by a ship that came down the coast past Mazagan. Storms took that ship, buffeting it on and on helplessly; then the slaves rose and killed those that remained of the Moors.

In slave hands, with none to guide, the ship met more storm, and came at last ashore of a night, here among the islands. Three lived—Melusine, old Felicia, and another slave named Diego, who was crippled by hurts, but was a crafty and cunning man. They thought they were on some Moorish coast, taking all blacks to be Moors, and acted accordingly.

"Diego made them think we were gods," she said. "A few goats, that were aboard our ship, reached that island yonder, and in time they multiplied. Diego did many things with their skins, and their flesh fed us, and their milk. We do not lack here."

Carvalho comprehended finally that the blacks had never seen these three as they were, so craftily had Diego played on the superstition of the savages. Both women, forced to every artifice to sustain life, became expert swimmers, and for them Diego made the queer mantles of goatskin.

"I'll show you." She stood up and regarded him gravely. "Turn around and don't look until I call."

Carvalho obeyed implicitly; he was still in awe of her; his better instincts were roused by her loveliness and her trust. When she called, he turned and saw her in the water, with one of the skin mantles wrapped about her, and her gown lying on the sand. She showed him how, thus wrapped, she could swim without her limbs being seen, or how the mantle could be put back in a roll if need were.

This was the explanation of the "gods" which had impressed blacks and whites alike....

For Carvalho, a new existence now began, an existence touched with wonder and bitter work and hard days and terror; for when he wakened next morning, he found Melusine tossing with fever, in the hut she occupied alone.

Of leechcraft he knew very little. He could only use his common sense, which was not too extensive, and trust that careful tending and her own iron constitution would pull her through. She weakened with the days, and passed into delirium; the fever burned out and recurred again until she was but a thin wasted shadow, and all her loveliness a radiant shroud that presaged death.

Death, however, came not.

AS THE days wore on, the young man became a different person. The gay, daredevil cavalier was quickly lost. The Carvalho who remained was a shaggy bearded man plagued by a devil of anxiety and torment, accomplishing the impossible. For the crippled Diego who lay under a wooden slab, he attained a fervent admiration, in view of all that poor devil had accomplished and so little to do with.

A hand-ax, an old crossbow with half a dozen bolts, a knife—nothing else, except a few bits of wreckage; with these Carvalho carried on. Responsibility was his, for the first time in life. By his hands, they two must live: fish from the reefs and pools, flesh from the goats, yams from the ground and fruits from the trees. The blacks, on the mainland, piled their offerings near the rivermouth and twice Carvalho went over in the frail skiff and brought back a load of fruits, at dead of night.

He tended Melusine carefully, gently, ceaselessly. His naked feet grew hard, and his body grew hard; his mind, too, grew hard, and his character firm. But tenderness deepened in him none the less. At first, he aided her from pity and manhood, but

later from love. When the day came that she could sit up and
move about, they celebrated her recovery joyously together. The
weeks flitted on, and she grew once more into her strength and
radiant beauty; tattered garments saved from the wreckage were
clothes enough.

A L L   T H I S   while Carvalho saw no other human thing, for
the blacks shunned these islets inside the cape. Melusine tried
to teach him the use of the goatskin mantles, but he was not at
ease in the water, thus enveloped; he left the trick to her.

The ducats of Venice? There were none. Diego had plundered
a few coins before the wreckage was scattered by the waves;
nothing else. More than once Melusine mentioned some mysterious work on which Diego had been engaged, before he died;
Carvalho thought little of it, until one day he learned that the
spot lay somewhere amid the thickets at the seaward end of the
island. He set forth to explore and find it, from idle curiosity.

Hours later, he came upon the spot, and life was changed
abruptly.

It lay close to the shore; in the months since Diego died
suddenly from some poisonous thing he had eaten, weather
had not affected anything. A clearing, made among the trees,
was growing up again; and in the clearing, bottom side up, was a
boat. Evidently, Diego had kept the matter secret lest he provoke
hope that might be hopeless.

Carvalho stared wide-eyed; with a hoarse cry, he ran upon
the boat and examined it. Much work had been done, much
remained to do. Here, it seemed, Diego had plundered the
wreckage to great purpose, having amassed bits of wood and
some cakes of hard tar and sundry other things.

Tears of joy silvered Carvalho's shaggy beard. When he had
found the boat sound and good, the worst damage repaired, and
under it some casks for water, he turned and went running back
to camp. He found Melusine cooking, dragged her away with
him, and presently showed her the boat.

"Salvation!" he cried. "Salvation, do you understand? We can get away from here!"

"Whither?" she asked, with no elation. "Only to fall into the hands of savage men?"

This checked him; there was sense to what she said.

"At least, this craft can dare the surf and the sea, which is more than the little skin float can," he rejoined. "We'll not go for the sake of going, dear lady; but here's work to do. If other men come, if Moors come, then we're not caught and trapped."

Always in his mind had grown the fear of other men coming and talking with the black chief, and seeing that golden ducat hanging at his neck. The Portuguese had humored the blacks, but others might not; they would investigate the island of gods, where grew golden Venetian coins—precisely as Carvalho himself had come to investigate.

He fell to upon the boat, which was stoutly built of Portugal oak; he labored with crude tools from dawn to night, and the work grew under his hand, slowly but surely. All his savage energy went into this task.

Now it must be said that these two, being in love, admitted it freely and joyously and as a sacred thing, taking an oath before a cross placed in the sand. They knelt hand in hand before it, and plighted their troth for life and life eternal; and Carvalho did not doubt that Fray Marcos would account this a good deed well done. That the friar would pass upon the matter was not unlikely, since the three ships would return this way on their voyage home....

Carvalho lost count of days. The labor on the boat drew forward; they got the seams well and duly tight, and together managed to launch the craft. It floated stanchly; there was a mast, with cordage, but the canvas Diego had salvaged was all rotted. Two goats remained on the other islet, and the milch-goats here; these Carvalho killed, and from their skins made a sail that was heavy but would serve.

HE WAS fitting this sail to the mast of an afternoon, when
a sound reached them. His head jerked up.

"A gun!" he exclaimed. "Melusine! Quickly!"

Together they plunged into a path that led across the island
to the land side. They emerged, and stood panting, hand in
hand. At the river-mouth was a ship, indeed; but fear leaped in
Carvalho as he eyed her. It was one of his own three ships, torn
and rent by shot, her rigging all awry; and the men aboard her
were not the men he knew.

"Moors!" said he, squinting across the sunlight at the tiny
figures. A boat was going ashore, where a crowd of blacks were
collected. "The Moors have taken our ship, and have put in here
to water and refit. Ah—watch!"

The ship's side bloomed smoke; from the boat more arose. The
Moors landed, and with the sound of gunfire drifting across the
water, attacked the blacks. Many of these, including their chief,
were slain, and many others captured and taken for slaves; and
the sun went down upon that bloody work.

Two Moors came splashing in; Carvalho engaged these with sword and dirk.

Carvalho knew well that evil destiny had come upon him; he sat sorrowing that night, for the fate of his comrades. Very early in the morning he swam over toward the ship and heard voices, and so made certain these men were Moors.

Coming back, he worked at the boat, putting aboard her the casks of water and all else that was worth taking, with the mast and hide sail. She was small, and to tempt the horizon of the sea with her would be mad folly; but she might serve to take them elsewhere along the coast, during the next night. He hoped against hope in this respect; and hope failed.

For, halfway through the day, he descried a pinnace that had towed behind the caravel, coming over toward the island. A big, bluff open boat, her mast broken off by battle, a dozen men at her oars, others crowded in till she was low in the water.

Carvalho ran for the creek entrance. He descried Melusine out between the islands with the goatskin mantle about her; at his shout, she headed in for shore, but she was some distance off. The boat rounded the end of the island as she came. The Moors yelled madly and loosed arrows, but she reached the shallows, threw off the mantle, and dived for the shelter of the trees where Carvalho stood with his weapons.

"Get to shelter and stay hid," said he, winding up the crossbow. A sudden savage light sprang in his eyes. "Ha! Look at that! And look at that man—Luis Gonzaga! Luis, I say!"

Things happened all at once. He had caught sight of a naked white man at the bow oar, one of his own old comrades, now enslaved with the caravel's capture; at the same instant, he saw

the pinnace lurch. She was a hundred yards out from shore. The
tide was low, and her bluff bow rose high upon a reef, and she
tilted.

"Gonzaga!" shouted Carvalho, "It's I, Carvalho! Over and
swim for it, man!"

The slave, who had been master gunner aboard the caravel,
sprang up. Men were tumbling all about; the Moors were in
utmost confusion, and he was overboard and swimming before
any of them understood the matter. Then the Moorish leader
stood up and bent a bow; but before he loosed the shaft, the
heavy twang of Carvalho's crossbow sang upon the air; the quarrel drove through the armored Moor from breast to back, and
he toppled into the water.

LUIS GONZAGA splashed through the water like a
madman. A pistolet roared, but the ball missed. Bowmen recovered balance and poised to shoot; again the crossbow twanged,
and this time the massive quarrel pierced two Moors and pinned
them in death.

"Too bad your Diego didn't rescue more quarrels!" said
Carvalho, as Melusine, in her tattered gown, appeared beside
him. "Back! To cover! Here comes death!"

The pinnace was hard and fast on the reef; by reason of the
island, the Moors on the caravel could not see what happened
here, and by reason of the distance could hear nothing. Those
aboard the pinnace, yelling furiously to Allah, were now loosing
a storm of shafts, directed chiefly at Carvalho; he slipped aside,
and the angry arrows whipped all around him. Luis Gonzaga
ducked in the shallows and escaped that storm also.

Three of the heavy Genoese quarrels were left, thick-shanked
and iron-headed. Carvalho cranked the bow, laid quarrel in
groove, and aimed carefully. To the clang, screams arose; it
pierced one man, hurt another.

The furious Moors, their light armor and mesh-coats glinting in the late afternoon light, plied bows again, made frenzied
efforts to get the pinnace loose, and could not. Gonzaga stum-

bled ashore, arrows whistling after him, and ducked for shelter under the greenery.

"Carvalho! Man, we thought you dead! Good God—who's this?" He started back and crossed himself, at sight of Melusine.

"My wife," said Carvalho. "Take cover before they spit you!"

He cranked the arm of the crossbow. Two quarrels remained, and he made the most of them. By this time, the Moors had lost taste for the death that struck them down. They came over the pinnace's stern into the water, swords and knives in teeth, and struck out. Some few remained aboard, trying to work off the pinnace with the heavy sweeps.

CARVALHO THREW the crossbow to the sands.

"That's done, but I'm not," he said, and took rapier in one hand, dagger in the other. He drew back, letting the bowmen spend useless shafts trying to find him, and looked at the rescued gunner. "What happened, Luis? How did they take the ship?"

"We were heading back here," said Gonzaga, panting, "and we met four of them. One we sank. One fled. Two others laid the caravel aboard and took us before their damned craft sank under them—our other two ships were too sorely battered to give aid or chase. I'm one of the few left alive. They came over here to investigate the talk of gods and the Venetian gold and put me in to row, with other slaves."

"Then the other two ships are safe?"

"Aye," said Gonzaga, "but badly cut up. They're just the other side of the cape, over yonder—"

"Ha! St. John!" shouted Carvalho, and went striding out across the beach. An arrow flicked at him and missed. Another sang past his ear; then no more, for the first of the Moors was on his feet and plunging ashore, and the bowmen on the pinnace dared fire no longer.

THE MOOR came wading in, but Carvalho waded out to meet him and thus had the advantage of footing and breath and height.

"Allah!" yelled the Moor. The rapier pricked through his throat and changed the yell to a bubbling groan, and the swarthy warrior pitched over.

Two others came splashing in, hot behind him. Carvalho engaged these with sword and dirk, the tide swirling around knees and ankles. One Moor lost footing, and the dagger smote down through his back. The other man, slashed across the eyes by the sword-point, turned away and went reeling up to the beach, holding a hand across his eyes and screaming.

Luis Gonzaga brained him with the heavy crossbow and took his weapons, but Carvalho did not see this, for now he was backing away, three of the Moors leaping at him.

There he fought them warily, looking into the dark bearded faces, meeting the savage eyes, giving thrust for thrust, parrying with the long dagger, keeping away from them with swift feet. One took a thrust and went down. Two others came splashing up to take his place, and had cut Carvalho off from any retreat, when suddenly Gonzaga was in upon them with a yell and a thirsty blade.

Now befell work of the deadliest, the sunset glinting from fast-whipping steel, the sand flying underfoot. Carvalho kept to the wet strip above the low tidemark, thus having solid footing. Blood was running down his face from a slash over the head, his arms were bleeding, Luis Gonzaga was down with a ripped thigh; but the Moors fared worst. Two died quickly, a third coughed his life away, another was hamstrung and crippled like a screaming horse. One stumbled; Gonzaga grappled him and stabbed him as they rolled in the hot white sand.

Then it was over. These were devils, not men, cried the Moors, and gave back. Besides, the men in the pinnace were yelling at them—they had her off, floating, but she was taking water fast and most of their sweeps had drifted away. So those that remained turned about and plunged again, swimming for her.

Gonzaga, having finished his man, put his point through the throat of the wounded Moor, and went staggering up the beach

for Melusine to bandage his hurt. Carvalho, panting, leaned on the red rapier and watched the pinnace go limping around the island end in the sunset glow.

In an hour or less, darkness would envelop earth and sea. In an hour or less, the land breeze would be up, blowing out to sea. In an hour or less, that pinnace would return, crowded with Moors—

"Carvalho!" Melusine came to him, with a wet rag and bits of cloth torn from her gown. "Your hurts—let me at them. Ah, poor man!"

"Poor Moors, you mean!" said Carvalho, with a fierce laugh as he regarded the corpses in the wash of the tide. She caught swiftly at his face, making him look her in the eyes.

"Listen! Did you hear what this man said?" She jerked her head toward Luis Gonzaga.

"Eh? What of it?"

"Everything!" She blazed with sudden excitement. "Your other two ships repairing their damages—there, there! Just the other side of the long cape! Don't you understand? We can put out in the boat now, when darkness comes down, and reach them with tomorrow's dawn—"

Carvalho started. He had failed to comprehend much that Gonzaga had uttered. Now he caught her meaning. His pulses leaped. With a quick movement, his hurt arm encircled her.

"Ha! By St. John, you've hit it! The Moors will land here. We'll put out from the other end of the island and be gone before they find us, in the darkness—"

The sun was gone under the ocean. Darkness stole down; the greenish sky deepened to blue, then the stars faded, everything faded. There was only a blank wall of stone.... Then the room lights flashed on again.

"WELL!" SAID Fletcher, with an air of satisfaction. "That's one of the best demonstrations I've ever obtained. It shows how the myth of mermaids arose, in this one variant of the story, and why, and the channel by which it reached the world. Like many another fable and legend, we owe it to protection."

"Protective coloration," corrected the Padre, smiling. "The genius of the oppressed. But what, may I ask, became of the two lovers?"

"I've been unable to obtain more information on that subject, at least directly," said Norman Fletcher. He took another paper from his instrument-board and handed it over. "But here's the indirect answer. A curious old engraving that came from Portuguese sources."

OUR FOURSOME clustered about the engraving, showing two subjects. One, to a casual glance, looked something like a flying fish. The other showed a rather horrible monster, until one inspected it more closely and perceived that it was actually a mermaid, holding back a sort of mantle.

"Why—upon my word!" exclaimed the Padre. "This is actually an illustration of your story, Fletcher! It represents the mermaid enfolded in her mantle, viewed from above; and also viewed from below, with the mantle thrown back!"

Fletcher nodded.

"Precisely. One of the few documentary evidences extant, in

regard to such fables. With due allowance for a confoundedly poor artist, he got his details from an eye-witness. Undoubtedly, from Carvalho or his wife. Naturally, they would keep quiet about her own part in the matter—in those days, anything that smacked of wizardry led to the stake."

We examined the two pictures. Heise, the banker, grunted and settled back in his chair.

"I still claim it's all nonsense," he said stubbornly. "This thing we've just seen—what was it, Fletcher? A magic-lantern trick? Of course it wasn't real."

There was a rather nasty undertone in his voice. Norman Fletcher, smoothing back his white hair, replied with his usual affability.

"You've heard the old story, Mr. Heise, about the yokel who viewed a giraffe for the first time, in a circus parade. 'There just ain't no sech animile!' said he, and stuck to it. You are of course entitled to your opinion, for which I have the greatest deference."

And Heise had the grace to blush.

THE SERPENT-PEOPLE

THE FINAL DRAMATIC STORY—OF THIS BAKER'S DOZEN OF WORLD-
WIDE MYTHS AND LEGENDS MADE REAL AND REASONABLE—IN
THE THOUGHT-PROVOKING SERIES "TRUMPETS FROM OBLIVION."

I RANG OFF, and got into touch with all the members
of the Inventors' Club I could reach. Dinner, a final demonstration of Fletcher's wizardry, and a special announcement to
our club—something, I gathered, of great moment. For Fletcher
was leaving us, was going to Washington as a member of the
war-defense committee. War, or the threat of war, plays the devil
with all of us, as he said. If the present threat came true, our club
would end in the army.

Nearly the whole crowd got together that evening. Fletcher
had given many demonstrations of his ability to bring back
scenes from the past, on the theory that light and sound never
die. His process was unknown to us; as the effect was apparently
a remarkable variant of television, which Fletcher emphatically
denied, we concluded that it was evolved from his work with
high-frequency and ultrasonic currents.

At first we had laid it to illusion. But this, with Norman
Fletcher, was impossible. He ranked with the foremost electrical brains alive. His genius had made the Pan-American
Corporation the greatest unit on earth. Now that it was turned
to government service with the national defense program,
predictions were freely made that any nation attempting to
measure barbaric might against Yankee wits would get a shocking surprise; and this was no joke.

During the afternoon Hopkins, the president of the Inventors' Club, called me. Old Hop had been a professional magician

before he retired on invention royalties; he had traveled widely, and had lived long in the Orient. He knew his stuff.

"You know," he said over the phone, "that Norman Fletcher

has turned this apparently useless but fascinating invention of his, to the purpose of proving that all the legends and fables of mankind have some factual basis."

"He's done a good job of proving it," I answered.

"Sure. Well, he called me, asking that I suggest a subject for demonstration tonight. I gave him a lulu! It's the legend of snake-men or serpent-people."

"Never heard of it," I rejoined, more crossly than kindly.

"A legend deeply rooted in India, whence the Portuguese brought it; and it bulks large in Buddhist tradition. In Angkor and other ruined cities of IndoChina, the carvings show how widespread was the belief in Nagas, as they're called—a cobra, see? It's supposed that some original race in those parts had the name, and worshiped the cobra; and when the Khmer race came along and conquered that part of Asia, they took over the belief. But the Khmer race has vanished now, and who knows the truth? Might be interesting."

I assented mechanically and hung up, rather disgusted with old Hop for proposing so asinine a legend. Snakes did not appeal to me. I took occasion to look up the matter, however, and discovered that belief in snake people extended everywhere, even to American Indians, not to mention the Garden and Eve and the Serpent: People who could command snakes, people who could change into snakes, and so forth. There were a lot of variations there....

Being a bachelor, Norman Fletcher lived at the Pan-American laboratories, where they had built him a gorgeous place of his own. A round dozen of us drove out from the city that evening, and Fletcher greeted us with his beaming hospitality.

The dinner was a rare one, and the wines were elaborate; it was, said Fletcher, a very special occasion. He had an announcement for us, but preferred to make it after the demonstration; he predicted that it would surprise us considerably.

The meal over, we lighted cigars and followed our host to the laboratory—his own private workshop, within high gaunt walls of stone. We took the easy-chairs facing one of those stone walls. Coffee and liqueurs were served, and we were left alone. Fletcher sat at his control-board, an instrument like an organ of many manuals, the keys of which controlled his lights and tubes. There was no other apparatus visible.

White-haired, urbane, genial, the old Yankee surveyed us with a twinkle in his eye.

"Invariably, you look around for apparatus," he observed amusedly. "Yet there is none. It's all here, here!"—tapping the keys under his fingers. "Here are the tubes, here's the magic, the illusion, the trickery you've sought so long and vainly to find!"

He was gently poking fun at us now. He went on more seriously:

"Mr. Hopkins, I believe you are a master magician. Did you ever see the most famous trick in the world—the rope trick of India?"

Hopkins laughed. "No; and no one has ever seen it. No reward has ever produced it on any stage, in any part of the world. It's one of those things talked about but never seen, like the sea-serpent. Every magician knows this. It's an impossibility."

"You're to see it this evening," said Fletcher softly. "You've asked for the origin of the legend of serpent-people. I've had great difficulty, I must admit, in getting the language of ancient IndoChina transcribed—for I need make no further mystery, gentlemen. When I recapture some scene from the past, by use of these tubes, I recapture the language as well. Sometimes it is an unknown tongue, and I must translate it as seems best, in making and synchronizing the sound-track. So it happens now: You're to see the vast ancient cities of the Khmer race, or one of them; it takes us back a thousand years or more, when the land that is now all jungle was teeming with myriads of people. An Aryan race, brown and intelligent with the brains of more ancient India, but a race doomed to sudden death. The reason will appear. The rope-trick will appear. So will the origin of this singular legend, typified by the cobra, the serpent which expands its wide hood—"

HIS VOICE died out. The room lights had sunk to nothing, and on the stone wall before us was playing the yellowish radiance which we recognized. The section of wall on which this light played, gradually disintegrated. It dissolved before our eyes. We looked as through a window, not upon the exterior darkness, but upon a glowing sea of green, waving in sunlight and shadow—green trees lifting high crowns into the very heaven, incredibly tall, creating a sort of twilight below them.

Dwarfed by these enormous trees, an elephant padded along. A driver sat on his neck; a howdah of gold and scarlet was on his back, and in the howdah sat a young man whose dress flashed with gems. Now it was seen that the elephant followed a road of stone slabs, thirty feet wide and straight as an arrow. Water glimmered ahead; the road became a causeway and crossed it. A lake? No; merely a moat within stone walls—a moat a thousand feet wide that circled walls and vaguely enormous buildings lost within a leafy cover opposite. The young man leaned forward and spoke.

"Stop at the bridge! A chariot there, and those priests. Ask them."

The beast slowed. Ahead, at the end of the causeway, appeared a chariot and a group of priests, yellow-robed, with whom the driver was talking. Something else appeared, towering above them on either hand; this was the head of an enormous cobra carved in stone. On either side of the causeway lifted such a head, the body running along the causeway on either hand and upheld by stone figures of men, life-sized.

The soldier in the chariot, the priests, saluted the figure on the elephant.

"Greeting, Prince Varma!" cried the soldier in a lazy voice. Upon him, as upon the others, sat an air of listless indolence. The driver leaned far over.

"Where can we find the juggler Paswan, of whom all the people talk? The foreigner who came out of the jungle and does miracles?"

One of the priests made response. "I hear, lord, that he may be found at the old shrine of Siva, across town, where the priests have given him shelter."

The elephant moved on. Prince Varma looked at the uplifted cobra heads of stone, on either side, on a level with his eyes. Now it appeared that each head, representing a cobra with out-puffed hood, was composed of many smaller heads, perfect in each detail—a startling vision to one not accus-

tomed to this form of art. Prince Varma merely glanced at them and looked on, across the moat, to the gigantic walls that rose amid palm-trees—the city of Ayuthia, where the king, his father, ruled the Khmer people.

Others appeared on the causeway, multitudes of people, who made room for the elephant. Some saluted, others did not. They were flower-decked, laughing, jesting, yet in all their faces lay the same listless expression. Prince Varma was one of the few who showed energy in his chiseled features and dark eyes.

A fragrance that was not of the forest flowers and jungle creepers drifted down the causeway; the elephant flung up his trunk to it, distastefully. It grew stronger. It was the fragrance that hung above Ayuthia and other Khmer cities, day and night. Prince Varma spoke to his driver.

"Will it be difficult to find them at that shrine?"

"That depends, lord," replied the other. "The old shrine is small; it will not have more than twenty thousand people around it—a third the number of those who live about the larger shrines and downtown temples. The priests will know, however; this juggler has become famous in the past two weeks."

The city gates appeared, open as always in these days, guarded by indolent archers. People crowded everywhere in masses—laughing, merry, lackluster people, always smiling. The gates had platforms of stone, the height of a howdah, for nobles and princes to disembark, but the elephant did not pause. The soldiers saluted the prince, wagged their heads after his frowning passage, and muttered. Prince Varma was highly unpopular; in fact, he was hated because he tried to enforce discipline and instill spirit into the troops. Who needed such things? Khmer ruled the world. The whole wealth of eastern Asia was poured into these cities, and chiefly into Ayuthia. It was fifty years since the legions had done any fighting, so terrible was the Khmer name to others.

But in those fifty years, a warrior race had drifted close under the jungle trees.

Within the city, the fragrance became more perceptible, permeating the very air. One scarcely noted it at first, for sheer amazement; this seemed a home of gods, rather than of men. The wide street showed straight ahead, for miles. To right and left lifted masses of carven stonework in fantastic shapes of pierced galleries, each tier smaller than the tier below—gigantic erections of stone. No one lived in these immense structures; they housed shrines, or religious devotees, or were monuments to dead kings. The people lived around them in slight bamboo structures; people by the thousand and ten thousand to each one. And as the elephant advanced along the mighty stone street, whose slabs were rutted by the wheels of chariots across the centuries, the subtle fragrance in the air deepened ever.

Chariots, bodies of troops, laughing crowds filled the street and crowded the bazaars lining it. They all made free passage for the elephant; a good-natured people, it seemed, with laughter everywhere, and the clangor of bronze bells from the temples or clumping bamboo bells held by monks. Good-natured—why not? Everywhere towered coco palms, shutting out the sky; bananas, fruits of every kind, sprang profusely from the earth. Into Ayuthia poured tribute of riches from all countries, until gold was common as dirt, and precious gems were bartered for a pig, and artists used such things to decorate the carved walls. In Ayuthia was no crime, no care, no trouble; even life and death were of no account here.

For ten miles ran this street, amid uncounted multitudes of laughing listless folk, past temples that lifted enormous stone faces to the sky, past the huge central park of the palace, on toward the old shrine of Siva. And the subtle fragrance was everywhere. No one hurried.

AT THE ancient shrine, where about the crumbling towering temple huddled twenty thousand attendants and priests and slaves and guests, in their flimsy bamboo structures, were two people, vastly different from the half-million in this city. They occupied a small guest-house of the temple; just the two of them, with a servant.

The juggler was powerful in build, a forceful but suave energy in every line of his strong golden-bronze features. He, Raswan, was of the Cham people—that fierce warrior folk who had come out of the northern hills to the verge of civilization, and whose mailed fist was beginning to close on this doomed race. His daughter Silva was a small, delicate creature, lovely as a flower, her skin like old ivory; she seemed rather some sprite of the forest than a girl, so fragile and beautiful she was.

"Bah!" said Raswan with scornful glance, at some question from her. "This city is a hell-hole; I shall cleanse it with fire and

The girl shrank back, for the hooded head was rising!
Varma pointed to an opening in the stone flooring.

sword, I tell you! And sooner than you think, my girl. These
people must be wiped out to the last person!"

"Why?" She turned to him, pity in her eyes. "They're a
friendly, kindly people, father! They've made no war for two
generations and more."

"No, they've lost the art of defending their wealth," said
Raswan with thin mockery. "You've seen the temples, the
passages, the wondrous carvings; in all of them, have you ever
seen one hint of one indelicate subject?"

The girl frowned, lightly. "No; that's true. Never. Why?"

"Ask this reeking air about us," rasped her father, who seemed more warrior than juggler. "A decadent people, a plague on the earth! In the King's stables are elephants by the hundred, chariots by the thousand; a hundred thousand warriors garrison this place. Yet in one night, with a thousand of my men and four elephants, will I destroy this whole city and every soul in it."

"That doesn't answer my question, Father. About the carvings."

"Oh, that!" Raswan smiled grimly. "Opium. These people have lost all energy; look at their faces! They eat opium, burn opium, spend vast sums on the accursed drug. It's in their food; its incense is perpetually in their nostrils—temples, houses, men and women, babes at the breast, all are soaked in it from birth to death! If you and I didn't get out in the open jungle every sunrise, we'd sicken and die of the fumes around us."

"They're not all like that," murmured Silva. Her father laughed.

"Aye! That prince—Varma, was it? I grant you, he's of the old Khmer stock. Let me warn you, girl! I've brought you here and hidden you away, so that you'll see no more of him; take care! He's a degenerate like all of them, not a man. He may use fine words and have a hint of hot blood in him, but he'll go the way of—ah! What's this?"

He sat quiet, listening to sudden voices outside. The girl stared at him, rebellious yet shrinking, dominated by him. He dominated everything around, whether he wore the blue robe of a coolie, the saffron robe of a priest, or the jeweled robe of a king. His lean steely features were made for dominance. As a juggler, performing tricks for the temple crowd, he dominated that crowd completely. His character, his presence, was a force that was felt.

THE DOOR opened. A priest entered, bringing another man with him.

"They are here, lord; there sits the man you seek."

Prince Varma dismissed the priest. He flung one swift glance at Silva, then fastened his gaze on her father, and stepped forward. He was quite unflurried beneath that frowning, black-avised regard, and with a salute, seated himself, still meeting the steely eyes.

"I have found you," he said calmly.

"It is not by my desire," snapped Raswan. "You're a prince; my daughter is not for you. You have women by the thousand in your palaces. Go! Leave us in peace."

"That is impossible," the Prince rejoined lightly. "The memory of your daughter does not leave me in peace; during four days I've been quartering the jungle, the roads to the frontier, the river banks, the hills. I have talked with the Nagas, the cobra people. Do you know that my fathers who ruled this land were descendants of the Nagas? That is true."

"Are you drunk?" demanded Raswan.

The Prince smiled.

"Yes, when I look at the eyes of your daughter. But in your eyes I see a sword, and it is the royal sword of the Cham kings, hilted with ivory."

THE GIRL shrank suddenly, staring. The gaze of Raswan slitted keenly; in a trice, he wiped all expression from his face. The Prince still smiled, and waited. Suddenly, unexpectedly, it was he who dominated this room.

"What do you want here?" shot out Raswan.

"Food. A king does not poison the rice of a guest."

"Our food," rasped the juggler, "contains none of your accustomed drug."

"That is why I desire it; I never touch opium."

"Serve us," said Raswan to his daughter, and flung a sneer at the prince. "You're the only person in Ayuthia who can boast as much. Your father the king is a sodden wreck; your captains have never seen a battle; your soldiers, your very slaves, have no will or power. They drift like lotos leaves on a pond."

"That is true," murmured the Prince, his face setting hard. He watched Silva as she moved about with the servant, bringing rice and fruits. Raswan went on, harshly:

"You are in disgrace. Your people hate you because you try to stir them to work. Your soldiers hate you because you love discipline. Your very father and brothers detest you, because you try to make them govern the land."

"All true," said Prince Varma. "But I'm still descended from the Nagas."

"What do you mean by that?" demanded Raswan sharply. The prince shook his head.

"You'll discover that too late, juggler; I have magic more powerful than yours."

Raswan eyed him scornfully. The food was set before them; they began to eat. Prince Varma presently lifted eyes of calm challenge.

"Do you juggle tonight?"

"In an hour. For the last time."

"The king of the Cham warriors, juggling for the pleasure of Ayuthia!"

"Well? Who told you I was a king?"

"Yourself; your words, your looks, your ways. Parties of your warriors are encamped in the hills and in the jungle; you have horsemen and elephants ready. You're here, disguised, a spy. Why?"

Death quivered in the room, in the gaze of Raswan.

"You fool!" he said softly. "Do you expect to leave here alive, to warn your people?"

Prince Varma shrugged lightly. "Oh, warnings would do them no good; they've had plenty! All you say is true. There aren't five hundred men in the garrison worth their rice. Some of the regiments of archers haven't strung a bow in a year or two—and in olden days the Khmer archers were the greatest in the world! No; no use giving them any warnings. It's you I'm warning."

Raswan stiffened. The Prince spoke on, easily, without heat.

"My people aren't worth fighting for or saving. Let them perish! Your warriors are barbarians; I've learned much about them, about you. You, a king without sons, with one daughter whom you love above all the world. You, a little king of a little hill race, who spy upon Ayuthia and dream of looting this city, crammed with all the wealth of Asia! Well, because I also love your daughter, and because she loves me, I shall let you go. Tomorrow noon, be out of the city or take the consequences."

RASWAN CONTROLLED himself, though lightnings sat in his eyes.

"I've gained what I came here to learn, Prince Varma," said he softly.

"Aye? One thing you don't know." The Prince tossed a rice-ball into his mouth. "Why the images of Nagas are everywhere about the city. Why the royal family of Ayuthia is said to be descended from the serpent-people. What it means."

"Suppose you tell me," said Raswan.

His daughter was intent upon the two of them.

"Why not?" Varma smiled. "Look! Long ago the world was young. My ancestors took for their emblem the cobra, the Naga of a hundred and one heads. The legend arose that they were descendants of a lovely princess of the Nagas, who took human form. They encouraged this legend. Time and again, it saved them in crisis; this story of the serpent-people who lived under the earth. Behind it all was a secret, held precious in the family, given from father to son. So I received it, though of late generations it has meant nothing to my family. To me, it means much."

"What is it?" demanded the other harshly. The Prince wiped his lips and shook his head.

"Not now." He stood up. "I give you until tomorrow noon before I tell any that you're in the city. It would not be wise if you were to try and kill me now."

"That will come in due time," said Raswan grimly. He cocked his head, listening. "Ah! The drums! The ceremonies will soon begin. I must juggle for your people, and do tricks."

"I shall be there," said the Prince, and flung a smile at Silva. "And I shall prove that my magic is greater than yours, spy and juggler and king!"

So, pleasantly, he took his leave. Raswan sat for a space like a man carved in stone; he wakened, abruptly, and crooked his finger at his daughter.

"Go, make everything ready. Ha! I shall trick this rascal yet. Go, I say!"

She departed. Raswan beckoned the servant, who was a sturdy, deep-chested Cham, and utterly devoted to him.

"You must drop everything and leave the city at once, and find our men."

"Lord, the gates are never closed, and the guards pay no heed to anyone."

"Good. You know where my brother and the Cham princes are encamped, six miles outside of the city. Go to them, now, at once. Instead of striking a few days hence, as we planned, they're to strike before dawn—and without fail! This very night."

The eyes of the Cham flashed. He gestured understanding.

"Here are the orders," went on Raswan. "One elephant to each gate; the gates are open, but the elephant must push down the gate-towers, which are old and ruinous. One party to each of the four gates; and each party must bring fire. Explain that this whole city is built of flimsy bamboo, like this house; these structures form solid masses about the temples.

"Once inside the gates, set fire to the houses—quickly! Pause not to slay. Time enough for that later. Then rush down the four great streets to the palace in the center, and fire the stables. After that, nothing remains except to loot and kill. We have a thousand men close at hand. Send at once for another five thousand, who should reach here before tomorrow night—cavalry. Runners will take the word, from my brother. Understood?"

The Cham assented, and was gone from the room like a shadow.

UPON THE night air, the sickly-sweet odor of opium lay heavy. This old shrine of Siva, one of the first structures built when the ancient city was new, had an enormous open court before its central portico. This portico was reached by two terraces. On the first terrace beside the steps stood two stone lions of monstrous size. On the second and upper terrace, before the temple entrance, were two of the enormous stone Nagas, amazingly carven. Each of those great uplifted cobra-hoods was composed of hundreds of tiny cobra figures, crested and puffed out and most intricately chiseled, like lacework: the bodies formed the frontal edge of the terrace.

Dancing girls and musicians were upon the terraces now, posturing silently to the low throb of drums. From inside the building, whose carven facade mounted into upper darkness, voices chorused the sacred texts, for worship and instruction went on ceaselessly. People were gathering in the open court, eternal smiles upon languid lips, flower-wreaths everywhere; flowers eked out the universal garb of both sexes—the sampot, a twisted length of silk, artfully arranged.

More people, ill and halt and maimed, were flocking in from the temple-hospital up the street—a larger, newer structure with some forty thousand permanent attendants. The men and women flocked in serried masses, moving listlessly, floating rather than walking. There was no hurry, no pushing, no crowding. Life was like that in Ayuthia, drugged to the very soul. The air was heavy with opium incense.

Now, at a pause in the dancing, slaves set up an enormous candle on either side of the Nagas before the entry. These candles were huge cylinders of bamboo, stuffed with fats and incense; as they burned, the fragrance of opium drifted ever more heavily.

Gold and jewels were everywhere. While Britain, across the world, was still a Roman province, the wealth of all the Far East had been pouring into the cities of the Khmers, and now it still poured in uncounted. The temple dancers, in their stylized costumes, were coruscating with rare gems.

A harsh gong lifted brazen clamor to the shadowed balconies above. It was close to midnight. Raswan appeared suddenly between the two Nagas and the gigantic candles; he was naked except for a loin-cloth—a brawny, magnificent figure of muscular ease, at which the crowded people gaped curiously, and applauded with faint excitement. His daughter appeared beside him, a slim and delicate shape, sampot twisted about her body. She handed him a sampot of flowing silk, and stepped away.

Other lights were extinguished; the two huge drugged candles gave sufficient light on the spot where the juggler stood. All else merged into obscurity. A figure slipped out of the temple, came over to the towering Naga on the right, and stood in its shadow. Prince Varma stood lost to sight, unobserved, and watchful.

As a juggler, Raswan was exceptional. In deft silence, he began his tricks, and his personality dominated the scene immediately. When he smiled, the crowd broke into laughter. When he waited, tense, the crowd swayed in suspense. These people loved tricks of magic and juggling, and Ayuthia had seen the best on earth, but never a man such as this. Raswan performed none of the usual and simple feats; everything he did was extraordinary. When he retired and came back wearing a Chinese robe, and proceeded to the Chinese "production" tricks, the materialization of objects from thin air, applause swept the massed throngs.

FOR AN hour or more he held them. The whole court and street behind was a sea of faces; the crowd was jammed thickly, impenetrably, yet the utmost good humor prevailed. In Ayuthia were no quarrels, no lost tempers.

Stripped again of his Chinese robe, Raswan knelt and prayed to the gods. He rose, and cast the silken sampot on the ground; he jerked it away, and in the lighted space was seen a coiled rope, a thick and heavy rope that lifted in air as though pulled by some invisible hand. It uncoiled and went up and up until it was lost in the shadowed carvings far above. Then it settled and became firm, like a rope of stone.

Raswan motioned his daughter. She went to the rope; her light, lithe shape swarmed up its pillared length with ease, became dim among the shadows above, and vanished. With one sudden fierce cry, Raswan flung down the sampot anew, and then jerked it away. Two men, two warriors, uprose from the ground, naked blades held between their teeth. They swarmed up furiously, swiftly.

They too were lost in the weaving shadows. From some-

where far above came a wailing shriek, a cry of agony. Even Varma, knowing it all to be a trick, thrilled and stiffened in sharp surmise. Something thudded on the ground—a hand, lopped off at the wrist. Something else fell, and a gasp went up as Raswan lifted and displayed it. The head of his daughter. Another hand, a foot. One by one, the portions of her body fell to earth. Women cried out and sickened. Men swayed with fear and dismay, but Raswan smiled and gestured reassuringly.

He collected all the portions of the girl's body, and over them spread the silken sampot. He waved his hand, and the rope unlimbered, began to descend; it came down and coiled as it came, until there was only a coil of rope on the ground. Then Raswan knelt again and prayed aloud to Siva, and stood up. With a momentary hesitation, he reached out to the sampot. Suddenly he caught it up and jerked it away.

Silva rose to her feet, unhurt, smiling. Quickly, Raswan flung the sampot over the coiled rope, and jerked it up. The rope was gone.

Applause burst forth. For once, the listless people were moved to real emotion. Flowers were thrown at the two. Masses of flowers fell about them. Jewels and ornaments showered around them.

Then, suddenly, a silence spread. A dread, incredulous silence. A woman shrieked out in wild horror. Raswan turned about, and took a step backward.

That enormous stone Naga on the right, the cobra's head composed of a thousand tiny heads, was moving!

The carven stone seemed to undulate. It moved upward as though the Naga had come to life and were lifting its head. Figures burst across the terrace—priests, shrieking out in horrible mad panic. What happened there beside the Naga, was hard to say; a dim shape moved, the daughter of the juggler screamed something. Then the great stone head moved again and settled into place, and the earth trembled to the movement.

RASWAN TURNED, peering about. His voice lifted; it lifted in alarm, in sharp terror. He had no answer, except from the frightened cries of the crowd. His daughter had disappeared. From the shrine behind him, a dozen archers appeared and closed up around him; they were smiling, and their officer was smiling, as he saluted the juggler.

"My daughter!" cried out Raswan. "Where is she?"

"I know not, lord," said the officer amiably. "But I have orders from Prince Varma to escort you home to your guesthouse, and to guard you there until noon tomorrow."

For one instant, the juggler was petrified. Then he broke into furious words, furious actions. Escape, he could not. There was something unearthly and horrible in the smiling refusal of the archers to answer force with force, in their refusal to heed him or his words. Only when he flew into a mad and insensate frenzy, when he produced a knife and stabbed at the officer— then they closed more tightly around him. Golden fetters were brought out and laid on his arms and legs. He screamed, shrieking wild words about death and destruction, attack by the Cham warriors—and ignoring him, smiling, unhurried, they forced him away and his hoarse desperation died out in the distance.

MEANWHILE, SILVA felt herself carried; she was enveloped in a mantle that muffled her cries. When she heard the voice of Prince Varma at her ear, she fell silent. He pulled the mantle away from her head, and she perceived that he was carrying her along a corridor, which ended in lighted chambers where lamps burned softly. A gasp escaped her, for these chambers were of a magnificent luxury such as she had never glimpsed.

Laughing, Varma set her on her feet, dropped the mantle, and looked into her eyes.

"You're my captive, precious lady!" he exclaimed gayly. "You vanished from beneath the very eyes of your father—"

"What's happened? Where am I?" she exclaimed.

"In your kingdom, my princess! The kingdom of the Nagas, the serpent-people, under the ground."

He stood silent, waiting; watching her, admiring her, giving her time to drink in the wonders all around. In all Ayuthia, only certain members of the royal family knew of this subterranean retreat; and most of them had forgotten about it.

It was a marvel from the days when slaves by the hundred thousand carved and toiled and died for the conquering Khmer princes. Human labor and wealth beyond calculation had made this place, far underground.

The walls were lined with carven stone; and, like the walls of the high temples above, every inch was sculptured. Here were laughing, fantastic little figures scuttling along; smiling temple dancers performed slow posturings; animals and Nagas—everywhere Nagas. Screens of intricately worked marble closed a vista of other chambers beyond. In the stone, gold had been run, filling the carven spaces here and there or solidly encasing the pilasters of columns, and everywhere was a sparkle of gems.

In the center of this room was set a table, heaped with fruits and wines, glimmering with golden dishes. At either side of this table, from the profusion of rich stuffs that covered the floor, lifted great Naga heads to the height of a man. The hoods and heads were composed of countless smaller heads, each one standing out full-chiseled, yet the whole forming one glorious cobra with distended hood. The serpent scales were exquisitely carved, and the lines filled with gold, the eyes of each tiny head were of ruby, and a profusion of other gems glittered from the flowing stone.

"My father!" Suddenly alarmed, the girl turned, hands clasped.

"He's quite safe." Varma smiled. "Be at ease, my dear. I've had him taken to your guest-house, under guard, until tomorrow noon; then he'll be sent back to your own people." He took her hands and kissed them. "My dear, my dear! You don't detest me?"

"You know better." Her glowing eyes warmed, her delicate features were radiant. "You're not like other princes, other warriors; when I first saw you—I knew! But there's much to be explained and understood, dear Varma."

"Much." He drew her to him. "Come, then; you must be tired. Sit and eat, talk, rest! We are alone. No slaves could be trusted with this secret."

"But what happened? How did I get here?"

He seated her at the table, and went to one of the two Nagas, and put out his hand.

"These are like the monster heads outside the shrine, Silva. They're not for ornament alone; watch!" Under his touch, the Naga moved. A cry broke from the girl; she shrank back, for that glorious hooded head was rising, undulating, rising! Then it stopped, and Varma pointed down, to an opening in the stone flooring.

"Even if this underground place were betrayed, or found and looted, there would remain the Khmer treasures, unfound—certain treasures stored away here in past ages. You see the boxes, here below? Gems and gold, safely packed away." He touched the stone head again, and it sank back into place. "So there's the secret for you!"

Her eyes drifted on the wonders around, as she sipped wine.

"But still I don't understand. There are no serpent-people, really?"

Varma laughed heartily. "Not even among the gods, my dear! More than once, my ancestors escaped war or revolution or sudden death, through such underground retreats as this. They fostered the legend of serpent-people. They conceived these wondrous Nagas. Two hundred years ago, the king who built the old shrine overhead, vanished during some struggle; he returned and recovered his throne, saying he had been among the serpent-folk. This place had saved him, you see. It's all symbolic, with a practical fund of wealth at hand, to boot."

She relaxed gradually, and her gaze rested upon his eager, alive features.

"You didn't know that my father was a king—at first?"

"No; but I knew you were the only woman I'd ever love," said Varma frankly. "Then I got reports from spies whom I keep on the frontier. I investigated. I took an elephant and went, myself. I got word of armed forces gathered, hidden, waiting. I found a man who knew the Cham king and described him minutely;

then I knew who your father was. And I came back, as you know."

"What are you going to do about it?" she asked.

"Escort him from the city, and marry you. If he wishes to make war, let him do so!"

Anxiety glimmered in her eyes. "But you don't understand. He planned a great raid on Ayuthia, a few days from now! That's why the warriors are gathered, ready—"

"I guessed as much," said Varma, calmly. "I'll have a talk with him before he leaves. I can't help these people of mine, you know; to them, life is a dream. They have no ambition, no will, no energy. All has been sapped from them by opium. Do you know what my ambition is?"

"I'd love to know—if it concerns me," she said, radiant once more.

"By the gods, you're most of it!" he cried. "I'd like to leave here forever, put this whole land away from me; take you, take the wealth that belongs to me, take the two or three warriors who love me, and go. For ever. North to the land of China, perhaps; or west to hither India, or on to the greater India beyond—"

Upon this their minds met; she was in a delighted flame on the instant. They were alone with love, and the future opened out before them in a glorious sheen of achievement; ambition arose, shooting like arrows at half-glimpsed marks. They talked of the things they would do afar, of strange sights and the marvels of the world, of what they together would accomplish in new lands beyond the horizon.

So the hours fled away.

IN THE guest-house King Raswan lay fettered in his golden chains, with anguish and terror increasing upon him. The archer guards smoked opium, or ate opium, and threw dice languidly, or gossiped. When his desperate voice beat at them, they merely smiled. When he offered gold and wealth if they would take messages quickly, they laughed and ignored his words. At last,

he became silent—a baffled man upon whose brain beat the horrors of futility, with certain knowledge of what was coming.

AT DAWN, the careless guards at each of the four great city gates saw the same thing happen:

Across the causeway bridging the enormous moat came an elephant silently padding along. He was a war elephant in full panoply, armored, with an armored howdah on his back. Behind him came a small following of men, dimly seen—not above a few hundred. Some party of royal hunters returning, the guards supposed. They paid but scant heed.

The elephant came to the gates, and there turned aside, and lowering his head, put it against the great guard-tower. Now the

*"The Naga people—the waters have rushed in
upon them; and they are dead! The Nagas are the
gods of the earth! Away from this accursed spot!"*

guards saw that the men on his back were Chams, and a trumpet
blew alarm. Too late! The tower was groaning and shaking. It
began to crumble, and with a roar collapsed in shattering ruin.
The Chams drew great scarlet-lacquered bows, and their long
black shafts drove afar, as the elephant charged across the ruins
and the screaming guards. Behind came the little column of
armored men and scattered quickly, fire-brands waving alight in
their hands. The elephant charged on, on down the wide empty

street of stone, and behind lifted the roaring crackle of flames
and the thin screams of the dying.

On, on to the peaceful center of the far-flung city, where as yet
no alarm reached. Here the elephants met, from each of the four
streets. Their riders came to earth and scattered. A few sleepy
guards appeared; the black shafts flew, the yell arose, the Khmer
trumpets blared, drums began to throb upon the daylight.

Then the crackle of flames arose. In a flash, a sea of fire was
sweeping across the enclosures around the palace, as though
answering the ruddy light of fire in the north and south, east
and west. Above the roar of flames, above the screams of men,
above the drums and trumpets, lifted the frightful trumpeting
of elephants in panic. They came bursting from the royal stables,
huge towering shapes gone mad with fear—not a dozen nor a
score, but a hundred or more lordly bulls, trumpeting terror,
charging blindly away in all directions, trampling everything
underfoot. Some went headlong into temple buildings and died
amid the ruins, but most of them scattered out to avoid flames,
met other flames and were turned away, and in blind horror went
careering on to destruction.

The whole city, for miles, was now a sea of fire and a tumult
of frenzied sound, made up of innumerable human voices and
the explosions of bamboo joints. The flimsy structures flared up
everywhere, in a flame that consumed swiftly and flew on; there
were no heavy structures to burn slowly. The rising bulk of the
temples were of solid stone. To these the people fled by thousands, clinging everywhere like ants in a stricken ant-heap. Some
one thought, here and there, to open the sluices that the waters
of the moat might come in and flood the lower portions of the
city. Multitudes who had escaped the flames, drowned here.

The sun rose upon a scene of smoking ruin, hideous death
and destruction. The Chams, unhurried, slaughtered every living
thing in the palace buildings, and then turned to the butcher-
ing of the hapless folk huddled in the high temples. Here and
there elephants were careering about, some blinded, all of them

gone mad; but the strangest thing of all was seen near the old shrine of Siva.

At this point the water was flooding in fast over the ground and stirring the litter of ruin and corpses which were piled high everywhere. An elephant, the mightiest bull of the royal stables, a gigantic beast with gold-tipped tusks, was stuck fast. His hind parts had broken through the earth, and he was trying frantically to pull himself free, his trunk upflung, scream upon scream trumpeting in frenzy.

The Cham captains gathered to look upon him, thinking he had fallen into some pit. As they looked, as the waters came rushing down more thickly, the gigantic beast, with a supremely agonized effort, pulled himself free. His hindquarters came up and out. As they did so, with a vast sucking sound, the water swirled and eddied and lowered; it seemed drawn into the very earth.

"L O O K, L O O K!" shouted the Chams, pointing to the elephant. "Look!"

They saw that blood was dribbling from wounds in his belly and legs; these were not hurts, but wounds. The water was no longer being sucked down; it rolled over everything in a placid wash of dead bodies. The Cham captains looked one at another.

"The Naga people!" said one, and the others nodded. "The bull broke through into the dwellings of the serpent-people! It was the Nagas who wounded him, and now the waters have rushed in upon them all, and they are dead. The Nagas are the gods of the earth; away from this accursed spot! Away! Find King Raswan!"

But him they found not, then nor ever.

T H E P A L L of smoke, the sweetish fragrance of opium, grew less; they all blurred and vanished, towering buildings and high trees. The lights of the room clicked on. We sat there, hardly realizing that it was ended, relaxing with some difficulty.

"By heavens!" blurted some one. "Then the two of 'em died, down there! Drowned like rats, they were!"

The earnest tension of the voice provoked a smile or two. Norman Fletcher left his controls and turned to face us, an envelope in his hand.

"My friends, you've seen the last demonstration of this invention that I shall give you," he said gravely, and we hushed to hear his words. "I'm off to Washington in the morning; when I shall return here is doubtful. We have witnessed many remarkable scenes from the past, thanks to this apparatus of mine, in company; I have enjoyed knowing you all, more than I can say.

"Here, Mr. Hopkins," and he handed the envelope to Old Hop, "is an attested copy of my will; I ask you to keep it. In the event of my death, I am bequeathing to the Inventors' Club this apparatus of mine, with full instructions for its use. If I live, as I expect to live, I shall some day bring the apparatus to better perfection and then hand it over to you gentlemen. But one never knows, in times like these; therefore, if anything should happen to me, I want you to have this invention as a token of friendship and esteem from one who valued highly his association with you all."

But I did not join in the outburst, as the others gathered around him. I was still thinking of those two caught down below, broken in upon and trapped, in the midst of love and dreams and golden ambitions, all lost and brought to naught.

Suddenly I found Norman Fletcher at my side, his hand on my shoulder.

"I know what's in your mind," he said gently. "Reflect on this, my friend: if there were no hell, what were the use of heaven? If we all gained our ambitions and brought our dreams to fruition—what good were dreams or ambitions? Good night."

ABOUT THE AUTHOR

H. BEDFORD-JONES is a Canadian by birth, but not by profession, having removed to the United States at the age of one year. For over twenty years he has been more or less profitably engaged in writing and traveling. As he has seldom resided in one place longer than a year or so and is a person of retiring habits, he is somewhat a man of mystery; more than once he has suffered from unscrupulous gentlemen who impersonated him—one of whom murdered a wife and was subsequently shot by the police, luckily after losing his alias.

The real Bedford-Jones is an elderly man, whose gray hair and precise attire give him rather the appearance of a retired foreign diplomat. His hobby is stamp collecting, and his collection of Japan is said to be one of the finest in existence. At present writing he is en route to Morocco, and when this appears in print he will probably be somewhere on the Mojave Desert in company with Erle Stanley Gardner.

Questioned as to the main facts in his life, he declared there was only one main fact, but it was not for publication; that his life had been uneventful except for numerous financial losses, and that his only adventures lay in evading adventurers. In his younger years he was something of an athlete, but the encroachments of age preclude any active pursuits except that of motoring. He is usually to be found poring over his stamps, working at his typewriter, or laboring in his California rose garden, which is one of the sights of Cathedral Cañon, near Palm Springs.